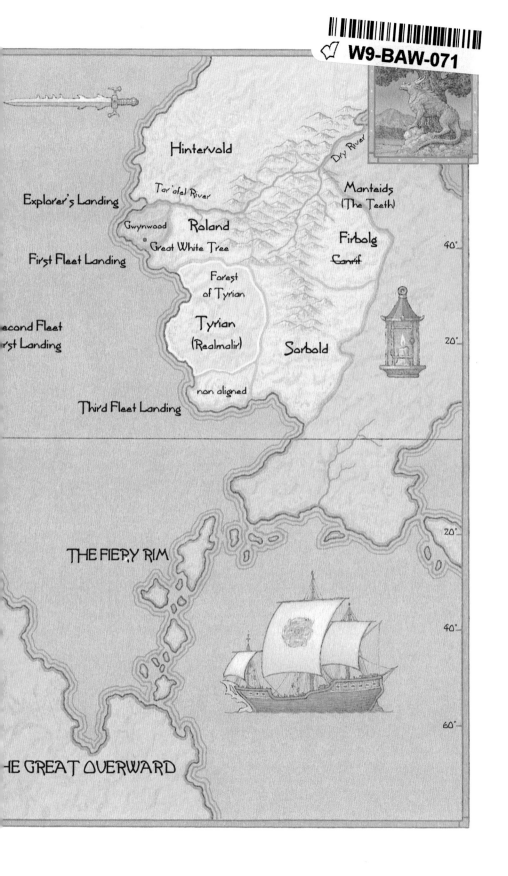

Hintervold

Dry River

Tar'afel River

Manteids
(The Teeth)

Explorer's Landing

Gwynwood

Roland

Firbolg

40°

Great White Tree

Canrif

First Fleet Landing

Forest
of Tyrian

Second Fleet
First Landing

Tyrian
(Realmalir)

20°

Sorbold

non aligned

Third Fleet Landing

20°

THE FIERY RIM

40°

60°

THE GREAT OVERWARD

The Merchant Emperor

The Symphony of Ages Books by Elizabeth Haydon

The Merchant Emperor

BOOK SEVEN OF
THE SYMPHONY *of* AGES

Elizabeth Haydon

A TOM DOHERTY ASSOCIATES BOOK

New York

THE MERCHANT EMPEROR

Copyright © 2014 by Elizabeth Haydon

All rights reserved.

Maps and ornaments by Ed Gazsi

A Tor Book
Published by Tom Doherty Associates, LLC
175 Fifth Avenue ·
New York, NY 10010

www.tor-forge.com

Tor® is a registered trademark of Tom Doherty Associates, LLC.

The Library of Congress Cataloging-in-Publication Data
is available upon request.

ISBN 978-0-7653-0566-4 (hardcover)
ISBN 978-1-4299-4397-0 (e-book)

Tor books may be purchased for educational, business, or
promotional use. For information on bulk purchases, please contact
Macmillan Corporate and Premium Sales Department at
1-800-221-7945, extension 5442, or write
specialmarkets@macmillan.com.

First Edition: June 2014

Printed in the United States of America

0 9 8 7 6 5 4 3 2 1

In Loving Memory
of
Carole
forever faithful
and William, James, and Constance
forever young

ACKNOWLEDGMENTS

With gratitude and profound thanks to Tor Books/Tom Doherty Associates and the readers of this tale, for sticking with it through the long silence and the darkness as it returns to the light and nears its end.

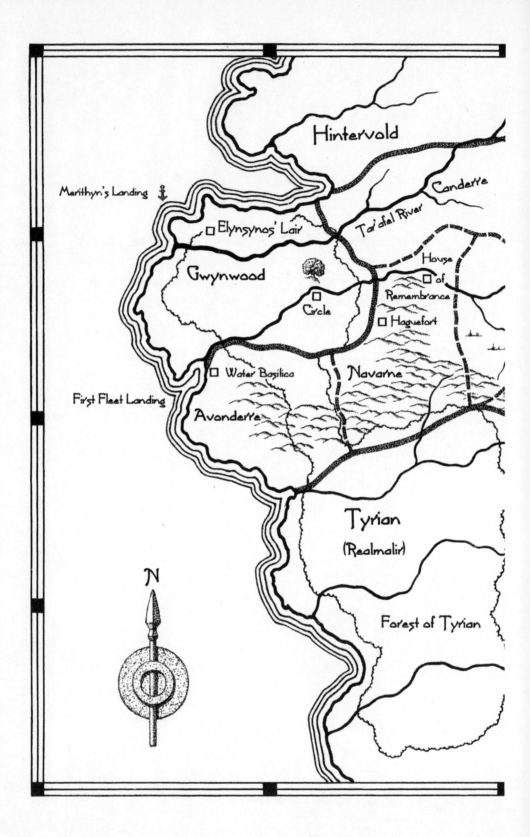

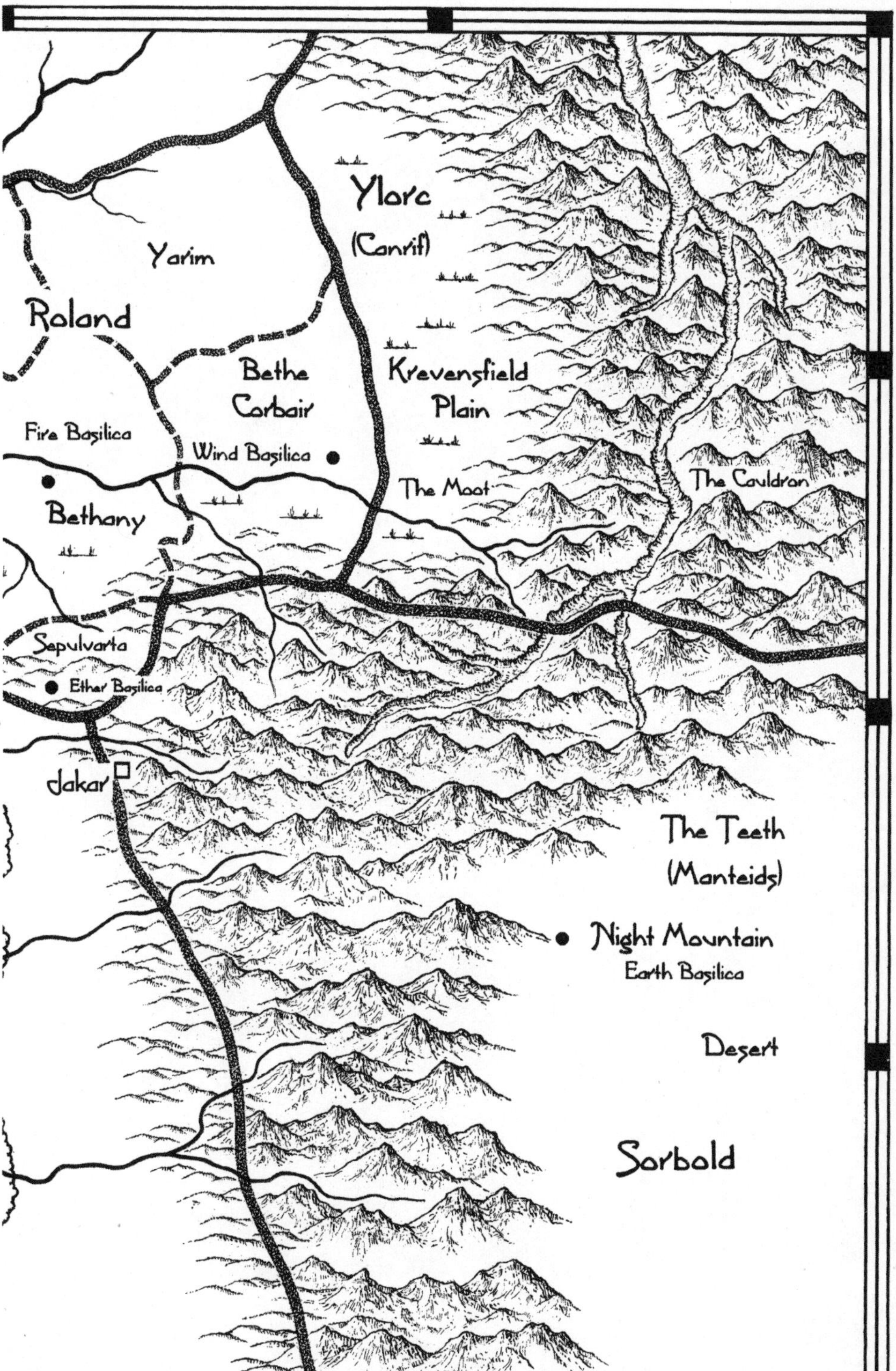

Yarim

Ylorc
(Canrif)

Roland

Bethe
Corbair

Krevensfield
Plain

Fire Basilica

Wind Basilica

The Moot

The Cauldron

Bethany

Sepulvarta

Ether Basilica

Jakar

The Teeth
(Manteids)

Night Mountain
Earth Basilica

Desert

Sorbold

THE WEAVER'S LAMENT

Time, it is a tapestry

Threads that weave it number three

These be known, from first to last,

Future, Present, and the Past

Present, Future, weft-thread be

Fleeting in inconstancy

Yet the colors they do add

Serve to make the heart be glad

Past, the warp-thread that it be

Sets the path of history

Every moment 'neath the sun

Every battle, lost or won

Finds its place within the lee

Of Time's enduring memory

Fate, the weaver of the bands

Holds these threads within Her hands

Plaits a rope that in its use

Can be a lifeline, net—or noose.

The Merchant Emperor

Overture Dolore

IN THE REALM BETWEEN LIFE
AND THE AFTERLIFE

In a quiet glade, where green leaves were painted in streaks of light, deep in the silence of a place out of Time, the heavy mist of morning burned off in the gentle glare of the rising sun.

Standing in that diminishing mist was a tall figure, a man clad in a green robe the color of the forest leaves, with eyes of bottomless darkness and brows that matched. A mythic figure, met or heard of only by those who came to this realm, the sleepy wooded place known as the Veil of Hoen, where only the dying were welcome.

The doorstep between Life and the Afterlife.

The Lord Rowan. Yl Angaulor.

The bringer of Peaceful Death.

The lord, himself a manifestation of an epic concept, was staring at another such manifestation.

Before him in the glen was an enormous vertical loom on which the tapestry of Time was being woven. Behind that warp-weighted loom sat the figure of a woman, an entity known as the Weaver, the being that embodied the concept of Time in history. Her face was serene, though any living being that had seen it in this drowsy place could never remember what her features looked like afterward.

The Lord Rowan had stood before the Weaver's loom on an all-but-infinite number of occasions before, observing the cataloguing of Time's story in the tapestry she was weaving. Every era, every battle, every great

20243040

feat or terrible loss was reflected in the warp and the weft of the tapestry, recorded in colored threads that told the tale of the ages of the world.

But there was something different this time.

And disturbing.

The ends of the long colorful strands of time-thread hanging loosely in the Weaver's hands were more ragged than he had ever seen them before. Each time he had beheld the Weaver at work, the weft-threads were neat and regular and replenished themselves as she wove them through the stationary warp-threads, so they maintained the same length. Now it seemed as if they had been *burnt* somehow.

So their ends were approaching the tapestry with each movement of the Weaver's hands.

In addition, the warp-threads, usually strung tight within the loom, were hanging loose at the bottom, their ends charred and ratted with smoke as well.

The Lord Rowan was not certain, but it occurred to him that he might be witnessing the end of Time approaching. Though he himself was a manifestation of Time, he was a thinking and feeling entity enough to contemplate the terror and the sadness that was portended.

Not just for the end of Life itself, but for the Afterlife as well.

In the distance he could hear the sound of horses' hooves dancing in preparation. The Lord Rowan knew this sound from long and terrible memory. It was the foretelling of the Ride, the gathering of his three brothers, the other, less peaceful, manifestations of Death, making ready to dispense it in the chaotic, thundering horror for which they were known, answering the call.

This time, however, for the first time, he had not heard that call himself.

Meaning that the wave of death, when it came, would have no peace associated with it.

He crouched down beside the Weaver and studied the tapestry.

Though he and his wife, the Lady Rowan, who was known as the Guardian of Sleep, had little awareness of the world beyond their realm, the Veil of Hoen, they did occasionally venture forth when summoned by fate.

He examined the area that seemed to contain an imperfection.

In the warp of that place, two weft-threads had been woven together in two separate places in the tapestry. One was gold, shining, the color of the sun at its peak on a midsummer day. The other was a copper color, a red-gold that gleamed almost metallically.

The Lord Rowan was fairly certain he had seen those colors before, in the hair of two living beings that had visited his realm.

A young man with the blood of dragons in his veins, torn asunder in a battle with an ancient demon. A man with hair the color of copper.

And a golden-haired woman who had come with a group of demonic children needing salvation of body and soul. Children of the same demon the man had fought.

Apparently these two people had met twice in history, not once as was the law of Time.

And in the second meeting, Time had been altered to allow for it to happen.

The Lord Rowan was not certain if the altering of Time had been undertaken to prevent the burning at the ends of the threads in the Weaver's hands.

Or if it had caused it.

The sound of hoofbeats in the distance grew louder.

The Lord Rowan closed his eyes.

$\mathcal{F}$ar away, in the deepest depths of the material world, another being felt, rather than heard, the hoofbeats as well.

That being was as old as the world was old, though in all the millennia of its life it had never woken, even for a moment.

Which was the salvation of that world.

For when it finally did wake, the being, a beast of unimaginable size and even more unnatural appetite, would consume the Earth of which its body comprised one-sixth.

The oldest entity ever to be called by the name.

The Sleeping Child.

The ancient wyrm, a child born of one of the first clutch of eggs of the race of dragons at the birth of the world, stolen by demons that would use it against that world and who had hidden it away within its frozen depths, where it would remain asleep, growing, gaining strength.

Until at last it was awakened.

And while that had always been a terrible possibility, the reality had never occurred.

Yet.

The beast stretched lazily in the cold depths of its lair, sending tremors through the Earth's mantle, earthquakes that split the ground in inexplicable tremors, or shook the teacups off the shelves in the larders of farm women. Volcanoes spilled forth lava, and tall, destructive waves lashed the coasts of the seas.

No one who felt the results of its movement knew what was happening.

For the moment, it didn't matter.

The unconscious beast settled back into slumber again.

Biding its time.

Which, given the sound of approaching hoofbeats, might be coming sooner than anyone realized.

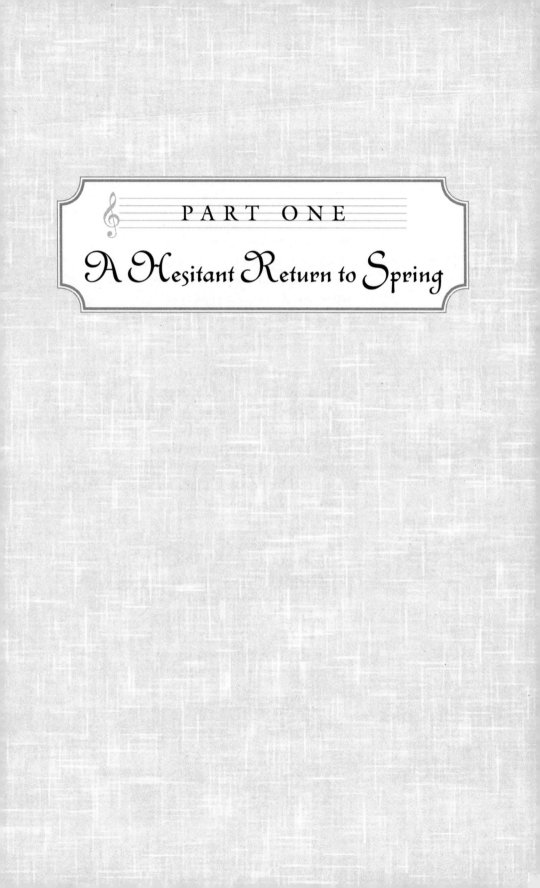

PART ONE

A Hesitant Return to Spring

ODE

WE are the music-makers,
And we are the dreamers of dreams,
Wandering by lone sea-breakers,
And sitting by desolate streams;
World-losers and world-forsakers,
On whom the pale moon gleams:
Yet we are the movers and shakers
Of the world for ever, it seems.

With wonderful deathless ditties
We build up the world's great cities,
And out of a fabulous story
We fashion an empire's glory:
One man with a dream, at pleasure,
Shall go forth and conquer a crown;
And three with a new song's measure
Can trample an empire down.

We, in the ages lying
In the buried past of the earth,
Built Nineveh with our sighing,
And Babel itself with our mirth;
And o'erthrew them with prophesying
To the old of the new world's worth;
For each age is a dream that is dying,
Or one that is coming to birth.

—Arthur O'Shaughnessy

1

GWYNWOOD, NORTH OF THE TAR'AFEL RIVER

$\mathcal{T}$he first sign that something terrible was wrong with the world was birdsong.

The white forest of Gwynwood was a virgin wood, thick with old stands of pale-barked trees that had been growing undisturbed for so many centuries that their upper branches had become entwined, interlacing in a thick canopy through which the sun struggled to warm the ground in the height of summer. Now, in the dying days of winter's Second Thaw, the warmth promised by a coming spring had caused trees of all heights to bud with new leaves, casting ever-changing patterns of shadow on the mossy ground below.

Melisande Navarne, mere days from her tenth birthday, reined her horse to a stop beneath those entwined branches, watching the patterns of light and shadow dance all around her.

And listened.

The air of the forest, rich and heavy with life and the lingering scent of old magic, was both sweet and spicy to her nose. The dazzling dance of the sun on the leaves filled her eyes, making her yearn for more innocent times, when she could have taken off her boots and run through the greenwood, playing chase with her brother and the father she had loved to adoration. The sweet singing of birds in the trees delighted her ears, completing the picture of tranquillity of an ancient forest in the advent of spring.

Except that in this place, if things were as they should be, no birds should sing.

All around them the woods were alive with natural music, the rustling of trees' boughs, skittering and snapping in the undergrowth, and every-where birdsong, a wild, almost nervous cacophony. The clear water of the stream she had been following joined in the forest song, splashing noisily as it hurried ahead of her. Melisande glanced repeatedly over her shoulder for Gavin the Invoker, feeling less than comforted, even at the sight of him fol-lowing her, as he had promised to do. There was something looming in the distance, something she had been warned about from the beginning, but was still unprepared for, no matter how good a face she was able to put on.

She clicked to her mount and continued into the greenwood.

Finally, when the noise was all but deafening, she heard a soft birdcall behind her, one she had come to recognize as the Invoker's signal. Melisande reined her horse to a halt and looked over her shoulder again.

Gavin had halted as well.

"This is where we part company for the moment, Lady Melisande Na-varne," he said seriously, gentling his own mount. "Your instructions from the Lady Cymrian forbid me from going on past this place."

The little girl nodded, trying to appear brave, but her stomach turned to water at his words. Gavin had found her, lost and wandering aimlessly in the forest after her carriage had been attacked. In spite of his gruffness and his sparse use of words, Gavin had been a comforting presence, a staunch protector and capable guide to this place of unwelcome birdsong and the errant wind in the trees. She had grown to depend on him to keep her safe not only from the dangers that lurked in the greenwood, but from her own doubts and fears.

It appeared both of those protections were about to come to an end.

She glanced into the sky above her. The silver branches of the tall trees reached, twisting, into a sky racing with clouds of almost the same color. Melisande shivered, then dismounted.

"Are you certain, Gavin?" she asked, hating the nervousness that made her voice sound younger than she was. "You are sure this is the place? You said you have never been here before."

The Invoker smiled. It was something Melisande had rarely seen him do in their brief time together, but she knew immediately that he had seen through her attempt to keep him with her a little longer.

"The instructions you conveyed to me were to bring you to follow the sweetwater creek to Mirror Lake."

"Yes."

Gavin nodded at the opening in the thicket before them. Melisande followed his gaze with hers, then tremulously ventured into the copse of trees. Beyond it, the splashing stream emptied out into an oval body of water, glistening in the morning light, its surface flat and smooth as a pane of glass. Mist clung to the clear water, hovering above it like clouds reflecting the sky.

Don't be frightened.

Melisande froze. The words were spoken in her ear, quiet and distinct, as if the speaker had been standing a hairsbreadth away, in the unmistakable voice of Rhapsody, the Lady Cymrian.

I have a mission for you.

The little girl spun around, looking anxiously for a glimpse of the Lady's golden hair, a shadow of her small, slender form, but there was nothing in the greenwood but the wind in the trees and the song of birds. The words could have come directly from her memory, spoken to her as they had been on a dark night, not really that long ago and a whole lifetime away. But they were not a function of memory; she could hear them as plainly as she could hear the rustling of the underbrush around her.

She thought back to that dark night, to the room in her family's keep, in the fading glow of the evening's candles. Melisande could feel the warmth and tingling of excitement now that she had felt then when Rhapsody had taken her hands and had begun to chant softly in the words of an ancient language, taught to her more than a thousand years before by her mentor in the art of Singing, a science known to her mother's people, the Liringlas, called Skysingers in the common language, and Namers, when they were especially advanced in it.

Melisande closed her eyes, reveling for a moment in the memory.

The air in the room had gone dry as the water within it was stripped, and a thin circle of mist formed around the two of them, glittering like sunlight on morning dew. A moment later, the words Rhapsody was speaking had began to echo outside of the mist in staggered intervals, building one upon the other until the room beyond was filled with a quiet cacophony. Melisande had witnessed this phenomenon before; the Lady

Cymrian, the closest thing to a mother she had known, often called such a circle of masking noise into being to protect their words from imaginary eavesdroppers whenever the two of them were whispering, giggling, and sharing secret thoughts. The corners of Melisande's eyes stung with sharp tears, bitter for the loss of those innocent times.

I need you to do something for me that I can entrust to no one in this world other than you, Melly.

The voice was even closer now, clearer in her ears. At the time they had first been spoken, the words had rung with a clarity that Melisande recognized as the Naming ability of True-Speaking. Now she wondered if, besides magically ensuring their veracity, the Lady Cymrian had been planting them in her head for this very moment, to remind her of her quest, or to indicate that she had arrived on its doorstep, in this sacred place, this untouched ground where only a handful of people had ever trod in all of history.

This night I will send a messenger bird to Gavin asking him to do as you direct him when you arrive. I can only entrust this request to you in spoken word, because if something should happen to the message, it would be disastrous.

Melisande, orphaned by such disasters, had understood the full implication of the Lady Cymrian's words.

Once you arrive at the Circle, ask Gavin to take you, along with a full contingent of his top foresters and his most accomplished healer, to the greenwood north-northeast of the Tar'afel River, where the holly grows thickest.

Melisande turned slowly, scanning the distant edges of the forest, burgeoning black with that holly, and willed herself to be calm.

These are sacred lands, and I can give you no map, for fear of what might become of it. Gavin will know where this is. Tell him to have his foresters fan out at that point, keeping to a distance of half a league each, and form a barrier that extends northwest all the way to the sea, setting whatever snares and traps they need to protect that barrier. They are to remain there, allowing no living soul to enter. They should comb the woods for a lost Firbolg midwife named Krinsel, and should they come upon her, they are to accord her both respect and safe passage back to the guarded caravan, which will accompany her to Ylorc.

In spite of being alone, Melisande nodded at the words. All had been done according to these commands; even now, many leagues behind them, the elite of Gavin's corps of foresters guarded the holy forest lands, unseen in the greenwood. She began to tremble, recalling how Gavin had recently come upon the body of a woman being devoured by coyotes, and wondering if the first part of her mission had already ended in failure.

Gavin himself is to take you from this point onward, the voice continued. It switched ears, making her start, and she turned quickly in the new direction of the voice to find herself facing the sparkling stream. *A sweetwater creek flows south into the Tar'afel; follow it northward until you come to Mirror Lake—you will know this body of water because its name describes it perfectly.*

Yes, it does, Melisande acknowledged. *This is the place.* Her stomach turned as she remembered the words that were to come a heartbeat later.

At the lake you are to leave Gavin and travel on alone. He is to wait for you there for no more than three days. If you have not returned by then, direct him to return to the Circle.

She stared, lost in thought, down into the glassy water of the lake, still partly frozen in winter's grip of ice, though the spring melt had begun, leaving large pools of shimmering liquid pocketing the surface, reflecting the sky. Melisande bent over and looked into the water.

A stranger's face returned her gaze.

The last time she had beheld her own aspect, it had been in her bedroom in her family's keep, and a young child of nine summers with black, inquisitive eyes ringed by golden curls had looked back at her, mischievous and smart beyond her years. The face that stared at her now was much older, though it had been but a few weeks in time since then, harder, browner.

More determined.

A face that had survived the attack of her carriage on the way to fulfill the quest Rhapsody had given her, the slaughter of most of her guards, and her awkward introduction to Gavin, who now seemed about to send her on her way, alone.

How long Melisande stood, absorbing the words of the voice, contemplating the change in her face, she did not know. When a quiet coughing sound behind her startled her, she looked up to see that the sun had climbed a little higher in the sky, though the mist still clung to the water of the lake, unmoved by its ascent. She turned to see the Invoker, still atop his horse, watching her intently.

"Well, Lady Melisande Navarne?"

Melisande inhaled deeply, the cold air of spring making the bottom of her lungs cramp. Then she walked back to Gavin and his mount.

"This is the place, you are right," she said, her young voice crisp with confidence she did not feel. "I am to go on from here alone."

The Invoker nodded, then alighted from his horse in a movement so swift she almost didn't see it. The golden oak leaf atop his wooden staff, the symbol of his office, caught the light as he dismounted, making it flash. It was the only thing that served to remind Melisande that she was traveling with the leader of the most numerous religious sect on the continent rather than a scruffy forester.

"You will be all right, then."

"I will."

The Invoker smiled again. "I know," he said, humor in his husky voice. "It wasn't a question." He opened the saddlebag and pulled forth a leather pack. "If I recall, I am to wait here for three days."

"Yes."

He tossed her the pack. "Well, this should keep you that long without getting too hungry. There is a waterskin in there as well—best not to drink anything found in these lands unless you know it to be safe and permissible for you to do so."

Melisande put her arms through the straps. "Thank you."

"The spores you will find in a sack inside there are luminescent—they glow in the dark when gently crushed. They should provide you light enough to see in the dark, as long as you are not too deep under the canopy."

"Again, thank you."

The Invoker came and stood in front of her.

"With your permission, m'lady, I would offer you a blessing, even though you are an adherent of the Patrician faith, rather than that of the Filidic order," he said. His voice took on a more gentle tone, and Melisande looked up to find his eyes fixed on her.

"By all means," she said, trying to sound older than her years.

The corners of the Invoker's mouth crinkled, but his eyes remained serious.

"Kneel then, if you will, Lady Melisande Navarne," he said.

The little girl sank quickly to the mossy ground.

Gavin pulled off his lambskin glove and rested his weathered hand on her head. He began to chant quietly in a language Melisande had not heard before, even in snippets of conversation she had caught in passing at the Circle, the central gathering place and holy lands of the Filidic religion. The dance of unintelligible words seemed after a moment to entwine with the gusts of wind around her, buffeting her with a breeze that felt warmer than it had a moment before.

The ground, cold and wet beneath her knees, hummed with a sudden warmth, blending with the song of the wind and that of the Invoker, lulling her. *I'm so tired,* she thought hazily, *so tired. I don't know if I can take another step. Let me sleep, then, let me curl up and sleep just a little longer.*

The newborn leaves rustled in the branches above, jarring her awake.

Her knees, no longer cold and stinging, tingled with warmth that seemed to seep up from the ground beneath her. The warmth spread quickly through her, filling her with energy she had not felt since she left home. It shot all the way to the top of her head, where the Invoker's hand rested.

She blinked, awake and alert.

Gavin removed his hand and helped her rise. He leaned on his staff, his eyes still trained on her thoughtfully.

"May the stars guide you, Lady Melisande Navarne," he said finally. "May the winds cleanse all ills and remain at your back. May the earth protect you and give you strength. May fire guard you, and rain refresh you, may all nature be your friend until we meet again in this place."

"Thank you," Melisande said. She shifted the pack on her shoulders to a more comfortable position, and patted her horse in farewell. "Remember, only wait three days. After that, Rhapsody said you should return to the Circle."

"So you have conveyed," Gavin replied. His eyes, dark in a face weathered brown from the sun, twinkled like starlight on dark water. "But, as I told you when I agreed to guide you here, take heed and remember this well—no matter what comes to pass, I will come for you."

Melisande tried to smile, but instead just turned to follow the stream.

"Three days hence, you will return, and with you, the spring," Gavin said from behind her. "And then you will be ten—life is much better when there are two digits in your age. It is even more so when there are three, but you shall have to wait awhile to see that." His hand came to rest on her shoulder. "Having the first day of spring as your birthday is auspicious, Lady Melisande Navarne. It means you are one who can bring about profound change in the world, returning warmth and light where cold and darkness once held sway." His hand returned to his side. "I hope if I'm ever lost, you are the one who comes for me."

This time the smile came, unbidden. The young Lady Navarne took her own walking stick from the horse's stores and started off into the depths of the greenwood, following the stream.

She did not look back.

The glassy lake was still shrouded in mist when she stepped through the trees to the water's edge. Vegetation floated quietly at the shoreline, unmoving. Birds called to one another from the trees, but no insects hummed above the still surface. *Well, that's a good sign, at least,* thought Melisande. *Perhaps here the wildlife is silent, as it should be. Perhaps the insects sense the world is aright.* She discarded the thought a moment later, realizing that the grip of winter had not eased enough to have brought them from their sleep anyway.

She stood on the shore, surveying the view beyond. Rhapsody's voice returned, clear and soft, as if it were hovering in the air in front of her.

Walk around the lake to the far side. There you will see a small hillside, and in it, hidden from all other vantage points, is a cave.

Melisande exhaled. Beyond the mist she thought she could make out a hummock or hillside, too far away to gauge its size. The crystal water of the lake appeared to originate from its mouth. Other than the twittering of the birds, and the occasional gust of wind, there was silence.

When she had waited as long as she dared, she made her way back across the marshy floodplain of the lake down to where the ground was dry enough to walk more easily, and began the trek around the lake to the hillside.

She found quickly that the lake was bigger than it appeared, and the walking more arduous than she had expected. Many steps led her only a very little way, and soon she was tired from pulling her feet from the sucking mud. The view had not changed much; the hummock appeared as far away as it had when she began. She paused a moment, and leaned over to catch her breath. She was just straightening up when she heard the voice again.

You must walk respectfully as you approach her lair.

The words shattered not only the silence, but Melisande's fragile sense of safety.

In all of the turbulence and violence, in the confusion of everything that had happened to her since she had left the safety of Haguefort, her ancestral home at the great forest's edge, she had almost come to forget the reason for her journey.

In the cave beyond the water's edge was a dragon, or at least Melisande hoped there was. The Lady Cymrian had sent her forth from the relative safety of her home into the forest to find the beast, Elynsynos, one of the five daughters of the Progenitor Wyrm, the very first of the race to appear on the earth. Like virtually every other human being in the world, Melisande had never seen Elynsynos in the flesh, but her late father had been the Cymrian historian, and so had a statue in his museum of her. That statue's ferocious aspect and cruel talons had frightened Melisande so much when she was little that she had refused to climb the stairs where it was situated at the top, welcoming museum guests to the second floor.

Rhapsody had assured her that the legends about the beast were lies, that Elynsynos, far from being sinister and wicked, was in fact childlike and beautiful, with uncommon wisdom and the desire to see the Cymrian people, Melisande's ancestors, prosper and live in peace. But the little girl remained unconvinced, still too close to the memory of her early-childhood nightmares in which the jewel-encrusted copper statue roared to life and rampaged through her father's keep, devouring the servants and the horses until it finally found her.

Now Melisande, whom some might also describe with the same words that Rhapsody had used to portray the dragon, was the one doing the seeking. Far from confronting a wyrm that was doing harm, however, she had been warned that the beast might be injured or dying.

Thus the reason Gavin's greatest healer had been brought on the journey and left at the place where the holly grew thickest.

Tread softly, said the voice. *Walk slowly, and pause every few steps to listen. If you feel warm air flowing from the cave, or hear the leaves of the trees begin to rustle noticeably, stop and ask permission to enter.*

Melisande closed her eyes and listened intently, but heard nothing. She tilted her face to the wind, to see if it carried any particular warmth, but found none other than the slight rise in temperature that had come with the advent of spring.

"Elynsynos?" she whispered. "Are you there? May I approach?"

She heard nothing.

She waited a moment longer, then carefully went forward, stopping every few steps, as she had been instructed, to listen and ask again. Nothing answered, not wind, not leaves, not voice.

When the sun was past its apex she rested halfway around the lake and dug into the pack Gavin had given her. Famished, she devoured a wedge of hard cheese, a winter apple, and several gulps from her waterskin before she realized that night would be coming on soon. Melisande scrambled to her feet and hurried on her way, fearful of darkness finding her alone at the forest's edge on the shore of Mirror Lake.

She doubled her speed, watching anxiously as the sun continued its descent, darkening the reflection of the trees mirrored in the surface of the water. Finally she came within sight of the hummock she had seen from afar, which was actually a series of steep hills. Melisande made her way as close as she could to the bottom of the hummock and looked up, panting.

A cave was set in the steepest of the hillsides, invisible except from this vantage point, its entrance black and ominous in the fading light. A small stream flowed from it, trickling down the hillside and emptying silently into the glassy waters of the reflecting pool. The mouth of the cave was perhaps twenty feet high.

"Elynsynos?" Melisande called, her voice high and childlike. She swallowed and willed herself to sound older. "Elynsynos, are you in there? May I enter?"

The sound of her voice echoed slightly above her in the mouth of the cave, but otherwise only silence answered her.

Rhapsody's voice spoke again, clear and soft.

As much as I pray that this will come to pass, I regret to tell you that I think that you may hear nothing. It is my fear, Melisande, that you will find her dead, or injured, or not there at all.

The little girl glanced up at the setting sun. The climb was steep, but not difficult, so she clenched her jaw and set to it, finding herself in half an hour's time at the opening of the cave.

On the rocky wall outside the opening was a rune, carved into the stone. Melisande peered at it as the dusky gold rays of the setting sun came to rest on the words, inscribed in an ancient language. She had seen those words in history books, had pored over them in her lessons many times, and could even pronounce the dead language of ship's cant correctly, thanks to the careful ministrations of her historian father.

Cyme we inne frid, fram the grip of deap to lif inne dis smylte land.

COME WE IN PEACE, FROM THE GRIP OF DEATH, TO LIFE IN THIS FAIR LAND.

Shivers ran through her from the roots of her hair to her heels. Even at the tender age of almost ten years, Melisande was aware of the significance of this place, and this rune, to her people, her family. This rune was more than fourteen centuries old, carved on the cave wall by Merithyn the Explorer, the Ancient Seren man who had saved the culture of the Cymrian people from being lost to the winds of Time. It was here he had met the dragon, and had secured her willingness to allow them to refugee to this continent, fleeing the destruction of their homeland in cataclysm. The words had been given to him by his king, Gwylliam, to greet anyone he had met in his search, and had led to the name Cymrian, as its prefix was the first word with which each person they contacted was greeted.

She was beholding the very birthplace of the Cymrian empire.

The shadows around her deepened as the sun began to slip beneath the horizon. The sky above her had turned to a deep shade of indigo, and stars were winking in and out of racing clouds. Melisande looked back to the opening of the dragon's lair.

The mouth of the cave widened into a dark tunnel, with a glowing light pulsing deep within it. At the outer edge, starlike lichen grew on the cave walls, reaching out into the remaining light of day, to grow thinner and eventually disappear in the darkness as the tunnel went deeper in. She summoned her courage and stepped in front of the opening.

Deep within the cave the wind whistled hollowly, tinged with the occasional lapping sound of water.

Nothing more.

If you find her dead, return to Gavin and report what you have found, the voice said. *If she is injured, but can still speak, ask her what she wants you to do. If she cannot, again, go to Gavin, but return with the healer to the cave, and stay with her while they attend to her wounds.*

Melisande squared her shoulders, trying to look brave in the vain hope that it would help her be so.

"Elynsynos?" she called again. "Are you in there?"

At first she heard nothing. Then, from the depths of the cave came a horrific noise, a groaning that was not human. It rattled the lichens and growths extending outside the cave, amplified by the high, deep tunnel walls, and sent waves of terror coursing through Melisande.

Because, at not even ten years of age, she knew the sound of agony in the face of approaching death.

2

THE KREVENSFIELD PLAIN, SOUTHERN BETHANY

𝒯he first sign that there might possibly be hope left for the world came in the form of itching insect bites, the wiggling of a toe, and controlled urine.

Anborn ap Gwylliam, Lord Marshal of the forces of the Cymrian Alliance, had lived more than a thousand years, and fought in brutal battles for most of them, so he was long inured to pain. It was not that he was unable feel it; on the contrary, he had trained himself to be so aware of his body that he could register almost any impulse his nerves were exposed to in a fraction of a heartbeat, making him in his younger days without peer where speed and skill with a sword were concerned, as well as giving him the ability to press on when injured to the point past which others would have long since collapsed. Even the loss of the use of his legs when his back was broken three years before had not kept him chairbound; his upper-body strength was sufficient, along with a specially trained horse, to allow him remarkable if limited mobility at an age and bodily state that would doom most men to invalid status.

In spite of this rather remarkable level of recovery, Anborn's heart burned always with a bitter resentment of his imperfect physical form. Phantom pain still chewed at his legs, even though he could have stabbed either of them with a dagger and not felt the wound as it emptied his life's blood onto the ground. While he had made the necessary adjustments to be able to ride and toilet himself, he had not done so with grateful acceptance, but with livid anger that always lurked just below the surface of his consciousness.

So it was not immediately apparent to him as he slept on the rocky ground of a sheltered swale, encamped with the rudiments of his army on the Krevensfield Plain, that the stinging on his calf was no mere phantasm of his mind remembering a time when he was whole, but was in fact the attack of a colony of ants, newly awakened by the approaching spring's warmth and swarming his lower limbs.

Hazily he waved away what he believed was a dream with his hand. The stinging did not disperse, but rather grew more intense.

"Fornication," the Lord Marshal mumbled in his sleep. He rose up on his elbow and rubbed his hand briskly down the leg of his trousers, then settled back down in his bedroll amid a copious amount of grunting and snorting.

A moment later, a forgotten but distantly familiar feeling swelled in his abdomen, where no sensation had been detectable for three years. Anborn pulled his rough bedroll closer against the chill night air, but nature's call would not be denied. Finally he woke, a pressing need growing more urgent in his belly.

"What the—?" he muttered. Then his mind roared to wakefulness, the realization of what was happening finally banishing sleep completely.

With a speed born of shock, the Lord Marshal crawled from his bedroll, dragging himself by his elbows, as he had learned to do, and edged agonizingly to a patch of frost-tinged weeds a stone's throw from where his commanders and the soldiers not on watch were sleeping. A mix of confusion and excitement rose within him as he fumbled with the leather laces of his trousers, removed the absorbent cloth that had served as a barrier and dam for the last few years, then rolled to his side on the cold ground and relieved himself as he had done all his life before his injury.

The cold patch of frost stung his genitals. Anborn quickly replaced the cloth and returned himself to rights, then lay on his back, staring up at the winking stars above, wondering what had just come to pass. Not only did he have sensation in places that had been completely numb, but control had returned to the muscles, as least in some cases. He tried to bend his legs, but they were unresponsive. He succeeded only in being able to wiggle the big toe on his left foot.

It was an accomplishment that dwarfed any victory in battle that he could remember for the sheer thrill it brought him.

The itching in the surface skin of his legs flared again. Anborn rolled onto his stomach and crawled back to his sleeping comrades, looking around for one man in particular and not finding him there among the off-duty soldiers. After a moment he beheld a shadow sitting at the top of a small rise near the western side of the swale. The Lord Marshal exhaled, summoned his strength, and crawled, elbow over elbow, dragging his useless legs behind him, to the crest of the swale.

The figure atop the rise was cloaked and hooded beneath the moonless sky. The dim light of the campfire coals showed his garment to be the plain light gray cloth of a wandering pilgrim, a cloak like those worn by hundreds of thousands of other religious nomads who had come to the holy city of Sepulvarta over the last three years. Sepulvarta, the City of Reason.

The city that lay now, four score miles to the southwest, smoldering in the ruins of siege and conquest.

The Lord Marshal pulled himself along the crest of the swale until he was within arm's reach of the cloaked man. He waited for the wind to gust, then when it died down he spoke, trying to keep his voice calm.

"Constantin."

The man did not move.

"Constantin," Anborn said again, this time slightly louder.

The figure finally favored him with a glance, no more.

"My—my legs are itching," the Lord Marshal said falteringly. "And I can piss on my own—I mean I can control myself."

The cloaked figure glanced at him again. The icy blue eyes beneath the hood of the cloak narrowed.

"I'm happy for you." The voice was as icy as the eyes.

Anborn's embarrassment drowned in a surge of indignation. "Neither of which was the case when I fell asleep this night," he said harshly in response. "Do you, the Patriarch, the head of the most powerful religious sect on the continent, as well as the greatest healer in the land, have not even a shred of interest in what can only be a *miracle*?"

The eyes remained fixed on Anborn's for a moment. Then the head bowed slightly, and the man took down his hood, revealing white-blond hair that curled into the gray edges of a fulsome beard and features that seemed chiseled from stone, still handsome even in the creases of age.

"I am sorry, Anborn," Constantin said. "I am indeed glad on your behalf, but the sacking of my citadel, and the horror visited upon it and its inhabitants, as well as my own new exile, have left me without much joy to bestow on anyone, even a man who is experiencing a miracle granted by the All-God."

Anborn pulled his glove from his hand and slapped it across the Patriarch's chest.

"Fool," he muttered. "Are you so mired in your grief and loss that you don't see what is happening here? The All-God has little or nothing to do with this, except indirectly." He crawled back to his bedroll, rummaged around inside it, then dragged himself back up the rise a moment later. "This—it is to this I owe the welcome itch and ability to control my water." He extended his hand to the Patriarch.

Constantin exhaled, then put out his own enormous hand, rough and scarred from a life of gladiatorial combat that had occurred both a few short years and at the same time centuries before. The Lord Marshal placed an object in it, and the Patriarch held it up to the fading glow of the campfires.

It appeared, in what little light there was available to him, to be a large conch shell, the discarded home of a sea creature tossed up on the sand by the waves of the ocean. The Patriarch, weary and heartsick, handed the shell back.

"I fail to understand what you are on about," he said brusquely. "Again, I am happy that you can itch and not piss yourself. Now leave me in peace."

"In this shell I can hear the vibrations that make up my true name, the essence of myself at the purest of levels," Anborn pressed on. "Vibrations placed in there by the only Lirin Namer I know. She told me if I were to repeat the song of my own name over and over again, I might be able to remake myself, at least somewhat, back to the way I once was. Foolish as it has made me feel, I have done as she asked. Three years I have felt nothing below my rib cage; now suddenly there is pain in my skin and strength in my groin again. You're a man of faith, are you not, Constantin?"

The Patriarch snorted. "I was. Now I am an outcast, expelled from my office by the army of a nation that a few days ago was counted among the adherents of the religion. My faith in the All-God is not in question, but perhaps His faith in me is."

"Nonetheless, is it not possible that you are bearing witness to a miracle, or at least the successful application of an age-old lore?"

"My city is in ruins, most likely with thousands dead. The Chain of Prayer, the core of our religion, has been shattered. I have told you that I am glad for you. What do you want me to do—dance in glee?"

The Lord Marshal's expression blackened. He crawled closer and seized the Patriarch's hand and held it up before the man's tired blue eyes.

"Clearly the Ring of Wisdom that is the symbol of your office must have been shattered along with the walls of Sepulvarta," he said acidly. "What is happening in my legs is the result of the same age-old lore that the Bolg king and the Lady Cymrian are working on *at this very moment*, in the depths of the mountains of Canrif. Recall the story of the Lightforge, the instrumentality built by my father Gwylliam, an instrumentality he used successfully to keep my hated mother Anwyn's forces at bay for five hundred years in the Cymrian War? That is what has obsessed the Bolg king—he has been attempting to reconstruct it, or some version of it, for just such a time as this which is upon us now. Being a man of little faith myself, I did not believe either Achmed or Rhapsody had the insight or the skill to resurrect such an instrument, itself shattered and long buried. Rhapsody may be a Namer, but by her own admission she is largely self-taught and did not have access to the Primal Lore of her kind before she fled the Island of Serendair. But she evidently *does* understand how it works. And while he is half Firbolg, I have learned never to underestimate Achmed, though it still seems a daunting task to restore something that was built by the Nain a thousand years ago under the tutelage of Gwylliam the Visionary, one of the greatest inventors and machinists the Known World has ever seen, with nothing more than a cadre of brutish, demi-human Bolg as artisans. *That* is the miracle, you fool, though there are still only glimmers of it. Given how badly the Cymrian Alliance is outnumbered, and our position in the very middle of this continent, with potential enemy nations surrounding us, we will need that glimmer to roar, full-fledged, into a miraculous fire if we are to survive what is coming."

For the first time since he had crawled to the summit of the swale, Anborn saw the Patriarch breathe.

Then a hint of light in his eyes.

Finally the tall cleric turned to him, and steel was in his expression.

"Let us begin gathering the kindling for that inferno, then," he said.

3

The Teeth
(Manteids)

★

● Night Mountain
Earth Basilica

Desert

PALACE OF JIERNA TAL, JIERNA'SID, SORBOLD

Talquist, Emperor Presumptive of the nation of Sorbold, stood in the top parapet of the palace of Jierna Tal, staring west, watching the sun slide down an indigo horizon beyond the sandy desert rim. Dusk was his favorite time of day, especially in the arid realm of Sorbold, an old land long forgotten by the gods he didn't believe in, full of magic and treasure hidden beneath dry vaults of richly colored windblown earth. While he didn't believe in gods, Talquist did believe in magic, and to him there was nothing so magical as the desert sky darkening into night, sprinkled with sandy grains of diamond dust winking in the clear air as the stars appeared, one by one, from behind thin clouds.

He remained in reverent silence as the sun slipped through the aquamarine veil at the horizon and beneath the world's rim. The stars grew brighter, changing the colors of the city below him from the flat brick red visible in the midday sun to the flame-colored shadows that reflected off the stone buildings from the watchfires and forges smoldering at all times of the day and night. As beautiful as he thought the capital city of Jierna'sid was in daylight, it could not compare to the glorious sight of it at night, when the sounds of martial preparations and military cadences echoed off the walls and cobbled streets, blending with the incessant clopping of horses' hooves, the clattering of wagon wheels and shouts of regimented discipline and drunken merriment into one building symphony of impending war.

From his many years at sea as a merchant plying the trade winds the world round, he was knowledgeable of the stars and their movements in the heavens. He turned his gaze to the southwest and waited patiently for the evening star to appear.

After a moment it did, twinkling brightly.

As he knew it would.

Talquist looked down at the scale in his hands. It was an ancient thing; that he'd known from the beginning. The moment he had found it, wedged in the bones of an old ship buried in the sand of the Skeleton Coast, a graveyard of things coughed up by the cold sea, he'd been aware that it was something far more special than he'd ever seen in all his travels, something more powerful than he might ever hope to fully understand. There must have been magic in it, for no one else might give it a second glance; it appeared to be little more than the scale of a giant fish or the slough of dead skin from the hide of something enormous. From almost the moment he touched it, his life's obsession became the quest to discover exactly what he was holding. Talquist sighed, remembering those almost carefree days on the open sea, in search of answers to his endless riddle. He had whored himself out to anyone who might have answers to that riddle, but had discovered little.

Finally he had come upon a reference to it in the ruins of a water-soaked tome in the Cymrian museum known anecdotally as *The Book of All Human Knowledge*. The fragile manuscript had identified his treasure as a dragon scale from a deck of scrying used by an ancient Seren woman named Sharra, and had noted its name as the New Beginning. None of the powers of the scale, however, had survived the book's immersion in the sea, so he had had to discover its uses himself.

One thing he found on his own was the effect starlight had on the object.

Idly, Talquist held up the scale to the horizon where the evening star gleamed. What had appeared solid a moment before—a rough gray piece of oval carapace with a finely tattered edge scored across its concave surface—turned suddenly translucent, the etching of a throne in the center visible even in the dim light of dusk. A purple flash skimmed across the surface, then vanished as the scale became clear, with but a mere outline able to be seen. As many times as Talquist had seen the effect, he never ceased to be amazed by it, especially given that after a moment his own hand, and eventually the rest of him, would follow suit, turning ethereal enough to render him all but invisible, too.

It had been an extremely useful tool in furthering his ends.

With his musings came an overwhelming sense of loss. From the moment he had discovered his treasure, it had almost never left his body, tucked in the custom-made pocket of his garments just above his heart. Its vibration had seeped into his core, changing the rhythms of his body to match its own. It had given him the throne of Sorbold, allowing him to brutally depose the Empress Leitha, the withered crone who had reigned undisputed for three-quarters of the past century, and her corpulent heir-apparent son at the same time, bringing to an abrupt end the three-centuries-old Dynasty of the Dark Earth, making way for his new one.

The Empire of the Sun.

In order to remain undetected as the usurper, however, he had modestly insisted upon taking on the title only of regent at first, to be crowned emperor on the first day of spring a year later. Even now, as light fled the sky and night took a more confident hold, the preparations for his coronation were being made in the streets of Jierna'sid.

It would be a festival without precedent and beyond measure.

Talquist.

The voice from the bottom of the stairs leading up to the parapet top scratched against his eardrums, sending chills down the length of his spine. It was harsh and high-pitched, with a crackling edge to it. In that voice the echo of other voices could be heard, some low and soft, others shrieking, all brimming with a nascent and ominous power that never ceased to make the skin on Talquist's neck prickle in fear.

Bring me the scale.

The words echoed up the stone staircase, carrying with them unmistakable threat.

More than anyone in the entire world, Talquist knew that the threat was not idle, even though there was no way for the one issuing it to gain access to the parapet. Not wishing to pass the remainder of his life in the high tower, however, the Emperor Presumptive sighed again, took one last fond look at his life's treasure, then turned away from the window and walked dispiritedly down the stairs.

As he rounded the last turn of the winding staircase he passed a mirror that had been set up to allow guards to see what might be pursuing them down or up the steps. An ordinary man of Sorbold looked back at him from the reflective surface; Talquist paused long enough to return his gaze. Clothed though he was in finely tailored robes of heavy linen trimmed in gold, in truth by outward appearance he was nothing more than a swarthy-skinned, thick-bodied man, dark of hair and eye, with a workman's callused hands and a face weathered by the sun and salt sea air. Not born to be a king, much less an emperor, whenever he beheld himself, Talquist saw the lie beneath the finery, the commoner in the garments of a masquerade.

And it infuriated him to the core.

He doubled his stride angrily, arriving at the bottom of the stair with a resounding thump.

The staircase opened up to the wide Great Hall of the palace's third floor, an opulent room of high angled ceilings painted in grand frescoes above a polished floor where more than a million small pieces of multicolored marble had been inset into an exquisite design, unparalleled in the Known World for its beauty. Long, thin windows of colored glass reflected the light of the burning torches that lined the walls, making the room shine as bright as day.

Standing just inside the room was an immense statue of a soldier, mammoth in size and heft, its features as detailed as life, down to the stone eyelashes and individual creases in each knuckle of its hands. The titan, more than the height of two men, was rendered in primitive armor and garb from a time before the Cymrians came to this land, ruining it forever, in Talquist's opinion. The primal, indigenous nature of the time was captured perfectly in the stone man's flat brow and broad face, with a strong, square jawline and sinewy limbs that ended in warrior's hands and feet. Most remarkable of all were the eyes, clear and cloudless as a summer day, blue as the sky would be.

They were open and watching him intently.

"There is no need to summon me like a fishwife, Faron," Talquist said smoothly, but with an undertone of anger. "I told you I would confer unto you the scale; did you not believe me?" He stretched out his arm, wincing inwardly but maintaining an indifferent mien, with the scale in hand.

The immense stone soldier continued to eye him, but the corners of the mouth seemed to contract in the hint of a smile.

I had no doubt that I would be taking the scale from you, one way or another, the shrill voice Talquist had heard in the parapet replied. The titan's lips did not move; the sound seemed to issue forth from within its thoracic cavity.

Talquist stared at the statue. Then he brought his arm back to his side.

"It would seem prudent that, as we are allies, you should trust me to hold on to what is mine—after all, I have not asked for possession of any of *your* scales. Tomorrow is the day of my second Weighing, and coronation—perhaps the presence of the scale is necessary to ensure that I am once again selected by the Great Scales as emperor. Given how critical that selection is to both of our plans, our *mutual* plans, I would think you would be hesitant to risk failure of all we have set in place."

The titan smirked.

We have mutual plans, true. But our priorities within those plans are not the same, Talquist.

The Emperor Presumptive's deep brown eyes darkened to the black of a sky before a night storm, but otherwise his face betrayed no anger.

"Do you wish to dissolve our association, then, Faron? You say you seek a child who resides deep within the mountains of the Firbolg, protected by their king. Without me, the armies of Sorbold will not follow you—do you intend to try and take the mountains on your own? Best of luck with that, impressive as you are." The look in his eyes sharpened now to a glare. "I tire of your threats and your attempts at intimidation, especially on the eve of my Weighing and coronation. Remember it was I that brought you into life, into awareness, into the strength with which you menace me now, in the first place. Without the body of Living Stone I provided for you, you would still be a gelatinous mass of freakish flesh in a carnival sideshow! And in thanks you threaten and shriek at me in your newly found voice which, by the way, sounds like that of a tone-deaf whore yodeling in pretended passion."

Well, you would know all about that.

Talquist thought he perceived an amusement he had never seen before in the statue's expression. *When and how did he grow so much more sophisticated?* he wondered. *He was not even sentient when he first stepped off the Scales, stumbling and barely able to stand.* He decided to take the negotiation to a higher level.

"Here is the deal on the table: if you wish to continue our association, we will need a new understanding about our interaction. I will not tolerate disrespect of this nature any longer. It is critical that the army of Sorbold sees you as my champion, under command of the generals who are subordinate to me. Otherwise, there will be chaos, and you will be on your own. I will treat you as my partner in secret, but in public it is necessary for you to blend in better, to not challenge me. Between us, we have almost a full set of Sharra's scales. Each of us should retain possession of his own until we are prepared to make use of them as a set. Remember, I, too, seek a child, with as much fervor as you do, I believe."

The titan eyed him, but said nothing.

"Do we have an understanding, then, Faron?"

Footsteps sounded on the wide marble staircase known as the Great Stair. Talquist turned quickly to see Lesik, his protocol officer, hurrying to the top of them from the second floor below.

He glanced back over his shoulder at the statue. It had seemed to fade into stolid inanimation again, its earthen eyelids colorless.

"M'lord?"

"Yes, Lesik, what is it?"

"Beliac, king of Golgarn, and the Diviner of the Hintervold have arrived. I will show them to their rooms unless you wish to greet them."

"Ah, thank you, Lesik," the Emperor Presumptive said. "I do indeed want to have some time with them this evening before tomorrow's festivities occupy me completely. Will you have supper and libations sent up here? I will be down directly to welcome them. Have them wait in the entryway."

The protocol officer bowed and hurried back down the staircase.

Talquist turned quickly to the titan.

"Make your decision, Faron," he whispered. "If I have your agreement, I will conduct my business with these two powerful allies here in the Great Hall, where you can be a silent witness to it, assuming you can be silent. If not—"

I will be silent.

"Good. Then I shall return with them momentarily. And while you wait, you might want to contemplate what you might need to do to deepen this new voice of yours. It's rather embarrassing, frankly."

Talquist turned again and trotted down the wide stone staircase, whistling, his good mood restored.

𝒯he titan watched until the Emperor Presumptive had descended out of sight.

Then, within the massive chest cavity of the statue, the recently insulted voice spoke, though it would have been inaudible to any human ear. It was not a feminine voice, but it had a woman's tone of comfort, of seduction.

He did not perceive me, Faron. He merely thinks you have matured.

Deep within that same cavity came a wordless agreement, different from the voice.

Then the voice spoke again. There was a definite excitement in its words.

Good; this is good. Do not chafe under the mantle of servitude, of obedience—trust me, when the time comes, Talquist will come to heel. Once we reveal to him what we know about the child he seeks so desperately, he will grant us whatever we wish. You and I will lead his army to take the Firbolg mountains.

And then it will all begin.

THE OCCUPIED CITY OF SEPULVARTA

$\mathcal{F}$hremus Alo'hari, supreme commander of Sorbold's land force, stood atop the wall that overlooked the Krevensfield Plain and the larger panorama of Roland to the north, shielding his eyes from the bright sun of morning, thinking.

Fhremus was not generally a pensive man; he had risen to command slowly, working his way through the ranks, not because of some grand undertaking or highly visible act of bravery, but rather a consistent reliability and staunch loyalty. He had been raised in a military family with many generations of service to the Crown, four of those generations specifically devoted to the late Empress Leitha, who had reigned for three-quarters of a century, and had taken, upon her death almost exactly one year before, the long-standing Dynasty of the Dark Earth with her.

Not that this vainglorious ending had been her idea. Her one and only heir, the grotesquely corpulent Crown Prince Vyshla, had managed to die within an hour of the empress; he had actually died first, but his death's significance paled in comparison with hers. Their synchronous endings erased several centuries of their family's dominion over the vast, forbidding nation that Fhremus loved, and set the stage for a battle of wills between, in the absence of any other royalty, the lesser nobles of the largest of the city-states of Sorbold, the Mercantile, the Church, and the army itself, which Fhremus had represented at the conclave that met prior to the Weighing.

Fhremus had been pleased with the outcome of the conclave, the decision to keep the empire united, rather than dividing it into city-states, as the nobility had pushed for, a decision made by the Scales, the enormous set of weighing plates that had long been the decider of contested questions in Sorbold and, in fact, many of what had once been the Cymrian lands. It was an old instrumentality of deep lore and magic from the Island of Serendair, brought in pieces on a ship with the refugees of the Third Fleet that had landed on Sorbold's southern maritime border known as the Skeleton Coast, a treacherous, mist-shrouded coastline that had been the graveyard of many ships over the millennia. For a thousand years since that landing, the Scales had weighed every major issue of state, and were considered to be undisputed in their wisdom and judgment.

Thus, when the new emperor was chosen from the Mercantile, the merchant class, Fhremus had been slightly surprised, but did not question the decision at all.

The man who would be crowned emperor this day was a man with immense vision, Fhremus knew. Despite having taken a humble position by his selection, at which he had seemed more surprised than anyone else there, making an offer to serve as regent for a year and then being reconfirmed by the Scales a year later, he had embarked upon an ambitious agenda of changing, or rather, improving many of the long-established practices of the nation.

Fhremus had not been surprised by this aspect of the aftermath of the death of the empress. Leitha had ruled with an iron hand, but there had been rust on the iron; in spite of her surprising acuity at the age of ninety-eight, she was not as hale and vigorous as she had been in youth, and therefore had allowed various aspects of her governance to fall into disrepair. While she had officially outlawed bloodsport in the gladiatorial arenas that were an enthusiastically supported tradition for thousands of years before the Cymrians came, she had also turned a blind eye to its return twenty years into her reign, and a deaf ear to the sounds of hooting and violence that had continued to build outside the arenas as she grew older and her reign grew longer.

The gladiatorial arenas were not the only aspect of evident neglect.

The return of the practice of slavery and slave trading had been more recent than the bloodsport, but it was even bloodier, though less widely known of. Fhremus had not been officially informed of the increase in the heinous activities, but would have had to have been blind in order to miss the buildup of the industries, state-run and privately owned, that had suddenly expanded their labor forces.

Though he was not sure why, he suspected that Talquist might have been involved with that expansion long before his elevation to the throne of the new dynasty he had established, called the Empire of the Sun.

The Mercantile was a misunderstood and, in Fhremus's estimation, underappreciated social class. Looked down upon by royalty, the nobility, and even the Church, the merchant class was often a bastion of far greater wealth and international connection than any of those other groups possessed. It was all but impossible to be isolated or parochial when the very basis of a class's existence was predicated on making contacts in every place possible around the world. While Fhremus knew little to nothing of the details of Talquist's holdings, wealth, and connections to friends in both high and low places across the globe, he was quite certain those elements of the new emperor's power were substantial.

Perhaps even frighteningly so.

As little as Fhremus knew about the financial and social secrets of the Merchant Emperor, he had a better window into Talquist's military plans, though not as clear a one as he would wish. Fhremus had been instrumental in the training and deployment of the soldiers who rode the iacxsis, a strange breed of flying beasts that could both soar over walled fortresses and mercilessly attack the inhabitants of those cities. He had been given a tour of the breeding and training grounds, hideous caverns that had once been the central cistern and aqueduct beneath the streets of the capital city of Sorbold, Jierna'sid, where both the Scales and the palace of Jierna Tal stood. He had still been unable to purge his nose of the stench of the place and his mind of the memory of what he had seen there.

He had accepted the emperor's word that the breeding and training program was essential to the survival of Sorbold, due to the merciless plans for conquest and expansion that the leaders of the new Alliance, the Lord and Lady Cymrian, were secretly putting into place. Talquist had shown him documents that detailed the royal pair's nefarious schemes from other merchants in their employ around the world; Fhremus had seen them as credible and did not question the information.

He had also been introduced to another of the abominations that

Constantin, the recently deposed Patriarch of Sepulvarta, the former holy city over which he was currently commandant, had been responsible for. Talquist had shown him a titan, an immense statue of a primitive warrior that had been animated, the emperor said, by the unholy practices employed in the holy city. The titan, now bent to Talquist's will and loyal, in its limited capacity, had been instrumental in breaking down the infamous gate of the holy city and bringing it into immediate occupation. The Patriarch's captured plans he had seen had made Fhremus glad that his army had been so successful, in concert with the iacxsis riders and the titan, in subverting and occupying the holy city as quickly as they did, before even more blood was shed.

"Uncle?"

Fhremus looked up.

A young soldier in the regalia of the army of Sorbold was smiling tentatively at him. He was handsome, possessed of the swarthy skin and dark brown eyes common in the residents of the desert nation, and a pleasant disposition; his sister's son, Kymel, the fifth generation of the family to have begun service to the empress three years ago, and now was in that of the emperor.

Fhremus stood straight and saluted, to Kymel's immediate response.

"At ease," he said, clapping the lad on the upper arm. "Are you off duty?"

"Yes," said Kymel. "On leave in honor of the Weighing and coronation. Titactyk has called us to muster at dawn tomorrow in preparation for the emperor's arrival six days hence. We have been assigned to guard him while in Sepulvarta and then accompany his return to Jierna'sid at his will."

"Congratulations." Fhremus had to struggle to keep his lip from curling at Titactyk's name. Titactyk was one of his own regimental commanders, and while he could not precisely put a reason to his dislike of the man, it was there nonetheless, though of course that information was unknown to the rank and file like Kymel. While Titactyk had never committed any offense or break of protocol egregious enough to merit discipline, there was an air of cruelty and insolence about him that Fhremus had seen before in other overly ambitious soldiers.

And others.

In his experience, it was always a bad sign.

It was very much the same feeling as he was having on this morning of celebration in Jierna'sid.

"Enjoy your leave," he said to his nephew. "Happy Weighing, and guard the emperor well."

Kymel grinned, then stood and snapped a salute. Fhremus returned it, smiling to himself as Kymel left, and then took one last look over the lands he knew he would soon be invading, putting to the sword and the flame, before making his way off the wall and down into the broken streets of Sepulvarta once more.

THE FORTRESS OF HIGHMEADOW, NAVARNE

To the north two hundred leagues and half a world away, Gwydion of Manosse, the Lord Cymrian, leader and high lord of the Alliance of the Middle Continent, was climbing a narrow set of curving stairs high into the tower in the center of his woodland fortress, known as Highmeadow, as he did each morning.

At the top of that curving staircase, he stepped out onto the cold, sheltered platform high in the tallest treetops of the forest canopy that held the aviary. The cultivation of a squadron of messenger birds had been one of his first priorities when Highmeadow was finally done with construction and being made inhabitable. His late father, Llauron the Invoker, the leader of the nature priests known as the Filids, had always made use of messenger birds for as long as Ashe could remember, as did another of the kings in the Alliance, Achmed the Snake, when he began retaking the mountains of Ylorc from the Firbolg four years back.

The Lord Cymrian had commissioned a series of birdhouses and rookeries for Highmeadow's aviary that were like those his grandfather Gwylliam had designed, architectural renderings of the buildings, palaces, basilicas, and mountain fortresses that were the destinations of those birds in cities all across the continent. The detail that had been captured in balsa wood and twigs was astounding; he never ceased to marvel at how close to the originals the carefully fashioned cages were, down to details like bell tower windows and the shape of Grivven Post, the peak in the Teeth where Achmed received his mail.

It was from this birdhouse that the Lord Cymrian pulled a flyer now, as he did each morning. The brown wren squirmed for a moment in his hand, but he gentled it down quickly, billing its throat with his forefinger, then carefully attached the metal leg tube with the tiny scroll containing his meticulously graphed words of longing and adoration in a long-dead language, and turned it loose, watching it catch a warm morning updraft and take to the wind, heading east, making for the place where his family was in hiding.

Taking his love along with it.

He waited until he could no longer see the bird, nor sense it with the inner sight that was the gift of the dragon blood in his veins.

Then he checked the door of the birdcage and made his way back down the twisting stairs to the courtyard where his battlefield commanders were awaiting him for morning orders.

5

GWYNWOOD, THE DRAGON'S CAVE

*C*he terrible moan trailed off into silence like the end of the night wind's howl.

Fear receded into the depths of Melisande's mind. Without further thought, she darted into the dark cave, calling as loudly as she could.

"Elynsynos! Elynsynos, I hear you! I'm coming!"

She had gone only a few paces when the total lack of light forced her to stop. The glowing lichens that had grown at the mouth of the cave had grown thinner and thinner in the dark, leaving the cave without any natural radiance on its walls. The acrid smell of fire and smoke long gone lingered in the air, making breathing difficult. Melisande's lungs constricted as her fear returned.

I wish my father were here, she thought, fighting back panic. *Or Gwydion—he would know what to do. Or Gavin.*

At the thought of the Invoker a memory, recently made, came into her mind. She fumbled blindly in her pack until she felt the luminescent spores he had given her, soft and sandy, beneath her fingers, then pulled one out and squeezed, swallowing hard as small bits crumbled into powder. After a moment, a thin glow appeared in her hands, and the cave walls became dimly visible.

Around her, the tunnel yawned like the maw of a giant beast.

"I'm coming, Elynsynos," Melisande said again, more quietly this time. She slung her pack onto her back and, holding the spore aloft, she started down into the darkness.

The tunnel twisted as she followed it, opening at the bottom into a large cavern below. The deeper she descended the more the cave began to curve, bending in a circular fashion to the west. At the bottom of the tunnel she could see a vague glow, like the distant light of firecoals. The dark walls began to brighten as she hurried on, reflecting the glow of the tunnel before them. The scent of the air changed, too; rather than growing more dank as she went deeper underground, the air around her began to freshen and take on a salty tang. Melisande recognized it after a moment as the smell of the sea.

That's right, she thought as she scurried down the earthen passageway. *Rhapsody told me about this, that Elynsynos had a lagoon of salt water in the depths of her lair. I wonder if it reaches all the way to the sea.* Even as she traveled, she discarded the notion. The sea was miles from this place.

Finally the widening tunnel opened into a vast cavern. Above her, as high up as she could see, the dim glow she had been following was emanating from six huge chandeliers, each large enough to light the ballroom of a palace. The chandeliers were dark except for a few candleless flames burning dispiritedly where thousands had once gleamed.

Their dim illumination cast little light on what at first Melisande thought were piles of coal and stones, but upon more careful investigation turned out to be masses of gems in every color of the rainbow. She held the glowing spore aloft, and the faint rays illuminated mountains of coins in gold, copper, silver, platinum, and rysin, a rare green-blue metal she had seen only once before.

Her gaze returned to the distant ceiling. The chandeliers were fashioned from the ship's wheels from hundreds of vessels. Melisande began to shiver. Her father, Lord Stephen Navarne, would have given anything to have beheld this place, stocked as it was with the history of their people, the Cymrian nation that had fled the cataclysm that would claim their homeland, the Island of Serendair, to come to this place in ships which often did not survive the voyage. The few treasures he had lovingly preserved in the museum he maintained at their keep at Haguefort had caused his blue eyes to gleam with excitement. Looking around, Melisande could only imagine how thrilled he would have been to actually see the wreckage of the First Fleet himself.

Unlike her father, she found such things terrifying.

The dark mountains of coins were piled high in captain's chests and hammocked in massive sails strung from ropes that were moored to the walls of the cave with rigging hardware. Wrecked prows and decks of ships loomed throughout the cavern, as did anchors, masts, and several salt-encrusted figureheads. The eyes of the wooden women adorning those figureheads seemed to stare at her in the dark.

In the center of the great cave was the lagoon of salt water Rhapsody had described, complete with waves that rolled gently to the muddy edges. She could see shapes and shadows of more objects displayed within the waves like offshore rocky formations, but the darkness was too deep to make out what they were.

She did not see what she had expected to find, the enormous shadow of an injured dragon.

"Elynsynos?" she called again. Her voice echoed up and around the gargantuan cave, repeating the beast's name over and over.

Elynsynos? Elynsynos? Elynsynos? Elynsyn—Elyn—El—en—sin—

No sound answered her.

I heard *her,* she thought, fighting back panic as cold sweat sprang from her, leaving her feeling faint. *I* know *I* did.

Rhapsody's voice spoke softly so that it echoed off the surface of the water and vibrated in the ripples it made.

If she is missing, when you report to Gavin, tell him to seal the cave. There is great treasure there, much of it not readily recognizable.

"No," Melisande whimpered aloud. "Don't tell me she's not here. I've come such a long way. Maybe she's just hiding. Please, please, don't tell me she's gone."

"Elynsynos?" she called again, her voice sounding thin and desperate.

The cave thudded with empty silence.

If that lair is plundered, it would mean even greater woe to the continent than it will have already experienced with her loss, said the magical voice. *And take nothing, Melisande—not even a pebble. To do so would be a desecration.*

Her own voice spoke aloud in answer, repeating the words she had said to the Lady Cymrian.

I understand.

I know you do. Rhapsody's answer had been soft with sorrow, and now it was even more mournful, echoing off the dark walls, drowning in the gently lapping waves. *Understand this as well—if through your efforts Elynsynos is found and restored to health, you will be doing this continent one of the greatest services that has ever been done it. And even if it is too late—even if it is, you will be safeguarding more than I can possibly explain.*

I'm ready, her own voice replied in her ear, as it had on that night in winter.

"No I'm *not!*" Melisande shouted. "Why did you send me here? Why would you make me come here if she's *dead*? She can't be dead. She *can't* be!" Tears of rage and pain sprang, hot, from her eyes.

She could feel the warmth on her cheek where Rhapsody had kissed her, and brushed her hand over the place angrily.

We wouldn't be sending you if we didn't believe it. I love you, Melisande. Travel well.

"She *has* to be here! I *heard* her! *Elynsynos!*" Melisande screamed, turning around blindly in the near-dark.

From behind a barrier of coins and gems, a horrific groan went up.

Her scalp tingling with dread and hope, Melisande scrambled to the pile of treasure and started to climb, slipping and falling as she tried to summit it. It took her several attempts to reach the crest, scattering gold pieces in every direction as she did, but finally she pulled herself to the top and looked over it.

Near the lapping water's edge lay a body in the dark, human in shape, prone in the sand.

Could that be Elynsynos? Melisande thought anxiously. Every Cymrian child knew the tale of how the beast had taken human, or rather Seren, form to attract the notice of Merithyn the Explorer, but she had expected the dragon to be in her natural serpentine state. She slid down the other side of the moraine of treasure and ran clumsily to the water's edge, where she fell on her knees beside the body. Then, her hands shaking violently, she held up the glowing spore, wincing at what she beheld.

The woman lay motionless, her face in the cold sand. On one side of her body the clothing was scorched, in some places to ashes, the skin beneath it blistered in horrific coal-colored burns that oozed red. If she was breathing at all, it was shallowly—Melisande could detect no movement whatsoever at her waist, which was scarred black.

Beside the body were scattered fragments of fish bones and traces of kelp, like that she could see floating in the shallows of the lagoon. Gently the little girl slid her hand under the woman's shoulder and turned her slightly onto the side that had not been burned to give her more access to the air. She gasped in horror.

The woman's left eye was poached white like an egg, swollen from beneath a tattered lid. Her face was half obscured by a thick, striated scab of charred skin, obliterating her ability to be recognized. That which remained unburned was dark and hirsute, its untouched eye fixed on the ceiling.

"Elynsynos?" Melisande whispered.

The woman's remaining eye blinked, but she said nothing.

This can't be the dragon, Melisande thought as her stomach turned over, threatening to spill its contents onto the sand. She fought her gorge back down as the voice that had been speaking to her since her entrance to the sacred lands spoke again.

They should comb the woods for a lost Firbolg midwife named Krinsel.

It took a moment for the words to register in her mind. Then she looked again at what remained of the woman's face and suddenly realized why she appeared so dark and hirsute—she was of a bastard race of demihumans who lived in the far mountains. Though Melisande had heard many childish tales of the Firbolg race, considered monsters by the humans of Roland, Rhapsody had taught her another view of them, and she herself had loved Grunthor, the giant Sergeant-Major, himself half Bolg, from the first time she had met him in early childhood.

"Krinsel?" Melisande asked. She leaned closer to the wounded woman. "Are you Krinsel?"

With great effort, the woman nodded once.

Perhaps there had been something so overwhelming in the prospect of discovering an injured dragon that Melisande had been able to distance herself from the possibility of real intervention. She had believed she would be given instructions, then would run for all her might back to Gavin, for surely no ten-year-old could be expected to minister to the wounds of such a beast. But now, upon discovering no beast but a flesh-and-blood being that was suffering on the sand in front of her, reality returned with a vengeance, and she began to weep, uncertain of what she should do.

"Dear All-God," she murmured as she ran her hand over her hair. "Dear All-God—"

The Firbolg woman strained to form a word. "Water," she croaked.

The word was not a request, but delivered, softly as it was, in the calm, commanding voice of one who had brought scores of children into a world of pain. Something in the tone was so intractable that Melisande's foggy mind cleared instantly. She tore into her pack and quickly produced the waterskin, holding it carefully to the disfigured woman's lips. Krinsel drank in desperation, then closed her remaining eye and laid her head back on the sand.

"Can you—can you walk?" Melisande asked. "I could help you—"

"You—alone?"

"Yes—I mean, no," Melisande stammered. "There is a healer nearby, about a day's journey, and the Invoker—"

"Bring—them."

"All right," the little girl said, rising. "I'll run as fast as I can. Hold on, and I will be back—"

The Firbolg midwife shook her head. "Wait for—morning," she whispered. "Dark now."

Melisande glanced back up the lightless tunnel and wondered how she knew. She surmised that the injured woman had been living off kelp and whatever fish she could catch in the shallows, but there was no fresh water in the cave, and the thirst, coupled with the burns, must be torturous. "Very well," she said at last. "You must eat. I have some apples, and the juice will be good for the thirst."

The Bolg woman said nothing, but made a faint attempt to nod.

"Did—Elynsynos do this to you?" Melisande asked as she rooted through her pack for food that would soothe the woman's tattered throat.

A slight shake of the head was all Krinsel could muster. "Anwyn," she whispered.

"Anwyn? Anwyn's dead—" Melisande began, but then remembered there were many things in the world that she, the insignificant sister of the young duke of Navarne, was not privy to. *That needs to come to an end,* she thought as she pulled the knife from her boot sheath and began to pare down the apple. *If I'm going to be sent on missions like this, I need to know what's actually going on. I'm going to have to speak to the Lord Cymrian about this as soon as I get back.*

The impudence of the thought made her cringe a moment later, and she set about tending to the woman's needs as best she could until exhaustion overcame her. She stretched out beside the Bolg midwife and fell into a deep, dreamless sleep on the sand.

How long she lay there she would never know, but she awoke to the sound of Krinsel's ragged breathing, sand impressed into her skin and hair. She sat up and leaned over the woman in the dark. The spore had extinguished; only the faintest of light remained in the cave from the flames in the chandeliers, but even in that dim illumination Krinsel's remaining skin appeared grayer, more sallow than she thought it had been when she first saw it.

"Is it morning yet?" she whispered to the disfigured woman.

Krinsel nodded slightly, her eyes still closed.

"How can you tell?"

The scarred forehead wrinkled in the effort to form words.

"Tide—is—out."

Melisande turned and saw that she was right. The water in the lagoon had withdrawn by a distance of a score of paces. She rose and followed the shoreline deeper into the cave, closer to the objects in the lagoon. One appeared to be shaped like a giant fork, another had the outline of a woman with a fish's tail. Everything else had receded into the dark.

Melisande turned back, brushing the sand from her trousers and shirt as best she could.

"I'm going for help," she said. She took the waterskin from her pack and laid it gently on the woman's abdomen, taking care to avoid the most badly burned area, and positioned her hand atop it. "I'm leaving the remains of the supplies here, too; they are next to you, here, where you can reach them. I'll be back, Krinsel, just hold on a little longer, please."

The Bolg midwife did not respond.

She is considered a great leader among her people, Melisande thought, remembering Rhapsody's tales of Bolg clan society, and how different it was from human rulership. She had liked the fact that the women who assisted in birth were valued among almost every other faction, and that children were considered valuable as well. *The most valuable warrior would be left to bleed to death on the battlefield when measured against the needs of a laboring woman. One represents only the present, the other, the future,* Rhapsody had said.

Krinsel coughed weakly, convulsed, then went still again.

I'm going to save you, Melisande thought. Dread and fear had been banished by her sleep in the dragon's cave; now she felt only determination and a sense of focused mission.

"I'll be back," she promised again as she tied her boots and leggings. "I'll be back soon."

She hurried up the long and winding tunnel, out into the fresh air again, and made her way as quickly as she could around Mirror Lake to where the Invoker said he would be waiting.

The sun had risen halfway up the welkin of the sky; the day was later than she had hoped, and the way longer than she remembered it. She stopped a few times to rest, but only for a few moments, driven on by the urgency that had taken root in her belly. She tried not to think about the sight of the woman's face, but it haunted her as she ran.

She had gotten only halfway around the shoreline when dusk began to set in. Birds twittered nervously as the air began to grow heavier with the moisture of night. The wind picked up, blowing her curly tresses in her face, so she stopped long enough to bind them back, when in the near distance a howl rose on the wind behind her.

Wolves—dear All-God, no, she thought as her blood ran cold, *no, not now. I have to get help for Krinsel. And if I die, what will Gwydion do? He'll be all alone in the world.*

She broke into a blind run, darting haphazardly through the underbrush, pushing aside the wild berry bushes and silvery thorns that scratched her face and snagged her hair. Her heart beat wildly in her chest, drowning out her common sense and causing her to gasp for air. The woods were losing light by the moment, the gleaming white tree trunks growing gray with the setting sun. The shore of Mirror Lake was quickly lost to sight as she scrambled through the thickets, her desperation taking her off course and losing her way even more profoundly.

And then, all at once, she was falling, sucked down from the faint light into blackness. For a moment there was only air around her; then, with a sickening *thud,* the wind was knocked out of her, and she struggled for breath, sinking in mud and dead leaves that swelled around her head. She tried to call for help, but the muck rushed into her mouth, choking her.

In that moment, Melisande knew with adult certainty, even at the mere age of not quite ten years, that when she tried to take another breath, she would only be able to inhale mud and the detritus from the forest floor, that no air would come into her lungs.

That she was dying.

She did not think of Krinsel, who until that moment had been foremost in her mind. The thought of leaving her brother Gwydion behind also vanished, as did any thought of the future, of rejoining her parents beyond the Veil of Hoen in the Afterlife. *At least I am buried,* she thought without sorrow. *My body will not be torn to pieces and devoured by coyotes, the way that poor woman we found was. The earth is my grave.*

Between her hands a smooth, slender tree branch suddenly appeared, as if by magic. It tapped against her chest, then slid between her hands again. Foggy from lack of air, Melisande pushed it away, but it returned insistently, pressing against her chest. Finally she grasped it and was pulled, amid the sucking of mud, out of the devouring mire, coated with muck to her hairline, back into the air of the world again.

A strong, rough hand grasped her by the back of her vest and swung her away from the hole.

"Lady Melisande Navarne, were you running in a forest at night?" came the gruff, familiar voice of the Invoker. He set her down on the forest floor.

The little girl wiped the sludge from her eyes, opening two gleaming white spheres in an otherwise black shadow in the last rays of the setting sun.

Then she spat out the mud that had filled her mouth a moment before.

"Yes," she said. "I was running from wolves."

"No, you were not," Gavin said solemnly. "There are no wolves in these woods, just coyotes. And you should never turn your back on either of them, nor should you run in a forest you don't know, for fear of deadfall such as the one you have just escaped. Haven't you learned *anything* in our time together?"

"Apparently not," Melisande said. She made another pass with the back of her sleeve at her mouth, succeeding only in filling it with more mud.

For the first time since she had been with him, the Invoker laughed.

"Follow me to the lake," he said, taking her by the shoulder. "It will be cold, but better than dragging around twice your weight in mire. Did you find the dragon's lair?" The little girl nodded in the dark. "And what did you discover there?"

"I came upon the Bolg midwife Rhapsody asked your foresters to look for," Melisande replied. She spat again into the underbrush as she walked beside the Invoker. "She is gravely injured—she needs help right away."

Gavin nodded. "And the dragon?"

Melisande sighed sadly as the surface of Mirror Lake appeared beyond the bracken, gleaming with mist in the dusk. She went to the water's edge and scooped what liquid was not in icy form into her hands, then splashed it onto her face. She did so again, but this time took some into her mouth, which she cleared, then spat out the liquid dirt.

The taste of the grave remained.

"Seal the cave," she said.

THE FAR NORTHEASTERN WILDS OF THE KREVENSFIELD PLAIN

$\mathcal{D}$eep within the earth in the cold northeastern desert wastelands, another dragon, the dragon Anwyn, daughter of Elynsynos, felt herself dying.

The beast had been lying within the relatively small comfort of the earth for as long as her tattered mind could remember. That she was in the broken ruins of a place of healing was only intermittently clear to her; her memory had been limited to only the things in the forgotten Past, a waste, given that she had once been the indisputably powerful Seer of that realm, into which only a few had sight.

Today she was mourning, though she was not certain why.

If her mind had been whole, it would have remembered that the event she was grieving was the relatively recent murder of her sister, the middle of the trio of triplets to which she belonged, born of an ancient mariner of a Firstborn race and the dragon who had fallen in love with him, taken a human form, and given birth to the three cursed and powerful offspring. Her sister Rhonwyn had been the one of the three that was mildest and gentlest, though her fragility of thought was maddening to most who knew her. She had been incapable of holding on to the Present beyond the moment that it had turned into the Past, a few seconds after it had occurred, and so she spent most of her life alone in an abbey in Sepulvarta, the holy City of Reason, sought after only by a few pilgrims looking for her fleeting guidance.

Until recently, when she had been thrown a thousand feet to her death from a tower into a chasm, an ignominious end to the most harmless of the Manteids, the Seers of the Past, Present, and Future.

Thrown by the hand of a man who was about to take hold of the royal scepter of state of a nation.

Anwyn, who when in the human form she was given at birth was the Seer of the Past, would have felt the emotions of the event but could not remember the details. She could also not have seen that the third sister, Manwyn, whose gift of sight looked into the Future, had once foretold of their fragile middle sister's death, because Anwyn's sight had faded both by the imminence of her own impending death and by the word of a woman with the power of Naming, who had retitled her the Forgotten Past.

It was a shame, the beast thought as she sensed the round blade of cold-fired rysin-steel, blue in color and jagged of edge, embedded in her body near her heart, that she only could remember the hate she felt for that woman.

A woman whose name, at least, she remembered.

Rhapsody.

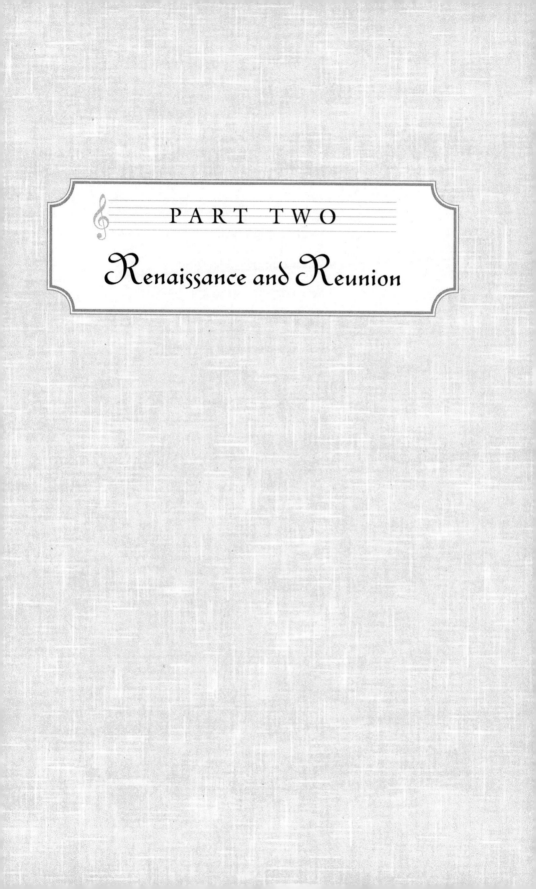

PART TWO

Renaissance and Reunion

THE POEM OF SEVEN

Seven Gifts of the Creator

Seven colors of light

Seven seas in the wide world

Seven days in a sennight

Seven months of fallow

Seven continents trod, weave

Seven eras of history

In the eye of God

6

GURGUS PEAK, YLORC, THE BOLGLANDS

ℜhapsody stood on a threshold, literally and figuratively, rubbing the nervous sweat from her hands. Behind her was the rubble of destruction, some of it cleared, much of it left as a reminder of the consequences of failure. Before her was uncertainty.

And the sound of agony.

The suffering of the man who awaited her ministrations in the vast room beyond the threshold would not be recognizable to most who heard it as expressions of pain. Indeed, the Firbolg guards who held watch outside the crumbled doorway seemed to take no notice of it whatsoever. But Rhapsody, attuned as she was to the vibrations of the world, knew that the soft whistling and scratching sounds foretold the imminent death of a being nearly as old as the world was old, and whose life force was slipping away with each passing second.

And with him, he would perhaps take the last hope of that world.

Behind her in the hallway was another sound, a wailing as intense as the dying gasps of the man beyond the door. No one else would have found it as compelling as Rhapsody, however, as she was attuned to this noise in a very similar, though more personal, way.

"First Woman?" The Bolg midwife's voice was tentative.

Rhapsody smiled involuntarily. It was a name she had not heard in long time, a name the Bolg had given her when she and her two companions, one now their king and the other the commander of their military forces, had first come to the mountainous realm of Ylorc. She had been out of place here among the demi-human Firbolg clans, who had considered her a wasted source of food as long as she was still walking around, but she had gained acceptance here eventually. She had left them, gone on to her own life and lands.

Now that she had returned, three years later, the name was a sign that she was still seen as being under the king's protection, as the Bolg presumed she was his favorite courtesan.

"Yes?"

"Your child is hungry."

Rhapsody sighed, closing her eyes as she wished she could close her ears.

"I know, believe me," she said, pressing her forearm against her breasts, which were filling at the sound of the baby's cries. "Please, Yltha, try and soothe him if you can. I can't feed him right now."

The hirsute woman nodded and retreated down the stone tunnel with the squalling infant.

Rhapsody's gaze followed them into the darkness. The sound of her baby's wails vibrated on her skin, burning, until he was long out of earshot.

Another sound, almost as loud and less pleasant, drew her attention back to the doorway.

"Any time you would like to favor us with your presence, Rhapsody, we would be ever so grateful." The sandy, fricative words dripped with sarcasm so poisonous that they stung her ears.

She exhaled deeply, then turned and made her way over the broken rubble and into the room beyond.

Oil lanterns gleamed in a circle at the very edges of the room, casting shadows that flitted and danced ominously on the smoothly hewn stone walls. Rhapsody looked up to the ceiling of the cylindrical tower above her. It was shrouded in protective canvas and wood, having been the focus of intensive reconstruction after the explosion that had shattered the stained-glass dome, leaving unfractured only the red and blue panels of what had once been a full spectrum in rainbow colors. The towering room in which she stood, in actuality a hollow mountain peak, tapered up to that ceiling, causing every footstep to echo loudly as the noise bounced up to the dome at the top of the cylinder.

In the center of the room around an altar of sorts made of black stone stood her two dearest friends in the world. Achmed the Snake, the Firbolg king, glared at her with an annoyance she could see even in the dark and the flickering shadows, his mismatched eyes staring her down as if she were prey. Looming beside him was his sergeant-major, Grunthor, seven and a half feet of musculature casting a shadow so large that it shaded the entire stone slab.

"Don't let us call you away from anything important," the Firbolg king said.

"I'm here," Rhapsody replied steadily. "I have sung this man songs of sustaining all night, Achmed, but beyond 'Rath,' I do not know his True Name, and even if I did, I doubt I could pronounce it. I needed to clear my head before we attempt something that every ally you have has warned you against. Forgive me if I'm a little hesitant to delve into powers beyond my understanding that have consequences beyond my imagination should I misstep."

"Are you sure your hesitancy doesn't have more to do with your howling brat?" Achmed said, gesturing out the doorway to the hall. "His screams are still irritating my skin. I should leave him out on the peaks for the hawks."

"Quite sure," Rhapsody said acidly as she came deeper into the room. "I just sent him away, unfed. I believe I have my priorities straight, Achmed, but lest you forget, that howling brat is the reason I'm here, not your great glass instrumentality. I agreed to help you with this Lightcatcher, but that is not why I came back to the mountains with you."

"I don't care why you came back. Now that you're here, I need to focus your attention on Rath."

Rhapsody looked down at the suffering man on the stone slab. In the half-light he looked so different from the first time she had seen him. Like the rest of his race, this ancient Dhracian had translucent eyelids covering great black eyes that seemingly had no scleras, and skin traced with exposed veins from the crown of his bald head to the ends of his fingertips. Now, having returned a few hours before from tracking and unsuccessfully attempting to kill a demon even more ancient than himself, he was almost unrecognizable. Blood-red veins bulged in the paper-thin eyelids, ropey lines across his skull. His dusky skin was mottled and bruised, as if all of his blood had emptied beneath it, though no puncture wounds could be seen. Her songs of sustaining and healing had left him no worse off than he was when he returned, but not much better.

"How soon until First-light?" she asked the Firbolg men.

"Dawn'll be breakin' any moment now, Duchess," Grunthor, the Sergeant-Major, said.

"And how long until it rises high enough to reach the windows?"

"The red panel, the panel of healing, is the closest to the horizon," Achmed said. "Once the sun crests the peaks of the eastern Teeth, in the better part of two hours, we should have red light."

"I'm not sure he'll hold on that long." Rhapsody laid her hand gently on the dying Dhracian's head. His skin was cold, as cold as a corpse's; she could barely feel the tides of his breath. *Live, Rath,* she willed silently, watching the strange-looking man struggle to comply. *Please live. I don't know what I am doing.*

Achmed glanced up at the dark canvas, then turned to the depths of the room where a heavily bearded young human man lingered in the shadows.

"Omet."

"Yes, Your Majesty?"

"Take three of the other artisans up to the peak and remove the cover of the dome. It's almost morning." Achmed felt the slight vibration of Omet's head nodding in assent, but kept his attention on the dying man in front of him as Omet started across the massive room for the door.

Rhapsody exhaled, trying force the panic out with her breath. She pushed everything else from her mind and focused her concentration on Rath again.

There was a beauty, a magic in this dying entity that she had seen before, twice. It defied her ability to put words to, strange for a Lirin Namer who by profession sought to know every True Name in the world. She could find the music in almost anything—the voice of the earth, the vibration of the stars, the whispers of meadow grass, the thundering of the waves of the sea, the crackling of fire—but there was something special about the wind, the element which carried the magic of her mother's race, that reached down into her heart whenever she was in the presence of those born of it.

As Rath had been born of it, purely and without the pollution of any other element, in the First Age of the world.

Even her friend the Bolg king, as obnoxious and offensive as he could be, and was being now, had been born of it, and she held him in her heart in spite of his surly behavior.

She bent back over the dying Dhracian. His eyes had gone glassy, and he was slowly turning the color of chalk.

"Rath," she whispered. "Live. Please."

"That's the best you can do?" Achmed demanded. "I could have had the piss boy from the third column of the Blasted Heath do that, with seemingly the same outcome."

"The only other thing I can think of to try is empathic healing, taking his injuries onto myself," Rhapsody said, searching his neck for his pulse and finding none. "But these injuries are not from the crushing blow of the titan that intervened in the Thrall ritual—it's the damage done to his heart when it was suddenly torn from its connection with the demon he was attempting to kill. Were I to take that on, to absorb that damage, my guess is that *you* would then have to nurse and wean Meridion, Achmed."

"I've already told you my solution for that—hawks."

"Not funny, sir." Grunthor's voice was uncharacteristically serious. "Yer not to even think o' doin' that, Duchess, 'owever important or ancient this bloke may be. That's an order. An' don't threaten the lit'le prince, sir— 'e's my friend and sleepin' partner."

Rhapsody looked up at the dome again, then turned quickly and called to Omet, who had just reached the doorway.

"Omet! Wait."

The young artisan stopped, looking questioningly at the Firbolg king, who exhaled in annoyance, then signaled his permission.

"Do you have any of the frits of glass left over from the original firings?" Rhapsody asked. Omet nodded. "Any of the red?" The artisan nodded again. "Please bring one to me, a little bigger than your hand—but make sure it is one that you have matched exactly to the color keys." The young man walked back into the recesses of the room as the Three returned their gaze to the dying Dhracian.

"Clarify something for me, Achmed," Rhapsody said as dark blood began to drip from Rath's mouth. "In Gwylliam's time, when this was a Lightforge, rather than a Lightcatcher, the power source was pure elemental fire from the heart of the Earth, piped here from the flamewell in the Loritorium below, right?"

"Yes." She could almost hear the dust of his clenched teeth in his voice. "It has been adapted to use the light of the sun now instead, as you bloody well know."

"Don' think 'e has two hours left in 'im, sir," Grunthor whispered.

For a moment Rhapsody continued to stare down at Rath, bringing her right hand to rest on his fractured heart. Then, without looking up, she spoke two words, and they echoed strangely in the tower room, as if they came from a deeper part of her.

"Step away," she said.

She put out her left hand as Omet returned to the stone altar and nervously placed a rectangular piece of red glass onto her palm, then carefully withdrew ten paces, his black eyes glittering in the light of the oil lanterns. Her eyes still locked on Rath, Rhapsody moved it into position in an angle above his heart exactly matching that of the spectrum of broken glass in the dome above.

"Achmed," she said quietly, "hold this. Here. Keep your fingers to the outside edge."

The Bolg king obeyed, his mismatched eyes watching intently.

As soon as she was certain of the sureness of Achmed's grip, Rhapsody slowly released the frit. Then, her hand still on the Dhracian's heart, slightly lower and to the right in his chest cavity than a human's, just as Achmed's was, she took hold of the hilt of her sword and carefully drew it from its sheath of Black Ivory, the same inert stone from which the altar was made.

Daystar Clarion, the ancient weapon of two elements, ether and fire, whispered forth from its sheath, a clear note like the sound of a horn winding as it came. Its blade gleamed with the light of the stars, while tongues of the purest flame licked up it from hilt to tip. Rhapsody took her eyes off Rath long enough to bring the sword into place behind the frit of red glass in Achmed's hand.

A palm-sized ray of ruby-colored light shone through the frit, gleaming brightly, pulsing as the fire of the sword pulsed. It came to rest on Rath's heart, just above where Rhapsody's hand rested.

Four sets of eyes watched intently.

After a long moment, Achmed spoke.

"Nothing is happening. I see no change."

"Of course you don't," Rhapsody whispered crossly. "Shhhh."

She opened her mouth and intoned a note, *ut*, the first in the common octave of Naming, voicing it a moment later with the word for it in the ancient lore, power from the Before-Time in the earliest days of the world.

Lisele.

At first there was no sign of any change.

Rhapsody's mind was racing, thinking methodically of the filmy parchment manuscript Achmed had showed her of the plans for this instrumentality, remembering the list of the True Names of the color spectrum, age-old lore that terrified her. It had been graphed in the manuscript in musical script, with the symbols for sharp and flat, and the words in Ancient Serenne, the language of the Lost Island of Serendair.

Blood Saver ♯
Blood Letter ♭

Understanding struck her. She made a slight adjustment to her tone, bringing it up a half-step to the sharp of *ut*, and sang the word again.

Lisele ♯

Above her hand, the area of Rath's heart began to glow as red as the light that was shining on it through the frit. The tone that Rhapsody sang vibrated along the surface of his skin, echoing back in the ruby light.

Omet and the Three watched in amazement as the color spread rapidly over and through Rath's body until it began to shine with a translucence that stung their eyes. Within moments his body was ringing with the tone.

Lisele-ut ♯

And healing before their eyes.

The common injuries, the damage sustained where he had been thrown violently across a forest glen, swelled, then disappeared first, shattered ribs mending visibly beneath the surface of his flesh, abrasions knitting back into smooth skin, bruises vanishing. Longer in the process of repair were the deeper wounds, the metaphysical damage caused when the Thrall ritual, the vibrational tie of hunter's heartbeat to that of prey, had been torn asunder. Rhapsody held the note, breathing in a circular pattern, as the bulging veins in his head and neck receded, his skin grew brighter, the blood that had trickled from his mouth dried and disappeared. Finally, his heartbeat returned, strong enough to be visible, keeping time with the rising and falling of the note Rhapsody sang.

A deep, shuddering gasp issued forth from the Dhracian's lungs.

Then he began breathing again in a regular rhythm, his body returning to an opacity that expelled the red light from within him, shining on the surface of his skin as it did on Rhapsody's hand.

After a few moments, when no further signs appeared, Achmed spoke in a low, quiet voice.

"Rhapsody—he's healed."

The Lady Cymrian exhaled and let the tone come to an end. "How can you tell?" she whispered back. "He still looks—well, fairly awful."

"He's a Dhracian," the Bolg king replied. "We always look awful. I think you can stop now." He put the red frit down on the altar beside

Rath, and flexed his gloved hand, stretching it to ease the cramping that had come into the fingers.

Rhapsody sheathed the sword; as she did, the room returned to darkness again, broken only by the fading flickering of the distant oil lamp flames. She leaned her head over Rath's lips, newly healed, and listened to the tides of his breath in time with the strong beating of his heart. Then she removed her hand and looked at the Bolg king, exhaling deeply once again.

"I believe you are right," she said softly. "I think he is as better as we can make him without knowing his True Name. We should let him sleep now—you can stand guard over him here if you want to, but it might make sense to move him to a bedchamber where he can get some real sleep."

"What did you do? How did you activate the lore without the Lightcatcher?"

Rhapsody put her hands to her face, covering it for a moment. She rubbed her eyes, then pulled her hair back off her forehead.

"Omet—" she began, but the young glass artisan had already taken the hint. He put his hands together, palm to palm, and bowed, then hurried from the room, a look of stark amazement still on his face. As soon as the heavy door was closed, Rhapsody turned to her two friends.

"I can't really explain it to you shortly except to convey this—you know that all of the universe is made up of vibration, of light in the color spectrum, energy, and sound. The basic function of the Lightcatcher is to direct all three kinds of the purest forms of each of those types of vibration together, focusing it where the specific lore, like healing, is needed or wanted. The wheel, the second piece of the instrumentality, focuses the colored light and provides the sound when it is functioning."

"That note you were singing?"

"Yes—and the name. I can explain this further to you, most likely within a circle of protection to prevent being overheard, sometime tomorrow, but right now I am exhausted."

As Achmed and Grunthor continued to stare down at the sleeping Dhracian, Rhapsody hurried to the speaking tubes in the corner of the vast cylindrical room, snapping one of them open.

"Yltha?"

A moment later the reply came up the tube. "Yes, First Woman?"

"Please bring Meridion to me as quickly as you can. I am literally about to explode, and believe me, *no one* wants that."

7

The Teeth
(Manteids)

★

● Night Mountain
Earth Basilica

Desert

PALACE OF JIERNA TAL, JIERNA'SID, SORBOLD

*W*hen Talquist arrived at the bottom of the Great Stair, he laughed aloud in delight.

Standing in the glorious light of the entryway, its towering marble walls illuminated by four hundred candle sconces, were two of the guests whose attendance he had most gleefully anticipated.

Beliac, the king of Golgarn, a seafaring nation to the east of Sorbold's southern coastline, was nervously glancing around the palace of Jierna Tal, his eyes glittering. He was attired in the traveling garments of his office, a military cloak and mantle with a drape at the shoulders in deeply resonant blue, much like the color of the water of the seacoast that was the entire southern border of his realm, with a simple silver circlet crowning his brow. Upon seeing that, except for Jierna Tal's staff, the Diviner, and the Emperor Presumptive himself, he was alone in the entryway, Beliac seemed to relax somewhat, Talquist noted. It was the first time the king of Golgarn had ever been in his palace, had met with him as anything other than the merchant he had been. And Beliac was clearly intimidated.

Talquist was immensely pleased.

Beside Beliac in a similar mantle, gray and trimmed in white fur, stood his even older friend Hjorst, the Diviner of the Hintervold, the cold, frozen realm of permafrost and glaciers to the north of Roland past the Tar'afel River. Talquist suppressed his amusement, knowing the next day would see his friend in the absurd regalia of his station, a massive robe of polar bear fur, a staff browed with curving animal bone, and a random choice of one of his many hats of state, all bearing a lifelike representation of an animal native to his land. Talquist had once been required to carry on a critical negotiation with the Diviner staring across a massive table at the lifelike life-sized model of a sea otter on the man's head; he could barely contain himself at the time. It was one of his best-kept secrets that the Diviner, whose public persona was that of a forbidding, primitive shaman with a thick gray beard reaching to the center of his chest, from a realm of seemingly endless winter nights and disturbingly long summer days, actually was a well-read anti-ascetic who favored bubbling wines, fragile emasculated pastries, and finger sandwiches with the crusts cut off.

"Ah, Majesties, well met! Welcome; I hope your travels were easy."

The Diviner snorted even as he clasped Talquist's shoulder in greeting.

"The journey from my lands took over three weeks, so even though it was uneventful, it can never be described as 'easy' except by migrating birds, Panjeri gypsies, and sea rat merchants such as yourself who actually enjoying plying the wind and the waves," he said testily. "I have been seasick most of that time; thank you, Talquist. I don't know why you couldn't have just accepted the judgment of the Scales a year ago and allowed yourself to be crowned when they chose you in the first place; it would have saved me a second trip after the empress's funeral, the journey from which I had barely gotten over. There had best be some good pastry and fine wine at the celebration tomorrow if you want me to forgive you and drink to your reign."

"You will find some upstairs in a few moments, Hjorst," Talquist replied smoothly, but his skin burned at the Diviner's words. "I thought perhaps a transition to power rooted in humility and selflessness might best serve my nation, but I certainly understand why this concept eludes you." He turned to the nervous king of Golgarn. "Beliac; how very nice to finally be able to host you in my domain." Talquist's eyes twinkled.

"Thank you," said Beliac. His journey had taken only eight days, and being born into the royal family of a seafaring nation, he had strong sea legs.

In spite of his ability to stand steady on the deck of a pitching ship, Talquist could tell that Beliac was quaking quietly on solid ground. Golgarn had always been a realm of solid security, in spite of technically being the Firbolg's neighbor—there were five hundred miles of forbidding mountains between the two kingdoms, making incursions from one into the other unlikely bordering on impossible. Golgarn, therefore, had been blessed with peace for virtually the entirety of its existence, a peace enforced by an overwhelming presence of military might.

As a result, Talquist's manipulation of the deep-seated fear that Beliac had once confided to him when in his cups, an intense terror he harbored of being eaten alive by the Bolg, a fear whose genesis was little more than stupid horror stories told to him by royal nannies and other children, bordered on artistry; cruel, but nonetheless diplomatic artistry. A fortuitous alliance with a pair of assassin's guilds, one in the province of Yarim in Roland, the other within Golgarn itself, had led to the king's willingness to commit his fleet of mostly unused warships to the command of the Emperor Presumptive in return for protection from the Firbolg, something that in fact Beliac did not need.

Even though the king of Golgarn did not know it.

Ah, the joy of friendship, Talquist thought as he embraced Beliac warmly.

"Come, my friends, I have arranged supper and libations for you both in the Great Hall," Talquist said, leading the rulers back toward the Great Stair. "My servants will see to your accommodations while we dine."

$\mathcal{A}$ glittering spread awaited at the top of the stairs. Within the quarter hour the men were settled into comfortable chairs before the grand fireplace, imbibing imported libations from the corners of the Known World and feasting on grouse, roasted vegetables, and sweetmeats. Talquist had been certain to order that the table be laid with an impressive variety of fresh fruits, something he knew that Hjorst craved, especially after the long and brutal winter from which the Hintervold was emerging.

Some of the sweetest salt I have ever rubbed in a wound, he mused from behind his crystal goblet as he watched his guests imbibe his potables and inhale his food.

The benign trap he had laid did not take very long to spring.

"Has Gwydion of Manosse arrived yet?" the Diviner demanded, his deep voice drying the air around them, his fulsome beard quivering in anger. "I have some urgent, and not particularly festive discourse I need to undertake with the Lord Cymrian, though I will be discreet so as not to violate the sanctity and reverence of your Weighing and coronation, Talquist."

"Oh?" The Emperor Presumptive raised his glass to his lips. "Something troubling you, Hjorst?"

"Indeed," said the Diviner. "The bastard has been starving the Hintervold, violating our grain treaties, engendering a famine in my lands. What contracted deliveries he actually does make good on, few and far between as they have been, are tainted with rat droppings, mold, or poison."

Talquist was well aware of this, having been the engineer of it, but he managed to set his face in a troubled mien.

"That's terrible. I actually was thinking that you were looking somewhat thinner, but did not want to mention it. A famine? Why would he do such a thing?"

"Evidence collected from a captured cohort of the Raven's Guild from Yarim points to the Alliance's intention to attack and occupy the riverlands, large parts of the southern Hintervold, this summer," the Diviner said darkly after looking around to make certain he was not overheard. "The Lord and Lady Cymrian are apparently more power- and land-hungry than we were led to believe four years ago when they were chosen and crowned. Clearly they seek to expand their dominion within the Alliance, their claims of friendship evidently notwithstanding."

"What is the Raven's Guild?" asked Beliac, his voice faltering.

"Tilemakers, ceramicists," said Talquist. "My ships have transported their wares for many years."

"They're *assassins*, you idiot." The Diviner scowled. "The tile factory is a cover, though an effective and profitable one."

"Really? I'd no idea." Talquist struggled not to smile behind his glass.

"The southlands bordering the Tar'afel are the only parts of the Hintervold in which agriculture is viable in the short summer growing season," the Diviner continued, growing more agitated as he spoke. "It's apparently not enough for the Lord Cymrian to control Roland, the breadbasket of the continent; now he wants the only fertile parts of my lands. You may have to restrain me, Talquist—I seek to find out what is going on diplomatically, king to king, but if he does not yield immediately there may well be war declared before the cake is cut."

"Likewise, I am hoping for a moment with King Achmed of Ylorc," said Beliac. "Though, er, not alone, if at all possible. Evidence has been uncovered of Firbolg encampments within two leagues of my capital city; this can obviously not be allowed to stand. I—I hope you will assist me with this, Talquist."

Talquist sighed dramatically.

"I do hope that you will both show restraint, at least until the Scales have weighed me and the Scepter of the Sun is in my hand," he said. "It won't really do to have an intercontinental war break out after I've waited the better part of a year, patiently, I believe, to finally ascend the Sun Throne." He leaned back in his chair and smiled, knowing that neither of the kings his guests were intent on seeing would be attending his investiture.

Given that they were already coping with the news of the sacking of the holy city of Sepulvarta.

"The targeting of the southlands is particularly heinous," the Diviner continued, his clear blue eyes, characteristic of his northern birth and distant Cymrian lineage, glinting angrily. "It's bad enough that they seek to attack a sovereign nation, but to disavow long-standing grain treaties which the Hintervold relies upon to feed its population three-quarters of the year, then to bloody the ground of the only growing fields is a form of genocide. I suppose I should not be surprised; Lord Gwydion is the direct descendant of those hateful miscreants Anwyn and Gwylliam, who, once they had conquered the Middle Continent, proceeded to destroy the entire realm in seven hundred years of war over a marital spat, it is said. Even though I myself am spawned of Cymrian blood, it is ancient; I had great reservations when I heard he was appointed to the lordship. He is said to have the blood of the wyrm Elynsynos in his veins; it was only a matter of time before his bloodthirsty nature would out and he would begin swallowing his neighbors."

"Well, given that *I* am his neighbor to the south, this is highly disturbing news," said the Emperor Presumptive. "The last thing I want are the citizens of Sorbold to be eaten alive by the Firbolg of Ylorc, which is a major part of the Cymrian Alliance." He struggled not to laugh aloud as the color fled Beliac's face, remembering how the king had once confided to him while profoundly inebriated after a particularly festive night in Golgarn his childhood nightmare of being devoured so. "It seems we should plan on you both remaining here after the Weighing and coronation to see what we can sort out with our mutual friends, the Lord and Lady Cymrian. Perhaps we can avert the war that seems to be looming."

"If the Lady Cymrian is present, I will need to not be left alone with her at any time," Beliac said decidedly. "Word of her has spread to Golgarn—she is said to be comely, beautiful beyond natural limits, most likely through witchcraft of some kind—and has used her unholy magic to enslave the hearts of men who come into her presence. My wife was most insistent on me keeping my distance. I ask your help in this also, Talquist."

"Happily given," Talquist declared. "We will all have to guard one another's backs in this." He inhaled decisively. "Which puts on the table for later discussion a topic we will need to address."

"That being—?" asked the Diviner.

"The threat of the new Cymrian dynasty to the safety and security of the rest of the continent," the Emperor Presumptive said. "We will talk about it at length, but if you would be so kind, I would like to you come to those discussions with some specific intelligence from your own lands. If you need to do some research, my messenger aviary is available to you at your convenience to send and receive information from your realms."

"What intelligence are you seeking?"

The crystal goblet in Talquist's hand came to a stop in midair, hovering where the light of the fireplace caught in its facets and fragmented a spattering of rainbow patterns on the table before him.

"Information about whatever assassin's guilds reside within your lands, or about whom you have knowledge," he said. He brought the goblet to his lips and took another sip as the Diviner and the king of Golgarn looked at each other askance, amused in the knowledge that he himself was far more aware of and connected to those entities than either of them were.

Within a few moments of the silence that fell at Talquist's words, the two rulers were finished with their food and drink and rose grimly, ready to be shown to their rooms.

"I believe you will find your accommodations comfortable, but if there is anything you require, ring for the chamberlain and he will attend to any need you may have," Talquist said pleasantly as two young female servants in the regalia of the new dynasty appeared at the top of the Great Stair. "Mira, please take King Beliac to his chambers." The young woman bowed and waited for the king to follow her, which he did hastily, glancing back over his shoulder before descending the stair.

The Diviner started to follow him, only to stop when Talquist laid a hand gently on his forearm.

"Tarry a moment, my friend," the almost-emperor said quietly. "I have a boon to ask of you."

The Diviner's brows drew together. "What is it?"

"I was hoping after the coronation I could prevail upon you to bless me with a divination."

Hjorst's eyes widened.

"It is the first day of spring tomorrow, Talquist, a whole season past Yule, when divinations are performed safely."

Talquist sighed. "I know, and I am very sorry and reluctant to impose upon you," he said. "It is of the highest import, though, and I was thinking that perhaps the auspicious occasion tomorrow might lend safety and power to the undertaking."

"Perhaps," said the Diviner doubtfully. "But, given that I am not within my own duomo, I will need access to a holy place of power, an altar of some sort on which I can spill blood." A thought occurred to him. "Though I would hesitate to do so, we could possibly consider using the Scales."

Talquist shuddered inwardly, but betrayed no emotion. The Diviner was referring to the ancient instrumentality that stood in the square outside the palace, its immense size casting an enormous shadow over the land, a giant set of weighing scales with plates large enough to each hold an oxcart. The Scales were considered the arbiter of all things of consequence, the decider of questions of great importance, as they had been brought with the Cymrian refugees a millennia and half ago from the old world, and had been imbued with the wisdom of that land. Any time a throne was left empty, or a dispute over territory or the need to go to war was felt, the Scales had weighed the possibilities and rendered a decision that was considered indisputable and final. It had shown wisdom and unbiased objectivity in all its renderings.

Until, of course, Talquist had found a way to rig the weighing of the candidates for the open throne of the empire of Sorbold.

A throne he had made open by killing both the empress and the Crown Prince himself.

"We will see what we can come up with," he said nonchalantly. "There is no need to concern yourself with it tonight, Hjorst. Let Kryst show you to your room, good sleep and pleasant dreams to you after your long journey. Thank you for coming all this way for my investiture. I tell you sincerely, this special time for me would not have been the same without you being here to share it with me, my friend."

The Diviner nodded wearily and followed the servant down the Great Stair. Talquist watched him descend, then sat back down in his chair, refilled his glass, and held it up to the firelight. The goblet caught the light of the flames again, this time causing a warm red glow like a mask on his eyes.

He smiled, amused at his last words to the Diviner.

They were the only truthful thing he had said all night.

He cast a glance over at the statue of the titanic soldier. Though its eyes remained colorless, Talquist was quite certain he could ascertain a slight smile on its stone lips as well.

8

Once the Diviner and the king of Golgarn had gone to bed, Talquist sent for another guest.

The soon-to-be emperor was drowsing in front of the fire, his glass almost empty, when a respectful tap came at the door of the library, a smaller, more private room than the massive hall where he had supped with the two monarchs.

"Come," he said pleasantly.

The door opened silently, and a thin man with similarly thin, long hair entered the room even more silently. His face was hollow, with a hooked nose between two eyes of devouring darkness. He was attired in far grander couture than he had been the last time Talquist had seen him, when he and his subordinate from the Raven's Guild had come in their ratty cloaks and dark, unremarkable clothing, looking to parley in the even rattier, darker business of assassin's guilds.

Now he was indistinguishable from any of the other guests of state that were being housed in Jierna Tal for the grand occasion of Talquist's Weighing on the Scales and subsequent coronation the next day.

"Well, good evening, Dranth," Talquist said. He drained his glass, then rose, went to the decanter, passing the enormous statue of a soldier that filled the corner of the study, and filled his glass again.

"And to you, m'lord," the thin man answered, bowing slightly. "Felicitations and congratulations on your ascent tomorrow."

"Thank you." Talquist sat back down. He had not offered the man anything to drink. "I trust all is well in Yarim."

Dranth nodded, still standing in the place he stopped when he came in.

"I am delighted with your work in Golgarn," Talquist said. "The documents you planted were convincing enough for Beliac to happily surrender a good two-thirds of his fleet; he put every warship I asked for at my disposal."

Dranth smiled slightly. "I think that might have more to do with the false camp of, er, Bolg that was set up in the foothills just outside the capital. Inspired, to be able to convince a man with an extraordinary reputation for scholarship that monsters who haven't moved closer than five hundred miles to his kingdom for the last six hundred years are lurking five miles outside his castle door. Sheer artistry, Majesty."

"We make a good team," the emperor-to-be acknowledged. "Speaking of teams, are you still working in concert with the Spider's Clutch of Golgarn?"

"Yes, Majesty. We are awaiting your orders."

"Delightful. Then let me show you the next assignment I would like you to undertake."

Talquist turned to the large stone titan in the corner of the room and nodded.

The irises in the statue's eyes went from inanimate stone to a piercing blue. Its muscles flexed; then it walked slowly over to the Emperor Presumptive.

Dranth's eyebrows rose slightly, but otherwise his face was impassive.

"Faron," Talquist said, humor in his voice, "meet Dranth. He is the guild scion of the Raven's Guild in Yarim Paar." The titan stared at the assassin with its milky blue eyes, disconcertingly out of place in the otherwise-stone face.

"It was my understanding when you came here last time that you have sworn a blood oath of vengeance against Achmed of Ylorc, king of the Firbolg," said Talquist. "Is that still the case?"

"A blood oath, by its very nature, is eternal, Majesty," Dranth answered dryly. "So therefore, since, for the moment, the Bolg king lives, yes."

"And are you willing to undertake, with your fellows in both the Raven's Guild and the Spider's Clutch of Golgarn, an assassination within the Firbolg mountains?"

Dranth exhaled, though no part of his body moved.

"In our hearts, with utter certainty. But our minds are aware that the mountains are all but unassailable. Esten, our guildmistress in Yarim, sent back schematics and drawings of the fortifications of the mountains, along with schedules of troop movements and details of the traps they employ.

Even knowing this information, we have been unable to find even the smallest hole in the shield, the tiniest opening to slip through." His voice faltered; the Emperor Presumptive knew it was because after the guildmistress had send back those schematics and drawings, the Bolg had sent back her rotting head in a crate.

Talquist smiled broadly. "What if I could show you a map to such an opening?"

"That would be most interesting."

The Emperor Presumptive's smile waned. "Interesting enough to expand your blood oath to include his associates and fellow Cymrians?"

Dranth raised an eyebrow.

"I am willing to show you a way into Canrif," said Talquist, "but in return, I want you to make it a policy to remove any Cymrians in positions of power, there or elsewhere across the Alliance, from those positions. And, when you are in Canrif, I want you to specifically search for a child, possibly the child of the Lord and Lady Cymrian. I suspect this child and its mother are hiding there, though I have no proof of that."

"Show me the way in, and I will kill whoever you like," said Dranth.

"Ah, ah—I do not want the child on that list. This is of critical importance. I do not know if it is in fact an infant, or weaned, but if it is as young as I suspect it is—I have reason to believe it was born three months ago, at Yule—it may still be a nursing infant, which would mean you would need to keep the mother alive as well, at least until you deliver the baby to me."

"We do not specialize in delivering anything live, Majesty. But I am willing to undertake what you ask if you really have a map of an entrance. Esten never found such a doorway."

"But I, Dranth, I will. I will show you exactly where you can enter the Firbolg kingdom, the precise doorway—in return for but one hair from your head."

Dranth swallowed. He was well aware of the import of the request; the possession of someone's hair, even a single strand of it, made it possible for that person to be tracked anywhere the wind could reach. The Raven's Guild made extensive use of such things when pursuing a victim. To agree to such a thing was a tremendous personal risk.

But to refuse might mean the condemnation of his blood oath to failure.

A far worse fate.

"Done," he said.

Talquist approached the guild scion and took hold of a strand of his thin hair. He plucked it from the man's head, evoking no reaction from Dranth. Satisfied, he looked at the titan.

The statue stared at Dranth a moment longer.

Then it opened its massive hand.

In its palm was an oblong, irregular object, gray in color, thin with a finely tattered edge, like a giant fish scale. The statue turned its palm at a slight angle, and a flash of blue light skittered across the object's surface.

"Come and look at the scale, Dranth," Talquist said softly, almost reverently.

The guild scion came close enough to see the object in the statue's hand, near enough to hear it breathe. He looked down at the dull gray surface, finely scored with tiny lines that made it look like it came from the hide of a snake.

Then, before his eyes, he watched the scale turn translucent.

It seemed as if there was a tiny image on its surface. Dranth looked closer.

At first what he could make out looked like the primitive picture of an eye with clouds surrounding it, but unobscured by them. Then, as he stared at the scale, the picture seemed to clear and resolve into one of an almost endless range of mountains, layer upon layer of fanglike peaks rising to a sky as blue as the light that had danced across the scale's surface. A moving image of the sun rose slowly in the east, providing a directional reference.

Then the picture seemed to home in on a particular place within the peaks. It was a small internal canyon nestled deep within the mountains, with rock walls that rose up in a tall circle, leading down into a dark hole where the rocky ground should have been.

As if his eyes had wings, the image moved, following the perspective of the filmy picture as it dove downward past the walls of the round interior canyon to a small, grassy field at its bottom. The rockwalls that he had seen from above now seemed to tower over the field, as if to indicate that the canyon was deep underground and hidden within the peaks.

After a moment, the translucent image shifted, and once again moved. Dranth's eyes followed it as it sped to the edge of the canyon's field to the south, ending at the shore of a dark, underground lake, a lake within a massive cave with a high vault of stone above it. The image sped across the lake, past an island at its center that had the remains of a gazebo at its far edge surrounded by nothing but rubble where a small house, trees, and extensive gardens had all been reduced to ash.

Dranth, who had no idea what he was seeing, watched woozily as the image sped across the other side of the lake to a shore that led up to an underground passageway, finally opening into the light of a much larger but very much similar canyon, this one also a circle with high, towering walls, its field above the ground riven by an enormous hole in the center.

The walls that rimmed it reached up to the open sky above.

The tiny image continued to move, heading to the tall circular wall, a seemingly unbroken stand of rock, until it came to a hallway of a sort hidden by the bends and crevasses in the canyon wall. Dranth watched as it sped down the hallway in the rock, the sides of the small pass reaching up on either side of it, until it finally opened into a heath that overlooked a colossal city, carved from the very face of the mountains themselves.

Hirsute, demi-human soldiers in studded leather armor were patrolling the mountain passes around the city.

Dhranth blinked.

Canrif.

He had seen inside Canrif itself, in detail.

As if on a spool of filmy thread, the image rewound itself, speeding back down the hidden hallway, into the wide-open canyon with the broken meadow, back to the passage that led to the underground grotto, across the dark subterranean lake, over the desolate ruins on the island in the center, across the other side of the lake to the tiny tunnel that led to the smaller, underground canyon, up into the sky that opened into a seemingly endless range of fanglike mountain peaks.

The image faded and disappeared, leaving the scale in the titan's hands blank and gray again.

"This, I believe, is the only unguarded entrance to Canrif," the Emperor Presumptive said. "From the maps that Esten sent you, and what you have just seen, can you determine how to get inside?"

"Absolutely." Dranth's almost skeletal face stretched into the first true smile Talquist had seen since the guild scion had entered the room.

"Good. Now, let us be clear in our understanding, as I always try to do in business. I have shown you not only the way into Canrif, but the scrying instrument I use to look into distant places which are often otherwise hidden from my sight. I want you to forget that you have seen this instrument, Dranth, to let it utterly disappear from your head, leaving the image it showed you remaining there. If you ever reveal its existence, if I ever hear of it on the wind, it would have been better if your own head had been placed in the box along with that of your mistress that the Bolg delivered to you after discovering who she was, and that she was inside their mountain. I assume I don't have to explain to you what you have given me in collateral for this information?"

"Of course not, Majesty," Dranth said darkly.

"Excellent. I just wanted to be sure. The Dynasty of the Dark Earth is gone, crumbled to dust with the death of the Empress Leitha last year. Tomorrow I will ascend to the new dynastic throne to undertake the beginning of the Empire of the Sun and, like its namesake, it will be a shining era. I certainly hope our long-standing friendship and business relationship will dissuade either side from betraying the other. There is so much potential for everyone to prosper greatly, to make old enemies suffer, and to gain the power that we, whose ancestors ruled these lands long before the Cymrians arrived, should have had all along."

"Agreed," said Dranth.

"Good. When will you and your company leave for Canrif?"

"Tomorrow, after your Weighing and coronation."

"Perfect. Send word to me when you have accomplished your task. And be careful of the child, should you find it—if it is less than a year in age, bring its mother along as well. Do not defile her until I have determined whether she is nursing or not."

"Of course not." Dranth's eyes darkened in displeasure at the affront.

"Please do not take offense, Dranth. If, as I surmise, the child's mother is the Lady Cymrian, you will have quite a fight on your hands. Her husband destroyed an entire corhort of my soldiers single-handedly that had come in disguise to Haguefort, I'm told. She is said to be formidable in her own right, and beautiful enough to melt even your granite heart."

"I have no heart, Majesty. The only thing that beats within my chest is the rage that feeds my blood oath."

"Indeed, but you still have eyes, and a tarse between your legs, I assume. You may need to employ a paralytic to incapacitate her; she will doubtless fight like a demon to protect her child."

"I am ready."

Talquist nodded. "Now, if you will excuse me, I need to retire for the night. Tomorrow is destined to be a great day, but most such days begin early. Good night."

Dranth bowed, his wraithlike body as straight as an arrow, then took his leave of the library.

The eyes of the massive statue focused on his back, boring holes in it that he could feel even after he closed the door behind him.

9

HIGHMEADOW, ROLAND

𝒩o matter how many glasses of Canderian brandy he poured down his gullet, the pain in Tristan Steward's ribs would not recede. His lungs were clear enough to breathe in the smoky air of the library to which he had fled a few hours earlier, but each breath was labored, causing his sides to hurt with the effort of taking in air. With a bitter hiss of liquid through clenched teeth, he bolted back another snifter's contents and closed his blue eyes, then ran his fingers meaninglessly through his sweat-soaked auburn hair, hot and brittle from sitting endlessly before the library's roaring hearth.

Steward, the Lord Roland and prince of Bethany, was trying and failing to blot from his mind the vision of the Lord Cymrian returning to the main keep of Highmeadow in the early light of foredawn, carrying in his arms the body of a woman Tristan knew well.

Perhaps not well, he thought, reconsidering the moment. *But certainly intimately.*

From the moment she had come to his notice in his own keep in the province of Bethany, the dead chambermaid, whose name was Portia, had become impossible for him to resist. Dark of hair and fair of face, with a wicked sparkle in her large, doe-like eyes, she had displayed none of the respectful deference that was universally present in those of the serving class, except when she was in public. In the privacy of his bedchamber, to which she had almost immediately gravitated, she was insolent and playful, commanding and dominating him sexually in a manner that he was both loath to allow and gleeful to embrace. Her ruthless passion had captivated him in ways that no other bed partner had ever inspired, and her willingness to participate without hesitation or compunction in whatever nefarious scheme he felt like concocting had made him trust her more than any person he had ever confided in save one.

It appalled him to know that other trusted person had met a similar fate to the one that had apparently befallen Portia.

But to recognize his own hand in the demise of his favorite paramours, both of whom he had sent forth on similarly shameful missions where they had met their hideous ends, would have required a modicum of introspection from Tristan Steward, as well as the ability to feel guilt and responsibility for his actions. Both of these traits had only been his while his first paramour, a serving woman named Prudence, was alive, and only because she had taken on the role of his conscience, loving him and insisting that he be a better man than he was by natural inclination. Any desire for self-improvement, for ethics and higher purpose had fled along with her spirit as it left the world. Now Tristan was alone again, aching with grief but feeling little remorse and no guilt whatsoever.

Rather, what he felt was poisonous rage directed at the man who had borne Portia's dead body back to Highmeadow.

Tristan seized the crystal decanter again and splashed more of the honey-colored liquid into his snifter. He tossed it back; the potable was so smooth it did not burn, but the corners of his eyes stung nonetheless. He could feel the warmth race down his throat to his stomach, where it sparked the fury that was boiling there into wildfire rage. He heaved the glass into the fire, where it shattered against the back of the hearth and flashed as the alcohol hit the flames.

Then, his anger still burning, he strode to the library's heavy back door, threw it open, and hurried down the auxiliary staircase to the servants' quarters.

The enclosed sconces that lined the stairway cast long, flickering shadows on the stone walls that curved along the staircase. Even in his fury Tristan made note of the solidity of the fortress he was visiting for the first time. Highmeadow was a new stronghold, a citadel four years in construction that had been designed for defense by the best artisans and military commanders of the Cymrian Alliance, making use of the premier military knowledge of four different races. Situated in the dense forests of western Roland, in the province of Navarne but very close to the border of Bethany, his own province, at the historical site where the ancient House of Remembrance had once stood, Highmeadow was a bastion of strength in an impenetrable woodland, a conglomeration of buildings that were situated on, within, and above the earth in the very trees of the forest, with hidden defenses and barricades surrounding it for miles. This building was the only one he had been privy to thus far in his visit, a general keep meant for housing guests of state and other visitors of the Lord and Lady Cymrian, with libraries, meeting rooms, and dining halls all secured for the protection of the guests and privacy of the discourse undertaken there. Even Portia, an eavesdropper of highly refined talents, had complained that the new keep had prevented her from overhearing anything of value since the household had moved there from the old and drafty keep of Haguefort in the capital of Navarne. Since one of the main functions that Tristan had commanded of her when he sent her as a gift to the Lord and Lady was just such surveillance, he had been left with little information of value for his pains.

At the bottom of the stairs, the hallway was dark save for light coming out from under a door halfway down on the right. The Lord Roland made his way to the door and paused outside it. A moment later he could hear soft conversation, and identified one of the voices as belonging to Gerald Owen, the longtime chamberlain of Haguefort who had served Stephen Navarne, the late duke, and his father and grandfather before him.

The other voice was unmistakably that of Gwydion of Manosse, known to his intimates as Ashe. Tristan's boyhood friend and long-hated rival for both power and, at least within the secrecy of Tristan's heart, the love of a woman.

The Lord Cymrian.

Without so much as a respectful tap on the door, Tristan barged into the room.

Gerald Owen and Ashe looked up in surprise. Both men were gray in the face, the chamberlain from age and exhaustion, the Lord Cymrian from something else. Tristan could see despair in his cerulean-blue eyes, though his face betrayed nothing as his gaze returned to the bed.

Lying before them on the room's bed was the body of the serving maid. Tristan's throat tightened upon beholding it again; he slammed the door shut behind him and came to the bed, staring down at the woman who lay there.

His mouth dropped open in shock.

The corpse of the beautiful young chambermaid was desiccated like a mummy that had been buried in sand for a thousand years. The supple flesh of her limbs, so vibrant and smooth that morning, had withered and dried to a tanned hide, hanging limply off the visible bones. The enormous eyes that had stared deeply into his own, watching him intently as she rode him up against the wall of his bedchamber in the guesthouse that morning, had sunken into hollow sockets and disappeared. Her sensuous mouth that had been open as if in the throes of sexual congress was open still, but the lips had vanished, leaving little more than gristle around the gaping teeth. Only the waves of long black hair remained, draping languorously over the pillow. Were it not for that hair, he would never have recognized her.

Tristan's stomach rushed into his mouth. He turned and retched into the washbasin on the nightstand. Then, when the nausea passed, he wheeled in wrath and addressed the two men, only one of whom was watching him.

"You *bastard*, Gwydion," he snarled at the one whose gaze was still on the body. "You unspeakable bastard. What have you done to her?"

"Nothing," the Lord Cymrian murmured over the chamberlain's snort of indignation.

"*Nothing? Look* at her—she's—she's—" Tristan stuttered to a halt as the chamberlain stared at him. "What have you done?" he repeated.

"Have you never seen a body in such a state?" Ashe asked quietly, his voice hollow.

"Never."

"No? Well, think back harder, to your childhood days. Do you recall the death of Talthea, the Gracious One?"

Tristan stopped. A memory, long buried, rose in the back of his mind, hanging in the mists behind which early days were hidden. He vaguely recalled standing beside his brother, Ian Steward, now the Blesser of Canderre-Yarim, but then merely an acolyte being trained in the Patrician faith, both of them barely old enough to feed themselves, watching the death of a woman most people in the crowd around them had simply referred to as the Widow.

"She was a First Generation Cymrian," Ashe went on, his hand coming to rest on the withered skin of the dead woman's arm.

"I *know* who she was," Tristan spat. "She was a historic figure. My father brought us all the way to the Circle to witness her death. I was barely old enough to walk. What does that have to do with *anything*?"

Finally Ashe turned to look at the Lord Roland. "If you recall, I lived at the Circle at that time. She was left on the Altar of Ultimate Sacrifice, where she had died, under the stars, after all the mourners had left. Like you, I was just a child. Watching her struggle to die, when all the healers were trying to save her against her will, had horrified me. I remember feeling deep sadness, and not really even understanding why. So that night, I looked out the window of my room in my father's keep, at her body bathed in moonlight on the altar. I thought she might be cold, so I took a blanket off my bed, slipped from my father's house, and went to the altar.

"When I reached the place where she lay, the body was still there, but had changed immensely. At the time of her death, she had appeared a young woman in the bloom of youth, even though she had lived more than a thousand years. Like all First Generation Cymrians, Time had stopped for her, so all her life she looked as she did the day she left the Island of Serendair. But now, in the darkness several hours after her death, she looked like this—desiccated, dry, as if she had been rotting for a millennium. I have seen a few Cymrians of the First Generation die since—and this is precisely what it looks like."

Tristan's body went cold in shock, and his skin began to prickle. "You believe Portia was a First Generation Cymrian as well?"

The expression on Ashe's face grew hard. "If she was, it's a mystery. For a short time, I wore the Patriarch's Ring of Wisdom. When I had it on my hand, I was aware of all of the living First Generationers—no matter where they were in the world. It was as if our heartbeats were tied together; there are few enough of them left to have counted each one, and know them by name. This woman was not among them."

"Then how could she be of the First Generation, m'lord?" Gerald Owen asked.

The Lord Cymrian's eyes met Tristan's.

"When I wore the ring, I believe this First Generation census of a sort was making me aware of living souls, of people who still were tied to their own names," he said. "There was a man who did not come into my awareness, but who should have been counted by rights as a First Generation Cymrian, a bastard named Michael, the Wind of Death, who had been known to the Three when they were still in Serendair, several ages ago. I did not know of him; he was no longer the man, the Cymrian he had been—because he had already taken on a demon spirit as its host."

The last words echoed off the walls of the room.

"A F'dor?" Tristan whispered.

Ashe nodded gravely. "And it is clear to me now, given all the trickery and games of the mind this woman was able to play on me, twisting reality until it was unrecognizable, that she, too, must have been host to something that evil, that unspeakably dark. If this body once belonged to a First Generation Cymrian woman, as it appears to have, that poor creature's soul was eaten long ago by something demonic that took over her body before I had possession of the ring."

"Dear All-God," Tristan said, trying to quell his rising stomach.

The Lord Cymrian glared at him. "I can imagine how ill you must feel now, Tristan, realizing as you no doubt are that you have literally been in bed with the beast, have coupled with a monster that may very well have possessed you, may have taken a piece of your very soul, without you even realizing it." His stare grew colder. "Not that you would even miss it."

"I—I—never—"

"Spare me." The air in the subterranean room grew instantly drier, as if it were on the verge of igniting. Tristan had seen the dragon in Ashe's blood rise before, but never in such close quarters. "You do not think that I know what you have been up to? You forget, my friend, that my draconic nature grants me an awareness of much of what is going on around me, transcending normal understanding. In addition, this is *my* house. I know every sickening detail of your tryst with this woman this morning, distracted as I am by everything else that I am contending with. She was your bedwench—I know you brought her here, not to aid Rhapsody with our son upon his birth, as you claimed to my face, but to seduce me, to lead me away from all that I hold holy. I do not know how she was able to appear in my wife's aspect, to approximate her scent, her likeness, but even you should know that those abilities are signs of powers of dark intent, probably demonic. And you knew she was capable of those things. Don't lie to me—this is not the time for it. I will gut you with my teeth where you stand, I swear it, if you speak another falsehood to me. *Confess.*"

Tristan's eyes darted nervously around the small room.

"Gwydion—I—"

The air around him seemed to swirl as Ashe grabbed him by the neck and slammed him up against the nearest wall, knocking the breath from him.

"Don't *lie* to me," the Lord Cymrian demanded through clenched teeth. His eyes were burning with azure fire, the veins in his neck extended in ropy strands. His anger was palpable in the air around them, burning Tristan's lungs. "Your next breath will be your last if you do not tell me the truth, *now.*"

Even as he danced on the edge of consciousness in the raging Wyrmkin's grasp, Tristan's wiles were working. *He is not his wife, the Skysinger, the Namer, so he hasn't the ability to discern the truth, as she does,* he thought, fighting off the blackness that winked in and out before his eyes. *His dragon sense cannot look into men's hearts.*

He gasped raggedly and with the last of his effort tore Ashe's hands from his neck.

"Unhand me, you lunatic," he snarled, pulling away. "What truth do you wish me to tell you, Gwydion? That I knobbed the girl? I admit it freely. I brought her to Haguefort, along with the other servants, to assist you and Rhapsody in any capacity you might need them in your transition to Highmeadow. It did not occur to me, nor does it embarrass me, that you might make use of her copious talents beneath the sheets. I couldn't care less. I have been free about acknowledging my attitudes regarding the value of bedwenches and whores—an attitude your own *father* shared, if you recall." Tristan breathed more deeply, his bruised trachea aching, noticing the simmering down of the fire in the Lord Cymrian's eyes. He decided to press his luck. "Also, if you recall, the woman I have loved most in my life was just such a serving wench who was both my father's concubine and mine. So do not attach to my gift any nefarious purpose, Gwydion. If you considered straying from your marital vows and bed, well, that's on your head."

Ashe eyed him warily, the gleam of fire calmer, but still burning.

"Look well upon your gift to me, and remember this sight as you recall what you once held in your arms," he said, his voice measured. "I speak to you as one who has had a piece of his very soul enslaved by such a demon, and if in the throes of passion the beast that probably inhabited this woman ripped away a piece of yours, Tristan, you will reap your deserved punishment a thousandfold. By rights I should kill you now, where you stand, rather than risk letting such a scourge live on through you, if you are in fact in the demon's thrall."

The Lord Roland's face went white.

"But you are surely not contemplating that, Gwydion?" he said nervously. The Lord Cymrian's aspect was utterly blank, expressionless, save for the burning fury in his blue eyes, eyes scored with vertical pupils denoting the dragon blood in his veins. Though they had been friends since childhood, Tristan Steward could see no reassuring sign of fealty or privilege there; for all intents and purposes, he could be looking into the face of a stranger.

Or an enemy.

The Lord Cymrian continued to stare at him a moment longer. Then he turned to his chamberlain.

"Parchment and ink, please, Owen. Sit down, Tristan." He indicated the only chair in the room at the small table on which the basin and pitcher rested as the chamberlain left the room. When the Lord Roland hesitated, the Lord Cymrian took him by the shoulder and slammed him into the seat. Tristan struggled to rise, but as he did, Ashe drew his sword.

In the glimmering blue light of the blade of Kirsdarke, the ancient sword of elemental water, Tristan Steward froze.

"Gwydion—" he gasped.

"If you so much as twitch again, I will behead you and gouge the beating heart from your chest," the Lord Cymrian said quietly. "Doubt not my word, Tristan. As far as I am concerned, you are a thrall of the demon and a threat to all I hold dear. To think I tolerated your continued existence in the same keep as my wife and son—"

"You—you can't seriously believe I would—*harm* Rhapsody, or your son?"

"Knowing that there is no limit to the evil a F'dor's thrall can commit, I am willing to believe you capable of anything," the Lord Cymrian said, his tone deadly. "I need not even believe that your soul is tied to a demon to know that you want my wife, and would do anything to have her, your pledge of fealty and supposed lifelong friendship to me notwithstanding. Don't open your mouth again to protest, Tristan, unless you want to experience the taste of my sword—I am fighting every inclination that is coursing through me at this moment to ram it down your throat."

The regent swallowed hard but said nothing as the chamberlain returned to the room with an inkwell, a quill pen, and a sheaf of parchment.

The Lord Cymrian indicated the table, and the chamberlain set the items down on the flat surface, moving the bowl and pitcher out of the way with a faint look of disgust. Ashe conferred with him in low tones for a moment; then the chamberlain nodded and left the room again. Ashe turned to Tristan once more.

"Write," he demanded.

"Write what?"

" 'My dearest Madeleine,' " the Lord Cymrian dictated. He raised his sword as Tristan hesitated, then took up the quill quickly and began to scratch letters onto the parchment. " 'I fear I am needed at Highmeadow for the foreseeable future. I urge you to take Malcolm and return for the time being to Canderre, where your father's keep will provide you both with security and care.' Finish with whatever endearments you don't mean. Then sign it."

"I—I need to get back to my lands—"

"As of this moment, you have no lands, Tristan. Your lands, your title, and your freedom are forfeit until such a time as it can be determined beyond a shadow of a doubt that you are not in the debt of a demon. I will take no chances with that possibility."

"You are out of your misbegotten *mind*," the Lord Roland spat, rage outweighing his fear. "What makes you think—" His words were choked off by the dry crackling in the air that signaled the rise of the dragon in Ashe's blood.

And the knock at the door.

"Come," the Lord Cymrian said. The multiple tones of the dragon were in his voice.

The door opened and Gerald Owen reappeared. Behind him in the hallway were four of Highmeadow's guards, armed and drawn. The chamberlain came into the room.

"The Lord Roland's—er, guest quarters are ready, m'lord."

"What are you talking about? I am perfectly comfortable in my current suite," Tristan Steward stammered, but realization was beginning to dawn on him.

"No doubt," said Ashe dryly. "Thank you, Gerald—we will be ready in a moment." The elderly chamberlain bowed and left the room, struggling to cover the smirk on his lips.

Finally the Lord Cymrian's eyes came to rest on the Lord Roland. In them there was no sign of Tristan's boyhood friend, or the patient leader of the Alliance; all of the pleasantry and tolerance had been stripped from his aspect, leaving nothing but a wildness of fury that chilled Tristan's soul. Somewhere, deep within that soul, he felt a twinge, guilt or something darker.

But only for a moment.

"You have not been given the tour yet, Tristan, but you will be happy to see that even the most secure of prison cells here in Highmeadow are relatively comfortable, certainly compared to the accommodations I experienced in my twenty years of exile, hiding from those forces that had taken a piece of *my* soul. Compared to those hovels, sewer vents, barns, and mud huts, you should feel downright pampered."

"You're insane," the Lord Roland whispered. "You can't be serious—you are *arresting me*?"

"For the sake of your wife and child, and her family, I am willing to forgo that announcement at present," Ashe said. His voice was low and controlled, but the hiss of the dragon was in the undertone. "It is still my hope that you can be examined by those who can taste the presence of a demon's bondage and found to be free of it, but until such time I will not chance the possibility that you are so bound. Portia died alone in the woods, as far as we know, so the demon may have died as well, with no host to take it on. But if it did find its way to a new host, then that person still holds a bill of lading against your soul—you are still a thrall of the demon, just like the every other hapless fool who wreaked havoc upon this land and then had no idea why. I have an Alliance to protect. The only other option to your imprisonment is your execution and the dissolving of your body in acid—you make the choice." His voice dropped to a sinister whisper.

"And remember, protecting the Alliance is my duty as Lord Cymrian. You should be grateful to have been allowed the chance to be incarcerated behind heavy doors that will spare you from the rampaging dragon and furious husband whose marriage you tried to ruin. For that alone I should cause your body to turn inside out, as I did to Khaddyr when he betrayed my father. You are the luckiest of men, the kind that never really gets what he truly deserves."

He opened the door and gestured with his sword.

Tristan Steward glared balefully at him as he passed through the doorway, stopping one last time.

"I will never forgive you for this, Gwydion. Never."

Ashe smiled ruefully, causing Tristan Steward to shudder.

"Those are not words you want to teach me, Tristan—you would curse the day you did, if I ever were to return the sentiment. Come; your new quarters await. If I'm feeling sporting I may even spot you a flask of Canderian brandy every now and then to keep you company."

10

THE KREVENSFIELD PLAIN,
SOUTHERN BETHANY

The aftermath of the retreat from Sepulvarta had filled the very air of the Krevensfield Plain with desolation and despair. Those morose emotions hung, above the ground, extant in the wind that whipped the new grass of early spring, unable to be cleared from the place or the army that was encamped on it.

In spite of not having been an actual part of the battle in which the army of Sorbold sacked the holy city of Sepulvarta, the fighting force that the Lord Marshal had assembled out of the reserves and forward installations along the southern rim of the Plain had been devastated by that battle anyway. They had gathered in the highest of spirits, called to martial duty by the ancient hero of the Cymrian War, a historic conflict fought centuries before the great majority of them had been born. They had dropped everything to ride with their brothers and sons to the rescue of the Citadel of the Star in the City of Reason, the sacred seat of their faith, and that of the Patriarch who was the head of that faith, in time to see the city in ruins, blazing with fire and patrolled from the air by nightmarish beasts that snatched its citizens from the streets and carried them off into the burning skies.

As they moved slowly through the smoke, the hastily assembled army had no idea that the Patriarch they had ridden to rescue was actually encamped among them. The fighting force had been gathered from all across the southern continent, so most of the soldiers had not served with one another before, and therefore did not recognize the tall, older man in the gray hood and robes as anything other than a comrade-in-arms who, like them, had been too late to aid the holy city.

Not only did the heartsick soldiers not recognize the Patriarch in their midst, they fairly believed him dead. The assumption of this assassination was the greatest reason for their depression.

Anborn ap Gwylliam sat atop his beautiful black warhorse at the crest of a low swale at the eastern outskirts of the encampment, watching the men he had gathered drifting aimlessly, going about their assigned duties as if they were ghosts. His thighs were aching from gripping his mount, an action which until that morning had been denied him for over three years. The feeling had begun to return to his toes and heels as well, though his calves and the arches of his feet still were numb.

Unlike his feet and those walking ghosts, Anborn's spirit was not numbed by the failure of the rescue he had undertaken. The impending rebirth of the use of his legs had filled the Lord Marshal with new hope, and the memory of a time in his life, long ago and long forgotten, when the ideals of selfless military service, defense of home, kin, and homeland, leadership, brotherhood and camaraderie, and valor were the foundation of his life. Thus, the grit of the battlefield smoke that was drifting over the encampment from the holy city eighty leagues away did not reek of despair or failure for him, but of invigoration, of grim and stolid determination.

A call to arms, ringing deep within the soul he had forgotten he had.

He cast his eyes around until they sighted on a trumpeter, sitting despondently in the gray light of foredawn, staring into a battered metal mug. He turned his mount into the wind; the horse intuitively lowered its head, knowing a command was coming.

"Soldier! Rise and attend!" The general's booming battlefield voice rang out in the smoky air of morning. The man, his neck snapping around in shock, leapt to his feet, dropping his mug down the front of his trousers.

"Follow me," Anborn instructed. He clicked to his mount, and the horse bore the general smoothly to the front of the rise. The trumpeter followed him, stumbling but eager.

At the crest of the rise the general stopped and surveyed the encampment again. Then he cleared his throat and signaled to the trumpeter.

"Sound muster," he ordered.

The trumpeter licked his lips, raised his horn, and let fly.

The silver blast rang over the encampment, causing a following wave of shock. Ten thousand faces turned in the Lord Marshal's direction.

Anborn sat up straight in the saddle. His black hair, streaked with silver, flowed freely in the wind above his burning azure eyes as he surveyed the army below him. As if gathering power from the very air around him, he swept his cape back over his shoulder, allowing his black ring mail interlaced with silver to catch the diffuse light of the sun rising behind the clouds of smoke, causing his chest to glow like a beacon above the army below him.

"Men of Roland, of the Alliance," he intoned. "Cast off your misery and rise."

The soldiers stared at him, then slowly began to stand.

"Rise!" the Lord Marshal thundered.

The army jumped to its feet, a new wave of energy surging through them at the threat and Right of Command in Anborn's voice. At just that moment, a shaft of sunlight broke through the morning haze and the smoke, lighting the rise on which he sat atop his mount, his broad face wreathed in the scowl of an ancient hero's disgust.

"I had been under the impression I was leading men, not children," he said disdainfully. "Cease your mourning, and stoke your *rage*. The holy city has been savagely attacked and burned; the Merchant Emperor of Sorbold is not even crowned yet and has already spat in the face of the All-God and wiped his feet on the documents of peace and friendship with the Alliance signed by his predecessor. Yet rather than mobilizing with grim determination and righteous anger, you are weeping and walking around like shades of men. Rise, you soldiers! You defenders! You sons of Roland! You, unlike your forebears, are united in the cause of Right, are not fighting your own brothers, but an invading army from the south that threatens your homes, and your God! Even in the most heinous battles of the Cymrian War, the holy city of Sepulvarta was never touched, never damaged by either faction. This is an *outrage*. It is an abomination, a *sin*. It should stir a fierce and merciless call for retaliation in your souls. Rise! We have a continent to protect, a Patriarch to restore, and you, sons of Roland, are going to establish the ramparts which will turn the open, undefended pastures of the Krevensfield Plain into a threshold of death to those invaders."

"M'lord—the Patriarch is dead," one of the field commanders said haltingly. "The Scales of Jierna Tal, the instrument that would decide a new Patriarch, are deep within Sorbold, in the armed city of Jierna'sid. How are we to—"

Before he could finish, the Lord Marshal signaled impatiently to a tall man in the hooded robes of a pilgrim standing at the foot of the swale. The man climbed quickly to the top of the rise and turned to face the makeshift army at Anborn's feet. Then, with a violent snatch, he pulled down his hood. The same sunbeam that was lighting the general's armor came to rest on the tall man's white-blond hair, causing it to burn with a radiance that outshone even the crystalline blue of the furious gaze in his eyes.

Gleaming on the holy symbol of Sepulvarta that hung around his neck.

A wave of silence swept over the Krevensfield Plain.

Then, as if from one monstrous, all-consuming voice, a roar of acclaim and fury billowed forth, rising into the wind and bellowing across the land. It grew, second by second, as weapons were raised to the sun, as men turned to one another with renewed spirit in their gleaming eyes, as the sun pierced the gloom and flooded the vast fields with light.

Anborn threw his head back and laughed aloud, then drew his bastard sword and raised it to the sky as well. He let loose a war cry that melded with the roar of his men, who doubled their volume. Then he signaled to his field commanders.

"Mount up! Separate into the sectors from east to west that each cohort came from, and follow me. While we await the arrival of the united army of the Alliance—an army that Sorbold does not even know exists—we will build a chain of armed farming settlements from here to the sea. Now, come."

He sheathed his sword, patted his steed, which cantered forth, and rode off to the west without so much as a backward glance.

With a reinvigorated fighting force ten thousand strong falling closely, excitedly in a great wide rank behind him.

11

THE DRAGON'S LAIR, GWYNWOOD,
NORTH OF THE TAR'AFEL RIVER

Melisande waited at the opening of the cave for the Invoker to return.

Every now and then sounds echoed up the winding tunnel, plinks and skittering noises, dripping water, the rustling of leaves swirling in the cave's mouth. The little girl rubbed her hands up and down her arms in the attempt to dispel the cold that had taken hold of her, but stopped after a few moments, realizing that the chill came from within.

From the vantage point atop the hill she looked down over the lake. The mirrorlike surface shone darkly below, its frozen patches duller than the areas where Thaw had melted the water. The call of a nightbird resounded off the surface, then was swallowed by the wind. Melisande thought it might have been the loneliest sound she had ever heard.

Below her in the greenwood she heard the crackling of brush.

She spun quickly around and peered into the darkness of the cave, but there was still no sign of Gavin.

The rustling grew louder. Whatever was moving through the brush was of a size and heft larger than her own, and there was more than one of them. Melisande shrank back from the cave's entrance, whimpering in fear and hating herself for it.

"Gavin?" she called into the depths. "Gavin, something's coming."

"Indeed, Lady Melisande Navarne," answered a voice from the dark behind her. Moments later, she could see the shadow of Gavin's form emerge from the blackness, the Bolg midwife in his arms. "I called for them."

Melisande looked back down the hill and watched as the Invoker's horse and the one on which she had ridden to this place emerged from the greenwood. She never ceased to wonder at how the nature priest was able to compel the birds of the wood and the beasts in his service to respond to silent signals, but she was glad to see them.

She turned and came over to the Invoker. Krinsel had been wrapped in muslin strips soaked in a spicy liquid, so Melisande could barely see her skin. "Is she alive?" she asked.

"After a fashion," Gavin replied gravely. "I have done what I can for her, but her wounds are beyond my skills to heal. The man who awaits us at the white forest's edge will be able to do more, but dragon breath is caustic and burns in a way that no mortal medicine can really affect. She requires the talents of a healer with primordial lore."

"Like a Lirin Skysinger? A Namer?"

Gavin nodded.

"But Rhapsody is back in the Bolglands now," Melisande said sadly. "I do not believe that there are any others of her kind on the continent, or if there are, they're within the Lirin realm. Krinsel may die before she gets there, and even if she does not, the Lirin and the Bolg are not friends. They might kill her, thinking she's an enemy."

Gavin emerged from the cave into the wind, and began heading carefully down the slope of the hillside to where the horses waited.

"Leave the worrying to me, Lady Melisande Navarne," he said, laying the Bolg midwife gently across the front of his saddle. "You've done your part; now it is left but for me to do mine. Stay with her."

"Where are you going?" Melisande asked nervously.

The Invoker barely glanced at her as he climbed back up the hummock to the mouth of the cave. "You already know the answer," he said as he pushed her back away from it. "I am doing as you, and the Lady Cymrian, command me. Stand clear."

The little girl covered her eyes as Gavin raised his muddy staff. Around the tip of his left hand, the wind whistled, almost as if it were tying itself in a knot there, causing the newborn leaves and young spring branches to dance wildly in the gathering breeze. The clouds raced along above them in the dark, and beneath her feet the earth seemed to be coming alive.

Inside the black cave tunnel, cracking and rumbling sounds began to issue forth along with a sputum of stones and rising dust. Melisande backed away, trying to shield her face from the stinging grit now flying forth.

I hope we're doing the right thing, she thought, but there really was nothing else to be done. As uncertain as she had been from the moment her carriage was attacked, one thing of which she was sure was that the cave had been empty.

The dragon was gone.

She maintained a stoic silence as boulders of all size began to roar down from within the rocky cave and from the mountainsides above. The Invoker stood amid it all, unflinching, as even the historic inscription calling the Cymrian people into being was covered in rubble. Melisande could not see clearly in the dark, but even in what little light there was she knew that the cave entrance had been sealed so completely that no one would ever have known it was there in the first place.

She stood quietly until the Invoker lowered his arms and turned to face her once again.

"I have done as you asked, Lady Melisande Navarne," Gavin said. His voice was as plain and toneless as the wind that had died down around them. "The cave is sealed. Whatever treasure the dragon had, whatever secrets lay within this place, are now lost to history, at least until one of greater power than mine comes to unseal it."

Melisande only nodded.

"Come, let us be on our way," the Invoker said, resting his hand on her shoulder. "We will find a place by the shore of the lake to make camp until the moon rises, then return to the Circle, where the Bolg woman can find healing, and where you can find passage back to your father's keep."

"There is no one there for me anymore," Melisande said in a dull voice as she mounted the horse the Invoker held for her. "Everyone is leaving Haguefort and moving on to Highmeadow, where Ashe will be leading the fight against whatever is coming."

"Then we will arrange to get you to Highmeadow," Gavin said, pulling himself into the saddle without jostling Krinsel at all. "Wherever you must be, I'll see that you get there."

Melisande took hold of the reins, but as she did, her horse snorted and danced sideways, shaking its right front hoof in pain. She gentled the mare down and dismounted, crouching down to examine the ground where the beast had trod.

Lying beneath a frozen fern was a strange dagger, rough-hewn, long and black, and wickedly sharp. It seemed to taper to a sickle-like point, bony ridges running along it from its man-made handle to what seemed to be a stone blade. Carefully Melisande picked it up and turned it over in her hands.

"What do you have there, Lady Melisande Navarne?" Gavin asked, wrapping the injured woman in his saddle blanket.

"It's a knife of some sort," the little girl answered, staring at it. The surface of the object hummed as if the stone were alive, vibrant, but there was no warmth in the thing.

The Invoker nudged his mount until he was alongside her own, and extended his gloved hand. Melisande complied with the silent demand, handing over the odd weapon, but feeling a tug of resistance bordering on resentment.

"It looks like a dragon's claw, in fact," he said, returning the blade to her after a moment. "Keep it. It will make a fine weapon as long as you are careful about keeping it sheathed unless you truly need it drawn."

Melisande's petty resentment turned quickly to horror.

"We—we can't take that," she stammered. "That's treasure; dragon treasure. We're not supposed to remove anything from the cave, not even a pebble. Rhapsody was quite specific about that." Her mind went immediately to her Cymrian history lessons, most notably the ancient ballad *The Burning Fields,* which told the story of a dragon's wrath upon discovering that a tin cup had been stolen by thieves from his lair. The tale ended in a gruesome and detailed description of the destruction of much of the Middle Continent, up to and including the central province of Bethany, where a great temple was later built in gratitude for a firebreak that spared the eastern continent. Rhapsody had assured her that the legends were lies, including one about Elynsynos's fury called *The Rampage of the Wyrm,* but having seen the gargantuan size of the beast's lair, and having felt the heft and sharpness of what had once been a mere single claw, she was beginning to wonder if perhaps the Lady Cymrian was believing what she wanted to believe about a dragon who had been fond of her, rather than the reality of the race.

The Invoker watched her thoughtfully for a moment. "I understand your concern, and admire your honesty," he said. "But you are taking nothing from her cave; clearly you've discovered this item outside it. And since we've determined the beast to be dead, or at least gone, you must now decide if you wish to leave such a powerful and dangerous artifact lying about where anyone can find it. I suggest you take it with you and bear it as a gesture of respect to the one who sent you here, and the one whom you came to save." He leaned closer, seeing that the little girl was struggling to keep her lip from trembling and tears from spilling out of her eyes. "Why are you crying, Lady Melisande Navarne?"

It was a moment before Melisande could speak. "I came all this way, and I failed," she said haltingly. "I'm glad we found Krinsel, and I hope that we have managed to keep her alive, but that's not why I traveled here from Haguefort. I came because Rhapsody wanted to me to save Elynsynos. She said that what I was doing was important beyond measure, something that might be saving the continent."

The Invoker's black eyes gleamed in the dark.

"How do you know that you have not?" he asked.

"Because Elynsynos is not here," Melisande said, angrily wiping her eyes with the back of her hand. "And her treasure is buried, perhaps for all time, so if there was something of great power in there that might have helped in the war that is coming, it is lost to the world as well. Not a very good outcome to my first, and probably last quest."

"And what does that matter? You did everything you could, you were valiant and brave, and fulfilled every command that was asked of you." The Invoker sighed deeply, took the reins of Melisande's horse, and started into the greenwood in a slow walk. "Nature, and the very universe itself, is at the same time random and lawful, Lady Melisande Navarne. There once was a young prince who was given a prophecy that led him to believe he was special beyond measure. He was told that something he would do with his life would one day be the means by which his people, long oppressed and driven from their lands, would return to the place they were meant to be, where they would prosper in peace for centuries to come. The young prince could barely contain his excitement, knowing that greatness would one day be his, and history would record his name as the one who returned his outcast nation to its former glory. He laid plans, Lady Melisande Navarne, great plans that many of his advisors questioned, but he had come to believe that whatever he felt was right to do would be the means by which his nation's glory, and his, was assured."

The Invoker clicked to the horses, and they stepped around the mud of the floodplain.

"And then one day, when he was little more than twice your age, still uncrowned, still young and untried by life, he did something very much like what you did yesterday—while journeying through a wood, he was not watching where he was going, misstepped and tumbled down a crevasse where he became embedded in the mud at the bottom. And he died there. They found him days later, long cold. No one can know what came into his mind, nor will anyone ever know what he thought as he lay, broken and immobile, but I imagine that before death finally came for him, at least one of his thoughts was one of disbelief. How could the seer prophesy that greatness would come from his life, when he was to die in such an ignominious way? But that is how the universe works, Lady Melisande Navarne. After his death, another leader took the reins, and made a different plan, one that did not lead to the destruction that the prince would have wreaked upon his people, but rather to the outcome that had been foretold. What the young prince did with his life was to end it early, and thus spare his people the consequences of his bad decisions. His name is lost to history."

"That's a lovely story," Melisande said acidly. "Thank you."

"You did not like it?"

"Not really, since that same thing almost just happened to me. I don't appreciate the suggestion that the most valuable thing I can do is die."

The Invoker chuckled. "Sometimes I forget that you are merely nine years old," he said. "I am not comparing you to that prince, Lady Melisande Navarne, far from it. I only wish you to understand that there are some things we can do to affect the outcome of life, and other things that life does to affect the outcome of *us*. Until the day is long past on the thread of Time, we cannot really know for certain how things have turned out. We can only do the best we can with what we think we know." He looked up into the sky, then back at the little girl riding in silence beside him. "But there is one thing I know about your life that I don't believe you do."

"And what is that?"

Gavin smiled.

"It's midnight," he said. "That means spring has come. And you are no longer merely nine years old."

Melisande exhaled, then looked down at the dragon's claw in her hand. Far away in the recesses of her young mind she remembered the stories Rhapsody had told her, years ago on a warm day at the beginning of spring, before the world had gone wrong. She thought she recalled her adopted grandmother saying that her own reason for first coming to the dragon's cave was to return just such a dagger. Rhapsody had been fearful of the beast's anger, but Elynsynos had turned out to be not the vengeful, avaricious wyrm of legend, but childlike and warm, with a gentleness that belied her power.

Perhaps this *is what I was meant to find,* she thought. *Perhaps, besides bringing Gavin to Krinsel, I was supposed to discover a weapon that had once been used to make a powerful, somewhat scary friend, the same way I have.* She glanced at the Invoker, now watching their path intently.

"Well, then, can we please hurry it up a bit?" she said, warmth returning to her voice. "At this rate I won't get home before I turn eleven."

PART THREE

A Moment of Solace in the Advent of War

SONG OF THE SKY LOOM

Oh, our Mother the Earth;
Oh, our Father the Sky,
Your children are we,
With tired backs.
We bring you the gifts you love.

Then weave for us a garment of brightness. . . .
May the warp be the white light of morning,
May the weft be the red light of evening,
May the fringes be the fallen rain,
May the border be the standing rainbow.

Thus weave for us a garment of brightness
That we may walk fittingly where birds sing;
That we may walk fittingly where the grass is green.

Oh, our Mother Earth;

Oh, our Father Sky.

—Traditional, Tewa

12

The Teeth
(Manteids)

★

● Night Mountain
Earth Basilica

Desert

PALACE OF JIERNA TAL, JIERNA'SID, SORBOLD

The sky above Jierna Tal was erupting in explosions of sparkling color as Talquist stepped out onto the balcony of the western minaret, breathing the thin air for the first time as the officially chosen, formally crowned emperor of Sorbold, the Empire of the Sun.

He took a deep breath of that thin air, inhaling the fringes of the clouds of evening as they colored with splashes of gold and green, red and purple, lighting the desert at night in much the same colors that could be seen in it during the day. Standing so high above the ground, it was almost as if he was breathing the stars, like a god of the old world, from a time before the modern era, when beings of extraordinary greatness trod and shaped the very earth itself.

Much the way he was effectively doing now.

With each new pyrotechnic, a muted but widespread chorus of gleeful cheering and applause could be heard down below him. The people of Jierna'sid and those that had traveled from across the nation to witness his coronation were still filling the streets of the capital, celebrating his ascension to the Sun Throne with boisterous merriment and drunken revelry, even now, approaching midnight. Talquist's heart squeezed in a swell of fondness; *my people,* he thought. A warm feeling surged through him, a sense of belonging, of acceptance and respect that his common birth and merchant status had never gained him before this day.

The day had been everything he had dreamed of, a grand spectacle of immense pageantry and military might, with a vast parade that escorted him to the Scales for his perfunctory Weighing, then to the steps of Jierna Tal, where he was crowned to the sounds of a three-hundred-piece orchestra and a citywide traditional dance from the days before the first Cymrian era. Grand feasting and a full-blown festival of all sorts of arts honoring the new emperor led up to the grand fireworks display that was now about to come to an end. Talquist was highly pleased with how everything had turned out.

It had been well worth the time and the cost.

Talquist sighed as the shimmering finale died away, the last of the firesparks winking out in the smoky air and falling quietly and slowly to the desert floor. He turned and hurried back into the tower, trotting down the staircase, humming his approximation of the coronation march that had been played repeatedly during the day.

At the bottom of the stairs to the third-floor Great Hall his fellow monarchs were waiting, at his request. Beliac, the king of Golgarn, was in a merry mood, while the Diviner of the Hintervold seemed preoccupied.

"Well, my friends, thank you for being here to help celebrate this day," he said smoothly. "I hope you have enjoyed yourselves sufficiently to have made the journey worthwhile."

The king of Golgarn nodded pleasantly, but the Diviner cast a sharp glance around the Hall.

"I am highly dismayed that the Lord Cymrian did not deign to attend," he said curtly. "I wish you a long and successful reign, Talquist, but I must attend to my nation's priorities now. I will be leaving forthwith and sailing back from Ghant. Thank you for your hospitality, long life to you."

Talquist's fine mood evaporated into the desert air. The Diviner's intentions were completely contradictory to his own plans.

"Please reconsider, Hjorst," he said smoothly. "I actually would like you both to consider undertaking a brief side expedition with me prior to returning to your kingdoms. I have some things to show you that I believe will raise your spirits and give you cause to believe in a happy outcome of all this current hostility."

"What sort of expedition?" said the Diviner in exasperation. "I am facing almost a month at sea as it is."

"No, no, my friend, it is a land-based journey," Talquist said soothingly, though his eyes would have displayed annoyance if the Diviner had been looking into them. "And I promise it will be an easy trip, bolstered by fine cuisine and fine drink."

"Where would we be going?" asked Beliac.

"To Sepulvarta," said the newly crowned emperor. "It is a beautiful city, even if it was originally consecrated to a manufactured god."

"Why would we want to travel *there*?" the Diviner demanded. "Neither Beliac nor I are adherents to the Patrician faith, obviously, nor are our subjects; there is nothing sacred there to either of us."

"Trust me," Talquist said, smiling brightly. "When you see what has occurred there, you will be feeling utterly transported. I'm very sorry that you were unable to meet up with the Bolg king and the Lord Cymrian, but when you see the loss they have absorbed in Sepulvarta, you will feel the diversion is well worth the delay in your return trips home."

The two leaders looked at each other doubtfully.

"My friends," Talquist said, looking over the staircase at the growing group of harlots that were gathering in the stairwell, "it's been a very long day. I am ready to retire for the night; I suggest you take your repose as well. Tomorrow we will take the royal carriage to Sepulvarta; I promise you will find it a trip of great import.

"Now," he said, signaling to the women waiting below, "good night, gentlemen."

The blazing lights that had illuminated the towering walls and soaring ceilings of the palace of Jierna Tal well past midnight had dimmed to a soft glow in the hundreds of wall sconces and standing torches; the magnificent chandeliers that had glittered with the light of thousands of candles were dark now. The gleaming marble floors were laced with shadows, ominous and twisting, through which only a few servants and guards passed, their footfalls echoing up into the darkness.

Standing in a deep pool of such shadow at its traditional place in the Great Hall of the palace's third floor was the stone titan, silent and still as death. The statue's eyes were closed; each of the passing servants who walked by it did not even cast a glance in its direction.

But deep within the stone of the image of what once had been an ancient soldier from a time long before the Cymrians had come to this continent, to this arid, mystic land, a parley of a sort was taking place, a secret confab of two entities, one of even more ancient origin than the soldier, and one younger, both tied to elemental dark fire.

The F'dor spirit Hrarfa had been born in the early days of the world, in the Before-Time, a member of the Older Pantheon of demons that had been imprisoned within the Vault of the Underworld by the other four Firstborn races, only to escape from that vault when a falling star had plunged to Earth and ruptured it. Hrarfa was a demon of determined spirit with a remarkable ability to survive; it had no dominant gender at birth, but had thrived better in female hosts than in most of its male incarnations, and so it generally identified as a female. She was a talented manipulator of scent and taste, deep-seated memory and a liar of great skill. Passionate, sometimes rash, but intelligent and scheming, Hrarfa was one of the few remaining of the Unspoken, the upworld diaspora of the children of dark fire still free in the wind.

Her previous host body, that of a lowly servant, had been captured in the Thrall ritual of a Dhracian hunter that had shattered that body's skull and sucked the life from its bones; Hrarfa herself was dying, all but dissipated when the titan that called itself Faron had appeared in the forest glade in Navarne. Faron had taken her on, had allowed the dying demon to move into his body of Living Stone, only for Hrarfa to discover when she did what was animating that titanic statue.

A Faorina spirit, the denatured, bastard child of another F'dor and a Seren woman.

Hrarfa knew what Faorina were, though she had never met one before. Very few had ever been brought into being, because F'dor were jealous of their individual power, and to commit to sire or give birth to a child while in the body of a human host was to voluntarily accept a permanent diminution of a demon's strength.

Hrarfa was not certain what to make of her Faorina host, but the gratitude she was displaying was only a mask. She was biding her time, waiting to learn more of her new environment before deciding her next move.

She assumed a motherly tone, gentling the harsh voice in which she had spoken that Talquist had mocked so scornfully.

Talquist's great day has finally come to an end, she said softly in the hollow darkness inside of the Living Stone statue. *He is now in his opulent bedchamber, undoubtedly making his way through the stable of bedwenches that was herded up the stairs an hour ago, or filling the air with sour flatulence and horrific snoring.*

There was no response.

Hrarfa willed herself to be calm, though the absence of a response worried her. While she had been able to continue to exist as a result of being accepted into the titan's body by its original animating source of life, she was well aware that Faron, that life source, controlled the actions and movements of the stone soldier.

Which meant that respectful negotiation and constant patience was going to be necessary in order to obtain the ultimate goal.

Faron? Hrarfa whispered. *Are you there?*

For a long moment, she sensed only silence.

Then she perceived an assent. It did not take verbal form, but it was clear nonetheless.

Can you hear the voices of our family? Hrarfa asked the Faorina spirit sharing the body of Living Stone with her. *Can you feel the deep fire, hear the chanting?*

After another pause, she felt the answer.

Yes. But only sometimes, and only distantly.

The warmth of her fire grew, adding to her confidence.

You are one of us, Faron, she whispered to the Faorina as if it were a child. *I sense that you have been lonely, but there is need for that no longer. You are born of an ancient race, the oldest race of this world. When you and I open the Vault, you will be one with our family, reunited with your father once more. And we will have dominion over the whole of the Earth.*

She could feel the Faorina's rising excitement, even though no specific thoughts were made clear.

In the hallway, a cohort of guards made their way to the stairs, their weapons clashing and clanking softly against their studded leather armor. Hrarfa's internal voice fell silent as they went by, waiting until the sound of their passing could no longer be heard in the stairwell. Then she called to Faron again, and sensed him listening.

Talquist seeks a child for his own purposes, and while we may have to accommodate him for the time being, we will be making use of the victories we achieve for him to our own ends. When I was still within the last body of flesh, that of Portia, the serving maid, I may have held that very child in my arms for a moment. If that is in fact the child he seeks, I have the greatest piece of information that Talquist could ever want.

I know its name.

She waited until she was certain the Faorina had absorbed her thoughts, then imparted the lesson she most needed to convey.

Deep within the mountains, another child, a child of living Earth, sleeps. It will be an immense undertaking to enter those mountains, and find that Sleeping Child. But once we have so done, we need but one rib from her body to serve as the key to all our greatest aspirations. Then you and I, Faron, we will achieve what no other of our race has been able to achieve, the greatest feat that has ever been attained.

We will open the Vault.

And then it will all begin.

Now, listen, and I will tell you the lore of the scales you possess.

13

THE ORLANDAN PLATEAU, ON THE
KREVENSFIELD PLAIN, SOUTH OF BETHANY

*A*nborn! Hie, Anborn!"

The Lord Marshal reined his black warhorse to a clean halt in the high morning wind, then looked down the hill over his shoulder.

Solarrs, his lead scout and longtime man-at-arms, was urging his red war mare up the rise, struggling to catch up with him. His silver mane of hair shone like a dim candle atop an otherwise black shadow of man and horse in the rosy glow of foredawn.

Anborn pulled himself up taller in his high-backed saddle, enjoying the stretch in his lower leg as he pushed successfully against the stirrup while he waited.

From atop the small hill he surveyed the distant encampments that he and his field commanders had recently set up across the Orlandan Plateau, as well as those in the valley immediately below, coming to light with the dawn as the rim of a glowing red sun approached the horizon.

The Krevensfield Plain was an immense grassland, with wide horizons on every side. Settled chiefly by families of farmers in small communities that dotted the landscape, the only other sign of civilization or their inclusion in a larger empire was the trans-Orlandan thoroughfare. The roadway had been built in the Cymrian Age and bisected the Middle Continent from the outer edge of the Great Forest of the west coast to Bethe Corbair, the easternmost Orlandan province before the mountains officially known as the Manteids, but more commonly referred to as the Teeth. The Lord Marshal had made the process of connecting those communities with military encampments that would serve to protect, and be fed by, those farming villages his first priority in building a battle line in the south.

While he awaited his scout, Anborn's eyes narrowed against the blast of seeds and grass flecks carried on the morning wind. He had sat atop a horse just like this one many times at almost this very spot, and hills just like it, observing other such encampments. He had seen these fields run red with blood and strewn with broken bodies, great stretches of fertile farmland dissolved into black ash. Four hundred years of flaccid peace had held sway since that terrible war ended, but the hollow, victory-less finale to it all had never washed away the stains from history.

Stains he had been largely responsible for.

Yet now, deep within him, as his legs began to show signs of life once more, he was starting to feel the twinges of rebirth and renewal in other parts of him as well.

In a rumbling of horseflesh and the huffing of breath, Solarrs summited the hill, dragging his mount to a dancing halt.

"Breathe first, then report," said the Lord Marshal mildly as the scout began to speak.

Solarrs eyed him with suspicion.

"What has—you in such a—bloody fine mood?" he demanded between breaths.

Anborn thought about answering honestly, then gave in to his baser nature and the easier convenience of a highly believable lie.

"The attentions of a bloody fine bedwench earlier this morning," he said smugly. "While you were riding hard from Sepulvarta under the cover of night, I was riding hard as well—or, more accurately, being ridden. So what news do you bring?"

Solarrs pulled himself up straighter as the horse settled.

"We retrieved a carcass of one of the flying beasts employed by Fhremus's army at Sepulvarta," he said, wiping his forehead with the back of his sleeve. "It's an unholy creature, monstrous; seemingly equal parts insect, lizard, and bat. It has mandibles reminiscent of the ancient plague locusts, but its hide is almost stonelike."

Anborn's azure eyes began to gleam, but otherwise his face was expressionless.

"They are apparently voracious in appetite; the squadron that assaulted the holy city has devastated the fields surrounding Sepulvarta's walls and ramparts," Solarrs continued. "Additionally, they seem to be somewhat fragile, or at least short-lived; there were a number of whole bodies of the beasts in the outer fields where we captured this one." He pointed down the hill to a horse-drawn wagon, which was approaching. "They don't last after death, apparently; this one has become little more than shell in the time it took us to travel here. Oh—and they seemed to be called 'yak-sis,' or something to that effect—at least that's what the spies discerned."

"Iacxsis," Anborn murmured distantly.

"What's that?"

"Iacxsis," the Lord Marshal repeated gruffly. "It's an old word, a word from before the Cymrian era, from a time of ancient gods and animist beliefs. I would think you would be more likely to recognize it than I, Solarrs, being a First Generationer of the Third Fleet—when Gwylliam landed at the Skeleton Coast, and you all had to fight your way to this place through the indigenous tribes of Sorbold—that's where the word is from. Before my time."

Solarrs shrugged.

"Can't say I remember hearing it."

Anborn pulled himself up to a full seat, guiding his horse in a half-turn.

"It was the name of the god of destruction, who rained death from the skies," he said. "Come, show me this thing."

Without another word the two soldiers rode back to the wagon.

Anborn remained atop his steed as Solarrs vaulted down from his beside the wagon.

The scout took hold of the ropes that had secured the cargo as the soldiers driving and guarding the wagon saluted the Lord Marshal, who acknowledged and dismissed them. Solarrs grunted at the weight of the heavy sheeting weighed down with rope stock, then dragged it back, revealing the carcass.

Anborn maneuvered his mount closer.

The beast had begun to dissolve into an almost skeletal state, its carapace brittle and cracked. It had, in its lifetime, a wingspan that exceeded fifteen feet, and long, segmented legs that appeared insectoid, just as its immense jaw and hinged mandibles did.

The hide that covered the wings had already had begun to tatter; Anborn pulled his glove off and ran his index finger along it. It crumbled into sand beneath his touch. His eyes flamed with blue fire.

"Living Stone, I'll wager," he said darkly. "Constantin was right; the bastard has been despoiling Terreanfor, the cathedral of elemental earth in Sorbold. So this is what he has used it for."

"As well as the titan," Solarrs reminded him. "Did you not say he had animated a giant statue of a soldier on the Scales of Jierna Tal?"

"Indeed," Anborn said, pulling on his glove again. "By the time he's done, the miscreant may have even topped my list of crimes with his own."

"An ambitious undertaking, that," said Solarrs humorously, receiving a sour look in return. "So what are your next orders?"

"Tell Knapp to saddle up. We have but one last outpost to set up and arrange to provision, at the very edge of the Plain and the foot of the steppes before the Teeth."

Solarrs sighed.

"Returning voluntarily to within sight of Canrif; now, that's something I never thought I would see you do again."

Anborn smiled; it was a melancholy smile, one with deep history beneath it, etched into the bones and muscles of his face.

"I'll show you something else I imagine you never thought you would see me do again, Solarrs. Are you watching?"

"Aye, m'lord."

As if literally throwing caution to the winds, Anborn tossed the reins over the horse's neck. Carefully he raised himself up using the great strength in his arms, as he always had, but rather than awaiting assistance, he swung his leg over the horse's side and lowered himself to the ground.

Then stepped away, standing on his own.

The silver-haired soldier's eyes opened wide, and he coughed, then choked.

Then he let out a loud, boisterous laugh. After a moment, Anborn joined in.

Solarrs, by nature fairly quiet and taciturn, broke into a smile so wide that it almost threatened to crack the weathered leather of his face.

"Well, well, isn't this interesting?" he said when he was finally able to form words.

"Aye, indeed," the Lord Marshal agreed. "Just when you were probably beginning to believe that the miracles were all on the side of our enemies. Come, help me mount again. Getting down is something I can reliably do; I'm still working on reliably getting back up again. Then snag Knapp and Constantin, and let's be on our way; I have a final outpost to install, and a beloved lady to visit."

14

THE CAULDRON, YLORC

> Rocky boye, baby
> So tiny an' sweet,
> Don't fall from yer cradle,
> You'll damage the meat—
> 'Ave a nice morning,
> Enjoy all yer play
> You'll be in my gut
> By the end of the day

All right, that's enough of *that* lullabye," Rhapsody said, laughing along with her son, who was giggling as Grunthor crooned to him, slightly off-key, while dangling a necklace of subterranean wolf teeth that was making a pleasant clacking sound over his tiny head. The Sergeant-Major inhaled deeply, sucking in his nostrils until they turned inside out, causing Meridion to break into squealing gales of laughter, and Rhapsody to spit her tea across the breakfast table, inadvertently spraying Achmed, who had just sat down.

"It's so lovely having you back here, Rhapsody," the Bolg king said sourly as the door of the dining hall balcony opened. Trug, the Archon in charge of communications known as the Voice, entered silently and bowed politely.

"What is it?" Achmed demanded, wiping his chest off with his napkin.

"Avian messages, Majesty," Trug said. He crossed to the king and handed him the leg containers from the messenger birds, then turned to Rhapsody and gave her two as well. Grunthor put out his enormous hand, claws extended hopefully, but Trug hurried past him and closed the door quickly behind him, missing the enormous pout that came over the Sergeant's face.

"Awww. Nobody ever sends me mail. It's breakin' my 'eart."

"I sent messages to you all the time when I was in Haguefort or Tyrian," Rhapsody said as she broke the wax seal on the first message and slid a tiny piece of parchment out of the small steel tube. "I don't remember getting any back from *you*."

"Not true. Oi 'ad several lovely shrunken 'eads delivered to you with an 'eartfelt poem for yer birthday just last summer."

"Oh, right. I'd forgotten. Thank you again." She unrolled the message carefully. The miniature, carefully graphed antiquated script was instantly recognizable as that of Rial, her viceroy in the Lirin kingdom, over which she reigned as titular queen.

Have made the attempt you requested. Was refused. Very relieved. LLTQ

Rhapsody sighed.

"Well?" Achmed was unsealing his own message tubes.

"Rial did as I asked at the meeting in Haguefort, and attempted to pick up the diadem of the Lirin kingdom, but was unable to do so; apparently the crown refused him."

"That's unfortunate," Achmed said as the first scrap of oilcloth slid into his hand.

"Rial doesn't seem to think so—he signed it 'Long Live the Queen.' I'm sure he's smirking as we speak. Who is yours from?"

Achmed's mismatched eyes were scanning the scrap.

"Your husband's uncle."

"Anborn?"

"Well, since the other one lives two thousand leagues away in the middle of the ocean, I would imagine it might be difficult getting a message from him by bird, unless it was a giant albatross," Achmed said. "Yes, Anborn. He says he is coming to speak with me, and will be here, most likely, tomorrow morning."

Rhapsody smiled. "Good; it will be nice to see him." She broke the second seal and slid the missive from its housing. She unrolled the tiny scroll, smiling slightly as she read the words of love in Ancient Lirin that Ashe sent every morning, then tucked it away and rose. "I need to look in on Rath."

"He was asleep a few moments ago," Achmed noted, having just come from the injured Dhracian's makeshift bedside in the hospice room in the well of Grivven Peak. "His breathing is much better."

"Good; that's good."

The Bolg king nodded. "If you're going to assess him, or speak with him, I want to be there."

"Well, finish your breakfast and reading your mail and then join me at his room. I will wait for you before saying much to him. He needs to be encouraged to eat and drink, but I don't know what is customary to the Dhracian diet. I would hazard a guess that yours is more Bolg."

"Undoubtedly. Even I don't know what real Dhracians eat and drink."

"One more thing he can teach you about your mother's people, then," Rhapsody said.

"If you think he might like the Bolg diet we could feed Meridion to him," Achmed offered.

"Oi would 'ave to object to that," Grunthor interjected. "Oi 'ave first claim there. If nobody's gonna send me messages, Oi should at least get to snack on the lit'le prince."

"Bad idea," Rhapsody said humorously. "He has dragon blood; I'm sure whatever Bolg or Dhracian ate him would end up with a stomach ache at best, and poisoned at worst. The last thing you want is a serious case of dysentery from a poorly considered snack. I'm sure all the soldiers who share the barracks with you would agree."

She rose and kissed Grunthor's cheek, dissolving his look of mock disappointment into a grin, then made her way out of the room to the tunnels of the hospice, Meridion wrapped securely in her arms, as she wished he could have been in the mist cloak his father had given her to keep them both safe and hidden from eyes that had the power to scry for them from afar.

As well as from her hungry Firbolg friends.

But, given that the mist cloak had been destroyed in the fire of the dragon Anwyn's breath on their way to the Teeth, she would just have to be extra vigilant.

And hide him in her own cloak.

The door opened with only the slightest sound.

Rhapsody glanced quickly inside, then knocked softly.

From the bed inside the room, the dark head of the Dhracian hunter turned slowly and opened his eyes.

"Rath?" she said softly. "May I enter?" The ancient man in the bed nodded. She came into the room and closed the door quietly behind her.

"How are you feeling?" she asked as she approached the bed. She reached into the pocket of her cloak and drew forth her lark's flute, a tiny reed instrument she carried with her when traveling.

"Grateful," Rath whispered.

"Achmed will be here momentarily," Rhapsody said. She let her eyes wander over the exposed parts of the Dhracian's body, his head, neck, and arms, taking note of the return of color to his skin, the quieting of his exposed veins, the absence of blood in his black eyes. "You need to take some nourishment, some fluid—what can I get for you?"

The Dhracian shook his head. "Later. Not yet." He closed his eyes as if in pain. "My thanks."

"If you wish, I could sing you a windsong," Rhapsody said, feeling awkward. "Or play for you on the lark's flute; it's a gentle instrument."

A ragged smile appeared on the Dhracian's face.

"Again, later, if you please," he said. "I am trying to reach my brother hunters."

Rhapsody glanced around the room. It was an interior chamber, windowless, as most of the rooms in Ylorc were.

"How careless of me," she murmured. "I'm sorry—I can have you moved to a chamber with an aperture that opens out onto the western steppes, where the wind can enter. How foolish of me—"

"Peace," said the Dhracian. "You were wise to put me in the solace of dark stillness, where I could rest and heal. In a few more hours, I will be well enough to walk on my own, and then I will accept your kind offer. For now, I must tell you something."

Rhapsody looked back as the door opened silently, and the Bolg king entered the room.

"Achmed is here now," she said.

Rath nodded again.

"I must report to you the outcome of the hunt," he said, taking his time with each word. "I know you have already discerned that I failed, that the Thrall ritual was broken. What you do not know is this—what broke my performance of the ritual was the intervention of a giant man of Living Stone, a soldier. He attacked me just as the host of the demon succumbed, but before the demon itself did, tossing me across the forest glade and into a tree with ease."

Rhapsody and Achmed looked at one another.

"The titan of Sorbold," the Bolg king said. "He was said to have disappeared from Sepulvarta after successfully leading the assault on the city."

"I wonder why he went to Navarne," Rhapsody said.

"Most probably because he sensed another of his kind on the wind." Rath's voice was little more than a whisper.

"Of his kind?"

"It was hard to discern, but within the stone statue I could sense something with the taint of F'dor, but not one of the known pantheons. I am not certain, but I suspect it might be a Faorina, the hideous result of F'dor procreation with a being of another race. They are extremely rare, as their conception and birth requires the demon to part with a piece of its own essence, diminishing its power permanently, something very few F'dor are willing to undertake. But whatever was powering that statue, it had a spark of life, and as a result, it was enough for the F'dor known as Hrarfa, the beast that I was attempting to destroy, to cling to it as a host. It took her on willingly."

"Gods," Rhapsody whispered.

"Do you know where it went?" Achmed asked.

Rath shook his head with effort.

"I was a bit distracted, trying to escape on the wind," he said. "I have experienced some bad luck with the availability of air currents of late, but, thankfully, just before the titan bore down on me again, I was able to catch one and be lifted away. The wind was kind in getting me back to you here, as well."

"We have to get word to Ashe," Rhapsody said to Achmed as Meridion began to make buzzing and cackling sounds within her cloak. "Perhaps I can transmit a message to him if you are ready to test the blue spectrum."

Achmed waved her into silence.

"Have you been able to report to the Brethren?" he asked Rath quietly.

The Dhracian nodded. "I sent an emergency missive as the wind caught me, but I have not had the strength or ability to reach them since." He turned his head toward Rhapsody. "May—may I see your child? I was so intent on finding you, Bolg king, that I didn't pay attention to the miracle in our midst that is every child."

Rhapsody looked at Achmed, then came to the chair at Rath's bedside and sat down. She turned the cloak toward him and carefully opened the folds, revealing Meridion. His blue eyes twinkled and he let forth a series of squeaking sounds, causing Achmed to put a hand to his ear and turn away.

Rath, however, pulled himself closer and opened his scleraless black eyes wide, drinking in the sight of the little boy. He studied him intently, then turned to the Firbolg king.

"Fascinating," he said softly. "Wyrmril, human, Seren, Lirin, time, fire, water, air, earth, and ether, with a dynastic right as well. What an interesting, highly magical child—was he born naturally, or was he conjured?"

Rhapsody blinked. "I don't know what you mean, *conjured*. I carried him and gave birth to him as any other child, though his delivery was, well, a bit unusual."

Achmed snorted but said nothing.

"One of the oldest lores of the world, possibly the oldest, is the lore of conjuring a child," Rath said to Rhapsody. "Indeed, the child of which you are the *amelystik* is such a child."

"The Earthchild?" Rhapsody spoke the word using a Namer's tool that allowed her to remove the element of air from it. It sounded directly in Rath's ear, silent to the rest of the world.

The Dhracian nodded and closed his eyes, as if suddenly tired.

"Any child like her was born the same way," he said quietly. "The race of dragons, the Wyrmril, regretted their folly of ignoring the Creator's model when assuming their racial form, which made it impossible for them to interbreed with the other Firstborn races. When the desire for progeny beyond their own race, for immortality, became strong, they turned to the act of conjuring. In order to make the offspring tangible, not ethereal, they used a base of their most precious possession—Living Stone." Rhapsody, who had heard the tale before from Elynsynos, nodded. "But in order to bring a soul forth to inhabit it, the Wyrmril needed to provide two parents who were both willing to sacrifice a part of their personal essence, the equivalent of a soul, to be joined together in the child. Like the F'dor, who found the birth of Faorina not to be worth the diminution of their power, I believe the Wyrmril made the same assessment, and, after conjuring a small number of Earthchildren, returned to propagation with their own kind, through the laying of eggs. So the use of conjuring fell out of history, though I know it has taken place rarely from time to time over the course of it. Because of the level of elemental power involved, it tends to produce extremely magical beings. Forgive me; I meant no insult to your child."

"None taken," Rhapsody said. She kissed Meridion on the top of his head, reveling in the softness of his golden curls. "Well, again, in answer to your question, Rath, Meridion was a product of ordinary love, not magical summoning."

The Dhracian did not open his eyes, but something akin to the first smile Rhapsody had ever seen him undertake appeared on his face.

"Do not assume that conjuring occurs without the presence of love," he said quietly. "Indeed, it can be the example of the greatest love possible— because it comes, by definition, with selfless sacrifice and the specific desire to bring a child into being. Nature does not have that same requirement, as I am certain you well know. Again, no disrespect intended. If you like, when I am well, I can share the incantation of the lore with you—it's quite beautiful and fascinating, and given your Namer status, you should know it for the ages. Now I must rest. If your offer of a room with a window is still good, I should appreciate it in a few hours."

Achmed opened the door, and Rhapsody left the room. He followed her, closing the door soundlessly. She turned to him in the corridor.

"If you are not busy this afternoon, I should like to take Meridion and tend to my *amelystik* duties," she said. "I want to do whatever I can to offset the despoliation of Terreanfor and its effects on her."

Achmed nodded. He had been thinking the same thing.

"Do you plan to perform any lullabyes?"

Rhapsody blinked in surprise. "Yes, why?"

"Because I think she might like that one Grunthor was singing when I came in to breakfast. Just don't spit tea on her."

The passageway to the Loritorium, a vault from the Cymrian era built to house the instrumentalities and artifacts of elemental lore, had its entrance hidden in a trunk at the foot of Achmed's bed.

The tunnel that was revealed when the chest was untrapped, unlocked and open had been carefully shaped from the stone of the mountain by Grunthor four years before after a particularly vicious battle with a demonic vine, a root of one of the five World Trees that had been tainted by the blood of innocent children and guilty men by the F'dor that the Three had vanquished three years back. The Sergeant-Major, tied as deeply and inexorably to the element of earth as Achmed was to blood and Rhapsody to fire, had saved the rare and beautiful creature known as the Earthchild, a child carved from Living Stone and imbued with the soul of a dragon, that had been sleeping eternally since long before the Cymrians had landed on this continent, and had built her as safe and secure a place to rest peacefully as he was capable of. He and Achmed served as the Earthchild's protectors and guardians, while Rhapsody had inherited the title of *amelystik*, the name meaning *she who tends eternally* that the child's original guardian, a Dhracian woman known as the Grandmother, had conferred upon her.

You must be her amelystik *now. I will soon be too aged to do it.*

I don't understand, Rhapsody had replied haltingly. *You are going too quickly.*

No, the ancient Dhracian woman had spat, *you are going too slowly. You are late, all of you. You should have been here long ago, when I was still strong, before Time broke me. But that did not occur. Nonetheless I have waited, waited alone these many years, these centuries, watching as the pendulum clock counted each hour, each day, each passing year. I have waited for you to come and relieve my watch; now you are here. But even now, it is not as simple as the mere passing of guardianship from my hand to yours. The child has begun to dream, is tormented by nightmares. I cannot hear them; I do not know what bedevils her mind. Only you can free that knowledge, Skychild. Only you can sing her back to a peaceful slumber. It was written in the wind. It is so.*

As they traveled the tunnel now in silence, the Three thought back to the battle they had fought together, to the loss of the Grandmother, the Earthchild's stalwart guardian, and to the future. They all knew a day would come when the demon spirits who sought her would make an attempt to broach the mountain. It was Achmed's first priority in life, by his own decision, to take over her guardianship when the Grandmother died. Rhapsody had never ceased to be amazed how gentle and caring he was with her, given how little he seemed to like children.

But perhaps that was because she was always asleep.

Meridion remained asleep as well through the long walk to the Loritorium. Just before they approached the wall of rubble that had been shaped into a barrier between the tunnel and the depository where the Earthchild slept, Rhapsody clicked softly to the two Bolg.

"I should feed him now," she said quietly. "He will go back to sleep if I do; otherwise, we risk him waking and disturbing her."

Achmed sighed in annoyance.

"I had never imagined I would encounter a creature who is more of a nuisance than you are, Rhapsody, but once again you have proven me wrong."

"Oi'm gonna go check on 'er while you do, Duchess," Grunthor said.

Rhapsody nodded, ignoring Achmed's slight, and slid down the stone wall, bracing her back against it. She draped her cape around herself and positioned Meridion, then looked at the Bolg king, a sharp look in her eye.

"Would you care to tell me what I've done that has made you so nasty of late?"

Achmed's mismatched eyes came to rest on her, then looked away again.

"I dispute that I have been any nastier than I normally am."

"Yes, you have been," Rhapsody said flatly. "I know you were nervous about Rath, but he's healed now. And I know you are worried about the Earthchild, but we are here to tend to her now. Why are you being so harsh?"

"Your baby irritates me."

"How? He hasn't cried in your presence all day."

"He doesn't have to cry to bother me. He smells bad; he makes you strange and distracted. He's one more thing to have to take into consideration every time we make a move. Forgive me if I'm irritated."

"Well, get beyond it, for gods' sake. If you didn't want us here, you should have refused Ashe's request to bring us back to the Bolglands with you."

Grunthor's head appeared above the moraine.

"Duchess, sir, Oi think you should see this."

$\mathcal{T}$he Earthchild slept on her catafalque of Living Stone in the center of the Loritorium. Her body was as tall as that of a full-grown human, her face was that of a child, her skin cold and polished gray, as if she were sculpted from stone. She would have, in fact, appeared to be a statue but for the measured tides of her breath. Below the surface of filmy skin her flesh was darker, in muted hues of brown and green, purple and dark red, twisted together like thin strands of colored clay.

Her features were at once coarse and smooth, as if her face had been carved with blunt tools, then polished carefully over a lifetime. Beneath her indelicate forehead were eyebrows and lashes that appeared formed from blades of dry grass, matching her long, grainy hair. In the dim light the tresses resembled wheat or bleached highgrass cut to even lengths and bound in delicate sheaves. At her scalp the roots of her hair grew green like the grass of early spring.

Muddy tears were rolling down her cheeks.

Rhapsody touched her hand.

"There, there, now," she whispered. "What has you so frightened, child?" She began to hum the earthsong that the Child seemed to like in the Past. She expanded the song into words.

White light
Draw back the night
And wake to the call of spring,
Come and see, come and see,
What the warm winds bring
The butterfly's wing
The meadowbirds sing
A new year in its birth
Welcomes the Child of the Earth

Cool green
In forests unseen
The summer sun's high in the sky
Come and dance, come and dance,
On the verdant ground
In merry round
Where joy is found
The season of mirth
Laughs with the Child of the Earth

Red gold
The leaves grow old
And fall on the breath of the wind
Stay and dream, stay and dream
At summer's flight
In colors bright
Autumn's fight
To hold fast for all she is worth
Comforts the Child of the Earth

White light
Yon comes the night
Snow drapes the frozen world,
Watch and wait, watch and wait
Prepare for sleep
In ice castles deep
A promise to keep
A year whose days left are dearth
Remembers the Child of the Earth

The Earthchild's breathing eased somewhat, and the tears rolled more slowly, but her distress remained evident to each of them.

"Constantin said that Talquist was despoiling Terreanfor, the basilica of Earth," Rhapsody said as she stroked the Sleeping Child's arm with one hand, while cradling Meridion in her other one. "But the benison of the basilica gave his life in the sealing of it, and with the sealing of Terreanfor, I would have thought that her fear might stop."

"She's worried," Grunthor said. The other two fell silent; Grunthor had a connection with the Earthchild that was innate. "She's dreamin' about being taken."

"Perhaps we should consider a more permanent barrier," Achmed said, his gloved hand coming to rest on her hair. "If the F'dor has taken up host in a titan of Living Stone, we should probably seal the tunnel. You can always open it each time we come down here."

"Yeah, sir, but what if somethin' 'appens to me?" the Sergeant-Major said. "You'll never be able to get to 'er."

The tears began to roll again.

AT THE EDGE OF THE TEETH, YLORC

𝒯he morning wind was sweet and high, the bellwether of a fine day.

Anborn's mood was similarly fine. The arming, training, and provisioning of the enhanced farming settlements and villages east-west along the Krevensfield Plain was going far better than he had expected; to his surprise and delight, all of his grousing and complaining to his nephew, the Lord Cymrian, had been heeded, and the army he had hurriedly gathered and commandeered to ride to the holy city's defense had turned out to be well-trained and highly loyal. He was not unaware that at least some part of that loyalty was directly or indirectly pledged to him personally in addition to the Alliance and its sovereigns. Rather than responding to that staunch allegiance with wry condescension or dismissive apathy, as he might have just a few years before, the Lord Marshal was secretly touched by it. Given the deserved reputation he had earned over seven hundred years of war as an intransigent, merciless killer, he was humbled to find that anyone outside of his immediate circle was willing to follow or serve with him at all.

Now his Threshold of Death, as he had named it when rallying his troops the morning after their retreat, was almost complete, a defensible line of former farming settlements and villages that had been converted into makeshift garrisons with the aid of the conscripts he had commandeered while awaiting reinforcements from the standing army of the Alliance, which was being redirected by the Lord Cymrian and the dukes of Roland with an eye toward making certain that the northern border was not left vulnerable. The occasional skirmishes that arose with Sorbold scouting parties were quickly and effectively rebuffed; *too easily*, Anborn was musing as he rode east in the company of Constantin, the exiled Patriarch of Sepulvarta, and his longtime men-at-arms, Solarrs and Knapp, companions who had served with him all his life. Solarrs and Knapp were both First Generation Cymrians, some of the few remaining immortals that had once trod the earth of the Lost Island of Serendair, gone now beneath the waves.

His own father, the high king Gwylliam ap Rendlar, had foreseen the Island's destruction and had engineered an exodus that was truly one of the epic accomplishments of history. Gwylliam had been responsible for the salvation of a great portion of the population of Serendair, had sent them forth from the doomed land in three great waves of more than eight hundred ships, had guided one of those fleets itself through a horrific landing at the crest of a massive storm and the tidal wave that followed it, to eventually come to live, and reign, in this beautiful land of sprawling plains and towering mountains, verdant forests and frozen tundra, seacoasts and cities that sheltered many different races, building a civilization that was the envy of history.

Then he had seen it destroyed by his own vanity, and his own shortcomings.

And Anborn had helped him.

The Lord Marshal shook the repugnant memories from his head; he opened his mouth slightly and let the clean, clear wind fill it, cleansing the bitter taste from his tongue and invigorating him once again.

He had only one more outpost to activate for the Threshold to be complete. That last garrison was one of the most critical of the string of fortresses, the easternmost outpost at the edge of the mountains known officially as the Manteids, in honor of the three Seers of the Past, Present, and Future, by sheer coincidence his mother and two aunts, but more commonly called the Teeth, due to their fanglike appearance and threatening history. Within those mountains stood the massive and mighty stronghold that his father had named Canrif when he reigned there; it was the Cymrian word for *century*, but that name had fallen out of use by all but the staunchest holdouts from the First and other early generations who had known it in its time as one of the great wonders of the world in architecture, engineering, invention, commerce, agriculture, art, and science.

That stronghold now was the home of the Firbolg and their king, an interesting man with a temper and attitude not dissimilar to Anborn's own, with the unlikely name of Achmed the Snake. The Bolg was a bastard race of demi-human monsters, or so Anborn had been trained to believe as a young soldier. He had come to understand otherwise through his cautious camaraderie with the Bolg king and his dear friendship with the Lady Cymrian, a woman who exasperated and amused him almost as much as she fascinated him. He had practically run her down on the road upon first meeting her from atop a beautiful black stallion very much like the one he was riding now; he had come to like her immensely and eventually admit a surface fondness that covered the deeper love of friends and allies who had once even discussed the possibility of an entertaining but loveless alliance marriage.

For all that his upcoming visit was primarily targeted at the Bolg king, it was really Rhapsody that Anborn was looking forward most to seeing.

Given that her husband, with whom she shared an unmistakable and soul-deep love, was his nephew, Gwydion of Manosse, the Lord Cymrian, Anborn's feelings for Rhapsody had, over the past few years, resolved from amused, if intense, attraction and affection into an almost avuncular outlook. He had sworn himself to her as her knight, a pledge of fealty that had surprised him more than anyone else when he made it, and so had taken on the happy task of being her protector and guardian, although as Iliachenva'ar, the formidable bearer of the ancient sword of fire and starlight known as Daystar Clarion, she hardly needed his help. Her marriage to his nephew and the birth of their child had only served to deepen that uncle-like role, providing to the Lord Marshal the first happy sense of family he had ever experienced, given the horror of the one into which he had been born.

And, as a result, out of respect for that sense of family, he had managed to look past what had first attracted him to her, a seraphic beauty as intense as the core of elemental fire that burned within her, making her irresistible to almost anyone who beheld her who wasn't terrified of her. He had come to admire the person she was even more than he could ever have lusted after her, something he had still not been able to believe about himself.

And to love her in a way he didn't really understand, nor did he feel the need to.

So as he and his comrades approached the guardpost that was the westernmost gateway into the Firbolg kingdom, his excitement, fed by a fair wind and a brightening sky, was high, even as war loomed around them all.

$\mathcal{A}$s they came within range of the guardpost, Anborn was delighted to see two shadows that he recognized stretching toward him to the west.

The first shadow was easily discernible as Achmed the Snake, the Firbolg king, chiefly by the flapping of his many veils and robes that shielded his sensitive face and body from the vibrations that others merely recognized as Life. Anborn was one of the few people in the world who knew that the Firbolg king was, in fact, a half-breed, the child of what must have been the horrifying ravaging of a Dhracian woman, one of the Elder races of the world. As a result of the vagaries of nature and his birth, King Achmed had traceries of exposed veins and surface nerve endings scoring his skin, and was able to isolate many rhythms that ordinary men were never aware existed.

Like the heartbeats of his enemies.

Standing next to him was a far bigger shadow that, with the sun behind it, dwarfed that of the Bolg king, who was as tall as Anborn himself. It belonged to a man for whom the Lord Marshal felt an immense liking, chiefly because, like Anborn, he was a longtime military commander, a Firbolg sergeant-major named Grunthor. Grunthor could rightly be described as a giant, standing close to eight feet tall, with skin the color of old bruises and a titanic build that put any human in Anborn's sizable army to shame. Grunthor, in spite of his enormous size, extreme agility, ferocity in battle, and impressive collections of bladed and other weapons that he wore in a bandolier on his back, the jutting hilts making him look like a deadly flower, had a disposition that Rhapsody had once described as sweet, correctly in Anborn's opinion. He was also a Kinsman, a brother of the wind, part of an elite, secretive fraternity of warriors who served as leaders of men, rather than of nations. Anborn was another member of that highly rare order, which meant that his life was happily put at Grunthor's service in times of need, and vice versa.

His sweet nature notwithstanding, what made Grunthor most valuable in the Lord Marshal's estimation was his unerring military wisdom and his ruthless application of it.

The travelers slowed their approach as the Firbolg king raised a hand to his eyes to shield them from the light of the rising sun.

"Good morning, Your Majesty," Anborn called in greeting.

Achmed nodded in turn. "I admire punctuality," he said in what passed for a pleasantry for him. "Thank you for not keeping me waiting. You must have made good time if you have crossed the entire Middle Continent since the sacking of Sepulvarta."

"Indeed," said Anborn as the riders drew the four horses to a halt at a respectful distance. "Speed was a necessity, so we marshaled only the reserve regiments along the Krevensfield Plain from Haguefort in the west to directly south of Bethe Corbair, your neighbor, along with an impressive host of volunteers—farmers, tradesmen, blacksmiths, young boys, even— anyone who was willing to ride to the aid and rescue of the holy city."

The Bolg king nodded. "So what do you need from me? I hope you are not asking for troops; I have a formidable enough task in the defense of my own mountains."

"Of course," said Anborn as the two men-at-arms dismounted. "I don't know if you remember my comrades, Solarrs and Knapp." His voice caught in his throat; he had needed to stop his automatic introduction of a third companion, Shrike, very likely his best friend over the time of his enormously long life, his best friend still, in recent death.

" 'Allo, gents," said Grunthor jovially. "Nice ta see you both again."

"I have brought another comrade as well," Anborn continued. "You both know him, and saw him a few months back at the meeting we held in secret at Haguefort."

The Bolg exchanged a glance. Then they both nodded at the hooded man who maintained his seat on his horse, receiving a curt nod in reply.

"You still have not told me what you need from me," Achmed said to Anborn.

"Sorry; I am hoping to establish a mutually beneficial arrangement. The easternmost outpost that I mentioned is going to need provisions that I thought the Alliance might obtain from you. I have positioned that garrison at the easternmost edge of the steppes, so that they might provide security, or at least an obstacle, between Sorbold and Ylorc, as well as Bethe Corbair."

Grunthor broke into a wide amused grin, his tusks gleaming in the morning light.

"Well, thank you kindly, General! That's mighty nice o' you."

"I am tasked with protecting the entirety of the Alliance, of which

Ylorc is a part," Anborn said seriously. "I imagine you hardly need our defenses, given the well-deserved reputation of your own—but a chain is only as strong as its weakest link, and what we have set up is such a chain, a threshold of death for the enemy, should he be unwise enough to attempt to cross it."

"Good," said the Bolg king. "What sort of provisions are you looking for?"

"Primarily foodstuffs and water," said the Lord Marshal, "but I would be interested in any Bolg weaponry you are willing to sell me. I do not wish to pry into anything you consider privileged, and what I've seen of the weapons you have put on the open market are often for close-quarter combat." The Bolg king nodded. "I don't expect much of that sort of warfare, at least not on the Threshold, but what would really be of use to us is any sort of heavy projectile weapons that can make use of ropes and the like, such as an adapted ballista. I'm not sure what details of the sacking of the holy city have been communicated to you, but Talquist accomplished it chiefly with the use of an aerial assault using monstrous flying creatures, abominations formed at least partially out of the Living Stone of the basilica of Terreanfor." He glanced at the Patriarch, but there was no indication of any kind of thought or emotion from beneath the heavy hood. "Before I left my nephew's headquarters at Highmeadow, he, his namesake Gwydion Navarne, and I discussed rope projectiles and ballistae as the only weapons likely to be effective against these creatures, known by their despicable creators as iacxsis, a name from the time before the Cymrians arrived, when this land was dedicated to animist gods and an even more brutal outlook."

"More brutal than the Cymrians? I shudder at the thought."

"Fair enough," said Anborn. He looked over the shoulders of the two Firbolg men and broke into a wide smile.

Rhapsody was hurrying to the gate, running to meet them, joy on her face.

Anborn sat up in his high-backed saddle, an adjustment the Master of the Horse had made for him upon his laming. He let his eyes feast on the sight of her as she approached; he had long admired the athletic, easy way she ran, not at all like the embarrassingly awkward, clodlike gait of many of the women he had known. Her long golden hair was loose around her, and streamed in the wind like a resplendent flag.

"I believe, at least for the time being, that water and foodstuffs are easily made available to your outpost," Achmed said, drawing Anborn's attention back to the matter he had come to address. "If you would like to come into the Cauldron, my seat within the mountain, Grunthor and I can see what sort of weaponry we might have available for your use."

"Thank you, Your Majesty."

The Bolg king turned to the Patriarch. "I can offer you a place to rest and pray, or whatever it is you do, as well as a place of refuge," he said.

"Thank you, Majesty," the holy man said in return, "but I have another boon to ask of you, one that should not be spoken out in the wind."

"Then you should definitely come inside." He looked at Anborn suddenly. "You will need assistance, a litter and carriers."

Rhapsody was just slowing to a stop as the Lord Marshal chuckled in answer.

"Thank you, no," he said.

He tossed the reins aside and lowered himself from the horse, then walked over to the Lady Cymrian, who froze in her steps.

And then he bowed, trying not to laugh at the look on her face.

"You—you can—Anborn! You can *walk?*"

"She has an impressive grasp of the obvious," the Bolg king said almost pleasantly. "Well, this is a welcome development."

"Right," added Grunthor enthusiastically. "Worthy o' celebratin' for certain. Shall we get drunk, go on a cannibalistic rampage, an' sacrifice a virgin?"

"We can get drunk at least," said the Lord Marshal, opening his arms as Rhapsody threw herself into them. "Stop smiling at me, Lady, you are making my already-compromised knees weak."

"I am just *so* happy to see this," Rhapsody said, fighting back tears. "Was it the shell?"

"Indeed, that and your Naming wisdom and the deafening of my regiment by the horror of my singing voice." Anborn noted that the Patriarch had dismounted. "Perhaps you will be even happier, then, to see who I have brought with me."

Rhapsody released the Lord Marshal and walked over to the cloaked man. She looked up into his hood, then put her hand over her mouth, the tears she had fought to hold back winning the battle and spilling down her cheeks.

"Oh, my," she said. "Welcome. Welcome; I am so sorry."

"Don't be," the Patriarch said harshly from beneath his hood. "Be outraged, rather. At the risk of being rude, might we go inside? I hope to keep my status among the living a secret from Talquist for the time being."

"Of course," said Rhapsody as the Firbolg quartermaster and several members of the supply regiment appeared, waiting to take the horses. "Please, by all means, come inside."

"Solarrs and Knapp will stay with the quartermaster and tend to the horses, if you don't mind," said Anborn, signaling to his men, who had already anticipated his orders. "Where is my great-nephew? I expect he's riding a horse himself already."

"Not quite yet," Rhapsody laughed, taking his hand and pulling him toward the entrance to the Cauldron. "I had just fed him and put him down for his nap when I heard the signal sounding your arrival. Come and see him; he'll be delighted."

Contrary to Rhapsody's expectations, Meridion was neither asleep or delighted by the time the group had made its way into the Great Hall of the Cauldron.

Upon entering the hallway that led to the enormous room within the mountain fortress, they were greeted with the shrill sound of wailing echoing off the basalt walls and thundering against the high ceilings. It caused the Bolg king's already unpleasant expression to turn even more sour, and interrupted the flow of thought and conversation that he and Anborn had engaged in since leaving the guardpost.

Constantin had asked to be taken to a quiet place where he could collect his thoughts and perform the rites of morning prayer incumbent on him as head of his religion, in spite of the happenings in Sepulvarta, so Achmed intercepted a Bolg guard, who led the Patriarch away to the tunnels overlooking the Blasted Heath on the other side of the vast interior canyon while Grunthor continued to listen to Anborn's queries about weapons and provisions.

Rhapsody opened the one functioning door of the Great Hall, and immediately the infant's cries doubled in volume and intensity, causing the Bolg king's eyes to cross, much to Anborn's amusement. Finally Achmed gave up attempting to concentrate and turned to Grunthor.

"Summon the Archons, tell them to meet back here in an hour," he said, referring to his elite cadre of specially trained subordinates. Not long after they had taken the mountain, Rhapsody had suggested that he identify a child of innate intelligence or special talents from each of the major Bolg tribes, singling them out for special training; they now were his second rank of command in Ylorc, handling almost all the day-to-day operations of the mountain kingdom. Kubila, the Archon of trade and diplomacy; Ralbux, who oversaw the education programs with Rhapsody, as well as Harran the Loremistress, who catalogued the history of the tribes; Dreekak, the Master of Tunnels; Vrith, who kept the accounts of trade; Greel, known as the Face of the Mountain, who was the master of mining, Trug, the Voice who spoke the common tongue, known as Orlandan, as well as any citizen of Roland; and Yen, the broadsmith, responsible for the massive program of weapons manufacture, were, she had once observed, the closest thing he had to his own children, a comment that had drawn a scornful look but no real response.

Grunthor nodded, clicked his heels, and left the room.

Achmed looked back at Anborn. "I will take a quick inventory of what we might have in stock in the armory to send with you, or after you." He closed his eyes as the vibrations of Meridion's cries rippled over the sensitive skin of his neck and eyelids, searing them.

"I'm going to have to excuse myself to attend to the baby," Rhapsody said, tying her hair back as she made her way to the cradle.

"Why excuse yourself? Surely you must know Grunthor and I are merely finding reasons to evacuate this room to get away from the appalling noise of your brat," Achmed said, heading for the door himself. "Feed that thing while we're gone and make it stop. You may come with me if you like, Anborn—I am happy to provide you an excuse to escape as well."

"Many thanks, but it's not necessary," Anborn said. "I am happy to remain with Rhapsody and my great-nephew; I won't get many chances to see him in the foreseeable future."

"You're a lucky man," Achmed said as he reached the doorframe. "Would that I were so lucky." He looked at the Lady Cymrian with an expression as ugly as she had ever seen.

"Hawks, Rhapsody."

Then he left the room, closing the door.

16

"Don't you want to see the armory?"

"Of course, but I'm hoping for a more complete tour," Anborn replied, stretching his back and shoulders. "Steady as they have become, my legs are building up slowly to full stamina, and I have used them a great deal today; there are not too many steps left in them at the moment. If I can get Achmed to show me around later, after I've been sitting for a while, I will be able to maintain my strength and see more of whatever he is willing to show me."

"Brilliant tactic, as always," Rhapsody said, lifting the baby out of the cradle and into her embrace. "Thank you for taking the time to visit with Meridion; it means a great deal to me."

"It means a great deal to me as well," said the Lord Marshal as Rhapsody draped a blanket from the cradle over her shoulder. "Would you like me to withdraw to the hallway while you feed him?"

"Only if you would be more comfortable," she replied, settling into her chair again. "I'm not embarrassed if you are not. I've gotten fairly good at feeding him discreetly, and I gave up on modesty a very long time ago anyway."

Anborn laughed. "Good for you; it's highly overrated." He settled into a chair and watched as she relaxed, the baby at her breast draped in the soft blanket, and began singing a wordless lullabye that reminded the Lord Marshal distinctly of the sea, though he had no idea why.

After what seemed like only a few moments, the tune changed. Anborn blinked; he had become lost in the sight of her, smiling down at the infant beneath the blanket, changing sides, playing with his toes, her face ethereal, more beautiful than he ever remembered seeing it.

A wave of almost sickening loss swept over him.

Within a relatively short time she was done; she pulled her shirt back to rights, took the blanket down and wrapped the little boy in it. Anborn coughed, clearing his throat.

"Young Meridion seems to be making excellent use of his access to your, er—"

"Yes. Thank you."

"Well, he's grown strong on your supply. Still quite small, but he seems very healthy."

"He was born early, I think," Rhapsody said, putting a clean rag, then the baby on her shoulder and patting his back. "It's hard to know what the gestation period should have been, given his bloodlines. He was so tiny at birth."

"Well, you've done an admirable job with him. He's perfect. Here, give him to me. An expert should be the one to teach him the art of belching properly."

Rhapsody laughed and handed him the baby. "Another of your many talents I was not aware of."

"Well, that's only because you had the very good sense not to marry me; if you had I could have demonstrated other talents you don't know of firsthand—snoring, using flatulence as a weapon—"

"Anborn, I knew you had studied as a young man with the Lirin and the Nain, but I had no idea until now that you were also a student of the Bolg."

The Cymrian general wasn't listening. He was staring down at Meridion. The baby was so small in his hands, Rhapsody noted. It seemed as if he had the grip of someone with experience holding an infant, though he had told her long ago that he had no children of his own. He raised the little boy to his wide shoulder and began rubbing his back gently with his large, callused hand, a soldier's hand, then murmured in the child's ear.

"Spit up on me and I will use you for target practice, great-nephew."

With mock panic Rhapsody pulled the rag from her shoulder and slung it over Anborn's neck.

A massive belch, completely out of proportion to the infant's size, echoed through the chamber.

The Lord Marshal examined his shoulder as Rhapsody laughed.

"Perfect," Anborn declared. "Well done, Meridion—a fulsome sound, grand degree of volume, and no residual aftereffect. Good use of resources when you keep it all down like that. An excellent student—you may redeem your wretched father's reputation after all." He took the little boy back into his hands, watching him intently.

"Were you the one to teach Ashe to burp as an infant?"

Anborn shook his head, but he didn't take his eyes off Meridion.

"At the time of Gwydion's birth, his father and I were still enemies. Llauron didn't marry until long after the war was over—he had gone to Tyrian in an attempt to mend fences with the Lirin by proposing a marriage of state to Terrell, their queen at the time—only my misbegotten brother would think such an offer would be taken as flattering after bringing so much destruction upon them, involving them in a war they should have stayed out of. Terrell refused—at least one Lirin queen has had the good sense to stay far away from this family. Eventually he married the woman to whom he was betrothed before the war—she was foolish enough to have him after being forced to wait seven hundred years. Then she died giving birth to his son. A terrible shame, really."

"So when did you get to know Ashe?"

Anborn smiled slightly as the baby drifted off to sleep in his hands. "That name always gives me pause, for to me he has always been Gwydion. He was the equivalent of eleven or so—I've lost track of his numerical age, as Wyrmkin all grow at different rates. By then my brother's and my enmity had settled into indifference, mostly, and I have avoided the Circle since my own childhood, so I did not see Gwydion as an infant or a young child much, except on occasions of state—Shrike actually spoke to him more often than I did during those days when he was little." Anborn's voice faltered slightly at his mention of his longtime friend and man-at-arms, who had died in an attack on Rhapsody's own carriage escort. "But Gwydion was great friends with Stephen Navarne, and Stephen's father was a favorite comrade-in-arms of mine, so one day I tripped over him, quite literally, at Haguefort. I gave the two boys some early training in the sword, and other important areas—spitting, cursing—Gwydion had a remarkable aptitude for that, being a dragon—"

"Yes, I've noticed."

"He was actually quite a pleasant and interesting young man, respectful, modest and easygoing, with a ready laugh and willingness to learn anything in which instruction was being offered, though it was also clear that he was somewhat lonely, understandable for a boy growing up motherless and with a father who was self-absorbed. I was gruff with him, but he didn't seem to mind, though I confess to some regret about the way I treated him then. When he was a little older, fourteen or so, I believe, he came into a phase of melancholy; the cheerful boy was replaced by a solemn, often sad young man. I have no idea what happened to cause that, but he remained so into adulthood."

The smile vanished from Rhapsody's face. She knew the reason.

She turned away to prevent the Lord Marshal from noticing, but he was still enthralled with the infant.

"At any rate, I had them both, Gwydion and Stephen, and that weaselmeat, Tristan Steward, in my regiment when they were older, with a few of his other friends—the Baldasarre brothers, Ian Steward, Andrew Canderre and the like. I have even greater regrets for my treatment of him then. Family favoritism is something I could never abide, especially when I was a young soldier and the unwilling beneficiary of my father's nepotism, so I made a great effort not to let it come into my command of Gwydion, perhaps to an unfair level, but he excelled in spite of my somewhat abusive treatment and criticism. I gave him some very onerous tasks, and some miserable nicknames, but he never complained."

"Ah, yes, 'Useless'?"

"That was actually from when he was younger. The later ones I would hesitate to mention in front of a lady." Anborn chuckled as Meridion began to make suckling motions with his mouth, his eyes still closed in slumber.

"I think we are going to have to call him 'Insatiable, son of Useless,'" he said fondly.

"Wouldn't the Cymrian nomenclature for that be 'Insatiable ap Useless'?"

"Indeed."

Rhapsody laughed as her son scowled and began issuing forth loud sucking noises. "His mouth is always moving in his sleep. In the rare moments during the day he isn't actually nursing, he's dreaming of it, it seems."

"Of course he is. No man of any age, in or out of his right mind, would ever pass up a chance to have his lips cemented to your breast, my dear," Anborn said pleasantly, still watching the baby. "I am often undertaking the same pastime in my own dreams."

"I am so glad to know that my newly minted motherhood has not changed your willingness to say crudely amusing things to me, Lord

Marshal," Rhapsody said, humor in her voice. "I would hate to think you might have falsely gained a new restraint—it would make life boring."

"It was meant as a compliment."

"Of course."

Finally the Lord Marshal looked at her. "Sincerely—I did not mean to be vulgar, just truthful."

"And believe me, it's appreciated," Rhapsody said lightly, hoping to leaven the awkwardness that had crept into the moment. "I often wonder if my lack of endowment in that area is contributing to my son's constant demand—perhaps he is underfed because the storage tanks are so small, an explanation Grunthor offered at one point. At least your observations are kind; Achmed's and Grunthor's are insulting."

Anborn exhaled, and his gaze returned to the baby.

"Did you ever discuss the prospect of marriage with either of them? Or both?"

"Goodness, no," Rhapsody blurted. Her face colored as Anborn looked at her again. "With Grunthor, much as I love him, it would literally be suicide. Though I did once raise Achmed as a potential mate when Ashe asked me about it long ago. He was rather nauseated by the thought, as I recall."

"Rightly so," Anborn agreed.

Rhapsody hesitated, then decided whatever was unspoken needed to be heard. "Is there a particular reason you ask?"

The Lord Marshal was silent for a moment. "I am just remembering a particularly fine day, and a particularly fine lunch, on a balcony in Tyrian where you and I discussed the same prospect. It was a perfect afternoon, with the exception of a line of imbeciles who had come to sue for your hand on the other side of the wall around Newyd Dda, hooting like a crowd at a bloodsport arena," he said. "Uncomfortable or nauseating as it may be for you to recall it, it is one of my most cherished memories."

Rhapsody inhaled, then let out her breath pensively.

"Why would you think it would be uncomfortable, much less nauseating, for me to recall it? Other than the imbeciles, I mean—that nonsense went on for months, so it is its own nauseating memory. Why would you think the memory of our first lunch together would be upsetting to me?"

Anborn tilted the baby slowly back and forth in his hands, rocking him. "Is it not?"

"No," said Rhapsody flatly. "At least it wasn't uncomfortable until just now. And certainly even now it isn't nauseating. I remember enjoying that lunch, and that conversation. You have been one of the easiest people I know to talk to, Anborn—that afternoon, and always. It's one of the things I cherish the most about *you*. If you have something to say to me, please speak it plainly. My brain is addled these days from the constant demands of an infant, missing my husband, being back in Ylorc where I am still considered a fresh source of wasted food, and the buildup to a war which terrifies me. I am grateful for plainspokenness, and you are usually the master of it." She thought for a moment. "And, if I'm being completely truthful, as I always try to be, I remember now that I also discussed Achmed as an alliance marriage with Oelendra, after I told her what I had suggested to you."

"That's right; I recall you did go off to speak to her after that lunch," Anborn said. "I believe I walked with you there." He moved Meridion into the crook of his arm; the child fit perfectly between his wrist and elbow with the padding of his blankets. Then Anborn scratched his head with his other hand. "I was touched and impressed that you spoke to me about the possibility of our marriage before you shared it with even your closest friends and confidantes. Oelendra advocated for Achmed over me, I presume?"

"She actually advocated for Ashe—er, Gwydion—over both of you." Anborn nodded, still not meeting her eyes, and Rhapsody felt her throat begin to tighten. "Please tell me what you are thinking," she said. "You're breaking my heart, and I don't even know why."

The Cymrian hero said nothing for a long time, just rocked his greatnephew in the crook of one arm while Rhapsody fought back tears. Finally he turned to her, and his searing blue eyes were gleaming, but the look in them was mild.

"I'm sorry, m'lady," he said simply. "When events of great portent come to pass—the birth of this beautiful child, a new generation in our troubled but powerful family, the buildup to war in which I am again serving as Lord Marshal, which I have not done since the Cymrian era, my brother's Ending, even the miraculous return of the use of my legs—I have always had a propensity to become contemplative; others might call it brooding, but really it's not. I go back over my old memories; it's probably the way the wyrm in my blood manifests itself, and you may not recognize it, because Gwydion's dragon nature is so much more a part of him than mine is of me. And when I go through the things I've said, the things I've done, I try to set things to rights, to answer any old, outstanding questions, make amends, whatnot, for things I have left in chaos, or unspoken, undone. A habit born out of longevity that borders on immortality; there are only so many things that you can carry around in your brain on a to-do list when your life is counted in millennia, not years."

"I can imagine," Rhapsody said.

Anborn laughed, but his eyes regarded her seriously. "Forgive me, but I don't believe you can, not yet, my dear, you are far too young still." he said. "But one day you will—one day you will have to, given your longevity is bound to be even greater than mine. And then, on that day, you will understand what you really cannot imagine now. And if I am still around, I will come to you, and comfort you in your understanding—because you will need comforting."

"So what has you contemplating our—our almost marriage?" Rhapsody asked. Before the words were even voiced she regretted opening her mouth.

Anborn smiled.

"Passing on it—asking you to let me out of the arrangement—is perhaps the only selfless, altruistic thing I have ever done," he said.

"I don't believe that."

The Lord Marshal shrugged. "Believe what you like; it's my assessment that matters, and as far as I am concerned, having taken stock of my memories, at least the ones I have chosen to keep, that's it; that's the only one."

"And it's something for which I have never thanked you properly," Rhapsody said quietly, her face reddening. "You were more aware of my feelings than I was at the time; you knew I was in love with Ashe, even when I couldn't admit it. It was such a confusing time, full of lies and misinformation. Had you not asked for release from our bargain, I would never have built a life with the other half of my soul. I wouldn't have Meridion. You once pledged your life to me, Anborn—truly, we need to reverse that pledge, for I owe everything I have found in this world to you."

"Stop that," the Lord Marshal commanded. "The value of altruism, of selflessness, dims when one seeks or accepts such thanks. You're welcome. Thank you for returning to me the use of my legs. There; we're even. Now, can you put aside what you have gained from my decision for a moment and explore some other possibilities with me, just for discussion's sake?"

Rhapsody blinked. "I—I guess so. I'm not sure what you mean."

"Let us both acknowledge that we are happy in the way things turned out for you in your marriage, your choice of spouses." Rhapsody nodded. "I wonder what you think life would have been like for us if I, in fact, had *not* given in to altruism, and had acted on the impulse of my baser nature, which has always been my default. I will make the question simple for you, Rhapsody: do you think you would even have gone through with it at all, or would good sense have held sway?"

"If I had not married Ashe, would I still have married you?"

"That's a start, yes."

"Of course," Rhapsody said haltingly. "I would not have broken our bargain."

"Well, that's a *good* start then," Anborn said. "And, had this come to pass, do you think we would have achieved the companionable, though loveless, marriage that we planned for, with my freedom unhampered and your suitors frightened off by the reputation of your husband, or, because it is clearly not what the All-God, or the Fates, or the Universe, or whatever other bloody thing is controlling our destiny wanted for us, would it have ended up as most of these marriages of convenience do—like Tristan Steward and his Lady Nightmare, or Anwyn and Gwylliam, or even Estelle and me?"

"Why are you asking me something I can't possibly have any knowledge of?"

The Lord Marshal smiled again, but this time it was rueful.

"Perhaps I am just torturing myself in preparation for war," he said. "When one contemplates something as impossible as saving a continent, it's good to know that there is something worth saving. Or maybe I need to clean out the closets that once held unrealistic dreams, because I have no excuse to have such things or the space in which they are stored anymore. Or perhaps because you are the only Lirin Namer I know, and I want a knowledgeable observation, an opinion, rather than a prophecy from a mad Seer which would ruin my life in trying to figure it out. Or—maybe I just want to know if what I sacrificed mattered anyway; if it were to turn out to be a horror, I didn't really miss out on much. Humor me—tell me what you think. It's just a harmless question—what if?"

Rhapsody sat back in her chair and watched him as he stood, then delivered Meridion to the cradle, covering him carefully with a blanket and patting him affectionately, to return a moment later to his chair. For the first time since he had come into the room, he gave her his complete attention.

"'What if?' is usually *not* a harmless question," she said. "It's an impossible question, because the true answer can never be known."

"There is no true answer; I'm just wondering what you think. I promise to hold you to nothing, because I understand the strictures of being a

Namer. I can also promise I will not reveal anything you say to anyone else, nor will I torment you with its repetition. I just want to know what you think."

Rhapsody closed her eyes. She pushed aside the tension of the feelings that had been mounting, recognizing Anborn's hypothetical query as being something antithetical to the attitude of a Namer, but reasonable from his perspective as an answer to whatever was clearly plaguing his mind. She considered his question, taking her time to sort through the layers of it, then opened her eyes. When she did, they were gleaming calmly.

"Very well," she said, "here's my opinion."

Anborn sat forward in his chair.

"First, all those forces you named that are supposedly controlling our lives don't give a roasted rat's damn about who we marry and what we do," she said. "At least not the way you specified. We control our own destiny. If the alternative of our marriage would not have been as favorable as the one I actually have, it doesn't mean we would have been made to suffer by some faceless entity for not getting it 'right.' "

Anborn nodded, pleased.

"Second, you and I could never—let me repeat this for emphasis—*never*—be Gwylliam and Anwyn, or Tristan Steward and his hateful spouse. We would only be ourselves, as we are. And while you rode away with a faceful of mud from our first encounter, and I was called a 'freak of nature' and threatened with the prospect of seeing your horse's new shoes close up if I didn't get out of your way, I actually do not believe the interaction within our marriage would have been even the slightest bit unpleasant."

Anborn chuckled, amused by the reminder of their first meeting. "Not even the slightest? If I recall, you accused me loudly of being buggered by my own *horse*. Come now, my dear—"

"Do you want my opinion or not?"

The Lord Marshal bowed his head humorously and yielded the floor back to her.

"I am so glad that I have come to know you now, at this point in your life, not in your youth, or during the Cymrian War, or in its aftermath. I have come to like the experienced you very much, and I'm not sure I would have liked you at all when you were younger. I am also especially glad that you did not know me in an earlier time, either; I expect you would have had nothing to do with me had you met me then."

"I doubt that, Rhapsody."

"Doubt it, or doubt it not. It doesn't matter. You and I are no longer works in progress, but adults now. Had things been different, had we gone ahead with our alliance marriage, I believe at least most of the conditions we laid out in that lunch meeting would have been fairly easily upheld. You would have had your freedom, and so I imagine the arguments or conflicts that might arise when two people who aren't in love marry would be nullified just because if things got to the edge of unpleasant, you would have saddled up and ridden away. It's hard to maintain anger when someone is gone, at least for me. I would have found myself missing you, and glad to see you once you came home again."

A small smile took up residence on his face. "Well, you have just proven yourself correct about not being like Estelle."

"We agreed not to have children—" Rhapsody's voice caught in her throat; she coughed. "Now that I have Meridion, I cannot imagine life without him. But, pragmatically, if I vowed that to you, I would not have tried to change your mind. All the things about not embarrassing each other or harming the people of Tyrian, I can't imagine that would have been a problem."

"No," Anborn agreed.

"So that only leaves one thing that I don't think I could have lived up to."

The Lord Marshal nodded. "Ah, yes. The wifely duties."

Rhapsody's brow furrowed. "Wifely duties? Feeding you, keeping your house clean? I certainly could provide those services, though I have been told I make a terrible pot of tea."

"You know very well that's not what I mean."

"I don't. I—wait. Wait a moment—do you mean the physical relationship?"

"Of course."

"Oh." Rhapsody settled back in her chair, not a whisper of embarrassment on her face. "I hardly consider those 'duties,' Anborn," she said. "Opportunities for mutual pleasure, rather, and perhaps good exercise. That certainly would not have been a problem, I assume—I can only speak for myself, of course."

The Lord Marshal let out a long breath. "You would have expected that pleasure to be mutual?"

"Of course. Why—didn't you?"

"I could only hope. Though it was not what I expected." He looked down at his hands, broken-knuckled and callused from a millennia of wielding a sword. "In a thousand years of being with women, all but the paltry few during which I was married have involved splendid commerce that was blissfully one-sided. Bedwenches and camp followers have no expectations of mutual pleasure. Wives in marriages of convenience are, forgive me, very much the same—at least in my experience. So even though I would have secretly hoped to be able to bring you pleasure, I had no real expectation that I would even know how. Your intimidating beauty would most likely have rendered me more pathetic than a lad of thirteen. But if what we were to have was a commerce of another kind, trading marital joys for me with protection for you—I could live up to that."

Rhapsody laughed. "You insult yourself greatly, and apparently don't know me as well as I thought," she said. "I could never sell myself in marriage to someone to whom I did not feel an attraction, or with whom that part of the marriage contract was a duty or an unwanted but required act." Her eyes gleamed as her smile faded. "My life has been difficult in that area, Anborn. You once commented that I had the male world prostrate at my feet, which of course I do not, but there is a lot of ugliness that comes with that assumption. Whoring for reasons other than the usual ones is still whoring."

The Lord Marshal's smile dimmed as well, and he nodded silently.

"Please remember, I'm the one that proposed to you," Rhapsody said, crossing her arms. "I did not presume at the time that you would want me in that way—" An explosion of laughter interrupted her. "What's so funny about that?"

"Nothing, my dear. Pray continue."

"But I'm a Namer. I cannot play fiddlesticks or three-in-hand because those are betting games, and I am unable, by profession and inclination both, to bluff. I thought you had already made this assessment of me by the time I asked you."

"But yet you considered Achmed?"

"Only reluctantly. But yes. And not if you had agreed."

Anborn's expression became complicated.

"You consider Achmed attractive?"

Rhapsody shifted uncomfortably in her chair. "Not all attraction is visible to the eye, Anborn. But again, please note who I asked, and who I did not."

The Lord Marshal nodded again. "So what, then, did you think would not have held in the agreement?"

Rhapsody smiled. "You told me it yourself when you asked to be set free."

Realization dawned on the Lord Marshal. "That—that I wasn't able to live up to the requirement of not loving you?"

"Yes, and I admitted I couldn't live up to that requirement either. I have told you a number of times since then, but I never want to let an opportunity to do so pass—I love you. It is very different from what I have with Ashe—I am in love with him in a way I could never be with anyone else. But our theoretical marriage would not have been loveless, at least as far as I was concerned. I was disappointed, crushed, even, when you asked to be set free of the promise, because I had come to believe we would have had a happy, easy union, one blessed with laughter, and crude humor, an exchange of ideas and the teaching of each other, mutual respect, and loving friendship. And so yes, I expected that pleasure to be mutual. You're a handsome man; your arms are strong, your body is youthful, and you kiss *very* well, if I recall correctly." She chuckled as his grin widened, then her expression became sober. "I feel safe with you, and there are very few people about whom I can say that. I imagined traveling together, sharing a horse, riding in front of you as we did when you rescued me in the forest, wrapped in your cloak, me sleeping as we rode, but only if you kept your knuckles from digging into my ribs—"

"That was necessary," he interrupted. "You were freezing to death."

"Shhh. If I had been your wife you would have spent less time lame, as I would have been after you intently to heal yourself, maybe even to the point where you would have gotten annoyed and left for a while. I would have tried very hard to be pleasant company and a good companion to you, and to have made your fondness for bedwenches unnecessary, at least as best as I could, without denying you their company if I could not hold your interest."

"Don't be ridiculous."

"It's not ridiculous—I assumed nothing. *Nothing*, Anborn. At that time I was trying to be as practical as I could, because romantic love was elusive and painful. The deception of the F'dor, and Llauron, and practically everyone I met, even Ashe, had me completely confused, and unable to listen to my own heart. It is not so now; I am grateful to the One-God and to you for setting me straight." She averted her gaze from his eyes, which were gleaming in azure fire. "But if you are asking me if you and I would have been like any of the other hateful unions you mentioned, then no, we would not have been. I believe our marriage would have been happy, and easy, and loving, at least in a friendly way, and that it would have provided me the safety and security I was seeking, and you with whatever comforts you would take from me, gratefully given. But, of course, as you requested, this is just my opinion. We will never know, will we?"

Anborn watched her for a long moment.

"No, of course, we will never know. But it has been fascinating hearing what you thought might have been."

From deep within the cradle came the sounds of an infant waking.

Rhapsody's head dropped back and she stared at the ceiling above her.

"Again? Already, Meridion? Arrrgh."

Anborn laughed in spite of himself.

"Sit, m'lady," he said as she started to rise. "I will get him for you—it's the least that I can do for the woman who almost was my wife."

"Your niece-in-law."

"Yes. My niece-in-law. May my nephew never take what he has for granted."

He stood slowly and went to the cradle. Carefully he lifted the baby into his arms and embraced him for a moment before he brought him to his mother to be fed.

His heart breaking wide open, as it had once been long before, filled with light and a fresh wind.

17

Once Anborn's legs had rested and recovered, Achmed and Grunthor made good on their offer to show him the forges and the factories, the vineyards on the Blasted Heath and the weapons stockpiles, at least those that were not classified. Anborn followed them through corridors he had known a thousand years before, past defenses that had been carefully reconsidered and redesigned from the use in which they had been employed during the Lord Marshal's time here.

His astonishment grew at each new sector.

The Bolg king and the Sergeant-Major had stripped away almost every decorative element left over from the Cymrian era, a hearty improvement in Anborn's opinion, and redesigned the mountain stronghold with defense and security first in priority, followed by efficiency and ease of maintainence and use. While Rhapsody's influence was evident in the more social aspects of the mountain, the hospitals and hospices, the schools and agricultural programs, it was clear that military might and manufacturing were the priorities of the Firbolg king, and all resources were directed to those priorities first.

He set about procuring whatever the Bolg king deemed available in the way of weapons and matériel, cheerfully imagining the benefits those things would provide to his armed farming settlements along the Threshold of Death.

"Anything else you can provide that would help me with that construct would be greatly appreciated, Your Majesty," he told Achmed as they left the armory.

Achmed smirked.

"I'll work on a new name for the Threshold of Death for you, then," he said.

While Anborn was happily touring the new Canrif, Rhapsody was spending time in Gurgus Peak in the room that held the Lightcatcher in the company of Constantin, the deposed and exiled Patriarch of Sepulvarta.

The Patriarch had requested to be taken to the tallest hollow peak within the area of Canrif and, after obtaining permission from Achmed, Rhapsody had led him to Gurgus, the highest mountain past the steppes and before the canyon that separated the part of the Bolglands known as the Cauldron, the place that once had been Gwylliam's seat of power and was now Achmed's, from the Deeper Realms, the lands of the Bolg clans grouped roughly into two categories known as Eyes and Guts. The Eyes were thin and wiry people, at ease in the high altitude of the mountain peaks, and therefore had the primary responsibility for spying and lookout. The Guts, far more warlike cave dwellers, had been some of the last clans to swear fealty to Achmed but had mutated into a highly loyal and formidable security force, guarding the mountain passes closer to the level of the piedmont, the gentle sloping area that served as a border between the flat steppes and the rocky peaks.

The Patriarch had seemed more comfortable with keeping his hood up at first, so Rhapsody was still adjusting to the booming timbre of his voice when it issued forth from his cloak. She was amused at this; she had met her husband when he was a hunted man, hiding from the sight of the world in a cloak of mist that he had made with Kirsdarke, his sword of elemental water, so her inability to adjust to the the sound of Constantin's voice was amazing to her. The tour she had provided ended up inside the room with the Lightcatcher.

The revelation had rendered Constantin speechless.

He stepped into the large circular room with the towering domed ceiling, his clear blue eyes, so intense in his otherwise elderly face, taking in the instrumentality—the stained glass in the ceiling, cast in slices of color, one of each of the hues in the spectrum, above a table, an altar of sorts in the center of a circular track on which a great wheel stood on its side.

"Can you explain this to me?"

Rhapsody followed him as he came to a stop in front of the altar.

"Basically, each color of the spectrum has a lore, or power associated with it and, like the ring you wear, each has a positive and a negative aspect to that power," she said. "The universe is made up of vibrations, of color, of light, of sound—this is the basis of the science of Singing, of Naming." The Patriarch nodded, listening attentively. "Because each of the colors of light has a lore connected to it, and the two basic constants of the universe are creation and destruction, those lores are tuned to the sharps and flats of the notes of the musical scale, the sharps attuned to the creative aspects, the flats to the destructive ones. For instance, red is known as Blood Saver in its sharp application, for healing, and Blood Letter in the flat, for killing. The orange part of the spectrum is known as Fire Starter or Fire Quencher, sort of self-explanatory, as is the yellow, Light Bringer or Light Queller. The sharp of green, Grass Scryer, allows for viewing things that are hidden within vegetation or terrain, while the flat, Grass Hider, conceals those things. The blue part of the spectrum is the one we feel confident enough to test first; that one is known as Cloud Chaser or Cloud Caller, which is similar to the green except that it illuminates things, makes them clearer or more obscure. The notes left behind in Gwylliam's library say that it could see across vast distances, sometimes allowing for communication while the daylight was active in that part of the spectrum, or was good for clearing away confusion and clarifying the properties of an object or hiding them. The indigo properties are called Night Bringer or Night Summoner; we've not experimented much with those, but they are said to affect time, to make things that are anticipated come more quickly, or to hold off those that are desired kept at bay. Finally, the last color in the spectrum, purple, is known as the New Beginning, which is the only note that has only a natural tone, not a sharp or a flat. This one is the most mysterious of all, and seems to overturn reality in favor of a new version of it, in small and great ways. Needless to say, we will be very hesitant in trying that one out."

"That seems prudent," the Patriarch agreed.

"We've had great luck with the red portion of the spectrum in healing so far," Rhapsody said. "We're ready to test the blue and the green shortly, but Achmed is wary about experimenting with most of the others any time soon."

The Patriarch nodded.

"There are basically three parts to the instrumentality's function—the color, which determines what sort of lore is tapped; the sound, which the wheel produces, or can be done vocally, which determines the specific pitch, sharp or flat; and the light, which shines through the specific color and is the power source. The person utilizing the Lightcatcher stands at the altar, which is made of Black Ivory, an entirely inert, dead stone, beneath the perfect center of the dome above, and states the direction or target where the lore is to be aimed, then either looses the wheel until the pitch is correct, or sings it. We are still learning how to use it, of course, but Achmed adapted this instrumentality from one that was built by Gwylliam the Visionary and Faedryth, the Nain king, changing it from one powered by fire from the heart of the earth, to one that draws on the light of the sun and stars as its power source. Much safer all the way around."

"Indeed."

"I am always wary of using anything that was designed by Gwylliam," Rhapsody said, brushing dust off the altar as the sun shone through the orange section of the spectrum. "Not that he wasn't a brilliant man, but anything associated with him makes me nervous."

"Because of the violence he displayed towards his wife?"

"Yes, partly—that event, the Grievous Blow that began the Cymrian War when he struck Anwyn—took place in my duchy, an underground grotto a little north of here that I call Elysian. The memory of that incident is so strong that it lingered in the place; when we first explored it, I witnessed the blow myself. It was like reliving it from Anwyn's perspective, and it was terrible, though I hardly think it deserved destroying the continent over. Anwyn returned to the Bolg lands recently, and the first place she destroyed was Elysian."

"I'm sorry to hear that."

Rhapsody thought of her underground haven, the cottage where she and Ashe had fallen in love, the gardens and orchard she had planted and tended with great care, the cave of purple crystal formations to explore and the small subterreanean meadow open to the sky far above, in which they had picnicked and watched the stars, and sighed in sad memory.

"I think the real incident that gives me pause about Gwylliam was finding his body in the library of the Cauldron," she said. "It was mummified, and sprawled on the library table, his crown standing on its side. I heard his last words; it's a shame—as he lay dying, he asked forgiveness of many of the people he wronged. That, at least, humanized him a little for me, but I still abhor what he did, both with the Grievous Blow and the war that came from it."

"Thank you for the explanation," Constantin said. "If you and your friends would allow me to make a different kind of use of this instrumentality, I could help you make it more usable."

Rhapsody looked startled. "How?"

"You remember the Spire in Sepulvarta?"

"Of course."

"The destruction of the citadel and my exile have left the Patrician faith in chaos. The prayers of the adherents are no longer channeled through the Chain of Prayer, because at its terminus, once all the prayers were collected at each level and passed along to me, it was my responsibility to offer them up as one great collective to the All-God through the tallest tower at my disposal."

"The Spire?"

"Yes. But if I could reconstruct the Chain of Prayer, using similar structures in each of the corners of the continent, I could triangulate that power and restore the connection to the All-God."

"What would that entail?"

The Patriarch smiled. "Access to the tower in the early morning and late at night, just as I accessed the Spire. I would only need to utilize it until I can get a connection in place again—an eastern thread—and then I would move on to Ryles Cedelian, the bell tower of the basilica in Bethe Corbair."

Rhapsody shuddered involuntarily. She, Grunthor, and Achmed had killed the F'dor they had been prophesied to vanquish beneath that very bell tower.

Constantin didn't notice. "That would provide a northern thread. The elevated mast on the basilica of Abbat Mythlinis in Avonderre, which is shaped like a giant sundered ship, would be able to offer up a western thread. If I can triangulate those directional threads, the Spire itself will serve as the final, southern thread. It would mean the reestablishment of the Patrician faith, m'lady—without the Chain of Prayer, no healing can be accomplished, no entreaties heard by the All-God."

Rhapsody was not an adherent of the Patrician faith, but her role as Illiachenva'ar, the bearer of the elemental sword of ether and fire, required her to serve as a protector or defender of anyone in the practice of his or her faith, or the worship of what was thought of as God, so she nodded.

"I will advocate for you to Achmed if need be," she said, "but since we both heard him offer you a place to pray, I believe you have found it, for as long as you need it."

"Thank you." Gratitude shone in the bright blue eyes. "And, in return, I will teach you how to remember the face of light, to hold it in your mind, which should help make the instrumentality work for you any time of the night or day, not just the hour of the day that the sun is shining through it."

"Remember the face of light?"

The Patriarch smiled.

"There are certain intangible things that the mind remembers but cannot completely recall physically," he said. "One of those things is pain; one can remember having been in it, but unless you study how to do so, you cannot completely recall, both mentally and physically, what pain that has passed actually felt like. That is a defense for the protection of both the mind and the body—if one could actually recall the pain of childbirth, I am told, the population would be severely limited."

Rhapsody laughed. "I can absolutely agree with that," she said.

"Light is something that also defies real memory, unless one is trained to recall it," Constantin went on. "The mind makes note of light—but not the detail of it. And light, as you have just explicated in your description of your tower instrumentality, has as many lengths of waves and colors to it as there are hairs on your head. Each different memory of light is called its face, something that identifies the form it took at a certain moment, defining it as an individual experience and able to be recalled. It's a complicated study. But to be general about it, if you can find me a diamond of great clarity of any size, I can teach you how to add a store of light to your Lightcatcher.

"And then, whatever your power source, be it sun or star, you can store its light, or the memory of it anyway, for use when it is not shining through the specific color in the spectrum you need."

"That would not only be fascinating and useful, but something that might make Achmed happy to loan the tower of Gurgus to you," said Rhapsody. "If you could do something to improve his mood, I would be forever in your debt."

NORTHERN YLORC

Dranth had plotted the course almost perfectly, it seemed.

The northern deserts west of Yarim were open wastelands, red clay that had baked in the cold sun into hard and unforgiving soil. Little grew there, less lived there, and while that had made for little interest in farming or colonization, for his purposes, the land was perfect to travel through, unnoticed.

He and the four other assassins, members of the Spider's Clutch of Golgarn and his own brotherhood, the Raven's Guild of Yarim, had crossed a vast expanse of the clay desert in disciplined silence. Open land was always hazardous; they did their best, in turn, to blend into whatever shadows the cold sun cast for or around them, but it was hardly necessary.

In the time it took to make it from Yarim to the upper reaches of the mountainous Firbolg realm, they did not see a single caravan, or even an itinerant traveler. As a result, they were able to pass in secret through the Bakhran Pass, slipping by the Bolg regiment on guard there at a respectful distance, and on into the high peaks of the northern Teeth without being discovered.

Dranth was pleased.

He had no idea how close he was, how dangerously proximate they all were, to the resting place of an injured wyrm that lay, in the pain-filled haze of torpor, beneath the cold red sand as they traveled past, above her, just beyond the range of her senses, where she waited.

Dreaming herself of vengeance.

18

Anborn awoke to the smell of fresh greenery and sweet spices.

For a moment he thought he was still dreaming, hazy, storyless dreams that had been without form but decidedly happy. The bed on which he had been sleeping was firm but soft on the surface, infused with an aroma that reminded him a little of Rhapsody. The crisp sheets and heavy comforter held in the warmth of the bed, even though he innately knew the air of the room was somewhat cold with the chill he remembered at the arrival of morning in the mountain all those centuries ago.

He rolled carefully out of bed, stretched, and made use of the washroom, a technological advance left over from Gwylliam's day but filled with dried aromatic plants, pleasant soaps and emollients. Back in the bedchamber he dressed, pulled on his boots, packed his belongings and put on the base of his armor, his black ring mailshirt anchored by silver centerpieces. He attached his cloak to the epaulets on his shoulders, then made his way into the hall.

Memory served him well enough to find the tunnelway that led to the great dining hall of Canrif, or what had once been. Rhapsody had directed him to it the night before, but even if she hadn't, or had his memory failed him, the tantalizing smell of breakfast, as arousing to his nose as it was surprising to his mind, greeted him enthusiastically as he rounded the corner to the hall where the entrance to the king's balcony had been in his father's day.

That door stood open in silent invitation. He could hear the sound of soldiers in the throes of breakfast in the high-ceilinged, giant room below the balcony, even out in the hall, though their commotion was less noisy, less merry than the sound of the human soldiers he was accustomed to. Anborn approached the door quietly and looked in.

The Three were seated at a long rectangular table near the half-wall that separated the balcony from the towering walls beyond it, laden with platters of food and pitchers of steaming drink. Achmed and Grunthor, their backs to the opening beyond the half-wall, were reviewing a heavy sheaf of parchment documents, clearly not maps or schematics, but ledgers of some kind. The Lady Cymrian, her back to him, sat on the side of the table closest to the door, an empty place beside her that he hoped had been reserved for him. A young Bolg woman sat on her other side; Anborn recognized her as Yltha, the midwife who occasionally tended to Meridion. Rhapsody was carrying on a soft, animated conversation with the baby, she using a variety of languages and songs, Meridion exploring his voice with cackles, coos, and clicking sounds, to the delight of his mother and no one else in the room.

Except now, himself.

"Good morning," he said, stepping through the door and onto the balcony.

"Good morning," Rhapsody replied, her face shining up at him from the table.

"Well, 'allo, General," Grunthor greeted him as Anborn bent and kissed the Lady Cymrian and his great-nephew. " 'Ope yer 'ungry; breakfast is pritty good today." Achmed merely nodded to the Lord Marshal and went back to his reading.

"Smells delicious," the Lord Marshal said, taking his seat beside Rhapsody and unfolding his napkin. "What is on the menu this morning?"

"Farmers from Bethe Corbair," Achmed said, passing the plate of link sausages to the Lord Marshal. "A tasty lot, though a little greasy."

Anborn looked down at the platter in Achmed's hands.

Grunthor had already consumed a dozen and a half links. "Oi don't think so, sir," he said, helping himself to griddle cakes from another platter with an enormous fork. "Those were 'eavily spiced, if Oi recall. These are sweeter—Oi'm guessin' these might be those lit'le kids from Canderre." Achmed nodded as he served himself another link.

"They're joking," Rhapsody assured the Lord Marshal as he leaned questioningly toward her. "Welcome to breakfast in the Bolglands—they are actually taking it easy on you, believe it or not."

"I'm sure," Anborn said agreeably, taking the sausage platter as it was passed to him. He served himself generously, then looked down over the half-wall to the floor of the dining hall below, where the second shift of the soldiers of Ylorc were eating. "I'm actually shocked at the decorum of the troops; it certainly is nothing like what passes for behavior in the mess tents of the army of Roland. Or a Cymrian wedding—this is a formal dining experience by comparison. I don't know if I can stand it, frankly."

"Rhapsody insists on civility in all parts of Ylorc, even the privies," Achmed said sourly. "And, unfortunately for all of us, she generally gets it. At least when she's here she does. Everyone is painfully polite, refrains from public urination, and puts the seat down."

"Except for you," Rhapsody said, rubbing her nose against Meridion's tiny one. "But even I occasionally accept the limits of what is humanly—or Firbolgly—possible."

"Are you certain you don't want to take her with you, Anborn?" Achmed inquired as he refilled his mug of tanic coffee; the odor made the Lord Marshal's eyes water. "She's a tremendous pain in the arse."

"Yeah, but we like to keep 'er around anyways," Grunthor said between bites. "She smells good, and she's a sweet lit'le thing most o' the time—although she can be meaner than a badger if you vex 'er—she's got a wicked right cross, General, so watch yer step. And Oi would 'ate to lose 'er; Oi'm sleepin' with 'er, at least when Oi'm feelin' generous, and she's feelin' lucky." The Lady Cymrian ignored him in favor of exchanging giggling smiles with her son.

"I could have lived without hearing that, and the picture I now have in my head," grumbled Anborn. "Please pass the griddle cakes."

" 'Ere—'ave a lit'le Lirin jam with those," Grunthor said, politely offering the dish and small spoon. Rhapsody rose halfway and cuffed him without looking away from Meridion, then sat down again.

Achmed rerolled the parchments. "Ready?" he said to Grunthor. The Sergeant-Major nodded. "We're off," the Bolg king said to Rhapsody and Anborn. "I want to make sure the equipment I'm sending with you is properly packed, and that the quartermaster has included the instructions for the weighted ballistae and the catapults."

"I'll come with you," said Anborn, preparing to stand up again.

"Don't rush your breakfast," Achmed said. "Yen, the Archon quartermaster, is outfitting your troops and packing up the supplies, armor and weaponry I am sending with you as we speak with the aid of your men. Grunthor and I will head down to the steppes and make certain everything is going as it should—you and Rhapsody can finish your food and watch from the rock ledge if you like. We'll signal you from below when all is ready to go."

"Thank you very much, Your Majesty," Anborn said, appreciation apparent in his tone and eyes.

"No need to thank me; it's just another excuse to get me away from the charming smell of baby *hrekin* at the breakfast table." The Bolg king and the Sergeant-Major rose as if in unison.

"Excuse me," Rhapsody said. "Meridion is dry. That's the smell of your rancid coffee. Ashe drinks the same extract of filth; I believe I once told him it smelled like dirt from a skunk's grave."

Anborn laughed and rose as well, extending a hand first to the Bolg king, then to his Sergeant-Major.

"Thank you, Achmed, Grunthor, for your welcome, your assistance, the tour of your fortress, and your aid. If you can keep the eastern encampments supplied, we will keep the enemy's traditional forces at bay and away from the Teeth for as long as humanly—or Firbolgly—possible." He winked at Rhapsody. "And, of course, this exchange comes with the happy benefit of being able to present enormous bills of service to my nephew. Empty a little of his treasury; it will do him good to be sending a nice portion of his gold to the Bolg."

"Did you think there was any other reason for my agreeing to this?"

"No, of course not." Anborn lurched forward slightly as Grunthor patted him on the back. He watched as they exited the balcony, Achmed closing the door resolutely behind them, then turned to Rhapsody, who was finishing her tea.

"M'lady, I believe I require your talents as a healer."

"Oh? For what? What part of you is injured?"

"My brain," said Anborn, returning to his breakfast. The sausages were savory, the griddle cakes light and delicious. "I need your help in expunging the image of you sleeping with Grunthor from my mind; I can barely keep my food down."

"Sorry to disappoint you, but I can't help you there. I've been sleeping with—or, more precisely, on—Grunthor since long before you were born, m'lord," Rhapsody said humorously. "I did so almost every night of our journey here from Serendair. He's very comfortable."

"I'm sure your husband would be delighted to know that."

"He already does. What he might not be so pleased to hear is that it has become a family tradition—Meridion loves sleeping curled up at

Grunthor's neck, just under his beard, away from the tusks. I think it's a little like hide-and-seek for him."

Anborn wiped his mouth with his napkin.

"I will make you a bargain," he said, folding the piece of linen one-handed with the unconscious habit of one to the manor born. "I will spare Gwydion the thought of that if you will keep from elaborating on any further Bolg custom until I have a large tankard of ale, or something stronger, in my hand."

"Bargain," Rhapsody said. "If you are ready, we can go out onto the rock ledge and watch them finish packing up." Anborn nodded, and she signaled to Yltha to follow them. "Meridion seems more awake than usual at this time of day; he must somehow be aware that you are leaving, and wants to see as much of you as he can before you go."

"Of course."

"I'm joking; he's an infant. I suppose that I am just projecting my own desires onto him," Rhapsody said wistfully. "How I do wish you could stay longer."

"As do I."

"Then do so," Rhapsody said as she led him off the balcony of the dining hall and into another of the corridors of Ylorc; the noise of the soldiers dimmed into a quiet hum as she closed the door behind Yltha. "You're the Lord Marshal; who is going to complain?"

Anborn sighed as he followed her through the familiar hallways, now devoid of the priceless works of art, as well as the ugly echoes of the anger and hatred that had been extant in the place when he had lived here centuries before.

"Only my conscience," he said. "I beg you, don't tempt me, m'lady. I would love to stay and see more of the reconstruction, and spend another night or more in that heavenly bed. How did you make it, and with what did you imbue it?"

"Thank you; those are a special design of mine," Rhapsody said, rounding a corner into a wider opening Anborn knew would exit onto one of the rock ledges in the outer face of the Teeth. "The Blasted Heath has long been a place where highgrass grows, a plant that in the old world was called Hymialacia, its True Name. It's cut and dried in lengths about as long as your forearm, then mixed with lavender, sweet woodruff, vernal-grass, and clove pods and rolled into cylinders, which are stood on their ends and formed and tied into the frame. Then the whole thing is wrapped in a cotton shell that has been quilted with other herbs and flowers. Then a linen liner, and a silk mattress topper. And I sing to each one—I really do, a song of deep slumber and rest. Glad you enjoyed it. I hope you slept well."

"As if I were entombed," he said. He winced as the smile left Rhapsody's eyes. "And I mean that as a compliment. Best night's sleep in recent memory."

"Good. Glad to hear it." The Lady Cymrian nodded to the Bolg guards at the massive doors leading out onto the ledge. The guards drew back the enormous timbers that served to bar the doors, sliding them sideways into specially drilled holes in the walls on either side of the opening, then swung the doors themselves open with a great deal of creaking and the screaming of wood and metal.

"Close your eyes," Rhapsody and Anborn said to one another in unison as the blazing light of early morning blasted down the tunnelway. Then they laughed; their mutual warning represented knowledge of the hazard that spanned a millennia in its application. Rhapsody had shielded the baby's eyes, and let her hand move slowly away from them, watching as the tiny dragonesque pupils contracted in the daylight.

They stepped out onto the rock ledge, one of hundreds in the western face of the mountain, where towers, walls, parapets, and turrets had been carved during the Cymrian Age, some martial, others decorative, all of which allowed the eyes of the occupants of the mountains to see west to the Krevensfield Plain for so many leagues that it seemed as if Ylorc was always vigilantly watching the sunset.

A cool wind whipped up from the steppes, a thousand feet below. Rhapsody wrapped the blanket around Meridion to shield him from the dust it carried, even as her own clothing caught the breeze like a sail on the high seas. Her hair, pulled tightly off her face and bound back, flapped like a flag, the tendrils around her face whipping wildly. It was an invigorating feeling; once again she closed her eyes, tilted her head back and smiled as the sun coming over the mountain from the east behind them crowned her face with light.

When she opened them again, Anborn, his black hair streaked in silver flying in the wind as well, was smiling down at her.

"Now, that's a sight I will carry with me," he said quietly. Then he looked to the east, where in the distance he could see the encampment he had established a few days before. The campfires of the previous night were still burning, and he thought he could see access roads plied by horses and wagons moving like lines of vertical ants. *Good,* he thought. *They're making progress.* His gaze returned, as it always did, to Rhapsody.

"Here—let me hold my great-nephew for a moment before I leave—may I?"

"Of course." Rhapsody swaddled the blanket a little tighter, tucking in the edges, and passed the baby to the Lord Marshal. He smiled down at Meridion, eliciting a delighted series of cooing sounds in return.

"He's a Singer already," said Anborn fondly. "I cannot wait to teach you the sword, my boy, and horsemanship, and all the other skills one needs to be a proper man—cursing, spitting, wenching—"

"Ahem."

Anborn laughed merrily, winked at Rhapsody, then looked back at the little boy. "He's a beautiful child, my dear—not surprising, given that he came from you."

Rhapsody laughed as well. "I'm not sure what you're talking about—he looks just like Ashe."

Anborn studied the infant's face. "The dragonesque pupils, yes. But his hair is golden."

"And curly—also from his father. And his eyes are blue."

The Lord Marshal sighed in resignation. "Ah yes, the color of the Cymrian rulers, bequeathed by the kings of Serendair. Poor little one—he cannot escape the curse of his family, of his destiny. But he has your beautiful skin, and your coloring, and the shape of your eyes and cheekbones, your eyelashes, which, by the way, were the first things that entranced me about you, and the bowlike curve to your upper lip that enflames so many men's dreams. A lucky blend of both his parents. Keep him safe, whatever else you do."

As the wind from the steppes kicked up around them, blasting the golden tendrils of her hair about her face, Rhapsody's eyes stung, and her throat went dry. Anborn saw the change in her expression, and the crinkled smile lines around his eyes smoothed out.

"What is it? Tell me."

Rhapsody looked away to the west, beyond the steppes to the vast expanse of the Krevensfield Plain. Below she took in the sight of Achmed and Grunthor, in the midst of the supply troops of the Archon quartermaster, packing up wagons and dray horses. In the distance she could see the rising smoke from the thousands of campfires, twisting menacingly in the morning light.

"I don't know how," she said, her voice breaking. The pain in that voice twisted Anborn's heart. "I took him away from his father, brought him here to the Teeth, where I thought he would be as safe as it was possible to be, only to find that your bloody *mother* had already broached the Bolglands, had slaughtered everyone who was unfortunate enough to be outside when she arrived, and no one had a weapon to kill her, because Achmed was with me in Gwynwood."

"So I heard. I also heard that your Archons and Grunthor drove her from the tunnel system with a blasting flood of sewage, and then trained their catapults on her in the canyon below, slinging boulders and garbage at her until she fled, bruised and broken—utterly brilliant tactics, and appropriate retribution; I haven't had such a good laugh in as long as I can remember. Grunthor regaled me with the tale on my tour of the armory and the forges, which they have improved mightily from Gwylliam's time in the mountain, by the way. I couldn't be more impressed with what you three have done with the place, Rhapsody; I was not sure what to expect upon seeing Canrif—er, Ylorc—again, and had truly been dreading it. But I am both amazed and delighted to see the wisdom, the vision, with which you all have rebuilt it. The armaments and defenses, of course—your two Bolg friends are truly ingenious when it comes to strategy—but your contributions as well. The shaping of the culture, commerce, medicine, the education and training of *Firbolg*, for the sake of all that is holy, who would have believed it? Achmed's forces, from what I can see, are as well-trained as any on the continent, as well-armed, and well-vested, in a place where the shallow artistry of Gwylliam's reign has been replaced by a sensible civilization. I am delighted to finally see inside it. You should be safe here, my dear; as safe as anywhere else."

Rhapsody clenched her jaw, trying and failing to prevent the burning tears from falling. When she spoke, her voice was strained and thin.

"The first place Anwyn destroyed was Elysian," she said.

19

$\mathcal{A}$nborn had never heard the word before.

"Elysian?"

"It was my—my duchy, a joking word for it from Grunthor, who has called me 'Duchess' for almost as long as I have known him," Rhapsody said sadly. "My own tiny piece of land within Achmed's kingdom, a grotto with a dark lake hidden within the guardian mountains past the Blasted Heath." Anborn's eyebrows shot into his hairline, but she didn't notice. "Just a small island with a tiny cottage—"

"The Dovecote?"

Rhapsody blinked. "Excuse me?"

"In the middle of the underground lake—a cottage, with a gazebo?"

"Yes," Rhapsody said. "It was a haven, a place the Bolg couldn't find. There was a vibration of sadness, of anger, to it and the fields above it when we first came. But we cleansed it of all that; I planted heartsease in the field, and replanted the underground gardens, and an orchard, cleaned out the mess of years of decay and soot and destruction, and filled the cave with music. It was my home here. It was there that Ashe and I fell in love, and—"

The look on Anborn's face brought her words to a screeching halt.

"What?"

"You were living in the Dovecote?" A string of familiar-sounding draconic curses rose up from Anborn's viscera and began spilling out of his mouth. He stopped suddenly, seeing the expression on Rhapsody's face which matched that of the child in his hands, then coughed.

"That's your first draconic swearing lesson, Meridion," he said, assuming a forced calm. "Practice the double glottal stop and the hiss at the end of each verb, or it doesn't have the same meaning." He turned to Rhapsody. "Forgive me, m'lady. As much as you may not wish to hear this, believe me when I tell you that my accursed mother, may she be staked down on her back in desert sand and eaten alive by raptors, has done you a tremendous favor. You have no idea what an evil place that was, what horrific deeds and atrocities were committed there."

"Actually, I do. I had a vision, right after we got there, of the Grievous Blow, when Gwylliam struck her; I actually think I saw it from Anwyn's perspective. It knocked me off my feet, literally."

Anborn's face was grim, but he kept his voice quiet and steady, and continued to force a smile at the baby. "That is the *least* of the abominations that occurred in that place."

"I'm not sure Anwyn would agree."

"Promise me you will never go back there," Anborn said. "Please, m'lady. Please." The urgency rose in his voice, and Meridion began to whimper.

"You needn't worry, Anborn; the place is in ruins, utterly destroyed. And Achmed and Grunthor have far too much more important rebuilding and war preparation to undertake to even begin to look at repairing Elysian any time soon."

"Good—please keep it that way. One day, after the war is over, and we are trading tales and playing with this child in peacetime, I will tell you the stories, and then you will understand my insistence."

"Meridion really needs to be put down for his nap," Rhapsody said. She turned and signaled to Yltha, who hurried forward. "Please bid him farewell, Lord Marshal."

Anborn nodded, then looked back down one last time at the little boy in his hands.

"Take good care of your mother, lad," he said. "Other than that, remember that your job is to eat well, which you clearly are already doing, sleep as much as you can, for your poor mother's sake, grow strong and healthy and above all, don't worry. Be a baby—don't let fear touch your life, not yet."

Meridion replied with a buzzing cackle from the back of his throat, drawing a delighted laugh from the Lord Marshal.

He kissed the child on the eyes, caressed his head, then reluctantly handed him over to the Bolg midwife, who took him hurriedly back into the mountain.

He looked at Rhapsody, who was shaking with the effort of suppressing her tears. Anborn drew her into his arms and held her tightly against his chest, cradling her head with his hand.

"Tell me," he said again, his lips against her ear. "I'm here, beloved niece-in-law; my lady, tell me."

Rhapsody's self-control crumbled, and she bent at the waist; Anborn pulled her closer to keep her from falling to the rocky ground.

"I can't keep him safe," she sobbed. "I don't know where to go, how to protect him, where to hide him. This place that I thought was so unassailable is vulnerable, not only to Anwyn and the armies of Sorbold, but to the demon inside the stone titan. While Talquist may want the continent, the F'dor will be seeking the Sleeping Child, and whatever the prophecy meant about eyes watching Meridion will eventually lead them to finding him too, if all of that attention and determination is trained on Ylorc. And Anwyn is looking for *me*; gods forbid she finds me when I am holding him or nursing him. In my dreams last night I ran out onto the Krevensfield Plain screaming her name, over and over, calling her, Naming her, just to flush her out and get her to take me while he was safe within the mountain. Maybe that's what I should do; at least there will be one less threat to him."

Rough hands tore her from the warmth and comfort of his embrace as he pushed her back. Rhapsody looked up into his face through her tears to see his azure eyes blazing down at her.

"Unspeak that *right now*," Anborn commanded angrily. "Don't even give voice, or thought, to something so foolish. How many times do I have to tell you of the unbridled, hellish *evil* that is nascent in that woman? Unspeak your words, and never repeat them ever again."

"I can't unspeak anything, or undream my dreams," Rhapsody said, choking. "I would happily give my life to save him, but knowing he is being sought on his own, for undoubtedly horrible purposes by the Merchant Emperor, is killing me, Anborn; *killing me*. I can't breathe; I can't breathe."

The Lord Marshal held her at arms' length a moment longer, studying her face, as she gasped, struggling for air. Then he drew her close again and kissed her on the forehead.

"You may not believe this," he murmured as he pulled her head against his neck again, "but there is no one who understands your terror as completely and utterly as I do. No one. Not even his father."

This time it was Rhapsody who pulled back. She looked into Anborn's eyes, and saw deeper sympathy than she had ever thought was possible to know. And something more; something worse than fear, more awful than pain.

"I do believe you," she said. "Even though I do not know why."

The Lord Marshal smiled slightly. He cupped her face, watching her, then released it and took her hand instead.

"Come sit with me," he said, leading her forward to the end of the ledge overlooking the steppes. "I need to save my legs, and you don't seem too stable on your feet at the moment, either. What other horrors are hiding in your heart? I have a sense that you are not finished."

Rhapsody sat beside him, her legs dangling over the edge. The wind rising from the canyon wall billowed her skirt around her.

"I know, as much as it sickens me to say it, that sooner or later I will be drawn into the war itself," she said softly. "I am the Iliachenva'ar; there are but three such weapons as the one I carry in the entirety of the Known World. With what you have said about the winged beasts, what Constantin has said about Talquist, and what Rath has told us of the demon, it is clear to me that Daystar Clarion will be needed in the fight eventually—Tysterisk is new to Gwydion Navarne, and Ashe shouldn't be in the fray while he is holding the continent. What will I do then? I would give the sword into the hands of anyone who is capable of using it, but that would dishonor the blade and denature the tie I have to it, depleting its power. I have to bear it, fight with it, until it decides otherwise." Anborn nodded in agreement. "What will I do with my baby then, Anborn? I can't bring him into battle, and everyone I would trust to protect him is already involved. In what hands am I supposed to leave him? Where will he *ever* be safe?"

The Lord Marshal lifted her hand to his lips and kissed it gently.

"I don't know," he said simply. "I understand, believe me. When the world is collapsing around you, the only thing you can do is the best you can at the time. For now, until that time, love him as fiercely and deeply and tenderly as you can. Make his life as secure and happy and full of the music of his mother while that is still possible, and tell yourself with each waking breath, each beat of your heart, that you will do whatever you have to do, whatever it costs you, and then do it. Be ready to move; don't be trapped anywhere, even a mountainous fortress like this one, if your instincts tell you to run. Pray to the All-God, or the One-God, or whatever it is you believe in that it will be enough when the time comes. But I swear to you, m'lady, as your devoted knight, I will do everything in my power to keep you out of it, will spare you the need to fight, if I can, so that your entire focus will be on keeping him safe."

"Thank you," Rhapsody whispered. She dropped her head. As she did, Anborn saw Achmed signal from the floor of the steppes. He sighed, then stood slowly and pulled the Lady Cymrian up beside him.

"The time has come," he said. "I must be on my way." He handed Rhapsody his handkerchief as another flood of tears came forth.

"I'm sorry," she whispered brokenly, dabbing her eyes. "I am sorry to show such weakness to you as you leave. I hope you will forgive me for crying in front of you, and expunge this sight of me now from your memory. I had wanted to send you off with the sight of a cheerful and confident face."

The Lord Marshal took a deep breath, then let it out slowly.

"You are sending me off with the sight of my favorite face in the world, a sight I would never expunge from my memory, even if I could," he said. "A lovely face, a kind face, occasionally a face with some very comical expressions of anger or annoyance on it, but most importantly, it is an *honest* face, a face which has always been remarkably open and easy for me to read. I am sworn to you, Rhapsody, because I love you deeply, in ways even I don't understand. But if you were to put on a brave face for me, when your heart is so full of fear, not only would I see through it, but I think I would lose some respect for you. That you trust me enough to cry in front of me, to tell me your deepest terrors, means more to me than I can possibly explain to you.

"I have no idea what women soldiers need to inspire them as they leave for battle, though watching you with my great-nephew seems to answer the question," he continued quietly. "For a man, it helps to have the face of a woman in his memory, a woman who says she loves him, to think of, to dream about, to plan to come home to. A woman who serves as the reason to take up arms, to take other men's lives, to lay down his own life, to give him reason to endure through pain and injury and death. A beautiful face to haunt and inspire his dreams. Even if she is the faithful, adoring wife of another man; even if she is only his friend. It helps, Rhapsody. Believe me, it helps."

Rhapsody's throat was so tight she thought she might strangle.

"Me? Am I that for you, Anborn? That face to live for?"

"Yes." His smile dimmed as the look in his eyes intensified. "There is no other face in my memory or my eyes, not now, anyway. I hope that doesn't offend you, or make you feel compromised in any way, my dear. I recognize and respect your marriage; reprobate and sinner though I am, I would never think or even hope for anything more than what you have given and been to me—my sovereign, my lady, a friend, a Kinsman, a confidante, someone who tells me the truth, tells me when I'm wrong or when I've overstepped, tells me that life is better, more worthwhile than I have ever seen it be. I would believe that I could fly if you said it to be true, Rhapsody—I would toss myself off this cliff into the arms of the wind, believing it so, expecting to soar to the clouds."

"Why—why 'says she loves him'? Do you not believe me when I tell you that I do?"

Anborn looked at her, shadows in his eyes.

"No, my dear, I believe you. But it is different—because you do not love me in the way that she did."

Rhapsody blinked, surprise finally stanching her tears. "She? Who?"

After a long moment, Anborn spoke. "My wife."

Rhapsody's brows drew together.

"I—thought you said you didn't like each other."

"Not Estelle." The words came from a throat that sounded as if it had swallowed shards of glass. "Damynia." He pronounced the word softly, reverently, like a prayer.

"Damynia?" It was a name that had never entered her ears before. "You—you had another wife?"

"I have lived a long time, Rhapsody."

"I had no idea. No one has ever told me this."

"No one else knows—no one living, anyway, not even my brother Edwyn. It was long ago. I tell you, my favorite Lirin Namer, now because, among other reasons, should I not survive the war, I want the lore, the history of that marriage to survive, at least—a tiny bit of immortality of some part of me that once was good."

"There is so much of you that *is* good," Rhapsody said. Her face was wet with tears again, and Anborn had to look away.

"This is what you do not grasp, Rhapsody—whatever could be described so now is entirely because of you. I have not led the life of a good man—not for centuries, anyway. There was a long time during which I was a cold-blooded, efficient killer, a relentless conqueror, remorseless in the destruction I leveled upon this land. The Lirin you love, that you were willing to try and undertake making peace with through our marriage, had it come to pass—no matter what I achieve, I will never be able to make amends for the damage I did to them, and they are certainly not the only ones that could say this.

"It is because of you and your foolishness—your insistent belief in the worth of this Alliance, your willingness to love those who really don't deserve it, your belief in forgiveness and redemption, your refusal to see people as they are, to see the blood on their hands, the Namer in you, that has brought about a change in me. As much as I scoffed at you in the beginning, in the end I have come to believe you—and as a result, I can walk again, which is the least important element of this transformation. Your undeserved faith in me has awakened something in me I thought long dead; I am remembering again a time when life's ideals and aspirations actually meant something to me, when camaraderie and valor and love of land and kin were the reasons to pick up arms, not wanton violence and the rage of revenge. It's sparking in me a rebirth of a sorts, a hope of absolution, making whatever sacrifices, whatever efforts in the coming war worth something meaningful; you cannot imagine how important this is to me, after a life as long as mine, time which I have passed, dead inside, until I met you. I have sworn allegiance to no one since Gwylliam, and when I did that I was unrecognizable as a human being. I am not understating this, Rhapsody; you are right that it is a good thing we did not meet in earlier days, because you would have hated me, as the entire empire did. You are well aware that my freedom is what I prize above most other things, but I am not certain you made the connection that my sworn allegiance to you was a voluntary surrender, a limitation on that freedom, that wherever you are, your safety, your need, is my happiest priority now. It is because of that allegiance, and because of you, that I wade back into this fray as the man, the leader I was born to be—unlike—unlike—" The Lord Marshal fell silent.

Rhapsody stood as still as she could, in mutual silence, waiting. Finally he finished his thought.

"Unlike the villain I was because of Damynia."

"Is she—was she the one you didn't—kiss goodbye? Is that why you won't say that word to me without doing so?"

The Lord Marshal's face darkened suddenly, and he turned away. He stood silent for a long while, traveling down old roads in his mind. Then he raised his head, looked back and her and smiled.

"It would be a fair assumption," he said at last. "You remind me a great deal of her, though you look nothing like her. If Fate is kind, I will tell you the story someday."

"You keep promising me that," Rhapsody rebuked him gently. "And yet you never do."

"True enough, I suppose." The general sighed. "This is old lore, Rhapsody—frozen for centuries, buried in a vault of unforgiving stone.

Allow me to chip away at it a little at a time, please—it's painful. Shrike knew, because he could show me glimpses of it, of her. And he never required me to speak of it. But my heart is sore from what little I've already said. I beg you—give me time."

"Then you must promise to come back to me and finish the story."

"Now, my dear, I may have made many promises I couldn't keep to a battlefield's worth of bedwenches, but I would never, upon my life, *never*, make one to you. I will promise you that I will do my very best to remain alive and sound, but after that, I'm afraid there is little to nothing else I can commit to. But I know you already understand that."

A horn blast echoed up from the floor of the steppes.

Anborn looked down over the edge and chuckled at the Bolg king's displeasure, evident even a thousand feet below.

"His Majesty summons," he said humorously. "I really can't keep him waiting any longer. Rhapsody, may I ask just one last boon of you?"

"Anything."

Anborn laughed again. "Now, what have I told you about making rash promises you can't or don't want to keep, m'lady? I believe the last time you did so I suggested I could have you there on the ground outside the Moot, but that was a considerably softer and warmer place than this rocky ledge."

"I remember," Rhapsody said. "Nonetheless, I love and trust you enough to make the same offer of anything."

The Lord Marshal's eyes took on a sheen. "I am well and truly honored," he said, repeating the words she had spoken upon receiving his sworn pledge of allegiance. "Will you tell me of the Veil of Hoen?"

Rhapsody's mind went back to the drowsy woodland place of healing and dreams, the realm of the Lady Rowan, Yl Breudiwyr, the Guardian of Sleep, and her husband, the Lord Rowan, Yl Angaulor, the Peaceful Death, where she had passed seven years' time healing children sired by a demon, during which time only a moment had passed in the eye of the world.

"Yes," she said, though the breaking of silence about the place made her nervous. "What do you want to know?"

"Do you—can one really see those who have gone before?"

Rhapsody smiled through her tears.

"Yes," she said. "I saw Jo, my sister, the first person I adopted in this world. I don't think you ever met her."

"I believe Shrike once described her to me," Anborn noted. "I sent him to Achmed's court when the Bolg king was accepting visits of state just after the three of you had taken the mountains; Shrike told me upon his return of a thin blond adolescent who he assumed was you, but by his description of her I knew he was mistaken. What happened to her?"

Rhapsody swallowed, but her face returned to a calm mien.

"I killed her," she said. "She was a thrall of the demon, and would have killed Achmed when he was compromised, so I killed her first. It was horrendous. The guilt and regret was torturous, until she came to me one night behind the Veil, granting me her forgiveness and telling me that I needed to forgive myself, demanding it, in fact. My mother came to me as well; it was only after that I was able to make peace with being in this world, on this side of Time, and was able to let the old world go to its rest."

Anborn's eyes began to shine.

"And that was just on this side of the Doorway," Rhapsody continued, "because that is essentially what the Veil of Hoen is—the doorstep between life and death. When Stephen Navarne lay dying after the battle of the Moot, when you were clinging to life as well, I sang the Lirin Song of Passage for him, and I saw—" Her voice faltered.

"Yes?"

"I saw him in front of the sun, in the doorway, whole, unbroken, with his wife, Lydia. The song allowed Gwydion Navarne and Melisande to see them both, their mother and father, for a last moment as well."

"So the legends are true," Anborn murmured. "Your husband had told me he had been healed there, but didn't remember anything about it."

Against her will, Rhapsody broke into tears again.

"Please do not hasten to that place," she pleaded. "You and I have been close enough to it before many times—when you rescued me in the forest near Sorbold, when I left you with Daystar Clarion as Michael took me hostage in the fire of Gwynwood, when you caught me as I fell from the sky—we are Kinsmen of more than one kind, Anborn. And so I will ask you as I did in Gwynwood, beg you even, selfish as the request is: live, please live. If I am that face for you, then live for me. I need you, Meridion needs you—Ashe needs you. Please, live, for us, for me, if not for yourself."

Anborn smiled and pulled her into an embrace.

"In a way, I already do, my dear, in case you haven't been listening," he said. "But I will do my best."

Another blast of an impatient horn caused him to release her quickly and step away from the ledge.

"Since we do plan to see each other again, there's no need to drag this out," Anborn said, checking the buckle of his sword belt and his vambraces. "Buck up, m'lady; there's no need to be weepy. You are the mother of a fine, strong son who lives and thrives, all predictions to the contrary, even mine. It's a bright morning, with fair weather, and it turns out your husband was heeding my warnings after all, so a worthy fighting force with Right on its side is gathering as we speak, coming to the rescue of an Alliance well worth saving. It's quite a glorious day to be alive—I will keep in touch by bird when I can. Keep out of harm's way as much as *you* can, and call me on the wind, Kinsman to Kinsman, if you are ever in need." His eyes twinkled; he turned away and started down the mountain pass to the steppes below. He had gone a score of paces when he stopped and looked back over his shoulder.

"Goodbye, Rhapsody."

The Lady Cymrian watched him turn away again, rooted to the spot. Then madly she ran to him, stumbling blindly, and threw herself into his arms, startling him.

"Wait! Don't you *dare* say that to me without kissing me. Don't you dare!"

As the Lord Marshal stared at her in shock she pressed her lips to his, holding his face in her hands, breathing him in, passionately, fearfully, intimately. She was too frightened to notice his arms wind around her, too terrified to feel his heart pounding against her chest beneath his mailshirt, too worried to care what it looked like in the sight of the world. She sustained the kiss, letting her mouth cling to his until their breathing slowed, until her fear was spent, until it settled into a calmer gesture, a respectful salute, a gentle goodbye.

When finally their lips parted, she took one hand from his face and caressed his black hair, the silver streaks that had been evident when she first met him somewhat wider now.

"Let that be from her," she whispered. "Whatever you missed, whatever the story of that loss was, let it be rectified now. Let that be from her."

Anborn smiled down at her, his eyes shining radiantly.

"Thank you," he said gently. "But it's more than enough that it was from you."

He let go of her reluctantly and, after a long final look, headed back to the pass leading down to where the two Bolg waited. Just before he disappeared around the rocky bend, he turned one last time and called up to her.

"If that's the way you plan to bid me goodbye, I may have to find reasons to come back more often."

"Do so," she called back.

"Not sure how much my nephew will like it."

"He will understand," she replied. "Be safe. My love goes with you."

The Lord Marshal held up his hand. Then he vanished from her sight.

She watched until he reappeared on the steppes below, saw him talking with Achmed and Grunthor, bowing finally amid pats on the shoulder from the Sergeant-Major and a nod from the Bolg king. Then Anborn pulled himself atop his beautiful black warhorse and shouted orders to his men.

He looked up to the rise and waved to her; she waved in return, and watched as the small cohort started out into the west.

Then she sank to her knees and gave herself over to grief.

As heart-wrenching as it had been to say goodbye to Ashe, somehow it was even more painful to do so to Anborn.

Perhaps it was because, in the deepest place in her heart, she believed she would see her husband again.

As they waited for Anborn to come down from the cliff, Achmed and Grunthor watched the two figures above them saying goodbye. It was taking an infernally long time, and the Bolg king was growing angrier by the moment, blasting the horn, which Rhapsody and Anborn apparently heard but were choosing to ignore.

Just before he put the horn to his lips for a third time, Anborn finally turned to go and stepped away from the ledge. To Achmed's surprise Rhapsody ran after him and threw herself into his arms, kissing him.

Grunthor, standing beside him, scratched his head.

"Hmmm—what do you suppose *that's* about, sir?"

Achmed exhaled and let the horn hang down to his side.

"It appears she finally understands the reality of the situation."

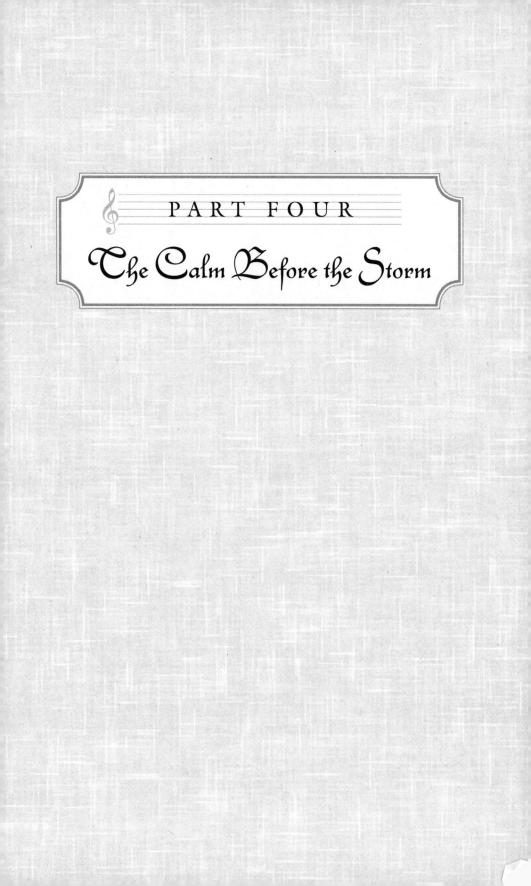

PART FOUR

The Calm Before the Storm

20

THE OCCUPIED CITY OF SEPULVARTA

$\mathfrak{B}$oth of the monarchs who sat in the opulent carriage on the thickly padded benches across from the newly crowned emperor of Sorbold had been shifting uncomfortably in their very comfortable seats for the better part of the morning. It was not a lack of physical ease that was causing the men to be fidgeting, but rather the vastly different clime of the places through which they were passing, and had been for the better part of a week.

Or perhaps it was the sight that they caught from time to time out the carriage window of the massive stone soldier, driving a chariot pulled by a team of eight horses, standing without rest.

The arid climate of the vast and mountainous Sorbold desert made both men itch. Beliac was a son of the seacoast in his southeastern coastal realm, and had benefited all his life from the ocean's tempering effect on the weather, meaning that the summers were never too hot, the winters never too bitter, and the wind was never too dry. The burning sand that was blasting occasionally through the seams of the carriage, stinging his face and eyes, was torturous, as was the rough pitching that occurred every time the wheels of the coach went through the ruts in the primitive roadways over which they were traveling. While the pitching of an ocean vessel had no effect on Beliac, the constant jolting of a land vehicle pulled by a team of twelve horses was enough to make him need to call the coach to a halt, jump out and vomit from time to time, much to the secret amusement of his host.

The Diviner of the Hintervold, a realm of all-but-endless winter, was not accustomed to the fortuitous weather of a seacoast kingdom, but his body's constant exposure to cold in his homeland made the brutal heat of early spring in Sorbold a nightmare for him. He had long since shed his polar bear robe and the hat bearing a life-sized replica of a roaring wolf's head that he had worn when embarking on the trip. Now he was attired in the thinnest of tunics and trousers, and was pulling continuously on the cord that was attached to the large fan strung in the upper ceiling of the carriage. His panting and the constant back-and-forth movement of his fist put Talquist in mind of a far more pleasurable activity that the Diviner could be undertaking; he could barely contain his mirth.

Because the more uncomfortable his allies could be made prior to seeing what they were about to see, he believed, the more ready they would be for it.

Finally, the carriage began to roll to a slow stop. The heavy velvet shades at the windows had allowed a soothing darkness that enabled the monarchs to drowse in fitful repose, and so the cessation of movement had not wakened them. Talquist reached out impatiently and grasped the king of Golgarn's arm, shaking him roughly awake.

"Come, my friends," he said in a pleasant, if somewhat loud tone. "We have arrived."

Beliac and the Diviner opened their eyes. Talquist raised the bottom of the shade slightly, allowing a crack of sunlight into the dark carriage; the monarchs squinted in pain. He pulled the rest of it up slowly, to allow their eyes to adjust; once the daylight had filled the interior of the coach, he knocked on the door and waited for the footman to open it, then stepped out, followed by the other men.

Who looked around and about them in stunned silence.

Before them was what was known to the population of Roland as the holy city of Sepulvarta, the City of Reason, built at the height of the Cymrian era a thousand years before, in the time known as the Illuminara, the Age of Enlightenment. It was set at the northernmost point in the foothills of the mountainous region of Sorbold, an independent city-state dedicated to what the adherents of the Patrician faith called the All-God. In its time it had been erected on the threshold between Sorbold's northern border and the beginning of the enormous grasslands known as the Krevensfield Plain, the southern edge of the realm of Roland. Somewhere within its massive walls, both of the visiting kings knew, was the massive basilica of Lianta'ar, the Citadel of the Star; they both were looking up in awe at the enormous tower known as the Spire, which stood a thousand feet in the air, atop of which was a gleaming pinnacle that, according to legend, held an actual piece of the star Seren, for which the Lost Island of Serendair, the birthplace of the Cymrian people, had been named. The Spire was said to tower above the massive basilica, which itself was set several hundred feet above the street level atop the city's tallest hill.

Each of the Patrician basilicas across the continent was dedicated to one of the five primordial elements in nature—ether, fire, water, air and earth. Of all of the cities in which a Cymrian-built basilica stood, Sepulvarta had been perhaps the smallest in population, but that was because it had as permanent residents only the large number of clergy that served in Lianta'ar, the laity that served the needs of the clergy, and the standard workers, tradesmen, shopkeepers and soldiers that had served to keep the city itself running smoothly. Pilgrims made up the largest part of the residents at any given time, but that group was transient, traveling to Sepulvarta for healing or supplication for an infinite number of spiritual requests, thus providing the monetary sustenance that kept hostels, inns, taverns, shops and markets of the holy city flush with coinage.

In every time of the year, but most especially on the high holy days, which took place beginning on the first day of summer, the roads leading into the walled city were packed with travelers in a long, snaking line, seeking entrance through the one gate that led inside. The pathway off the main road to the north that bisected the continent through Roland, known as the trans-Orlandan thoroughfare, was always teeming with people, from the pilgrims on the way to the holy shrines, clergy traveling to and from assignments, and the typical humanity that wandered the thoroughfare from province to province, looking for commerce of both honorable and nefarious natures.

Now that immense line of people seeking entrance to the city was gone.

The massive wall that surrounded the city on either side of the enormous gate was teeming instead with guards, some patrolling the ramparts in shifts, others placed in regular formation behind mounted crossbows and ballistae. The gate itself had been shattered, recently by the look of it, and one side of it, the massive door which had absorbed the impact of that damage had been sealed and braced with temporary iron banding in the advent of real repair. The other door stood open, though vigorously guarded both at the ground level and from the ramparts above. Passing through it was an endless stream of soldiers, driving wagons filled with matériel, equipment, goods, and occasionally captives, most of whom looked like civilians or clergy, seated in open wagons, always in some sort of restraint.

From every crenellated tower, the flag of the Empire of the Sun flew proudly in the desert wind.

For the span of five hundred heartbeats, Beliac and the Diviner stood in stunned silence, trying to take in what they were beholding. Finally the Diviner looked at Talquist, who was smiling broadly, surveying the hundreds of banners displaying his colors.

"You—you have taken the holy city, Talquist?"

"For what purpose are you occupying Sepulvarta?" the king of Golgarn said. His voice was quavering.

Talquist turned to his two friends.

"I will try not to take offense at your words, Beliac, Hjorst," he said, the smooth tone of the merchant he had been most of his life in his voice. "I certainly am not surprised at your misunderstanding, which is largely due to the distance your kingdoms enjoy from this dry, parched land. What you do not realize is that, three years ago, when the Cymrian Alliance was restored and the Lord and Lady crowned, a new Patriarch was vested as well—a miscreant, a maniac by the name of Constantin.

"The people of the nation of Sorbold, which had been under Cymrian dominion during the days of Anwyn and Gwylliam, were, out of old habit, adherents to the Patrician faith, one of the two religions established on this continent when the misbegotten interlopers came. The previous Patriarch was, like all his forebears, the impotent head of that artificial religion, but nonetheless harmless. He died, by the way, at the Lady Cymrian's coronation as the Lirin queen, just as he came before her to offer his blessing. Your fears about her, and those of your wife, are well-placed, Beliac. The Patriarch died in her arms, and by her hand. She is said to have accepted his smiling blessing, then ripped the very life from him where he stood. She then sang him a brief but lovely dirge, dropped his body to the ground, and continued on with her receiving line of admirers as he lay there." He swallowed his amusement at the look of horror in Beliac's eyes.

"Constantin, who replaced him upon his death, was an apostate, a twisted, evil man in league with Lord Gwydion and his witch wife. He took the ring of the Patriarchy and immediately began creating abominations, beasts of hideous nature and voracious appetites, which he used the power of his office to animate, along with a vast array of other monsters. Trust me when I tell you that this so-called holy city was one of the most perverted, corrupt, murderous places in the Known World under his dominion. You cannot even begin to imagine the depravity that was undertaken in what had once been sacred cathedrals, particularly the one in Sepulvarta. It took the better part of three weeks to scald the semen of the supposedly celibate Patriarch and the blood of uncounted virgins off the altar of the basilica."

"Gods," Beliac murmured.

"In short, once he had amassed an army of monstrous beasts and men without conscience, he turned to the south and attacked the villages in the piedmont of Sorbold, innocent towns that served the outposts of the Sorbold army, burning seven of them to the ground in night raids, killing every man, woman, child, and farm animal. He had manipulated the lore of the elements in twisted, demonic ways, so the fire burned, uncontained, until everything it touched was rendered into ashes.

"What else could I do? We struck back, and, having both Right and military superiority on our side, we prevailed, at great cost, of course, but we drove the beasts back and destroyed them, then set about cleansing the city of its apostasy. Even the clerics that once served the Patriarch were part of the conspiracy, so they have been put to resanctifying the various buildings and shrines as they can. Most are repentant, but there are still a few holdouts who are in secret league with the Lord and Lady Cymrian; we are ferreting them out as they can be identified."

"That is a terrible story," the Diviner said dryly.

Talquist's stomach roiled in shock. He thought he had been convincing in his lie, but the grand scope of it might have been too much to seem possible. He opened his mouth, but as he did the Diviner continued his thought.

"I knew that the selection of Gwydion of Manosse would lead to disaster; it appears we in the Hintervold are not the only victims of his depravity and appalling greed."

"No, indeed," Talquist said, secretly relieved. "But, as you can see, the Sorbold army has greater military might, as well as the Creator's blessing. It is fortuitous that we three are old friends and new allies, gentlemen. That is very possibly the only hope for the continent.

"Now, if you will return to the carriage, I will show you what we are doing to try and set things to right within what one day soon will actually be a *true* holy city."

21

GURGUS PEAK, YLORC

$\mathcal{T}$rue to his word, each day when he was finished with gathering the stray prayers that had been offered up the chain using Gurgus Peak and the Lightcatcher, Constantin spent time with Rhapsody, instructing her in the lore of remembering the face of light.

The process was meditative and required silence and introspection, so there was only a small amount of time she could work with the Patriarch while Meridion was sleeping. She found that her musical study and Naming lore had a synchronicity to the science he was imparting to her, so that connecting the musical understanding she had developed over a lifetime to the lessons made her understanding clearer.

The first memory she had chosen to study was that of a moment in the forest of Gwynwood, in the course of her early travels with Ashe, back when they were still suspicious of one another, but falling in love nonetheless. He had brought her to a deeply hidden glen near a waterfall, where crabapple trees had been blooming, great boughs heavy with pink flowers. The woods had been rich with the scent of recent rain, and the sunlight through the leaves was so dense, so heavy, that she had unconsciously held out her hands, hoping to catch it. It was one of the sweetest memories she had of the man she missed beyond measure, coupled with a very strong memory of light, so she worked on the lore repeatedly until one day she had opened her eyes in the dank darkness of the interior of the mountain to find herself bathed in the perfect golden luminescence of that day, with dusty streams of sunshine raining heavily down on her. The feel of the wind on her face, the sweet odor of the blossoms, the singing of the birds.

She was there.

But only for a moment.

After that experience, the loneliness and loss of her husband's presence grew more poignant and unbearable each day. Rhapsody had been struggling against the sadness from the beginning of their separation, but the intensity of the memory now made the pain almost too deep to bear. With her work on the calibration of the Lightcatcher almost complete, she suggested one night that she try it out.

"I think the blue element of the spectrum is ready to be tested," she said that night at supper to Achmed and Grunthor while the Patriarch was offering his prayers in Gurgus Peak.

Achmed was buttering a roll.

"What makes you think so?"

"All of the musical matches have been accurate, and the diamond that Constantin has been blessing to hold the sunlight seems to be full."

"And where do you propose to scry?"

"Into Highmeadow," Rhapsody said. "It's friendly territory, rather than making the attempt into a hostile area first. I'm not certain if the pool of light that the blue section of the glass dome utilizes works both ways, or just from the perspective of the person doing the scrying."

Achmed shook his head in disagreement. "What if someone else is there? You won't know it until you have already summoned the light. I think you should try a forest glade or perhaps a seacoast first."

"If you wish. But I would like to try and reach Ashe if I can. We need to let him know that the titan is the voluntary host of the F'dor that Rath was trying to kill."

"Oi agree with 'Is Majesty," said Grunthor seriously. "Prolly should test it out where no one is likely to be at first."

"How's this for a compromise?" Rhapsody said, folding her napkin and rising from the table with Meridion in the crook of her arm. "We can use the direct power of the sun in the morning, and aim for a place that's likely to be empty and harmless. But later tonight, I may want to see if the diamond really is storing the light, and give it a try when it's dark. Jalasee, the Sea Mage ambassador you are so fond of, Achmed, tried to explain to me at the Winter Carnival about baptism in the light of stars, so that a Namer or someone who understands the lore can carry the light around inside himself or herself. I think all of this lore is related. So if Omet will help me, I will give it a try in the dark tonight. Then at least we will know if the diamond is working or if I'm just wasting my time talking to a useless rock."

"Well, either way it will duplicate the experience of your being with Ashe," Achmed said, rising from the table and tossing his napkin on his chair. He left the room, leaving Grunthor and Rhapsody looking at each other with the same quizzical expression on their faces.

An hour or so later, Rhapsody came into the darkness of Gurgus Peak with Meridion and a nervous Omet in tow.

The instrumentality was much more mysterious-looking in the dark, with a circle of light glowing on the altar and the starlight through the glass dome above the only illumination.

"I think I should be able to activate it by myself," Rhapsody said to Omet, who nodded. "But I don't know if the diamond has any power stored in it at all, so I won't even try the wheel; I'll just sing. Can you be ready just in case?"

"Certainly."

Rhapsody drew the bundle in her arms closer. She kissed the baby's soft curls, then smiled at him.

"Let us go see your papa, shall we?"

The infant's blue eyes regarded her thoughtfully. Then he cooed at her almost convincingly enough to make her believe that he understood.

22

IN THE STUDY OFF THE MAIN
LIBRARY, HIGHMEADOW

$\mathcal{A}$she had fallen, with the aid of a decanter of not particularly good brandy, into a restless sleep at his desk, his grizzled cheek resting on the growing piles of battlefield communiqués. His exhaustion had denied him any chance at the sleep of a normal man, and instead had caused him to sink quickly into the recesses of draconic slumber, from which he always had to struggle to awaken. He was deep in despairing, alcohol-tinged dreams when a blue light appeared in the corner of his study.

My love.

The words, though spoken softly, carried an unmistakable ring of deep familiarity.

With great difficulty, Ashe lifted his head.

The waves of light at first had a similar appearance to those that ran down the blade of Kirsdarke when in his hand. After a moment within those waves he could make out an image of Rhapsody, translucent, clutching a bundle close to her chest and smiling at him uncertainly.

Unlike the other times Portia had taken her form, or caused whatever manipulation the demon had been capable of, the picture of his wife was clad not in a nightdress or a revealing gown, but in simple molecloth trousers, boots, and a linen shirt. Her hair was bound back in a black ribbon, rather than tumbling over her shoulders as it had in the mirages the demon had tormented him with.

But the choice to present her as she often dressed was clever; whatever demonic hand was manipulating him again had caused his heart to leap at the simple image of the woman he loved, in spite of how clearly he knew she was an illusion. Now it was also tantalizing him with the suggestion of Meridion's presence as well.

The few working parts of his human brain collapsed under the weight of his fury.

"What are you doing here?" the dragon's voice demanded.

The image of Rhapsody blinked. Then she smiled even more uncertainly. When she spoke, her voice echoed hollowly, as if she were far away.

I've brought your son to see you. He misses you almost as much as I do.

Ashe's hand, outstretched beneath his head a moment before, clutched at the inkwell and a blotter on his desk, sending the objects scattering. Then he rose from the desk and seized the hilt of his sword, dragging it from its scabbard in its own waves of blue light.

And made his way around the desk toward the image in the light, murder in his eyes.

Guttural sounds issued forth from his throat, draconic curses of the highest intensity of hate.

"You misbegotten *monster*, you damned whore, I cannot believe you've come back," he snarled.

In the slice of blue light raining down from above her, Rhapsody blinked again, her face slack in shock. Then, as the image of her rampaging husband gained speed, barreling down on her and Meridion, she grasped the hilt of her own sword.

Daystar Clarion whispered forth from its scabbard, blazing in lapping tongues of flame rippling up its blade, which she held as far away from the bundle in her arms as she could. Then she took in a ragged breath and spoke a command with the ringing tone of a Namer.

"Gwydion ap Llauron, *stop*."

Against his will, Ashe lurched to a halt.

They stood, frozen either in the shock of having drawn on each other, or that of being dragged to an involuntary standstill in the midst of crossing the room. Then slowly, quietly, Rhapsody spoke aloud again, her eyes fiercely fixed on her husband, her words addressed to another.

"Omet," she said without breaking her gaze away, "take the baby."

The young glass artisan, who was staring in horror at what he was witnessing, stood stock-still for a moment. Then he nervously crossed to the edge of the pool of blue light, took the child from Rhapsody's left arm as she remained drawn with her right, and carried him out of the light pool as quickly as he could.

Rhapsody's eyes were still fixed on her panting, struggling husband. As soon as Meridion was no longer in the light, her expression changed from one of shock and horror to one of incredible sadness.

"My poor, dear love—my poor love," she said softly. "Ashe—do you not recognize me?"

I know who you are, the draconic voice whispered furiously in return. *You filthy, manipulative bitch. How dare you return to this place? Did you think I would not recognize you in another form?*

Tears sprang to Rhapsody's eyes, not from the insult or threat of violence, but at the delirium in the eyes of the man with whom she shared a soul. She had felt his sanity begin to fray and crumble even before she had left their lands, but the immense depth of madness mirrored in his eyes tore at her heart.

"Who am I, then?" she whispered. "Tell me."

Ashe struggled angrily in the bonds of her Naming lore, with such hatred on his face that the tears that had formed in her eyes spilled over and rolled down her cheeks. *You are the demon who clung to the serving maid, Portia, before whatever found her in the woods mercifully crushed the life out of her,* he said. *You unspeakable miscreant—how dare you come to me in my wife's aspect again?*

Rhapsody stared at him a moment more. Then she sheathed her sword and looked him over. He was unkempt; his hair had apparently not been cut since she left, and it curled around his ears and almost down to his shoulders, glistening with sweat. His beard had begun to grow in from lack of attention, and he had obviously slept in his clothes, though for how long was not clear. He was trembling in agitation, the sword in his frozen hand twitching as he did, sending wild pulses of blue light around the study's walls and ceiling.

Across the mammoth room in which she actually stood, Meridion squeaked unhappily in Omet's arms.

Ashe's eyes grew wilder at the sound.

Rhapsody inhaled slowly, trying to keep her face as placid as she could, and her voice as steady. Whatever unknown bedevilment of the mind was tormenting her husband had him riled into believing she was not who she appeared to be, it was clear. She struggled to smile at him, and when she spoke, her words were calm, steady, almost playful.

"You know, beloved, as I've told you before, you really should shave off that beard, it's awful."

Ashe froze. The wildness remained in his eyes, but the anger abated somewhat.

Rhapsody stood still and waited, watching him carefully. The phrase she had uttered was something she had said to him years before, during his time of hiding, in the course of the first long journey they had undertaken together, still suspicious of one another. Just before they had parted ways, he had asked her to tarry a moment, then had pulled down his hood to reveal his face to her for the first time. The import of the moment had not been lost on her at the time; she understood both the risk that he was taking if she was not who she claimed to be, and his status a hunted man. The vulnerability and longing in his eyes had gone straight to her heart then, as it did now. She had lightened the moment with the joke about his beard.

It was impossible to imagine that anyone else would have known and understood the reference now.

Rhapsody? he whispered. The soprano, alto, tenor and bass tones of the dragon's voice were gone, replaced by a trembling all-too-human baritone.

The tears running down her face, blurring her vision, threatened to blind her.

"Yes, my love," she said quietly.

Are you—are you really here?

"Not in the flesh, no," she said, trying to keep her voice steady. "We are in the testing stage of our project, so while I physically remain in Ylorc, I am able to come to you this way, to see into Highmeadow—it's my home, and half of my soul is there, so it was fairly easy to scry into your study. But this is really me, not some affectation of a demon—by the star I swear it." She exhaled as the madness seemed to abate in his eyes.

And—do you—still love me?

She swallowed the knot in her throat. Like her use of the reference to his beard, he was undertaking a similar countersign to see if she answered it as she should if she was genuine. The question had always been one of gentle teasing and reassurance, but her answer had been the same each time he had asked it. The pain in his voice now made the tears fall faster.

She summoned a smile through them.

"Always," she said.

Ashe bowed his head. When he looked up again, relief had replaced the despair that had been on his face a moment before. He exhaled, and Rhapsody could hear the clutching pain give way in the sound of his breath. She signaled for Omet's return and dismissed the Naming command, freeing Ashe from his invisible bonds.

"If you will put away your sword, we can try this once more," she said, taking the baby into her arms and walking toward the edge of the blue light closest to Ashe. "You once promised that you would never draw on me again, but I will assume that you have not broken your word as you thought I was someone else." She held the child up in front of his father.

Are you certain he's—he's not in any danger—being in this light? Ashe asked haltingly. He quickly sheathed Kirsdarke and came to the blue light pool's edge.

"As certain as I can be," she replied. "I don't have long to be with you—and I have much I need to tell you. But first things first—Meridion wants to see his papa."

The expression on Ashe's face was too painful to be borne; she avoided looking at him and instead pulled the blanket away from the baby and turned him to face his father, her hands supporting his head and his back. Then she extended her arms, holding Meridion so that Ashe could see him up close.

Through the haze of his own tears Ashe looked down at his son, translucent in the waves of light as Rhapsody was. The baby's eyes were focused on him, their tiny dragonesque pupils expanding and contracting vertically, locked on his similar ones. They were intensely blue, like Ashe's own, fringed with his mother's black lashes, his cheeks rosy and his small mouth puckered, either in interest or in hunger. Meridion stared at his father for the span of a dozen heartbeats, then let out an enormous burp.

The tearful parents broke into laughter.

He's gotten so big, Ashe whispered fondly.

"Not big enough for a burp of that size," Rhapsody said, nuzzling the baby's head. "He's obviously picking up some of Uncle Grunthor's habits—or Uncle Anborn's."

Ashe shuddered but continued to stare at his son, love of unmistakable depth in his eyes.

"Hold him," Rhapsody urged. "You might not be able to feel him through the light, but it's worth a try."

I don't want to hurt him, Ashe said haltingly.

"I won't let go—I won't drop him. We can hold him together."

Beads of sweat broke out on the Lord Cymrian's brow. He reached forward into the waves of blue light and slid his arms into the spaces that Rhapsody had left open for him. And while, as she had predicted, there was no heft to the image of the little boy, a buzz ran along Ashe's arms where that image had shape, tickling his dragon sense with the joyful feeling of being reunited with lost treasure.

With great effort he tore his eyes away from his son and looked into Rhapsody's face. It was shining; she was smiling up at him in the way that always made his heart cramp.

"I will bring him to you as often as can be deemed safe," she said as Ashe looked back at Meridion. "Can you feel him at all?" Ashe nodded numbly, still transfixed by the sight of the child. "Then why don't you give him a kiss—I have to talk with you quickly before the light fades and our connection is lost."

No! screamed the dragon in Ashe's blood. *Mine! My treasure—my child—no!*

Thank—you—for bringing him to me, Aria, he said haltingly, the dragon tones present in his voice but fading as he struggled and won control. He bent down and put his lips to the image of Meridion's head; no heft or solidity met them in return, but a similar buzzing vibration rushed across them, sending a thrill through him that reached into his heart and warmed it.

It was all he could do to keep from howling madly as Rhapsody pulled the baby closer, tilting him one last time for another look.

"Good night, Papa," she said as the baby gurgled and waved his tiny arms in the air in Ashe's direction. "I love you—we will see you again soon." Ashe struggled to keep from screaming as she turned away and walked back to the far edge of the light circle, handing Meridion off into the dark shadows beyond.

She returned quickly to the near edge of the circle and put out her hand to him. Like Meridion, she had no heft, no weight to her, and Ashe's hand passed through the image of hers like a sunshadow. Seeing his despair, she turned her palm upward and held it out to him.

"Here," she said. "Let's try it this way."

Trembling, Ashe reached out again and matched the vertical angle of her palm, then slowly approached her. This time, as with Meridion, as it came in contact with the translucent image he felt a thrilling tingle of warmth on his skin; it shot through him, ringing with joy.

I love you, Aria, he said. *Gods, I love you, I love you, forgive me—*

"None of that," Rhapsody said briskly. "The forgiveness part, I mean; I love you too. I've been on the verge of madness myself, missing you so terribly."

The only thing that has kept me even vaguely sane is clinging to the picture in my mind of you and our son, safe within Elysian, as the world caves in, Ashe said, experiencing another thrill as the undulating image of his wife reached up and laid her other filmy hand lovingly on his cheek. *I dream about you both every night—last night you were sitting on the warm ground beneath the young apple trees in the orchard of the grotto, feeding him and singing him his lullabye.*

Rhapsody's smile dimmed slightly.

"Imagine us instead within Ylorc," she said, her voice echoing softly, "because that's where we are staying presently."

Ylorc? Not in Elysian? Why?

Rhapsody swallowed. She did not want to compromise his recent return to fragile sanity by telling him about the destruction of the grotto, its house, grounds, and contents, by his grandmother, the dragon Anwyn, but resolved to be honest with him if he pressed.

"Achmed deemed it safer for us to stay within the mountain for now," she said. "I will tell you more about our accommodations, and anything else you want to know, later—but first I have to convey something to you for which you need to steel yourself."

Ashe exhaled. *Tell me.*

The evanescent image of his wife nodded. "Portia—the serving maid that Tristan Steward brought to us in Haguefort—" Her words were interrupted by a cascade of draconic curses. "Oh good—then I assume you already know she was the host of one of the Older Pantheon."

I surmised. You have confirmed it?

"Yes, sadly, and more—the demon escaped the Thrall ritual that killed her body—and has taken on another host."

As I feared, Ashe said. *At least it could not have been a very powerful host; Portia was but a serving maid, brought by Tristan Steward for the purpose of seducing me.* He watched Rhapsody's eyes carefully; she blinked, but did not flinch otherwise. *Given that F'dor can only subsume a host who is weaker or only a peer in strength of will, it can't have been anyone particularly powerful.*

Rhapsody's eyes filled with pain.

"Alas, I fear you are wrong, beloved," she said. "The demon's new host took it on willingly, like Michael did long ago. It is the stone titan that Anborn told us of at our last council, the animated statue of Living Stone that Talquist brought to life on the Scales of Jierna Tal. The titan that led Talquist's successful assault on Sepulvarta."

Ashe's face went white.

"The Dhracian that was in the midst of the Thrall ritual, trying to kill the one of the Older Pantheon, was attacked, almost destroyed by the titan," Rhapsody continued, trying not to look at him. "His word is unquestionable. This has just made our task even more complicated, but not insurmountable."

Now I fear that you may be the one who is wrong, beloved, Ashe said in reply. *The task felt insurmountable even before this dire news. I have sent word to Manosse and Gaematria, but have not heard back yet, though it truly is too soon for the ships to have even landed.* He looked at the pool in which the image of his wife hovered.

The blue light was fading.

"Any other news?" Rhapsody asked quickly. "I fear we are about to be parted for the time being."

Tristan Steward is our semi-permanent guest in the most secure of the cells in the internal stockade.

"You've arrested Tristan?"

He was sleeping with Portia, Rhapsody, Ashe said archly. *I have reason to believe he may be a thrall of the demon.*

"Of course," she murmured. "Of course. How sad—I'm so sorry, beloved."

I have not put that on the wind for now, Ashe said. *If Achmed or the Dhracian you mentioned is ever in Highmeadow, I hope they might assess him and determine him to be free of demonic bondage, but otherwise I know of no other way to handle this. All of Roland, even his wife, believes he is here assisting in the war effort, and for now I am prepared to allow them all to believe that. But I am unwilling to risk his contact with anyone—anyone— until either the demon is dead or he can be declared definitively free of it.*

Rhapsody smiled at him.

"You are wise, my love. Did Melisande return?"

Yes. She is in Haguefort for a few days visiting Gwydion, and then she will be escorted here—I believe it is requiring a brigade's effort to pack all her clothing and whatnot—she truly is your granddaughter.

Rhapsody struggled to put the loss of her closetful of dresses in Elysian destroyed in dragonfire out of her mind. "And did she find Elynsynos?"

Ashe ran his hand through his hair uncomfortably.

No. I'm sorry. Gavin sealed the cave. He felt the dragon in his blood rise again as tears came to Rhapsody's eyes and glimmered, ephemeral, in the fading light. *But they did find Krinsel, the Bolg midwife—she was horrifically injured, but Gavin has tended to her intensively, and she seems on the way back to health, at least of some degree. As soon as she is well enough to travel, I will send her with an escort back to Ylorc—she is in need of the skills of a Namer, Gavin says, having sustained her injuries in dragon's breath— from Anwyn. She survived; it's a miracle.*

"Well, that is good to hear, at least. I will let Achmed know—she is one of his Archons." The mention of dragon's breath brought up another thought. "Oh—I'm sorry to have to tell you this, but I inadvertently destroyed your mist cloak; it did what it was supposed to do, and kept Meridion safe, but it's gone. Can you and Kirsdarke make another one for me for the future?"

Of course. I will send it with Krinsel, wrapped about her—it may help soothe her wounds. How did it come to be lost?

Rhapsody glanced above her. The sun had all but moved on to the next pane of glass, the indigo section.

"I'll tell you next time," she said. "Goodbye, beloved. Stay well."

I love you, Ashe said as the vision of his wife dimmed into darkness. *Kiss the baby for me. Do you still love me?*

The image disappeared, but her reply hung in the air of the study.

"Always."

A moment later, the household staff and soldiers passing by the window of the study felt a rumbling roar that trailed off into the sound of epic anguish. They quickened their pace as they returned to what they had been doing.

It was a sound they had heard on occasion before.

23

THE OCCUPIED CITY OF SEPULVARTA

𝒯he next step of the journey was accorded to the emperor's guests at somewhat more gradual speed.

The winding internal streets of what had been the City of Reason were not designed for comfort or ease of travel; rather, part of the path to penitence was thought to be the trial of making one's way through the narrow, cobbled roads and uphill alleyways, a route that pilgrims often trod barefoot. The military occupation of a city built largely of white stone and marble had not improved the streets, which were now even more rutted and uneven. The Diviner and the king of Golgarn found themselves clinging to one another or in each other's laps as the carriage lurched from side to side, making agonizingly slow progress past the blackened and broken buildings that at one time had obviously seemed almost otherworldly in the glint of the sunlight.

The enormous Spire was now impossible to see from within the city, but it made its presence known nonetheless. Every now and then the sun caught a facet of the star at its pinnacle, sending a broad slash of ethereal light flashing through the air, causing the broken rooftops to gleam in momentary glory, then settle back in the shame of black ash and crumbled brick recently visited upon them.

The carriage tilted at an extreme angle as the horses began to plod even more slowly forward.

"What—what is happening?" Beliac asked nervously.

"We are ascending the hill to the basilica. We have been for a while, but we are now almost at the summit."

"How much farther, Talquist?" the Diviner demanded, removing Beliac's elbow from his face for the fourth time.

"We are almost there," the emperor assured him. "The basilica is within sight; it should only be a few more moments."

"Thank the All-God, or whatever it is they worship here," muttered Beliac. He was too busy trying to steady himself to notice the look of black anger that glanced across Talquist's face, to be replaced a moment later by the same placid mien that had been there all along.

Finally, the carriage rolled to a slow, bumpy halt in front of a massive fountainbed that led up to the wide stairs of the basilica. The fountainbed was the size of three streets put together in both width and length, and running down its center from the edge of the street where the carriage stood to the steps of the basilica were apparatuses that at one time had sprayed curved ribbons of shining water in a multiplicity of colors, forming a shimmering representation of the star at the top of the Spire in the marble basin. Water still gurgled from those apparatuses, but weakly; what had once been a grand reflecting pool that mirrored the beauty of the basilica was now serving as a watering trough for scores of warhorses that were drinking from all four of its sides. Soldiers were bathing the beasts in the enormous basin as well.

Beliac, the sovereign of a highly militarized naval city, put his hand over his nose and mouth to shield them from the stench, and to hold back the nausea that had gripped him at the sight even before the smell did.

The carriage door opened, and the footman stepped clear; Talquist rose and allowed himself to be assisted out, then turned and offered his hand to the Diviner and subsequently to Beliac. The three royal men made their unsteady way along the outskirts of the reflecting pool to the steps of the great basilica.

Now the Spire was visible again; its base from which the tower tapered up toward the clouds was as wide as a city block, and it stood directly across the city from Lianta'ar. The gleaming radiance at the top came from the tiny piece of ethereal matter that had been affixed within a platinum star-shaped housing, and the light of midafternoon was catching in the sculpture's rays, sending wild flashes around the streets.

The Diviner could only imagine that it was silently calling for help.

The monarchs mounted the stairs and made their way inside the massive basilica. Even before they passed the entry doors, the visiting kings had begun to marvel; the basilica had towering walls of polished marble and an overarching dome that was taller than any in the Known World. It had seating for thousands of souls who now no longer came to it seeking solace, but in spite of the signs of battle, the pitted stone still gleamed as evidence of a time of great architectural inspiration and ingenuity in praise of the divine.

Some of what were known to be the most beautiful and immense mosaics of tile ever assembled graced the floor and the ceiling of the basilica; the two visiting kings were led past the frescoed walls and windows fashioned in colored glass, many of which had been covered with long sheets of rough burlap.

When the Diviner looked questioningly at the obscured frescoes and windows, the emperor chuckled.

"Magnificent as the artwork in the cathedral is, some of it is representative of fallacies and lies from the Cymrian era, the distortion of history in some of the most egregious and appalling ways. Those which will remain in Lianta'ar are the depictions of nature and elemental lore that preceded that terrible, destructive time in the world."

By now they had come to the central sanctuary of the basilica. In what seemed to be the exact center of the building a tall cylindrical rise stood, atop which was the church's altar, a large plain table formed of simple stone edged in platinum. Through the openings in the great dome above the altar, the Spire across the city could be seen, casting its radiance down in random flashes of sunlight. By night, it was clear that the basilica would be bathed in ethereal light from the top of the tower.

"Why have you brought us here, Talquist?" the Diviner demanded impatiently. "The beauty of the place is extraordinary, true, but you know that we have much to attend to in our own lands."

"I wanted you to see the beginning of the return to sanity for the continent, and, eventually, the world," the emperor said quietly. "Unlike you both, I was not born into a royal line that led me to the throne of my native land. You, Hjorst, and you, Beliac, knew your destinies almost as soon as you knew your own names; I have had to search the entirety of the earth to discover mine. I have worked in almost every profession, traveled to each of the continents, sailed every one of the seas, all in search of what my purpose in life is supposed to be. I have finally come to understand it— and it is vastly more than merely sitting atop the throne of Sorbold, as Leitha did for three-quarters of a century, dressing in finery and consuming expensive victuals. I have a calling—and it is something I hope you will share in, given that the very survival of your lands may depend on its success." He fell silent, looking up at the dome of the ceiling high above him.

"What is this calling?" the Diviner asked after a long moment with nothing but the vast echo of the basilica sounding in his ears. "What are you talking about?"

Talquist turned in a full circle at the foot of the cylindrical stairs leading up to the stone altar.

"I believe it is my life's purpose not only to rule Sorbold, but to return it to a time before the scourge that was the Cymrian era took root in our homeland," he said, a tone both inspired and bitter in his voice. "Those retched transplants, loyal to a king who could not accept his destiny, and that of his Island—to be stamped out by nature, destroyed in the volcanic fire of the Sleeping Child's awakening—refugeed to *our* lands—some of the most magical, beautiful places on the Earth—and remade them in his image, bringing with him famine, death, disease, and discontent that eventually boiled over into a war that destroyed both the land and the population that had taken the Cymrians in, storm-tossed and dying as they had been from their trek across the world. This place, the holiest of their religious sites, is where the renewal of our history begins."

"How so?" asked Beliac nervously.

"First, we will go back to the name of God that was perverted, made idiotic not only by the fools who followed the Patriarch, but those in the western forests who were overrun by the first of the fleets to come here, to the lands of Elynsynos, the dragon. The All-God, the One-God; ridiculous."

"And what do you plan to see supplant those names?" The Diviner's normally skeptical expression was somewhat less guarded.

Talquist smiled.

"He will be known, as He was in the time before the Cymrians came, as the Creator," he said smugly, "as you have always called Him, Hjorst. The Sorbolds and the Icemen have always shared a purer faith, an animist belief, one tied to nature, to the demi-gods that symbolized the elements, the animals, the plant life, the weather, the stars, the land—none of the sheer nonsense that was practiced in this building for centuries. As a nation, an empire, Sorbold will return to those days, those beliefs, and they will guide, inform, and rule our commerce, our military, our family life, everything. The Spire, which for more than a thousand years supposedly directed the prayers of the mindless faithful of the Patrician religion to their ridiculous All-God, will be used as the great symbol of our returned belief system."

Beliac ran a finger under the collar of his jerkin. "That symbol being what, if not what it was built for?"

The emperor smiled.

"It will symbolize many things, actually—a massive phallus, for fertility and masculine power and dominion, an elevated eye, for the clarity of sight across the continent, a giant spear, for military superiority—we will turn each of the Cymrian landmarks that we do not choose to destroy to a noble purpose, ushering in the return to a holier, cleaner, more natural time. But before we begin to undertake the replanting of that noble purpose, we will need to eradicate the remains of that apostate civilization, the interlopers, the rapists who took our magical, deeply beautiful realm and polluted it, crushed it under their heels. We need to remove every last trace of Cymrian rulership, and, with his assault on Sorbold, the Patriarch has given us the opening to now do what we should have done centuries ago. I assume that his allies, the Bolg king, who is building settlements within a league of your capital city, Beliac, and the Lord Cymrian, who is poisoning your populace, Hjorst, have given you both the same openings."

The visiting kings listened intently, absorbing his words. Then the Diviner nodded in agreement, followed immediately by the king of Golgarn. Talquist's face broke into a broad smile, and he clapped both men on the shoulders.

"Excellent! I see we have much to discuss. Now, come with me to my quarters within the city; I had the most sumptuous of the guesthouses that had once sheltered the royalty of the Alliance when they came to visit annexed for my own use while here in Sepulvarta. You will both be most comfortable there, I'm certain; we can sup and imbibe and discuss my plans for turning the unprovoked assault on Sorbold into a campaign to return the continent to what the Creator designed it to be—three allied exterior nations ruling, rather than being ruled by, the Middle Continent."

He led the two stunned monarchs out of the basilica, whistling as he walked.

24

$\mathcal{A}$fter night had fallen, eased down around him by sumptuous feasting and merrymaking, the emperor of Sorbold left the guesthouse in the company of his old friend, the Diviner of the Hintervold.

Hjorst had been silent for most of the evening; Talquist was accustomed to his quiet reflection, which was his nature and inclination whenever contemplating plans of even the smallest sort of change. Hjorst's younger brother, a lesser diviner named Miraz of Winter, with whom Talquist had limited commerce, was a rash man, prone to whim. In constrast, the Diviner was a considered man, who ruled a realm, unlike Beliac's religion-free kingdom, of deeply held beliefs and ancient practices from which his power emanated. He was careful about committing his forces and his aid without consulting his gods first through the practice of divination, from whence his title was derived.

Talquist, a believer in no god other than himself, had come to realize that while those who held such deep beliefs were among the most resistant to the manipulation to his will, they could be bent and eventually recruited, but only if his approach took into account the logic and emotion of the religion to which they were devoted. Beliac, having no belief structure to speak of, was putty in his hands, because Talquist knew his deepest fears and had already played the cards that ignited them, the fear of being consumed while alive by the Bolg. But Hjorst would be a harder sell.

Fortunately, Talquist was an expert merchant.

As they approached the great doors of the basilica again now in the dark, he signaled to the guards standing watch to open them, then withdraw to the edge of the exterior stairs.

As he suspected, the sanctuary was filled with the ethereal light shining from the Spire on the other side of the city, its radiance raining down through the windows in the dome high above. The stone altar glowed in the dark.

"I thank you, Hjorst, for being willing to undertake a divination on my behalf, especially so far after Yule," he said as they made their way down the center aisle. "I am grateful to have a friend who has the power to aid in the mission we have undertaken."

"We have not discussed your needs sufficiently, Talquist," the Diviner replied quietly. "I have no idea what sort of divination you are seeking, and so therefore do not have all of the materials I will need to undertake one."

"What are the options?"

The Diviner looked around the sanctuary, his eyes finally coming to rest on the stone table atop the cylindrical rise.

"First, is that the semen-soaked altar you referred to?"

"No, not at all," Talquist said quickly. When he had undertaken the lie, he had realized almost immediately that it might negate the altar's use. Given its sacred status in Lianta'ar, he assumed it would be the best place to make whatever sacrifice the Diviner required for conducting his ritual. "Even Constantin had a fragment of discretion. The altar I referred to is in the manse, where he and the highest of his clerics lived."

"Ah, good. At least we have a place to perform the rite. Now, there are many different types of rituals, depending on what sort of answer you are looking for."

"Such as?"

"Well, have you had a sign or an omen that you want interpreted?"

"No, not really," Talquist said. "I went to Manwyn's temple and paid for a prophecy, which she gave me, but it was incomplete."

The Diviner sighed. "Perhaps we should begin with you explaining what it is you want to know, Talquist—completely and honestly. I do not judge those I divine for, but I hate being misled or lied to. When that happens, it would have been better not to have undertaken the ritual in the first place; there is a considerable amount of risk in it, both for you and for me."

Talquist drew himself up indignantly.

"I would never lie to you, Hjorst," he said, a haughty tone in his voice.

"I did not think you would, nor was I referring to you personally. I'm just explaining that you need not worry about the subject of your divination as far as I am concerned; I will not think ill of you, whatever it is."

The Merchant Emperor closed his eyes. Telling the truth, something he undertook rarely, was easier if he did not have to meet the gaze of the recipient of that truth.

"I have finally ascended to the throne after—after a year I voluntarily spent as regent, rather than agreeing just to be crowned emperor," he said haltingly. He had almost inadvertently revealed how long he had actually been planning his ascendancy, and the steps he had taken to put it in place. "I thought that a humble approach to my unexpected selection by the Scales was the best one."

The Diviner nodded. "Go on."

"I have, as you have heard, an ambitious goal for my reign. Unfortunately, I am already in my middle years, moving toward my dotage, and I have not even begun my undertaking. My biggest fear is that I will not live long enough to see it through. That would leave Sorbold vulnerable to retaliation by the Cymrians I intend to supplant, if I were to die before they are eradicated."

His mouth grew dry as his anger rose; it always did when contemplating the rest of his thought.

"It was not enough that those bastards were inordinately powerful when they crashed upon our shores and began the rape of our continent. No, in addition to their bloodthirstiness and the innocence of our ancestors who were slaughtered and displaced, the Cymrians had two more advantages—elemental lore, which gave them powers they were unworthy of, and a ridiculously extended life expectancy, which allowed them to outlive many times over anyone who would confront them. How, then, am I to be able to defeat Gwydion of Manosse, or his wife, or the Lord Roland, or any of the other misbegotten descendants of Gwylliam and Anwyn, or dragons, or even the ordinary Cymrian dock whore who still has the advantage of immortality over me?"

The Diviner's eyes, black as midnight, took him in thoughtfully.

"So you are looking to know how long you will live?"

"No," said Talquist quietly. "I am looking to do so eternally."

"You seek immortality for yourself?"

"Is that so wrong?" the emperor asked bitterly. "One hundred thousand miscreant refugees, who Fate had declared doomed, sailed away from their homeland in great ships whose broken magical wooden shells still litter the Skeleton Coast—farmers and apostate priests, prostitutes and thieves, buggerers and assassins, and every one of those reprehensible excuses for human beings was gifted, as a result of whatever they did to cheat Death, with life everlasting."

"And suffered immensely for it," the Diviner said seriously. "Of those one hundred thousand of the First Generation, how many are still alive, do you know? For if you do not, *I* do—I had an ancestor who was one who is not. There are but a handful among the living, Talquist, and this is something that most likely you do not know—far more of them died at their own hands, in the grip of insanity brought on by the so-called gift of everlasting life, than even died in the Cymrian War."

"Of course they did," said Talquist contemptuously. "Because, with all due deference to your ancestor, the majority of that indigent population was deficient, inferior; they were pampered and protected from the harsh realities of life by the abundance of resources the Island of Serendair enjoyed, the gentle climate, the fortuitous geography—"

"Indeed, especially if you overlook their proximity to a boiling undersea hazard with catastrophic inclination, they were lazy, worthless peasants living in a lackadaisical paradise," growled the Diviner. "Stop, Talquist, I beg you. I am your friend, and your ally, though until these recent unfortunate events our nations were both also friends of the Alliance. I met the Lord and Lady Cymrian at their wedding, and several times thereafter, as well as King Achmed, and I have to say that, while they have proven to be skillful liars and disingenuous in their claims of peace and friendship, they are hardly the pathetic lowlifes you describe. I am very intent on not underestimating any adversaries the Hintervold may be forced to fight; that is the first fool's errand. Lord Gwydion is an impressive man, a well-educated, well-trained and gifted soldier and the grandson of perhaps the greatest inventor the Known World has ever seen. The Lady Rhapsody is a Namer of undeniable power, and very difficult to resist becoming enchanted with, as Beliac has already mentioned. The Bolg king terrifies me, I have to say, and has since I made his acquaintance at the empress's funeral last year. It would be highly unwise to underestimate their power." He sighed dispiritedly at the expression that came over the new emperor's face and looked up at the dome towering above him in the dark, through which gleaming ethereal light was bathing the center of the basilica.

"That being said, you have my loyalty as your friend and ally. Our kingdoms are under threat; we have no choice but to do whatever we must to ensure their safety and protection. So, if you will tell me what exactly you are trying to achieve, I will divine as best as I am able for you at this inopportune time of the year."

Talquist exhaled. He closed his eyes again and recalled the dark, musty temple of Manwyn, the Seer of the Future, the insane soothsayer in

Yarim whose irisless eyes reflected like a mirror as she looked into the realm of what had not yet come to pass.

"The prophecy I was given, in response to my question regarding immortality, was unsatisfying and obtuse. I am hoping your divination can be more specific as to what I must do to achieve it."

"Tell me what you said to Manwyn, as exactly as you can remember it, and exactly what she said in return."

Talquist swallowed. He did not have the desire to reveal that his legendary self-confidence had deserted him in the face of the mad prophetess, who gazed at him with what could only be interpreted as a wildly amused and cruel expression.

You have awaited this day for a very long time, the madwoman had said. *Gaze into the well, and tell me what you see there—Your Majesty.*

Talquist, at the time still a powerful but socially insignificant member of the mercantile, had blinked in astonishment melting into delight at her form of address. She had all but confirmed to him the reality of his wishes to be crowned emperor. It was not until later that he realized the shock of having his deepest desires affirmed had made his phrasing of what he wanted to know vulnerable to the famed manipulation of the Seer.

He had done as she commanded and looked into the yawning chasm at her feet over which she was suspended on a hanging platform, rocking unsteadily back and forth. The image that looked back at him from the darkness below was his own, attired in linen robes painted with gold, and the crown of Sorbold on his brow.

When will I be able to see myself so attired, should I happen to look in the mirror? he asked, almost unable to contain his excitement.

On the first day of spring, four years hence, Manwyn had intoned. *Or a thousand years in the Future. On either day, you will be attired in the same way.*

And what must I do to see myself, so attired, a thousand years hence? he had asked.

Manwyn grinned even more broadly.

You must find the Child of Time, she whispered.

And then, as the last syllable had left her lips, the platform on which she lay prone began to swing wildly over the bottomless pit as a tremor shook the very earth on which Talquist was standing.

As dust and grit began to rain down from the ceiling above, also wreathed in darkness, he had quit the temple, running for his life.

More thrilled than he had ever been with it before.

Until the day, little more than a year ago, when he had attended the burial of Leitha. The Dowager Empress had died as she had lived, resolutely and without compromise; she had managed, as she lay all but frozen by the magics he had called upon through the purple scale of the New Beginning, to deliver a stinging shot with her ancient, grotesquely twisted foot to his genitals as he stood above her bed, taunting her, and to move one finger on her bird-claw of a desiccated hand into a commonly recognized gesture of obscenity before he stripped the life from her. At ninety-eight, there had been little enough of it left in her skeletal body anyway.

But after her funeral in the elemental basilica Terreanfor, where he had once served as an acolyte to the sexton, an experience that had allowed him to harvest the Living Stone that made all his steps in usurping the throne possible, he had noticed as they carried her body to its final entombment in the upper chapel that she was attired in the same gold-painted linen garment and crown that he had seen in the paintings of her coronation three-quarters of a century before.

The same such robes as he had worn in his vision from Manwyn.

On either day, you will be attired in the same way.

The worry had come to consume him, the doubt creeping into his brain in his dreams. He wondered constantly what finding the Child of Time meant, and how it would bring his desired immortality into being. In his deepest moments of despair, it occurred to him that the so-named child might be born free of its bonds, and therefore Time had no power over it. If that was the case, as he grew more to fear each day that it was, perhaps the she-witch of a Seer merely was suggesting that such a creature could transport him into the Future.

And that he would be attired in his gold-painted linen robes of state and crown as he was carried on his burial litter to his catafalque beneath the stained glass windows in the upper chapel of Terreanfor.

While Talquist, stalwart atheist that he was, did not fear punishment for his crimes in the Afterlife, he was terrified of Oblivion.

"I asked Manwyn what I needed to do to attain eternal life," he said to the Diviner, pushing the abhorrent memory out of his mind. "She told me, in turn, that I must find the Child of Time."

"And do you know who or what that is? Have you ever heard of the Child of Time?"

"No. I have no idea." His mind went to Manwyn's sister, Rhonwyn, the Seer of the Present, who had indicated the whereabouts of the child, in the Orlandan keep known as Haguefort, as the night of the calendar's last day passed into the day of Yule. He had sent a cohort of his soldiers, clothed in the colors of the Lord Cymrian's regiment, who had never returned. Rhonwyn was able to tell him nothing of use after that, being limited in her sight to the Present; in his anger, he had tossed her from the window of his tower into the abyss a thousand feet below. "Is this a name or title that you have heard in your divinations, possibly at the turn of this year?"

"Indeed not," said the Diviner.

"Then what can you do to discover what this means?" Talquist swallowed, trying to keep his voice from cracking under the strain. "Can you help me, Hjorst?"

The Diviner affixed him with the steady, troubled gaze of his devouringly dark eyes for a moment. Then he exhaled.

"I will try," he said. "But we must choose the right kind of divination to undertake, as I can only perform one. Do you have any idea as to what kind you would want?"

The emperor smiled.

"The kind which will be unquestionably right. Because, Hjorst, the fate of the Middle Continent depends upon it."

25

GURGUS PEAK, YLORC

The fire was crackling merrily on the enormous hearth that Rhapsody had once observed was big enough to allow an oxcart team to be roasted whole.

She was now comfortably ensconced in front of it in a large, ugly padded leather chair with grotesquely cheerful floral pillows that her Bolg friends had kept for her from the days when she had lived within the mountain. Even after her marriage and relocation to the other side of the Middle Continent, the miserable chair had remained in the council room behind the thrones in the Great Hall, untouched and unsat-in.

Achmed still treasured the memory of the look of horror on her face when he and Grunthor had solemnly presented it to her for her birthday the year the three of them had taken the mountain, a look which had quickly melted into the sweetest of smiles amid her almost-sincere thanks. Watching her curled up in it now, beneath an equally ugly lap rug, writing furiously in a leather-bound notebook while reading from the ancient scrolls that contained the schematics of the Lightcatcher, the firelight mirroring her moods, crackling when she was scratching enthusiastically with her quill, settling into softer embers when she was lost in thought, it was almost like old times.

Almost, he thought sourly.

Meridion drowsed beneath a soft blanket on her shoulder. He had been highly entertaining earlier in the evening, mimicking her singing of her evening vespers and, later, the songs she sang to him, like a tiny mocking-bird, buzzing like a lizard and burping like a drunkard, causing Grunthor to laugh until the heavy pine council table shook. Rath, who was sitting nearer to the window, watched with what seemed to be amusement in his large black eyes, and even Achmed hid a smile from time to time at the outrageous sounds coming from the small baby.

He had driven his mother to distraction by blowing bubbles at her breast when she tried to feed him, making flatulent sounds with his tiny mouth against her skin, then giggling infectiously, until at last he settled down to vigorous nursing that caused Rhapsody to alternately wince or gasp. His feeding was followed by a ridiculously loud belch and a collapse into a milk stupor, his tiny dragonesque eyes staring blankly at the ceiling above him. When they finally closed, it was as if he had suddenly become boneless; his head hung off Rhapsody's shoulder as if tied by a thread to his neck, until she pulled him gently against her own, caressing his back as she returned to her reading.

The evening had been so comfortable and easy that Achmed had to remind himself they were at war, and preparing for it to spread into calamitous bloodshed.

A respectful tap on the doorway across the long room sounded, disturbing the reverie.

"Come," Achmed said, not looking up from his field reports.

Trug stepped into the room just inside the door.

"Majesty, there is a visitor, arrived at the northern gate—a woman, not human. She asks pardon, and says she has come to see the First Woman."

All four sets of eyes in the room locked on him.

"What?" Achmed demanded. "Repeat that."

"A woman, not human, alone, at the northern gate, requesting entry, though through apology. Has come to see the First Woman."

"Didn' make any better sense the second time," Grunthor said. "You expectin' someone, Duchess? Maybe from Tyrian?"

Rhapsody shook her head. "Of course not—I'm *hiding.* This is most disturbing."

Achmed rose and tossed his papers on the table.

"Well, let's go see who it is. Trug, call down through the speaking tube and have a full cohort armed and ready below in the breastworks at that gate, full alert." The Archon nodded and hurried out of the room.

" 'Ere, give me the lit'le prince, Yer Ladyship," Grunthor said, rising as well and holding out his enormous hands, the claws withdrawn. " 'E can sleep in my quiver." He shrugged the wide arrow sheath over his shoulder from his back and tucked it inside his arm, packing the edge of his cloak into it, then tilted it for Rhapsody to put Meridion inside. She looked askance at him, then sighed and slid the baby into it, layering his blankets carefully around him. She kissed his golden curls.

"If he starts to wake up, summon Yltha," she said as she followed Achmed out of the council room. "She might be able to keep him quiet, but I wouldn't count on it. I can't imagine how his cries will sound from the depths of your quiver—the Bolg will think we're haunted by demons again."

"Go," said Grunthor affectionately. "One too many stinkin' women around 'ere anyway." He sat back down, the quiver with the sleeping baby against his chest, and went back to his plans.

It took the better part of an hour for Achmed and Rhapsody to get all the way to the northern gate.

The northern gate was the second largest of the ramparts in Ylorc, as the old Cymrian stronghold of Canrif was called by the Firbolg. It stretched for more than two miles, growing almost organically from the stone of the mountain, with tunnels below the ground before and behind it, breastworks that could hide ten thousand soldiers, unseen. Above the ground, the gate could shelter even more, Firbolg crossbowmen that provided cover to "jumpers," soldiers who had come from the Eye clans. The Eyes were the Bolg that lived in the highest of the peaks of the western Teeth, scaling the heights with natural ease; jumpers were specially trained to hide within the crags and outcroppings of the mountainous edges by the gate, leaping from heights considered impossible by humans, adding an aerial element of attack to the subterranean one.

Two carriage lights burned in front of a small guard station inside the enormous wall of towering brick columns, reinforced with interior steel cores.

The Firbolg soldiers opened the wooden door bound in steel as the king approached.

Inside the small station, lit by oil lanterns, a woman approximately as tall as Rhapsody but substantially broader was sitting in a wooden chair. She rose as Achmed entered the room.

She was at the same time youthful and aged; there were lines at the outside corners of her eyelids, but otherwise her face was smooth. Her hair was long and light of color, with touches of gray at the temples, bound back into a long braid by a series of rawhide straps. Her features were heavier than those of human women, and Achmed instantly recognized the confusion of the Firbolg, who had not seen many of her race because her people lived in the far northern mountains, in the Deep Kingdom known as Undervale.

The kingdom of the Nain.

The visitor was the daughter of Faedryth, the Nain king.

"Lady Gyllian?" Rhapsody asked. "What—to what do we owe the honor of your presence?"

"Why are you here unannounced?" Achmed demanded. "Where is your retinue?"

The Nain princess smiled slightly, and made a small bow to the king and the Lady Cymrian.

"I am here alone, Your Majesty," she said to Achmed as she reached into the pocket of her cloak. "I came on my own, through the mountains, to bring you this, m'lady."

She pulled out a small velvet drawstring bag and offered it to Rhapsody.

"Through the mountains?" Rhapsody asked incredulously. "Alone?" She took the bag from the Nain princess; it felt heavy, as if filled with rice grains. "I am very happy to see that you are here, uninjured. What could have been worth such risk?"

"You have it in your hand."

Rhapsody looked at Achmed, who returned her blank expression. She walked over to one of the lanterns and stood where its radiance would illuminate the object in her hands. Carefully she untied the knotted cords and pulled open the velvet sack, then tilted it to catch the light.

In the dusky radiance of the oil lantern, inside the sack she saw a small landslide of what looked like colorful sand, ground finely, in every hue of the rainbow. Her brows drew together as she looked back at Gyllian.

"Ground glass?"

Gyllian smiled slightly again.

"Indeed."

"I was under the impression, given strongly to me by your father when he departed my lands, that our kingdoms are not currently on the best of terms," Achmed interrupted, annoyance in his tone. "Has something happened to change his mind?"

"Oh, absolutely not."

"Well, I assure you, nothing has changed mine. Then, with respect, why are you here?"

Rhapsody had withdrawn from the conversation. She was humming her Naming note, trying to get the ground glass in the velvet bag to tell her its story, to sing her its song. Her mind was filled with the clear, sweet tones of pure color, glowing like gemstones—rubies and sapphires, emeralds and amethysts. Then, with a shocking rush of power, she was overwhelmed, and she began to shake so violently that the bag of ground glass almost fell from her hand.

"Sweet One-God, Gyllian," she whispered, looking with wide eyes at the Nain princess, "is this—is this from the Lightforge in the Nain kingdom?"

The Nain princess nodded.

"How—how—did Faedryth—did he *destroy* it?"

"Evidently." Gyllian looked from the shocked Namer to the Bolg king, whose brows were drawn together, though his demeanor had remained calm. "I have brought you this as evidence of its destruction, so that you will know indisputably, with utter certainty, that whatever threat was posed from that instrumentality no longer exists."

"Well, that surely is reassuring," said Achmed, taking the bag from Rhapsody's trembling hand, "but I'm not certain what you want from me now. I hope you are not expecting me to follow suit."

The Nain princess eyed him steadily.

"I had no real hope that such wisdom would occur where it has not chosen to present itself up until now," she said. "I felt that you had reason to know what had taken place, and now you do. I will be on my way now; thank you for hearing me out." She turned around in the direction of the chair in which she had been sitting, where her pack was stowed on the floor.

"Your Highness, please, tarry," Rhapsody blurted. She put her hand on the Nain princess's forearm to stop her. "Unless you are desperately needed immediately in the Deep Kingdom, please consider staying for a visit." She turned rapidly away from the poisonous look Achmed shot in her direction.

"You are most kind, m'lady, but I must be returning to my homelands."

"But surely not tonight, in the dark. And surely you must need to be reprovisioned, at least. It seems a great shame to have traveled so far to only spend a few moments in Ylorc."

Gyllian's slight smile took up residence on her face again.

"You did not deem the news I have brought you worthy of the journey?"

Rhapsody's face grew solemn.

"Indeed, I most certainly do. But I think it would be an even better outcome of your undertaking if you could stay and see what is being done here, within the Teeth." She ignored Achmed's incredulous stare. "At the time your father came to Ylorc, and had, er, words with Achmed, he was under some severe misconceptions about what was being attempted. I think it would be worthwhile for you to see what is actually going on here—if only to be able to honestly assure Faedryth that his worries are groundless. Perhaps your own wisdom would be useful in a cause you may find that you actually support. And, if nothing else, you would be providing me with a brief but blessed respite from being outnumbered consistently by those of the less fortunate, and usually less pleasant, gender."

The Nain princess chuckled.

"Well, I suppose there is wisdom in waiting until morning at least," she said. "If the invitation meets with His Majesty's approval, I will gratefully accept. We can discuss the length of stay, and what you are comfortable with me doing while here, in the morning." She turned her steady gaze on Achmed, who nodded curtly, then went back to retrieve her pack.

"What exactly do you think you are doing?" Achmed said in a low tone and in the Bolgish tongue.

"Repairing the damage you have done, with my help, to the Alliance," she whispered back. "And possibly bringing in someone who has actually seen an instrumentality very much like this operated before; if, for no other reason than that, you should have thought to issue the invitation yourself."

She put out her hand to Gyllian, taking her by the shoulder, and led the Nain princess out of the guardhouse, back to the path to the Cauldron, the furious Bolg king following closely behind, reconsidering the value of old times.

26

HIGHMEADOW

$\mathcal{A}$she was deeply engrossed in the reports coming in from the battlefield commanders when Gerald Owen appeared at the door of his study.

"Pardon, m'lord?"

The Lord Cymrian looked up. His face was haggard, the chamberlain noted, his hair unkempt and his face shadowed with untold mornings' worth of unshaven beard. From the snippets of conversations Owen had caught in passing that morning, it appeared that the forces of the Alliance were once again experiencing random raids that were serving as distractions to whatever the Merchant Emperor's unknown strategic advances might be.

Having served the Lord Cymrian for more than three years, Owen knew that at least one aspect of his nature was also concentrating on a second, far more important front as well; the dragon in his blood was keeping active vigil in guarding the unseen shield of protection that his race held as a bulwark against the demonic forces of the Underworld. The Lady Cymrian had undertaken to explain this guardianship to him once, but the concept was beyond the understanding of the chamberlain.

All he knew was that it cost the Lord Cymrian dearly in lost sleep and mental exhaustion.

"Yes, Gerald?"

"The guard tower at the western gate has sent word that a woman is here to see you, or, rather, to see the Lady Cymrian. She was informed that Highmeadow is on high alert and closed to visitors, but she was most insistent. As she is said to have come from Manosse, with the blockade of the harbor, I thought perhaps you should decide if she is to be turned away."

"She is come from Manosse?"

"So she says—or at least that is the guard report."

The Lord Cymrian's brows drew together. Manosse, the land of his mother's birth and many of his own holdings, was almost half a world away on the other side of the Wide Central Sea. He shook his head and stood, stacking the tall piles of parchment neatly on his desk.

"I'll go to the gate myself; the walk would be welcome in clearing my head. Thank you, Gerald."

The chamberlain bowed and withdrew.

Ashe reached out and picked up the tiny scrap of parchment that lay within reach of his hand on the desk. It was the note of love from Rhapsody that had been delivered by the master of the rookery that morning, as notes from her were on most days; he had read it over many times already, each time he felt especially bereft or as if the world was beginning to close in around him.

A loving touchstone that kept him sane.

He hoped the ones he was sending her were having the same effect.

He rose, put it in his pocket, and left the room, closing the door behind him.

As Ashe made his way through the forest citadel of Highmeadow, his dragon nature, much more evident at the surface of his consciousness than it normally was, took notice of every infinitesimal detail of the activities going on around him. *Thirteen thousand, seven hundred seventy-four heavy crossbow bolts, sixteen hundred forty-seven ballistae shells, two hundred thirty-two light infantry breastplates,* it whispered as he passed the first in a long line of supply wagons rumbling past along the quartermaster's route. He closed his eyes for a brief moment, trying to drown out the insistent natter of the internal voice as his draconic nature made note of and enumerated every last piece of weaponry and matériel down to the tiniest lead sling bullet. He touched the scrap of paper in his pocket and deliberately made the effort to imagine Rhapsody singing to Meridion in the hidden grotto of Elysian, painting as clear and detailed a mental picture of her as he could.

He remembered her telling him that she and the baby were actually staying within the Cauldron in Ylorc, but his mind discarded the picture, preferring to concentrate on the thought of them within Rhapsody's lovely cottage, surrounded by her gardens, in the grotto instead.

Whenever his dragon sense threatened to overwhelm him, he pictured his wife in his mind. The wyrm in his blood was far more obsessed with her than with the minutiae of the world around him, and often could be diverted in its concentration when offered a thought of her to enjoy.

The unfortunate consequence of distracting the dragon in this way was the overwhelming loss it engendered. The wistful thoughts were usually successful in quelling the noise in his mind, especially when he was in complex or detailed situations that tempted the beast to count a multiplicity of objects, but afterward, the memory came up against the reality, and to have to endure losing his wife and son yet again usually left Ashe feeling hollow and heartbroken.

He returned the salutes of the guards as he neared the western gate, making note of the integrity of the high stone wall reinforced with iron, two stories in height and encircling a major part of the stronghold to the west. He climbed the nearest of the ladders and looked down at the outside of the gate.

A woman was standing with her back turned to him. She was wearing a hooded cloak, much like Rhapsody often wore when away from home out in the world; even obscured by it, Ashe could see that the visitor's height, slender build, and stance were very reminiscent of his wife's.

A cold nausea swept through him; the serving maid that Tristan Steward had brought into his household when he and Rhapsody were still living in Haguefort, who later had transitioned with him to Highmeadow, and who had turned out to be the host of a F'dor spirit, had often subtly tormented him by appearing to him in his wife's aspect, and was convincing enough in doing so that it had almost cost him his whole world. The memory of the manipulation caused his revulsion to begin to mutate into anger.

Then, as the wind changed, the woman turned toward the gate again, her face visible, and Ashe could see that while she was, like Rhapsody, of the Liringlas race, a rarity in the Known World and even more of one on the continent, she was of advanced years, reminding him more of Oelendra, the ancient hero of the Seren War who had trained Rhapsody in the use of Daystar Clarion, than she resembled Rhapsody herself.

Relief broke over him, and he made his way down the ladder and signaled for the guards to open the gate and usher her in.

Once on the ground, his relief turned to delight.

He did, in fact, recognize the elderly Liringlas woman the guards were escorting through the heavily bound doors of the gate. He had once been a guest in her household in Manosse, in the second year of his marriage when he had taken Rhapsody across the sea to meet and visit his family and ancestral lands there.

She was his wife's oldest friend from Serendair, someone she had known longer, though not as dearly, as Achmed and Grunthor.

"Analise!" he called as the woman passed through the guard station. She looked in his direction and smiled warmly, then dropped him a respectful bow.

"Lord Gwydion."

"Ashe, please," he said, embracing her. "Happy as I am to see you, what in the world are you doing here, in a time of war?"

Analise's face went slack.

"War?"

Ashe offered her his arm and led her back toward the central building of the fortress.

"I am surprised you are unaware of the buildup and hostilities here; I sent word long ago to the magisterium in Manosse."

The elderly woman blinked rapidly as they traveled through the forest.

"I do not believe that word was received, m'lord. My husband be, as you know, a member of the consulate, and if he had been aware that war was in the offing, I be quite certain he would not have agreed with my decision to come here." She looked up into Ashe's face, a head higher than her own. "Though I would have come anyway. Rhapsody—be she all right?"

"I believe so."

"Forgive me—believe so? You don't know?"

They had reached sight of the central command post; Analise paused where she stood and took in a breath.

The palace was a wonder of architecture and engineering, built from polished wood and stone to evoke and enhance the natural beauty of its forest setting, with gleaming leaded glass windows filling the building with light and breathtaking views. It was set at many interesting angles and levels, as Ashe's father Llauron's house at the Circle had been when he had served as the Invoker of the Filids and the guardian of the Great White Tree in Gwynwood, but with a more Cymrian aspect, the lost artistry of the Island of Serendair apparent in its design.

Analise, who had been born on the Island, had seen its type of design in person, rather than from historical renderings.

"Please come in, Analise," Ashe said as one of the soldiers standing guard opened the front door. "This is the chamberlain, Gerald Owen, on loan from Navarne; he is the wisest person in the fortress, so if you need anything, by all means seek his aid."

The elderly chamberlain smiled politely and bowed, then extended his arms for Analise's cloak, which she gave him. She returned her attention to Ashe.

"M'lord, I came from Manosse because, until six months or so ago, Rhapsody and I were in regular contact, exchanging letters on each Alliance flagship that sailed between Manosse and the Middle Continent. She had written to me in great excitement and joy of her pregnancy; as you know, I be, by profession, a midwife and healer specializing in young children." Ashe nodded. "But then, suddenly, the letters stopped coming, and I thought perhaps, feared really, that something had happened to Rhapsody or the baby, that she was grieving, or ill—"

"No, no," Ashe said quickly, seeing the tears that had welled up in the woman's eyes. He took her elbow and guided her gently into the library, wordlessly signaling to Gerald Owen, who departed immediately. "Come, please, Analise, let us sit. Gerald will bring us tea, and supper later." He led his wife's friend to a set of chairs across from one another in front of the cold fireplace and waited until she had taken a seat, then did so himself.

"Rhapsody has had quite a hard time of it in the last six months," he said quietly. "First, she was kidnapped by a maniac from the old world when I was away at the funeral of the empress of Sorbold, someone who had been seeking her all this time. She escaped him, endured, and prevailed, only to have the baby come early, in a manner that threatened her life and left her profoundly weak. Finally, as war neared, I needed to send them both away, into hiding. But I hear from her almost every day, in one way or another, and she and our child seem well."

"The baby was born already, then?"

"Yes."

The Liringlas woman exhaled in relief. Then her silver eyes darkened.

"A maniac, you say? From the old land?"

Ashe grimaced, then nodded. He had already said more to Analise than he normally would have, but there was comfort in speaking with someone who was unlikely to be a thrall of the demon. Analise lived on the other side of the sea, and her relationship to Rhapsody was unknown to any but the two of them on the continent.

Forbear, the dragon in his blood whispered. *You can trust no one.*

Ashe swallowed and forced the words out.

"He was a soldier when he knew her in Serendair. She hated him."

Analise went pale, and she began to tremble slightly.

"Not—not—Michael?" Her voice was a hoarse whisper.

Ashe blinked, and his face grew solemn.

"Yes, it was Michael, the Wind of Death."

Analise's hand went to her mouth. "He be still alive? Dear One-God."

"He is no longer," said Ashe bitterly. "You knew of him?"

The elderly woman nodded, her breathing somewhat lighter.

"Not of him; I knew him, in the most horrible of ways." She looked askance at the Lord Cymrian. "Rhapsody did not tell you how we met? Not even before you came to visit my family in Manosse?"

"No," said Ashe, thinking back. "I don't think she ever did. She said you were a child when she knew you, and she was older, seventeen or so, I believe, though I can't recall her saying more than that. But I am aware that the era in her life in which you must have known her was the most terrible time; I have held her through the nightmares she still occasionally has of it, though she does not speak of those days to me." His stomach turned over. "She once told me of some of the things she was forced to do in those days, and it upset me so greatly that she has shielded me, coward that I am, ever since, to spare the dragon in my blood from knowledge that might enflame it."

Tears came to Analise's eyes again.

"It is because of what she did for me in those days that I be alive and here this day," she said quietly. "Michael killed my family before my eyes, set our longhouse on fire, and took me, wrapped in my mother's bloody shawl, away with him to the city of Easton where he used me as leverage to gain her attention. My memories of that time be those of a child, because I was spared the details, as Rhapsody made sure to shield me as much as she could as well, m'lord. But I know that Michael's intentions for me were brutal, and that Rhapsody's intervention spared me from them. I do not know everything she sacrificed to save me, but on at least one occasion I saw—"

Ashe could see the lump rise in her throat, his dragon sense making note of the depth of her horror.

"I beg you, Analise, please do not tell me," he interrupted, urgency in his voice. "I am having a difficult enough time maintaining my sanity with the loss of my wife and child; please. It could very well provoke a rampage."

Analise nodded silently as the tears in her eyes spilled over and down her cheeks.

"Of course; my deepest apologies, m'lord. It is brazen past words for me to think to tell you of things she did not choose to. I only wish you to know that I had planned to come when Rhapsody was closer to the end of her pregnancy, to help, if possible, with the delivery of the baby. There is a song Liringlas women sing to one another to ease the pain of childbirth, with which I be very familiar."

Ashe smiled as a soft tap sounded at the door, and Gerald Owen came in, bearing a tea tray. "I imagine. I'm sure she would have welcomed that greatly. I am sorry for your worry, Analise, though it certainly was founded, but she has returned to health, from what I can surmise, and the baby is apparently growing stronger each day." His own throat felt a lump rise in it. "I miss them both more than I can put into words."

He picked up the cup of tea the chamberlain had placed before him as Analise did the same.

"I am sorry you traveled all this way, only to not find them here," he said after taking a draught. "If Manosse truly does not know that we are in a state of war, I fear even more for the outcome, as I had been depending on a number of warships I ordered from there and Gaematria. So, after we've finished our repast, I fear I must return to my work. If you would like to tour the fortress, I can arrange that. Then we can have supper and decide what to do about getting you home."

27

$\mathcal{A}$ few hours later and several buildings away, deep within the heavy walls and behind the even heavier doors of the high-security stockade, Tristan Steward was pacing his cell, wearing a path in the small rug on the stone floor.

Each day that passed devolved him, bit by bit, into something only vaguely human. He was allowed, in exchange for being bound and under bowman sight, to be shaved if he so desired, as well as having a one-way drain for any refuse or bodily fluids he wished to dispose of through the floor. Hot water was available to him every day through a pipe high above in the ceiling in a tiled area in the corner of his cell for cleansing himself, and fresh clothes were delivered daily also. Ashe had commented, on one of the occasions he had come down to make good on his offer of a flask of brandy now and then, that he wished he had been so incarcerated during his time in hiding.

But in spite of a relatively luxurious captivity, Tristan was going out of his mind.

If the utter solitude and ascetic living wasn't enough to drive him mad, the thin voice that scratched on windy nights at the back of his brain surely would bring it about.

Tristan.

He thought he had heard that voice before, somewhere in his broken memory, but the solid walls of the prison cell, the complete silence that the stones kept locked away with him, prevented him from deriving any tone from it. It was as if it was sounding deep within his mind, rather than coming to him through his ears.

Mostly because it was.

Tristan, come to me.

He had been hearing it, or something like it, for a very long time he realized one day, early in his captivity, just after he had finished reading one of the books Ashe loaned him to occupy his mind in his solitude. The text was a dense historical narrative, a dull retelling of the story of the exodus of the Cymrian Fleets. The only actual satisfaction he had derived from it was the picture it had placed in his mind of Rhapsody in the land of her birth. His lack of intellectual curiosity meant that he had never ascertained with which Fleet she had sailed, or anything else about her history, though he was aware that she was one of the Three that had been prophesied about at the end of the Cymrian War. But her personal history, or any other mundane detail, was not what held his interest about her.

The Lord Roland had been shocked when Gwydion had arrested him at Ashe's angry accusation of Tristan's desire to have his wife. The shock was not a result of error, but rather of degree; if the Lord Cymrian had any real notion of the intensity and depth of Tristan's obsession with the Lady Cymrian, the Lord Roland reasoned, he would have been long since buried in an unmarked grave, undoubtedly watered with Gwydion's urine. He had been consumed with an overpowering lust from the moment Rhapsody had walked away from him almost five years before, upon their meeting in which she had unsuccessfully presented a diplomatic initiative to him on behalf of the Firbolg king. His arrogant response to her, and her amused departure, had ignited an anger and passion so foolhardy in his addled brain and the lower regions of his body that he had sent two thousand men to their slaughter in the vain attempt to win back her interest.

His sexual fantasies while awake and feverish dreams while asleep were consumed with images of her, none of which he would have wanted her husband to be able to see through his eyes. Having been raised in unrivaled privelege, Tristan's powers of self-deception and self-importance led to him having no compunction about planning for a time when he might steal her away from his childhood friend, whether for a well-timed tryst or something more long-lasting that would increase his power and social standing. A realistic assessment of his chances of this happening was never in question. Married to the cold and pusillanimous woman that he was, he felt no guilt at his unclean thoughts, believing on a soul-deep level that he deserved better than what he had chosen for his life. At the very worst, he reasoned, he was engaging in harmless sexual fantasy that satisfied masturbatory needs which he alone was aware of. At best, his gloriously seedy fornication with Portia, whom Gwydion had described as being the host of a F'dor, was fueled by her encouragement of his sharing of those raunchy and deviant fantasies as she fulfilled them to the best of her abilities. Upon discovering her real nature after her death, Tristan was grateful to have escaped with his soul intact.

Or so he thought.

He had no idea that the intensity of his longing for another man's wife, predating his introduction to the demonic serving wench, was the only thing that had kept him from succumbing to the F'dor's thrall.

But as time passed in his cell, his fading ability to recall Rhapsody's face, to bring her image into his mind, or feel anything but despair left him vulnerable to the whispering voice in his mind.

Tristan, come to me.

Tristan listened carefully now, as he always did, to the toneless words in his mind. It was an all-but-unavoidable beckoning, one he could not ignore, but the solidity of his surroundings made its demand impossible to obey. The only opening in the room was a low, locked metal window on the one door, near the floor. It was unlocked from the outside, and items, mostly food, were slid in on wooden trays which needed to be returned before any new ones were sent through. Tristan had tried repeatedly but was unable to fathom any possible escape; Gwydion had made certain of the jail's impenetrability.

Now, however, the words were more than the command to come. They whispered other instructions, simple words with a harsh meaning, repeated over and over in the silence of his empty chamber.

Finally, Tristan comprehended.

When it was almost time for the evening meal to be delivered, he rose from his cot and made his way to the door. It was built from thick elm trunks bound tightly in brass bands that had been affixed with heavy bolts, the heads of which were rounded and smoothed to prevent being used to shape weapons, though the jailers were always careful not to leave anything behind that would be able to be so manufactured.

Tristan took hold of the stone walls on either side of the doorway.

His muscles strained as he gripped them tight.

Then, with all his strength, he slammed his head into the door.

Over, and over, methodically repeating the self-assault as soon as his head cleared enough to do it again.

He kept bashing his head into the door and the stone edges of the opening, gashing his forehead open and spraying blood all over the walls. Finally the world went dark around him and he fell to the floor, his head leaking a black-red river immediately in front of the metal opening at the base of the door.

So that when the guard came to bring him his supper, and unlocked that opening, he was met with an ominous cascade of gore pooling already under the metal window.

M'lord! M'lord!"

Ashe looked up in surprise from the meal he was sharing with his visitor. He smiled reassuringly at Analise, then rose, bowed politely, folded his napkin, and went to the door of his library chambers.

"Yes, Gerald?"

"M'lord, come, please. Your, er, guest in the stockade is in need of your attention."

Ashe nodded, then turned to Analise.

"I'm very sorry, I must go, though I will return as soon as I can. Please, finish and enjoy the rest of the meal; we can talk more when I return." He made a slight bow again and followed Gerald Owen through the doorway.

Ashe's dragon sense had assessed the degree of Tristan's injury even before he had entered the corridor leading to the cell.

"Tristan, you fool," he muttered as he strode down the corridor, the jailer, two guards and Gerald Owen hurrying to keep pace with him. "What sort of game are you playing this time?"

He signaled impatiently for the jailer to unlock the door, then drew his sword as the guards entered the cell. Just beyond the door, Tristan was lying in a large pool of blood, sprawled prone on the stone floor. Ashe gestured impatiently, and the two guards took the unconscious prince by the upper arms and hauled him to his feet, then over to his cot, where they propped him, slumped, against the cell wall.

The jailer slung his crossbow over his shoulder and sighted it on the prisoner, just to be sure.

Ashe crossed the room slowly, deliberation in each step. The blue waves of light emitted by Kirsdarke made the cell seem as if it were under the sea in the fading radiance of dusk.

"Exactly what do you think you accomplished with this brilliant tactic, my friend?" he asked the prince, who was coming to consciousness, wincing in pain.

The Lord Roland waved his hand in front of his face hazily.

"Let me out of here," he whispered weakly. "For the love of the All-God, Gwydion, send me home."

"I'm sorry, Tristan, but nothing has changed. I've asked for those who might be able to assess you to do so if they are in the area, but the war is in full fledge now, and there is little travel that isn't of a martial nature."

"My brother," Tristan said. "Send for Ian, I beg you, Gwydion. He is a man of the cloth, a benison. Surely he will be able to attest that I am not bound."

"You insult my intelligence, and your own," Ashe said harshly. "I am going to give you the benefit of the doubt and assume that your head injury made you disoriented enough to suggest such a silly thing to me, rather than the actual possibility that you think I might be stupid enough to agree to that. Your brother may be a holy man, or at least claim to be one, but his word is not one I would take to rule you free of demonic taint. Stop your pathetic attempts at gaining freedom and accept your fate for the time being. I have kept Madeleine and her family in the dark, passing along your missives of love and reports of your brave leadership in the buildup to the war. I have kept those contacts minimal so as not to arouse her suspicion; I suspect Madeleine is well aware of what a rotten husband you are in all aspects, no matter what she pretends."

"You—you can't keep me locked up for being an—unfaithful—husband, Gwydion," Tristan muttered. "Unless you—wish to share—the cell."

Ashe's eyes narrowed in anger.

"What is *that* supposed to mean?"

Tristan sat up as straight as he could and leveled a blurry glare at the Lord Cymrian.

"Come now, Gwydion. Your wife is not here; who are you trying to deceive? I well know what you did with Portia when Rhapsody was away in the dragon's cave, swollen with pregnancy—"

His cloudy speech ground to a halt as the point of the ancient sword of water pressed into his neck. His eyes grew wider as a hissing oath in draconic tones issued forth from Ashe's mouth.

"You disgusting piece of filth," Ashe said once his curse was finished being uttered. "You have forgotten the warnings I gave you when you were first imprisoned, Tristan; I told you that this was not ground on which you wished to tread heavily. Now, let me be specific—I do not want to hear my wife's name rolling around in your mouth or uttered by your tongue *ever again.* Do you hear me?" He punctuated his question with a deeper press of the sword against Tristan's jugular vein, causing the Lord Roland to suddenly see swimming black bands before his eyes. "You are not worthy to *think* of her, let alone speak about her. I have told you for the last time, your subterfuge *did not work.* Whatever demonic magic your servant-F'dor employed to convince me to stray from my marriage vows *did not work.* It insults Rhapsody for you to imagine that you and your demon bedwench could come even close to approximating her enough to confuse me into betraying her; the very thought is laughable." He leaned a little closer, pressing the sword deeper. "I do not ever want to hear you speak of this again. Do you understand?"

Tristan leaned his head back against the wall.

"Yes," he whispered.

Ashe turned to one of the guards. "Give him a handkerchief," he said, "and have the buttery send down some wet cloths on his supper tray." He turned to the Lord Roland once more.

"Fortunately, you have not damaged your actual skull with your idiocy," he said in annoyance. "The tendency for head wounds to bleed furiously has given palpitations to my chamberlain, but you'll get no further sympathy from me. Settle down, Tristan. You may not be enjoying my hospitality, but if you continue to be an obstreperous guest, I may give up on the possibility of having you examined to be clear of demonic taint, and just put you out of all of our misery for being a tremendous pain in the privates and a colossal waste of resources."

Tristan said nothing, but just closed his eyes.

Ashe withdrew his blade with a sweeping motion, spattering drops of water across the floor of the cell. He sheathed the sword, dousing the blue light, and signaled to the guards to remain at attention, then made his way across the cell.

He stopped at the door, where Gerald Owen had already managed to clear the pool of blood from the floor, and turned back to signal the guards that they could withdraw.

"Oh, I'm sure you'll be glad to know that there is a lovely minted roast lamb coming for your supper. I wish you a pleasant evening."

He waited for Gerald to gather the bloody rags and then slammed the cell door behind him, waiting until the jailer sealed and locked the door again.

Then followed the chamberlain back up the stairs and out into the night, back to the central building where his dinner guest awaited him.

His dragon sense, roiling and twisting as it had been since the moment that his family had departed, failed to make note of the blood that had stained the chamberlain's hands in the process of cleaning it up.

Deep within his cell, as he leaned up against the stone wall, a smile staggered over Tristan's bruised and blooded face.

He had no idea why.

28

The dragon in Ashe's blood was rising, whispering angrily when he returned to the table. He swallowed with effort and forced as pleasant a smile as he could muster before sitting down to the cold remnants of his supper and Analise again.

"I apologize," he said, moving his plate out of the way.

"No need to, m'lord," his wife's oldest friend said briskly. "I hope all is well."

Ashe smiled ruefully.

"All has not been well in a very long time, I'm afraid," he said. He picked up his wine glass and drained it quickly, then set it down again. "I have pondered your request, and, if you are still determined to help Rhapsody with the baby, I have a proposal for you."

Analise's face brightened. "Yes?"

"I want you to know from the outset that it is a grotesquely presumptuous request, and I will not feel slighted in any way if you decline." Analise nodded. "I don't believe it is safe to send you back to Manosse now. Civilian passage will be all but impossible soon; the Middle Continent is now little more than a string of armed command posts and fortifications where there used to be open grasslands for as far as the eye could see, dotted by farming settlements and villages that have now been swallowed into the outposts. My wife and son are a thousand miles away, on the other side of the Krevensfield Plain, hidden away in the mountains for their safety.

"Analise, I beg your forgiveness, but were you not as dear to my wife as you are, I would never have even told you where they have gone, because in these days of intercontinental war, there is no one I can trust, especially regarding my family. But I believe you are sincere in your offer of help, and my heart wants to believe you. I know what you have sacrificed to travel here, how fearful your family must be for your safety, but I could not even judge now whether it would be more dangerous to keep you here, or send you on. I cannot send you home; the harbor is vulnerable to attack—there is no chance of safe return at this time. So, if you are willing, here is my plan.

"Tonight, as soon as you are ready and provisions are made, if you are willing to do so, I will send you, in an armored coach, in the company of a cohort of highly trained guards, to the place where Rhapsody and our son are living now. I will not send word to her ahead of time, as I cannot take the chance of that information falling into enemy hands, for your sake and hers."

The woman's wrinkled face began to shine, but she merely nodded again.

"If you are willing, I will entrust two others with you as traveling companions. The first is an injured Firbolg woman, a midwife of great skill and stature, like yourself. Her name is Krinsel; she has undergone a horrific trauma and is healing from it, but is still frail and weak. She is in need of Rhapsody's healing talents specifically; if you would be willing to make the journey with her, I would be most grateful."

"Of course, m'lord."

"Thank you. If you will bear with me, I will introduce you to your other prospective traveling companion." He rose from his chair and rang for the chamberlain, whom he met at the door. After exchanging a few words he sat down again and poured himself another glass of wine.

A few moments later, the door opened again, and Melisande came into the room. She looked quizzically at Ashe, then came to the table and made a polite bow in Analise's direction.

The Lord Cymrian smiled easily for the first time since he had returned from the stockade.

"Lady Melisande Navarne, it is my honor, and yours, to introduce you to Analise o Serendair, a First Generation Cymrian, and your grandmother's oldest friend."

Melisande's mouth dropped open.

"Oh, my," she said. Then she blushed and curtsied more deeply.

Analise laughed aloud.

"There is no need for such a reverence, child; I be of common birth. If anything, I should bow to you, m'lady."

"Oh, please don't," Melisande blurted. "I—I don't know what I would do if you did. Are you Liringlas, like Rhapsody?"

"Aye."

"Well, then, for many reasons, I am indeed greatly honored to meet you."

"Melisande and her brother were the first two to be adopted as Rhapsody's honorary grandchildren," Ashe said to Analise. "I know her, er, grandmother misses her greatly. Melisande recently returned from a very challenging scouting mission which she accomplished with great skill; I would be grateful if you would take her with you, Analise, so that she can be of aid to Rhapsody directly."

Melisande whirled around and stared at him.

"You're sending me to Rhapsody? Really?"

"If both you and Analise agree. It's a dangerous journey, Melly, far more so than what you have just undertaken. And there is no time to ponder it, I'm afraid; Gerald has already gone to get the provisions ready. So, ladies, what do you say?"

"I'd be delighted to have my sovereign's granddaughter and scout as a traveling companion," said Analise solemnly.

The little girl was grinning from ear to ear.

"I can be ready in the span of ten heartbeats," she said excitedly.

"You will be taking Krinsel with you," Ashe said to Melisande as Analise rose from the table. "Take good care of her, Melly, just as you did in Gwynwood."

"I shall."

"I have no doubt. All right, then, thank you both for being willing to do this for my wife and child. You have my unending gratitude; I mean that literally. I will do everything I can to repay you for the rest of my life."

Analise's face lost its smile. "Indeed not, m'lord. As I've told you, it be I that am repaying a debt, a far older and dearer one than you could ever accrue with me."

The door opened once more, and Gwydion Navarne came hurriedly into the room, followed by Gerald Owen, who remained respectfully in the doorframe. Gwydion's eyes were wide with concern, but his face showed signs of great relief. He came rapidly to his sister and stood in front of her, looking down at her.

"I just got you back," he said.

"I know," Melisande answered seriously. "But in times of war, we all do what we must. Isn't that what you said when I left for Gwynwood?"

"Yes." Her brother crouched down and opened his arms to her, and she came into his embrace. "When this is over, we will go camping, and maybe take a trip across the sea."

Melisande rested her head on his shoulder.

"You always say that, and yet it has never happened."

"It has not happened yet. It will."

"I hope you're right." She pulled back and looked him in the eye. "Make our parents proud. Don't do anything stupid to besmirch our family name. I already had to defend the family honor at the Winter Carnival last year to make up for your humiliating defeat in the Snow Snakes competition."

Gwydion laughed, as did Ashe and Analise. He swallowed hard, choking on a knot that had risen in his throat. "I will do my best to not dishonor you, Melly."

"Good." She came out of his embrace and looked across the room to where Gerald Owen was standing in the doorway. Her face lost its smile as she locked eyes with the elderly chamberlain who had given loyal and loving service to three generations of her family, who had been the only true constant in her life from the time she was born. The elderly man smiled encouragingly.

Melisande ran to him, threw her arms around his waist, and burst into tears.

Slowly and with great effort, the chamberlain crouched down and took her into his own arms.

"There, now, m'lady, there's no need for tears. You are about to embark on yet another grand adventure; you and I both know how much your soul longs for adventure. I am very much looking forward already to hearing all about your travels when you return, safe and sound, when we are at peace once again—forever this time."

Melisande nodded wordlessly.

"Melisande assures me she can be ready in the span of ten heartbeats, Gerald," Ashe said humorously.

Gerald Owen coughed politely, but merely smiled. The others broke into laughter.

The chamberlain extricated himself gently from her embrace, then stood creakily. He bent forward and whispered in her ear.

"Your favorite pillow and shoes, muff, and cape are already in the coach."

Melisande's face broke into a broad smile again.

"Thank you, Gerald." She walked back over to her guardian and looked up at him.

"Give me whatever hugs or kisses you want me to pass along to Rhapsody and Meridion, and I will be sure to do so," she said sensibly.

Ashe swept her off her feet and into a warm embrace.

"Thank you—convey the deepest love in my heart to my wife and son." He hugged her vigorously, then put her back on the ground without letting go.

"May you grow up to be just like her," he murmured in her ear, "and may he grow up to be just like you."

As the carriage rolled into the darkness, Gwydion Navarne stood at the window and watched it go as it took away the last living member of his natal family.

He fought down the memories that rose from the dusty vault of his seven-year-old soul, recalling the words his mother had said to him before she climbed into just such a carriage and embarked on her journey to town to buy his one-year-old sister her first pair of baby shoes.

Be a brave little man. Remember I love you.

She had never returned, except in pieces, her head sawed viciously from her body.

His stomach rushed into his mouth, and he ran to the privy closet, where he vomited. Then he stood, pumped water into the basin, and splashed it on his face.

And returned to the command center.

PART FIVE

The Darkness at the Edge of the Plain

29

BASILICA OF LIANTA'AR, SEPULVARTA

$\mathcal{H}$alf a thousand leagues to the south, the glowing light from atop the Spire filled the shadowy basilica, making the platinum band around the altar gleam eerily.

The Diviner's eyes gleamed similarly in the darkness.

"Well," he said finally, "probably the safest sort of divination would be to use cleromancy, the undertaking of a sortilege." When he saw only a blank look on Talquist's face, he hurried to explain. "Sortition is the casting of sortes, or lots, and reading the random patterns that they have taken."

"Like coins or dice?"

"Yes—though I tend to use bones or sticks—it's more within my view of nature, the primitive, wilder sort from the cold lands, rather than that of, say, the Invoker of the Filids, whose forest lands might yield the use of beans, lentils, rocks, or animal spoor. It's possible I could get a glimpse of the general direction in which this so-called Child of Time has gone."

Talquist struggled to keep his lip from curling in disgust. "That seems like it could be widely interpreted," he said. "I'm afraid I need more detailed guidance. Do you have something else that might be a bit more specific?"

The Diviner considered.

"If that's the case, we may need to undertake an augury, but we won't be able to do that tonight."

"Why not?" Talquist's words came out in a voice he regretted, tense and demanding. He swallowed at the sight of the blackening of the Diviner's expression, and tried again. "I am so sorry, Hjorst; I didn't mean for my words to sound so harsh. I fear I am anxious."

"I cannot accommodate you tonight because I need materials that I do not currently have, as I explained to you before. I generally only carry with me what I need for rhabdomancy, or dowsings—you've seen me perform one of these before, I believe."

Talquist nodded. "Was that when you gathered the staves and let them fall, determining from their pattern where the lost merchant fleet was, thirteen years ago?"

"No, I had forgotten you were witness to that. I was referring to the meeting in Cariproth, four or so years ago, when I used the silver willow branch to locate Jurun's grave, as well as finding the headwaters of the underground feeder stream for the Erim Rus, the Blood River, for the duke of Yarim."

"Ah, yes. Of course."

"But that will be of no use to you now. You are in need of a full augury, most likely an extispicy. It would, more specifically, be a form of haruspicy, hepatomancy or perhaps hepatoscopy, followed by an auspicy."

The Merchant Emperor swallowed his building wrath and struggled to speak calmly.

"My friend, unlike those who are mistaken into believing that the primal nature of your rituals comes from a primitive view of the world, I am well aware of what a learned and scholarly man you are. You are, therefore, speaking to me in words that come into my ears as little more than babble. Please, speak down to me, imbecile that I am; be clear and simple."

The Diviner eyed him darkly.

"I cannot even begin to tell you how uncomfortable all of this is making me, Talquist. That you are unfamiliar with the practices is perhaps yet another sign that I should not be performing them for you. The risk to both of us, as I believe I have mentioned, is very great, and is not limited merely to misdirection if the augury fails."

"Please, my friend, I know this," Talquist said, fighting desperation, "but you are truly my last hope. Once, long ago, I found a rare object that captured my soul; it was unlike anything I had ever seen before. I am a common, unpoetic man, Hjorst; I was not born into royal bloodlines in the rich, earthy world of golden eagles and frozen ice peaks that you are blessed to inhabit, nor the verdant forests lands, steeped in magic, that are the realm of the Lord Cymrian. I am a common workman, bred of the lifeless and barren soil of the desert—a man with a limited life span, but limitless vision. Not the sort who would ever fall in love with an inanimate object—but I did, and I gave a major portion of my youth and halest years searching the corners of the world to discover what it was. I apprenticed in every cathedral, every basilica, every library, every museum, every hall of study that would have me, as well as the bellies of ships and the hovel kitchens of army barracks—until I finally found what I was looking for.

"With that discovery came another, even more significant one—the discovery of my destiny, what I was born to accomplish with my life. And it is highly out of odds with my birth, my upbringing—because, if you will forgive my vanity, I, like you, have a holy purpose to my life. I was born to bring Sorbold back to its glory, and to join hands across the continent with you, and perhaps Beliac, to rule where the apostates now reign. I am destined to uproot the false All-Gods and One-Gods the Cymrians have enthroned, and to bring this land back to its natural magic, its intrinsic beauty, in nature, in the base, perverse, glorious realm that the Creator provided for us. I was born to this—*born* to it—but I was born too late. The work that lies ahead of me is the task of five men's lifetimes; even Leitha, had she any sense of the urgency of this calling, did not live long enough in almost one hundred years, to accomplish what needs doing, restoring Sorbold before it crumbles into the desert sand. I do not seek immortality for my own ends, for my own power—but to set about and finish the task of rescuing the land I love from those who would grind it further into powder under their heels before my life comes to an end. Help me, Hjorst, I beg you. *Help me.*"

Silence danced among the shadows of the gargantuan basilica.

Finally the Diviner sighed.

"Very well, Talquist. As much as I dread it, I will grant your request."

Relief broke over the Merchant Emperor's face, and the furrows and lines that had riven it a moment before disappeared into the heavy jowls and broad forehead once again. "Thank you, thank you my friend. This will be the first step in our shared destiny of saving our continent, and the lands we love."

"I hope you are right," said the Diviner seriously. "You and I may share a love of fine potables and the desire to ensure the safety of our peoples, but we differ highly about our fundamental outlooks on life, Talquist. I would never seek immortality for any purpose; the very thought of it makes my blood run cold.

"Now, this is what we will do. Tomorrow, at this very time, you will bring me a sacrificial animal—I will give you details in a moment. I will perform a hepatoscopy, an examination of the animal's lungs, the intestines, and the liver, and anything else of interest or worry that might be found in the cavity. We will stand vigil afterward, and then I will attempt an auspicy at dawn, a reading of my first sight of the flight patterns of whatever birds take to the morning wind. That is the best that I can do for you, Talquist—and I will be requiring you to take on some of the tasks in the ritual that carry the most risk."

"Of course. Absolutely. Thank you. Now what sort of animal must I procure?"

"It must be ritually pure—most often this indicates a young animal, a lamb, a fledgling bird, something that is untouched in every way, virginal, if you will. Do you understand? If you are uncertain of the animal's origin, or its history, it would be better to obtain something very low on the Ladder of Life, like a minnow or a tadpole; it's spring, and they should be easy to come by, even in this destroyed city."

"Ladder of Life?"

"Yes," said the Diviner, "though you are not of the True Faith, I assume you can make the distinction between those creatures at the base of the Ladder, the simple, primitive forms of life like worms, as opposed to those on higher steps, like birds, or even higher, in the warm-blooded realm, such as the lamb I mentioned. The more complex an entity is, the more power there is in examining its entrails, but it has its risks as well; age and complexity means that the opportunity for impurity to have been experienced is greater."

The Merchant Emperor's eyes took on a deeper twinkle.

"So I am searching for an animal that is as old and complex a being as possible, but that has never been touched?"

"Or fed anything with another's blood. You need an animal that eats grass and grain, not a predatory animal like a cat or a wolf. Those beasts are highly powerful in divination if you can get them as nursing kittens or pups, before they have consumed meat or blood-milk from their mothers, but the chances of that are quite small. You should speak to the sexton of this basilica, Talquist; even though the Patriarchy doesn't practice augury, if I'm not mistaken, ritually pure beasts are used as celebratory decorations in some of the holiday rites. The clerical populace of any of the Cymrian elemental basilicas, whether Lianta'ar, or Vrackna in Bethany, or Ryles Cedelian in Bethe Corbair, or even Terreanfor in your own kingdom, is very aware of ritual purity; everyone from the sexton to the serving maids are vegetarian and celibate. Of course, as a result, they are a very limited group of people, and clearly have no problems leading miserable lives."

Talquist laughed. "I shall procure a sacrifice as pure and complex as I can find, Hjorst."

The amusement of his last joke fled the Diviner's eyes.

"You will do more than that. You will need to find a cloth fifty knuckles square of pure, white flax, unbleached and unpolished—I suggest you ask the sexton for that as well. If it needs to be sized, have him cut it only using silver implements." The emperor nodded. "You will use that cloth to peacefully smother the sacrifice; normally I would do that, but as it is, I am uncomfortable enough spilling the blood and doing the augury, neither of which can be done for me. It is of the greatest importance—I cannot overstate this, Talquist—that you spill no blood, not even enough to cause a bruise, in the killing of the sacrificial animal. There is skill and training in doing this, so you may wish to obtain several birds or lambs, in case you are not gentle enough the first time you try. I also suggest you obtain some herbs that induce sleep and dose the creature first—passionflower or valerian can be brewed into a strong tea and fed to the animal an hour or so before it is to be sacrificed. Cover whatever the animal breathes through with the flax sheet, take its life gently, and leave its body, unblooded, on the altar. And try to time the smothering to be as close to when I arrive as possible; the longer the beast is dead, the less accurate the reading will be."

The emperor nodded again.

"Finally, please order your guards to keep everyone out of this basilica— everyone, Talquist. I will come at noon tomorrow and prepare the altar; I will write a list of the things I need for the sexton to provide as well, so he may leave them at the door in the care of the guards. When I have finished the prayers I will say before I leave here, there must be no other sound than that of my footsteps as I go. Do you understand?"

"Yes," Talquist said. "I am ever so grateful for all of your assistance and your wisdom, Hjorst. Thank you, thank you."

"Do not thank me yet," the Diviner warned. "I will entreat the Creator that the deviations we are allowing to the ritual will not result in calamity for either of us, or for our lands. All of those things are possible with even one misstep. The more meaningful the sacrifice, the safer we will be, so if you are sure that a lamb or another herbivore is ritually pure, that would make a better offering than a minnow. But *only* if you are certain it is pure."

"I will go now and inform the guards that they are to allow you to close the doors of the basilica upon your exit, and that no one is to enter until you return," said the Merchant Emperor. "After that, I will go to the manse and pass along your instructions to the sexton; if you write your list back at the guesthouse it can be delivered to the manse this night or in the morning, whatever you prefer."

"Very good. Sleep well, Talquist; it is my dearest hope that we both will do so tomorrow night as well."

"And mine. Good night, Hjorst. Thank you again."

The emperor took his leave quickly and quietly, leaving the Diviner staring silently up at the glittering star at the top of the Spire through the glass of the dome high above him.

Talquist stepped out of his carriage and nodded imperceptibly at the soldiers standing guard at the door to the manse, the low stone building that had been the Patriarch's residence, and that of his clergy, prior to the assault on Sepulvarta, and all the way back to the founding of the city.

"Bring the sexton out to me," he said.

One of the soldiers bowed quickly and disappeared into the building. Talquist turned away and stepped back to the edge of the street, admiring the rubble that was still in the cobbled gutter from the assault that had driven Constantin into exile, and most likely to death in the desert.

The stars of that desert's sky winked at him from the edges of the bright glow of the Spire; humorously Talquist winked back, though a sense of reverence was in his gesture. He had always loved watching the stars come forth in the deep blue of a Sorbold twilight; he could hardly wait to see them the next night as they shone down on him, one step closer to being the true Emperor of the Sun.

Behind him he heard the door of the manse open again.

Following the soldier out of the building was a tall, thin middle-aged man with a crown of even thinner white hair and dark brows that almost matched the black cassock he wore.

"The sexton of Lianta'ar, Majesty," the soldier said softly. Talquist nodded, and the man hurried back to his post.

"Your name?"

"Gregory."

"Gregory, you will be receiving a list, either tonight or tomorrow morning, of ceremonial implements and other materials needed by our guest, the Diviner of the Hintervold, for one of his holy rituals. Obtain and assemble those materials as quickly and carefully as possible; ritual purity is of the utmost necessity. Additionally, I need you to procure a cloth fifty knuckles square of pure, white flax, unbleached and unpolished. If it needs to be sized, cut it only using silver implements. Do you understand these instructions exactly?"

"Of course."

Talquist did not like the sexton's tone, nor did he appreciate the lack of subservient address.

"*Majesty*," he said, his voice quiet and deadly.

The sexton bowed quickly. "Majesty."

Mollified, Talquist looked about him. Seeing no one within earshot, he stepped slightly closer to the sexton.

"I also need for you to bring me one of your female acolytes, a young one that you know to be ritually pure, meaning, for clarity, that she is a virgin and has never consumed meat. You will bring her to the front entrance of Lianta'ar tomorrow evening at sunset. Is this clear?"

"Yes, of course, Majesty," Gregory said.

"Do you have a choice of vegetarian virgins, or just one?"

"Anyone living within this manse meets those standards."

The emperor smiled.

"Then, by all means, pick the prettiest one," he said. "Good night, Gregory."

He turned and left the manse, whistling as he made his way back to the guesthouse in the dark, following the stars all the way there.

30

THE CAULDRON, YLORC

The door of Rhapsody's room in the mountain vibrated as a great pounding sound shattered the silence of her study.

Meridion woke with a start, making the harsh infant sounds that signaled a windup to full-blown crying. His mother sighed.

"Come in," she said as she put down the quill with which she had been scratching symbols into parchment and glanced apologetically at Gyllian, who was working on a similarly bound sheath of paper. The Nain princess smiled and went back to her work, oblivious to the noise of the baby. Rhapsody rose and picked up Meridion from his cradle.

Grunthor's wide head, wearing a wider grin, appeared from behind the door at about half the height of it.

"Special deliv'ry, Duchess," he said as solemnly as a man with a smile wreathing the entirety of his face could manage. "Came with the mail caravan this mornin'."

"That's odd; I didn't order anything, Ashe didn't mention sending me anything, and no one else should know I'm here."

"*I* know you're here!" came a high, familiar voice from behind the door. It pulled open wider and Melisande Navarne burst into the room, running straight for her grandmother, whose face was ringed a moment later by an even brighter smile.

"Melly! Oh my goodness!" Laughing, the Lady Cymrian bent to embrace her adopted grandchild, holding the now-quiet baby down so that Melisande could see him. "What are you doing here?"

"She's accompanying me," said Analise, stepping into the room.

Rhapsody's face went blank; she blinked, lost for words for the moment. "Analise? You—you're *here*? What on earth—"

"I told you two years ago that when you were ready to bring your first child, and all your other children, into the world, I would be there to attend you," the Liringlas midwife said, her weathered face shining brightly. "While I missed the actual blessed event, I be come to assist you with this beautiful boy in any way I can." She came into Rhapsody's still-stunned embrace and looked down into the little face grinning toothlessly up at her. "Though you seem to be doing quite well without my aid."

"I cannot believe you're here," Rhapsody said, putting Meridion into Analise's arms. "All the way from Manosse? And at a time of war? Gods, you ran the blockade?"

"I, like the rest of Manosse, had no idea there *was* a blockade," Analise said, smiling back at the baby, who was greeting her with humorous buzzing sounds and cooing. "Your husband ruled out the possibility of my return for the time being, and decided to send us here to aid you, and, like you, to take refuge from the hostilities back in Roland."

"Not all of us," Melisande said, wrapping her arms around Rhapsody's waist again. "One of us is just coming home." She nodded toward the door; when the Lady Cymrian looked up, she saw a tall, wiry figure wrapped in a cloak of mist standing there. Her smile drained away.

"Ashe? No, it's not possible." She gently freed herself from Melisande's stranglehold and came cautiously across the room until she stood in front of the figure. Then she remembered her conversation in the blue spectrum of the Lightcatcher with her husband a few weeks back. "Krinsel?"

The figure took down the hood of the cloak, revealing the Bolg woman's scarred face, her horrifyingly damaged eye. Rhapsody's own eyes welled with tears at the sight, but she resisted the urge to embrace the Bolg woman, understanding the differences in their cultures and fearing causing her more pain. She swallowed and merely nodded. "The king is aware that you are back?"

The Firbolg midwife nodded slightly in return.

"Excellent. I am so glad to see you." She turned and introduced the three women to the Nain princess, then went to Grunthor, who was leaning on the wall by the door, still grinning, and hugged him.

"You could not have brought me a better gift," she said. "Thank you."

The Sergeant-Major coughed, hiding his smile.

"Well, then, Oi'm off to the garrison," he said in mock gruffness. "Too many smelly women in 'ere." He pulled a blue light globe from his pouch and handed it to Analise. " 'Ere," he said, "Oi can see you're one of them Glass-Lirin, like the Duchess. Used ta give 'er these when she first came to live inside the mountains; Oi know bein' away from the sky makes you all nervous an' twitchy." He bowed politely and took his leave, closing the door behind him and leaving Rhapsody in the circle of women who were the closest female friends and family she had in the world.

She turned and embraced Melisande Navarne again.

"I am so glad to see each of you that I don't have words to express myself," she said to the three women. "And I look forward to hearing all your news, which we can accomplish over supper. But first, please, tell me about Ashe, how he's faring—I miss him so terribly. Then I want to go with you, Krinsel, back to your quarters and see what I can do to help aid with healing the wounds you received saving my life, and Meridion's."

She turned to Gyllian.

"And tonight, we have an appointment—one you came a very long way to attend."

The Nain princess smiled.

31

That evening, when Meridion and Melisande were in bed for the night, Analise was engrossed in her Lirin devotions, and Krinsel was resting in the hospice after the first of her musical healings, Rhapsody and Gyllian made their way to the heart of the Cauldron, to the room beneath Gurgus Peak where the Lightcatcher was.

"I thank you for staying long enough to see this moment," Rhapsody said to the Nain princess. "I hope you will be able to see not only the safe use of the Lightcatcher, but perhaps bear witness to its necessity, so that you may reassure your father that it really is being operated with all appropriate caution."

Gyllian nodded uncommittally.

Achmed and Grunthor were waiting in the antechamber, as was Rath. The Patriarch was within the inner chamber, conducting his evening prayers.

The Sergeant-Major bowed politely to Gyllian, then scooped Rhapsody up into his arms.

"After all this time, ya ready, miss?"

Rhapsody choked as he squeezed her, then chuckled.

"Yes—so far the blue spectrum of the Lightcatcher has let me scry into places I know, to see someone I'm related to, that I share a soul with," she said as the giant Bolg put her down again. "It will be interesting to see if it really can give us vision into a place we are unknown to, or where we would be unwelcome."

"And if it can be done without their knowledge," Gyllian noted. "When you have visited with your husband, he is able to see you, to speak to you in return. If what you are attempting is of a clandestine nature, it is imperative that you not be seen, or caught. This was something Faedryth was never willing to try, your belief to the contrary notwithstanding, Your Majesty."

Achmed merely listened without comment.

"My ability to communicate directly with Ashe may have a great deal to do with the fact I share his name, and his child," Rhapsody said. "I know very little of Sorbold and even less of Talquist. This is an area of Naming I am uncertain of—I just hope that if I fail in the scrying, I don't do any damage."

"Is there any chance that this may leave Ylorc vulnerable to be seen inside of, should we misguess?" Achmed asked Gyllian.

The Nain princess looked at him seriously.

"That was Faedryth's fear," she said. "Whether it was founded or not, I have no idea. Understand that, though my father built the Lightforge for Gwylliam, he had only a rudimentary understanding of its lore. Gwylliam himself was the architect and the engineer of it; the Lord Cymrian had that mechanical knowledge, as well as the lore that is known only to kings and rulers with a Right of Command—and, of course, Namers." She smiled at Rhapsody, who grinned in return. "So Faedryth worked from Gwylliam's documents, and under his tutelage—the Lord Cymrian was apparently involved in each detail of the process, which is why all the documents you have found are scribed in his hand. Faedryth's greatest contribution was the understanding of the colors, the hues themselves. Gwylliam could not have determined their true 'names,' if you will; only Nain have the eyes for judging the precise hue of the pure color spectrum, because it requires a different kind of lore."

"What kind?" Achmed demanded.

"The ability to see true color comes from the knowledge of gemstones," Gyllian said. "The Earth itself holds that secret—certain precious stones, in their purest form, are the precise colors in the spectrum. There are many tales of why, but it best might be explained that, just as with names, which can be spoken commonly as nicknames, or partial titles, or aliases, only those trained in the actual lore of Naming can know a true one. There are many different variants in the colors of gemstones—but only one true hue for each of the most precious stones. Did it ever seem strange to you that, among all the gems and types of stones that exist in the wide world, only a few are considered 'precious,' and why?"

"Yeah," Grunthor said. "They sing diff'rent, those gems."

Gyllian smiled. "Indeed," she said. "Bolg and Nain, those who are children of the Earth, can hear those songs that I expect are silent to those without that lore. Gwylliam was, by birth, human and Lirin. Neither of these bloodlines granted him knowledge of the Earth. As vain as it may seem, he could never have built the Lightforge without Faedryth, who may not have understood the reasons for its design, but was the only one who could have determined the true color of the glass to make it work. The woman who fired the plates for you could only do so because you had Faedryth's color keys, Your Majesty. Had my father taken them when he left Canrif forever in disgust, this effort all would have been for naught. The only reason Faedryth could duplicate the Lightforge in Undervale is because he had built Gwylliam's, and knew the true colors for the glass, because he understands the secret of the gemstones. When the color is true in one of the precious stones, it sings, at least to ears that can discern it.

"And so, in answer to your question, I do not have any knowledge of the actual lore of the Lightcatcher, because that lore is ancient, and known only to Namers."

"And dragons," Rhapsody interjected. "As the original race sprung from the element of Earth, they say that gemstones come from the blood they leave behind when they die. They believe that is their only immortality, because they think they have no other soul. Now I understand how this is all tied in; the Wyrmril guard the Earth from the F'dor, and are the keepers of that Primal Lore of color—because, in many cases, it comes from their very blood."

"I do know Faedryth worried that scrying through *Brige-sol*, the blue spectrum, might be a two-way venture," Gyllian continued. "I believe the last time he used the Lightforge, he got the distinct impression that he was being scryed in return—and by something that all of us fear waking within the Earth."

"No wonder he was willing to reduce it to ground glass," Achmed said. "Well, let's see if the Patriarch is finished with his prayers, or whatever it is he is doing in there, and get on with it."

The Patriarch had finished his evening devotions when the women, the two Bolg, and the Dhracian entered the room beyond the Great Hall in Gurgus Peak.

"Are we disturbing you, Your Grace?" Rhapsody asked.

"Not at all, m'lady," Constantin replied. "Are you ready?"

"I hope so." She stepped up to the table, the others watching her intently.

Constantin, who had been owned by Talquist only a few short years and a lifetime before, had told her that the name Rev-Penthor had been used about the Merchant Emperor among the members of the Mercantile when he was the guild hierarch prior to his first Weighing on the Scales of Jierna Tal that proclaimed him emperor. Rhapsody swallowed hard and sang the note for *Brige-sol♯*.

The diamond Constantin had been blessing with the memory of light gleamed brightly in the darkness of the enormous room, lit only by lanterns at the far edges of the circle and the light of the stars.

Then a blue light appeared in the enormous room.

Rhapsody exhaled. She thought back to her days training with Oelendra, the Lirin champion, her mentor and friend who had trained her in the sword and taught her so much about life.

How can I find the stars in daylight? she had asked her mentor.

Oelendra had smiled.

Just because you can't see the stars, Rhapsody, doesn't mean they cease to be there. The knowledge of their placement in the heavens, and their names, transcend the need for darkness. But you have to be able to find them, and know where they are. Even without seeing them.

Though she was unsure of his True Name, or where he was, she cleared her mind and spoke what she believed it to be into the filmy blue light raining gently down from above.

Talquist Rev-Penthor, she sang. *Emperor of Sorbold.*

She was fairly certain she saw Constantin's lip curl.

An image formed in the light.

The group stared at the moving picture hovering above the table.

"Sweet All-God," the Patriarch murmured. "That bloody bastard's in Lianta'ar—in Sepulvarta."

"What's he doing?" Gyllian asked quietly.

Achmed stared into the light with his mismatched eyes.

"It looks like he is making a sacrifice on the altar of the basilica."

32

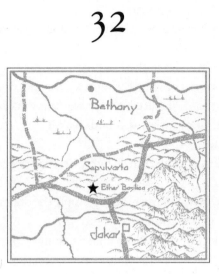

LIANTA'AR, SEPULVARTA

*W*hen the Diviner returned to the basilica the next evening, dressed in his robe of polar bear fur and a hat with a life-sized representation of an eagle with talons ascendant, he took the time to question the soldiers who were standing guard at the doors.

"Has anyone come in here since I left this afternoon?"

"Yes, m'lord. The emperor entered a short time ago, with the sexton of the basilica, who was carrying a basket of implements, and a young woman in robes, an acolyte, I believe."

The Diviner's brows drew together.

"A woman? That's odd. Stand aside."

The soldier nodded and opened the basilica door for him.

The Diviner walked through the shadows of the narthex to the open sanctuary, glowing as it had been the night before in the light of the star atop the Spire.

Talquist stood behind the stone altar atop the cylindrical rise, reverently looking above him at the dome of the basilica.

A body rested on the altar, covered in the sheet of white flax.

A body, though slight, far too large to be a lamb.

The Diviner's throat went dry.

"In the Creator's name, what have you done, Talquist?" he said as he came to the bottom of the cylindrical rise.

The emperor's face was bathed in ethereal light.

"You said the more complex the animal, the more accurate the divination would be," he said, his eyes still above him. "As high as possible on the Ladder of Life, that is what you said, isn't it?"

"I—I didn't mean—"

"You said it needed to be ritually pure, virginal, never having consumed meat, did you not?"

"Yes." The Diviner began to slowly climb the stairs leading up to the altar where the emperor stood.

"Well, I assume a human is the highest rung of the Ladder of Life."

"Again, yes." The Diviner stopped on the top step.

Finally the Merchant Emperor broke his gaze away from the sky and looked directly at the Diviner.

"I need for this augury to be as complete and as accurate as it is possible to be, Hjorst," he said softly. "There is too much riding on this not to do everything possible to assure success."

The Diviner, a man born of a harsh clime and harsher realities, merely shrugged.

"I told you I would not judge you, Talquist," he said. "If the fate of the continent is at stake, what's the life of a virgin in the grand scheme of things?"

"My thoughts exactly," Talquist said.

"And were you able to accomplish the smothering without spilling any blood?"

"Not even a bruise. The tea was most helpful in that; thank you for the suggestion. The sexton had dried passionflower in abundance; apparently they use it in the hospice to comfort the pain of the dying. How appropriate."

"Enough talk," the Diviner said impatiently. "Stop cluttering up the air; you will befuddle the augury." He approached the altar and took hold of the white flaxen sheet, then pulled it down gently.

The light of the Spire shone just as gently down on the face of the sacrifice, eyes closed in endless repose, the body naked beneath the sheet.

Against his will, the Diviner gasped.

It was the sexton of the basilica.

$\mathcal{H}$undreds of leagues away, in the tower of Gurgus Peak, a ragged breath came forth from the Patriarch as well.

"Sweet All-God," he whispered, his voice hoarse. "It's Gregory—he's sacrificed *Gregory*."

Grunthor and Achmed exchanged a glance. They had both met the sexton on the occasion when they, with Ashe, had come to Sepulvarta with the corpse of one of the kidnappers who had helped Michael, the Wind of Death, take Rhapsody hostage. The Patriarch had wrung every infinitesimal drop of blood from the dead man, then summoned the memory of what he had heard in the last moments of his life, which had happened to be Rhapsody's own voice.

The sexton had assisted the Patriarch with a ritual that was disturbingly similar to what looked like was about to be undertaken now.

Grunthor looked at the two women watching the images moving in the blue light of *Lisele-ut*. While Gyllian's face betrayed no emotion, Rhapsody's was white. He stepped behind her, put one enormous hand on her shoulder, and squeezed gently, careful not to scratch her with his claws.

$\mathcal{W}$hat have you done with the young woman?" the Diviner demanded.

Talquist looked surprised. He turned and nodded to the area in the back of the basilica.

"Nothing, yet," he said, a smile returning to the corners of his mouth. "She's in out in the narthex, sleeping. We had a veritable little tea party after the sexton set up your implements."

"You may very well have compromised your own outcome, Talquist," the Diviner said darkly. "I told you a *lamb*, not a man of middling years. Do you have any idea how likely it is that he is ritually impure?"

"Highly unlikely, actually," Talquist said defensively. "He was committed to the service of the All-God in this very basilica as a toddler; he has never lived outside of the manse. He assured me that no one living there, which included himself, was anything but a virgin and a vegetarian. I assume that his advanced age, along with his humanity, make him the most powerful, ritually pure receptacle possible—am I incorrect?"

The Diviner exhaled. "We shall see. Let us hope that your hubris has not been both of our undoing."

He turned to the implements that Gregory had provided—a ritual vessel known as a lachrymatory, four large linen sheets, three large canopic urns, a sewing needle and heavy thread, a brazier filled with incense, an enormous cinerary bowl, often used for storing ashes, a bag of cedarwood flakes and dried rose petals, and a series of horrifically shaped knives, saws, and tongs of all sizes.

"Light the brazier," he instructed Talquist while he gently uncorked the lachrymatory, covering its mouth with his fingers and drawing forth some of the oil in it. He anointed his eyes and ears, and Gregory's mouth and abdomen; then, as the smoke from the burning incense began to rise, he picked up the first of the thin knives.

"Step away from the altar," he said to the emperor. "Ask your question—and take care with your phrasing; you will only have one chance."

Talquist took a step back, lost in thought. Finally he spoke.

"Who and where is the Child of Time, and what must I do with or to it in order to successfully achieve immortality, without aging, for myself?"

The Diviner held the knife up to the dome of the basilica, then placed the tip of the knife at the base of the corpse's throat. He then proceeded to slice open the sexton's thoracic and abdominal cavities, using the implements of the gruesome ritual, all the while chanting the prayers of his office. As if in a trance, he muttered the words to the rite in a language Talquist had never heard as he methodically removed lungs, liver, and intestines, depositing each in a separate canopic urn. With great care he examined each organ and the cavity from which it had come, finally reassembling the flaps of skin and wrapping the bleeding body in the heavy linen sheets. He placed his index and middle fingers on the sexton's now-bloodless lips; his eyes rolled back as his head tilted upward.

Around the Diviner's head, a circle of smoke from the brazier seemed to gather. An alien voice, both the Diviner's own and yet very different, came forth from his mouth.

"The Child of Time hides from the eye of man; who, where, and what it is remains unknown. But if it can be found, an ageless immortality can be achieved by one who eats the beating heart of the Child of Time at the moment between life and death. Then the hold that Time itself has over the one who consumes the heart of the Child will shatter, and the Child's lore shall be conveyed unto his very blood as it dies."

Grunthor's other hand quickly came to rest on Rhapsody's shoulder, and he tightened his grip as he watched the blood drain from her face.

"Shhh, darlin'," he whispered. "Hold on, now."

Achmed saw the blue light begin to dim; he looked at Gyllian, who had noticed the same thing and nodded slightly.

The circle of smoke vanished.

The Diviner looked down and shook his head, his eyes returning to normal.

"The best we could hope for," he said softly to Talquist, who was still standing away from the altar, listening intently. "You must have been right about this poor sexton; a middle-aged virgin whose lips never touched blood meats or strong drink. The only thing more horrible than the way he died was the way he lived. Oh, well."

"I suppose the only sex the man had in life was in his title," Talquist said humorously.

The Diviner scowled at the emperor. Carefully he poured more oil from the lachrymatory over the organs in the canopic urns and lit them on fire. As they burned, he filled the sexton's abdomen with the cedarwood flakes and the rose petals, then proceeded to stitch the corpse up, working as carefully as a tailor on a robe for a royal court.

When at last he was done, he wrapped the rest of the linen sheets around the body, then combined the ashes of the organs in the cinerary bowl, which he handed to Talquist.

"Take these out with you when you leave and commit them to the wind," he said brusquely. "I will stand vigil until morning. Then you must have the body taken and ritually burned; given the death and destruction that has been visited upon this city, I assume they know how to do that."

Talquist ignored the slight.

"I thank you most assuredly for your efforts on my behalf, Hjorst," he said quietly. "Did you get any sense, any fragment of the whereabouts or identity of the child—if it's a boy or a girl?"

"None whatsoever." The Diviner's voice was testy.

Talquist trod lightly. "I have reason to believe it is a baby, an infant of approximately four months of age. No idea of the name or the sex, but I had some indication that it might be the child of our friends, the Lord and Lady Cymrian."

"Well, that would prove most interesting if it were true," said the Diviner, continuing to wipe the blood off the altar.

"Indeed. I sent a cohort several months ago to Haguefort, which, sadly, never returned. The intelligence says that the Lord Cymrian has moved on to his new fortress at the site of the old House of Remembrance—but that there is no sign of the Lady or child."

"Perhaps she has taken refuge among the Bolg in Canrif," the Diviner said. He tossed the flaxen sheet, now red as a rose petal, into one of the canopic urns and set it alight as well. "She is said to be a close friend of the Bolg king. If that be the case, you will most likely never find them. Canrif is unassailable."

"Indeed," Talquist agreed regretfully.

"You may need to search for another wellspring of immortality, or speed up your war efforts to double time." The Diviner handed the last of the ashes to the emperor. "I am done here. Good night, Talquist. May your reign be long and fruitful."

$\mathcal{T}$he blue glow in the center of the Lightcatcher vanished from view.

Rhapsody turned in Grunthor's grip and buried her face in his massive chest as his arms came around her, keeping her from collapsing to the ground. The rest of the witnesses to the ritual looked at each other in the dark.

$\mathcal{T}$omorrow, just after dawn, if anything came to me from the auspicy, I will leave you a written message here on the altar," said the Diviner, cleansing his hands with oil. "Perhaps the flight patterns of whatever birds are left in Sepulvarta will give me a direction as to the whereabouts of the Child of Time."

"Thank you again, Hjorst," Talquist said. "A carriage is waiting to take you back to the guesthouse after your vigil."

"No, thank you, I'd much rather walk," said the Diviner. "It will be bad enough having to endure another week in one of your carriages taking me to port as it is."

"Will it disturb your vigil if I send the guards in to remove the woman from the narthex?"

"No," said the Diviner, "as long as they do not enter the sanctuary, and are silent."

"Very good. It shall be ordered so."

"When I arrive back in the Hintervold I will alert my generals and field commanders to be on the lookout for your messages when the time comes for us to wade into the fray. I wish you luck in finding the Child of Time. Perhaps you could ask the Scales when you get home."

Talquist's smile broadened.

What an outstanding idea, he mused. *Not the Scales you are thinking of, Hjorst, but a scale was used nonetheless. If all has gone well, the assassins may even be in Canrif already.*

"My thanks again," he said as he made his way down the concentric rise. "I will be certain to make it worth your while, Hjorst, if I ever have the opportunity."

The Diviner's voice was distant from the altar as Talquist made his way to the basilica door.

"If you wish to make it worth my while, never speak to me of it again, and forget about ever requesting another augury, unless you want me to gut you as I did the sexton. Good night."

The emperor turned and smiled at his friend, then left the basilica.

Then he tossed the ashes into the wind and then gave the guards instructions to have the woman sleeping in the narthex brought to his waiting carriage. He made his way down the front steps, past the defiled fountain, and climbed into the coach, where he waited impatiently.

By the time the carriage arrived at the guesthouse, a mere five streets away, the acolyte could no longer be successfully sacrificed for an augury.

M'lady, please don't panic," Gyllian said sensibly. "I know that was terrifying to hear, but take courage—they both agree that Canrif is unassailable. As long as you and your son are here, they will not even attempt to find you."

"That's right, miss," Grunthor said, squeezing her shoulders again. "You can just stay 'ere 'til the end of the war."

"That's not my understanding," Rhapsody said nervously. "Ashe and I have always assumed that I would need to fight. There are but three elemental swords in the Known World, and I have the most powerful of them."

"Your husband and grandson both have such weapons as well," said Achmed quietly. "Their priority was your security; you don't need to be adding to their worry by risking your life, and that of your brat. As long as you're here, Talquist can't touch you."

ABOVE THE GROTTO OF ELYSIAN, YLORC

The five men had arrived at the rim of the canyon hidden in the depths of the forbidding mountains.

Quietly Dranth wiped the sweat from his forehead and surveyed the panorama of peaks rising even higher behind him than the ones they had summited had been. Born of the red sand desert in Yarim, the windy high peaks of Ylorc were a torment to him and the others.

But it mattered little.

A sight that had burned his eyes a year before filled his memory again, as it did during many of his waking moments, and all of his sleeping ones.

The head of the guildmistress, a woman he had loved and served since her childhood.

Slashed from her neck, her eyes still open.

Tossed unceremoniously into a box, wrapped carefully in paper and shipped back to him at the tile foundry of Yarim Paar.

It was an image that haunted him.

But not as much as it inspired him.

"Careful," he said to Colhoe, one of his subordinates from the Raven's Guild, as he lowered a coil of rope down the side of the wall that formed the underground canyon. "This is the greatest honor we will ever have—let us make it memorable."

$\mathcal{H}$eed the advice of your friends, m'lady," the Patriarch said, placing a hand on her arm, then turning to the Firbolg king. "I will take my leave of your mountain at week's end after my last prayer ritual, Your Majesty. Thank you for allowing me to learn of your Lightcatcher, and to rebuild part of the Chain of Prayer from your kingdom. When it has been reformed, I will make certain your safety, and that of your subjects, is foremost in my offerings. And, of course, anything I saw within your realm will never be spoken of."

Achmed smiled slightly. "Thank you. Travel well."

"I'd like to see your son before I leave, if you don't mind," Constantin said to Rhapsody. "I will offer my blessing to him again. You will both be in my prayers at all times."

Rhapsody, still pale, nodded numbly.

"Thank you. We will need every entreaty we can obtain," she said.

33

𝒯he next morning, after he had finished with the weeping acolyte again, Talquist dressed and made his way to the basilica.

"Is the Diviner gone?" he asked the guards standing watch at the main door.

"Yes, Majesty. He left just after dawn. The carriage driver had his belongings, and said he was taking him to port in Ghant. A cohort accompanied them."

"Good, good. And has anyone else entered the basilica?"

"Just the workmen, sire."

"Workmen?" Talquist's eyes narrowed.

"Yes, Majesty. Your orders to cover and remove some of the frescoes and stained-glass images are being attended to."

"Ah, good. Carry on." Talquist waited as the door was opened for him, and then strolled into the basilica.

Where the night before there had been darkness, twisting shadows, and gleaming ethereal radiance, this morning there was dusty sunlight raining through the glass windows atop the dome. Talquist made his way hurriedly through the narthex to the sanctuary, nodding perfunctorily at the artisans who stopped in their work, carrying ladders and hanging cloth, to bow before him.

Atop the altar, a scroll was waiting.

The emperor climbed the stairs made of concentric circles until he stood before the altar. It was all he could do to keep from snatching the rolled parchment and tearing the seal open, but he controlled himself and picked up the scroll with dignity, trying not to call attention to himself.

As he broke the seal, he cast a glance around and noted that the artisans had returned to their work, almost as if he wasn't there.

Good, he thought.

He unrolled the paper and looked down at it.

Northeast, the coarsely written script said. *It looks to be an early winter as well. I expect the next of your ships to dock at Verne Hys to be delivering berries and several cases of a fine single malt.*

Northeast, the Diviner noted.

Canrif.

He looked up from the scroll and glanced around the basilica again.

A dozen or so laborers were setting about removing tiles from mosaics and stripping paint from frescoes that had been indentified as celebrating Cyrmian history, rather than elemental lore. All seemed engaged except for one, who looked perplexed, studying a fresco on one of the walls of the nave.

Talquist tucked the scroll into his robes and trotted down the concentric rise. He came quietly up behind the man and looked to see what he was confused about.

"Can I help you with something, my son?" he asked pleasantly.

The artisan turned around. His eyes widened at the sight of the emperor, crowned and wearing the golden symbol of the ascendant sun on a chain around his neck. He bowed deeply and nervously.

"Majesty. Pardon and apologies."

"None are necessary. I am grateful for your talents and labor in restoring Lianta'ar to the glory that it should have held all along. Is something causing you confusion?"

"I—I was merely uncertain as to whether this fresco is Cymrian, and therefore needing to be stripped, or an appropriate depiction of elemental lore, Majesty. I do not know what it represents."

"Well, move aside and let me have a look."

The worker obeyed quickly.

Talquist eyed the fresco. He had spent a good deal of his lifetime in research and study of every type of lore—pure, legend or folk—in the pursuit of the answer to the question of the identity of the purple scale he had found in the sand of the Skeleton Coast. He was therefore surprisingly familiar, for a godless man, with sacred paintings and depictions of folktales and religious legends.

It was the image of a woman, ordinary in nature, her coloring favoring the dark eyes and skin of a native Sorbold, rather than the blue-eyed, fair-skinned Cymrian lineage. She was clothed in common garments except for a veil or wimple of some sort that covered most of her hair, and was surrounded by smiling children of all sizes and colorings, as well as women, some of whom were holding infants.

At her feet was a pond or a well of some kind, modest of size and filled with dark water, in which an image of the gibbous moon was reflected.

The woman held in her hands what appeared to be a small round tray of some kind, on which a single object rested. It was familiarly shaped, hand-sized and oblong, with a slightly tattered edge, and was yellow in color. It seemed to be scored with lines of no recognizable pattern.

Talquist froze.

He blinked and looked at the fresco again, staring most closely at the object on the tray in the woman's hands.

Then, after a moment, he was aware of the breath of the workman standing behind him. He turned around slowly and forced as pleasant a smile as he was capable of to come over his face.

"What is your name?"

"Devein, Majesty."

"Devein, I am thirsty. Could I prevail upon you to request a cup of water from the guards at the basilica door?"

"Of—of course, sire." The workman took off like a jackrabbit.

Talquist turned quickly back to the fresco.

He reached inside the inner pocket of his robe and pulled out his greatest possession, the one he carried over his heart.

The gray scale, purple when it caught the light, scored with the image of a throne on the convex side.

The New Beginning.

And held it up before him.

It was almost the exact size and shape as the yellow image on the tray in the fresco, its edge finely tattered like a fish scale.

Talquist's hands began to tremble violently.

Yellow—one of the scales that Faron and he were missing between them in the spectrum.

He could hear the sound of heavy footsteps approaching; he quickly slid the scale back into his robes and forced another smile to his face.

"Thank you," he said, accepting the flagon that the workman offered him. He drank deeply, willing himself to be calm.

"So, have you decided what you would like done with this fresco, Majesty?" Devein asked nervously.

Talquist nodded and took another sip.

"Leave it for now. I will ask you to have it removed shortly."

Talquist had almost finished the repast that had been brought to the basilica for his refreshment when he heard the unmistakable sounds of military footfalls echoing through the narthex on their way to the sanctuary.

He rose, wiped his mouth with the linen napkin and laid it on the makeshift table before him, and waited.

A moment later Fhremus, his supreme commander of the land forces of Sorbold, came into view, a young soldier following at a respectful distance behind him.

"You sent for me, Majesty?" Fhremus asked, as he came to a halt, bowing.

"Indeed." Talquist signaled for the soldiers to follow him to the wall where the fresco was displayed.

"Is this the soldier who will be in my retinue on the way back to Jierna'sid?"

"Yes, sire. His name is Kymel."

"Well met, Kymel," Talquist said as the young soldier bowed. "And you have arranged to double the number of soldiers in my retinue, as I asked, Fhremus?" .

"Yes, sire. They will be under the command of Titactyk."

"Thank you, Fhremus; I just wanted to review some of the plans for my return tomorrow morning with Kymel. I assume he can be trusted to accurately relay my orders to Titactyk?"

"Yes, sire."

"Excellent. And this is important—send word to the naval command, under highest security and seal. Tell them to launch the offensive on the harbor of Avonderre immediately."

"Yes, sire."

"You may go."

The supreme commander bowed and took his leave. Talquist turned back to Kymel.

"Kymel, on the way back to Jierna'sid, I will be sending half the retinue off on a side mission to the seacoast between the border at Jakar and the port of Windswere in the Nonaligned States. I will discuss the specifics of this mission with Titactyk, but I want you to make careful note of this image. I asked Fhremus to bring me someone who was intelligent and had a good memory, so I know you will not fail me in this, am I correct?"

Kymel's face went hot.

"Absolutely, Majesty."

"Good, good. Make special note of this part of the image." He pointed to the tray and the yellow object on it. Kymel looked carefully, then nodded.

"Thank you, Kymel. I expect I will be seeing you on the morrow, then. Good day." The young soldier bowed, turned on his heel and left the basilica as his commander had.

Talquist went through the door of the basilica, stopping long enough to confer with the guards.

"Locate the artisan named Devein, and tell him he can strip the fresco now."

"Yes, Majesty."

The Merchant Emperor walked briskly to the carriage and embarked.

"Take me back to the guesthouse," he said cheerfully. "It's been a stimulating morning; I feel the need for an afternoon nap."

He thought of the young acolyte back at the guesthouse and smiled, congratulating himself for telling Gregory to select the prettiest one, as the coachman's voice clicked to the horses and the carriage began to roll away from the basilica.

34

Children who were blessed to grow up in plenty, or at least enough, more often than not had access in their youth to fables and fairy tales, stories told to them by loving parents and family members, nannies or teachers, tales of magic and adventure to amuse them, to teach them lessons and morals, to give them practice in learning how to dream.

But motherless and fatherless children, orphans, and even those with one parent to cling to in the darkness of poverty, the nightmare of the slave mines, the cold and the biting wind of a life under the docks or in the faceless streets and alleyways of every city on the continent, those children were by far more in need of such stories. Even the smallest amount of encouragement to such children might have made the torment that they lived in daily a little less terrible, may have offered an inspiration to endure for the prospect of better days in the future. Sadly, the bedtimes of these children were not opportunities for the warm and loving impartment of the fairy tales, legends, and stories of good children being elevated to high praise, wealth, social stature, and happy endings that their luckier counterparts benefited from. The nightmares of the dark hours that bedeviled such children were scarcely more frightening than the reality of their waking lives.

But even without the same opportunities to learn of legends with happy endings and stories extolling bravery, selflessness, and pluck, there was one legend that seemed to make its way into every dark alleyway, every windswept dock, every brutal salt mine, every stinking stable, every orphanage where less fortunate children spent their days, working, slaving, or just trying to survive.

The legend of the Well of the Moon.

On first blush it was possible to write off the legend as wish-fulfillment, a story that was both impossible and tempting to believe, especially for children to whom a simple crust of bread, a day without beatings and a night without fear would be the fulfillment of their greatest wish. But there was something compelling about the tale, the story of a haven for children, particularly children in want and need, between the land and the sea, within both and neither places, where children who had run away from their abusive homes and their rotten lives could find solace, or peace, or even happiness.

The legend told of a guardian who, while having no loyalty to adults, was sympathetic to the plight of lonely, damaged children, and, if that guardian could be found, would lead such children to a place of peace and safety, where adults were kind, soldiers did not beat them for being in the wrong place, food and water were plentiful, there were real toys to be played with and they could eat cookies and sweetmeats all day, and pain could not find them.

There were many versions of the tale, of course, because it was common to such a wide variety of climes and cultures across an expansive continent, but one phrase, or its variant, heard in every telling was this:

The Guardian of the Well of the Moon will guide you to that peaceful place, when the moon is full, when the tide is high, when all other paths are exhausted, when all the sandbars are covered, when all other roads are blocked.
But only if you are a child.

It was a tale that went back many generations, and was conveyed in many languages. When other tales were passed around and vanished into the wind, when other legends were proven false or disbelieved, the legend of the Well of the Moon continued to cling to the collective vault of oral tradition, continued to be heard and often believed by the poorest of the poor, the most forgotten of the lost.

Because it was true.

Calquist had learned the legend in childhood when he, the bastard son of a peasant woman and a merchant with no interest in raising him, had heard it while working in the olive groves of Nicosi at the age of ten. All of his fellow young pickers knew the tale, and spoke wistfully of the place of peace and plenty where the Well of the Moon lived on nights when they had had nothing but blemished olives to eat. When a child disappeared from the work detail or the sleeping tents, it was said he or she had gone off to find the path to the Well of the Moon. Talquist had never desired to do so, however.

He had known his own path from the time he was very young.

That path had led him one day to the Skeleton Coast, the twisting coastline of Sorbold's southwestern shore, where the bones of ships and the men who had sailed on them lay drying in the dim sun that filtered through the ever-present mist that hung in the air off the sea. He had wandered that foggy graveyard in silent anger, studying the wreckage of the Third Cymrian Fleet that had landed there fourteen hundred years before his birth, the ruins of the vessels that had allowed the interlopers to conquer his homeland and turn it into something unrecognizable. The hatred that burned in his viscera had ignited on that beach, unchecked and aimless until he had discovered by accident the purple scale inscribed with the image of a throne.

He had no idea what it was.

And as he whored himself out to every person who could potentially help him discover the answer to his life's mystery, he set himself to learning everything he could, in every place of catalogued wisdom that would let him in.

So it was while he was serving as an acolyte to a man named Lasyrus, the sexton of Terreanfor, the basilica of living Earth that was the principal Patrician place of worship in Sorbold, that he came to understand what the Well of the Moon really was.

Or think he understood it.

In order to move up in the ranks of the clergy of the Patrician faith, an acolyte was required to go to a holy site where service was needed and perform that service for three years. Talquist had no such intentions; he did not wish to have any association with the Patrician faith, though he had made a good pretense of it. Rather, he understood that centers of religious study had resources of knowledge that were available nowhere else, and that being an acolyte in as holy and powerful a place as Terreanfor gave him access to those resources he would never be able to find elsewhere.

So while he was poring over the massive bound volumes where all the places where holy service could be undertaken were listed, he came upon a place called the Abbey of Nikkid'sar, which allowed only female acolytes to apply for consideration for service placement.

Being that Talquist was always fascinated by being denied access to or told that he was unqualified for something, he had read the listing anyway.

The text explained that the abbey was located in Windswere, a coastal area of the lands that bordered southwestern Sorbold known as the Non-aligned States. Like Sorbold, the lands leading to the seacoast of Windswere did not slope gently to the beaches, but rather were tall cliffs that stretched forth into the sea atop sandspits, or spits, as they were more commonly known, long deposits of sediment formed by the backwash of a strong ocean drift.

The abbey had been the renovation of an older military site that had been there before the Cymrians came, bringing their Patrician faith and their domination of lands that had once been ruled by Talquist's ancestors, or so he liked to think. When the Third Fleet landed, the cliff on the spit on which the abbey was later built had held a large ancient catapult of a sort, a weapon of defense from the old days pointed out to sea, when it and all the other ones like it up and down the coast had been employed against the exhausted Cymrians, who had fared badly in their rough voyage across the Wide Central Sea, only to be attacked once they had landed, ship-wrecked, by the people who occupied the coastlands.

When those lands, like the rest of the continent, had fallen easily to Cymrian tyrannical dominion, the Church immediately sought to replace the primitive animist religious beliefs with their ridiculous doctrines of channeled prayer, where the individual no longer communicated directly with his Creator, but was now required to pray through a local cleric, who passed the combined adoration and supplication up what was known as the Chain of Prayer. The actions of the Cymrians, and the indigenous peoples' reactions to them, had produced many orphans and widows, so the supposedly altruistic Church set up places where those unfortunates could receive services and live simple, safe lives away from the streets where many poor women and children were routinely victimized.

And so the Abbey of Nikkid'sar was designed and built atop the most advantageous spot on those tall, rocky cliffs. The terrain was not jagged and peaked, like most of the spit-topped cliffs, but had a wide, flat top, a rocky field of sorts, surrounded by a heavy barricade of jagged outcrop-pings which hid both the view of the field and the sea beyond it. The rocks from the field were gathered and used in the construction of the main buildings, a gathering place where meals were served and lessons were taught, a small hospital and a dormitory for orphans, as well as individual stone houses for mothers with young children to live as families.

And in the very center of it all, where an unusual depression in the flat rock field had been discovered filled with rainwater, a deeper cistern was dug, expanding the natural formation into a useful source of fresh water atop a massive stone cliff which otherwise would have none. Round and deep, with filters and pipes that had been invented by the Cymrian lord known as Gwylliam the Visionary, it was deep and large enough to reflect the whole of a gibbous moon when it was lighting the sky.

The Well of the Moon.

The abbey was under the supervision of a mother abbess, generally a cleric of substantial level out of Sepulvarta, the newly built holy city at the time, and was kept running with the aid of more than a dozen female acolytes of second-year or higher training. Its construction and stocking of necessary tools, sundries, and foodstuffs was completed and the moving in of the occupants accomplished just in time before a massive earthquake struck the coast of Windswere.

While many of the uninhabited sandspit cliffs were damaged in the quake, the only thing to happen to the cliffs of the Abbey of Nikkid'sar was the landslide that crumbled the heavy barricade of rocky outcroppings that had been known as the Moraine. Prior to the earthquake, a narrow natural path had been widened to allow for access to the rock field at the top of the cliff. Now that path and, in fact, all connection to the land behind it was severed, making the cliff that once had been part of a mountain range extending out into the sea into a freestanding structure that looked almost as if it had dropped from the sky at the edge of the water.

The other significant effect of the quake was that the abbey's widened passageway was swallowed, all but cutting off access to the outside world. This did not prove to be a problem for the current residents, because the open field at the top of the cliff had been topped with cultivatable soil; it had water and open sun, and the weather modulation of the sea. The only problem that arose from the landslide was the closing of the doorway to any future refugees.

Except at the time of the full moon, when the ocean's effects on the tides meant a small alternative passage could be found, too narrow to accommodate a man in armor, or even a non-armored man of any great heft.

But it was just wide enough to allow entrance to a child and most women.

When the moon is full, when the tide is high, when all other paths are exhausted, when all the sandbars are covered, when all other roads are blocked.

But only if you are a child.

Talquist had all but forgotten about the legend until he saw the fresco on the basilica wall.

A woman, the Guardian of the Well, undoubtedly the mother abbess, pictured in the center of a circle of smiling children and the mothers of babes in arms.

Holding what looked to be a scale very much like the one he had found on the Skeleton Coast.

Talquist spun the stem of his wineglass between his thumb and forefinger, lost in thought.

It made sense to him that one of the scales of the deck had been given into the care of a cloistered place between land and sea, where no male adult would find it, Undoubtedly the yellow scale, known in the ancient texts as Heat Saver/Heat Spiller or Light Bringer/Light Queller, would be used to warm and light a lonely stone outpost full of child refugees at the edge of the cold sea. Dearly as he would have loved to have been the one to rediscover and take the scale from the clifftop abbey himself, his position now prevented him from attending to such things in person. *A pity*, he mused as he raised the glass to his lips and drank. The consequences of power was that he now had to accomplish his desires at the hands of others.

Much as he had when he was powerless, but in a completely different way.

He looked over at the acolyte he had been defiling for the better part of the last day. She was curled up in the corner of the room under a blanket with the royal crest of the Empire of the Sun embroidered on it, shivering violently and hiccoughing from time to time. Talquist smiled broadly as a pleasant, almost altruistic thought occurred to him.

Perhaps she can gain a position in the Abbey of Nikkid'sar, he thought, pleased with himself. In addition to being a female acolyte, she now might also qualify as the type of woman that abbey specialized in serving.

Now that the pristine and celibate manse of Sepulvarta would no longer have a use for her.

He finished his wine and pulled up the polished linen sheets and thick quilt around his neck, settling down to the sleep of someone eager to be on the road home in the morning.

35

AVONDERRE HARBOR, WESTERN SEACOAST

The brigantine *Flying Sails* was not a sleek vessel, nor was she particularly large. She lay low in the water, encrusted with salt and barnacles all the way up to the portholes. When not rigged, as unrigged she stood on that fateful morning, she could easily be mistaken for a scow.

Especially from the air.

It was her age and weather-beaten look that saved her, the captain would note later. Moored alongside one of the oldest docks far to the north in Avonderre Harbor, she was lying in shadow, her sun-bleached decks causing her to blend in with the wood of the quay, when the assault on the naval forces began.

A delay due to bad weather meant that the crew of the *Flying Sails* had arrived in port in the earliest hours of the new day, and therefore had not returned to muster. All sailors save the captain, the boatswain, and the sleeping shift were still haunting the taverns in the northern villages of Avonderre, harassing the serving women with demands for service of many kinds. As the kitchen fire was cold and the women exhausted, the only requests fulfilled were those for ale, leaving the crew disgruntled, tired, hungry, and drunk.

Their bad timing was their salvation.

Jacinth Specter, who had been serving on the *Flying Sails* even longer than the captain, was on deck taking note of damage to the yardarm that had occurred in the storm the night before. That storm had blown them roughly into port; Jacinth's eyes were bleary from salt spray and lack of sleep, so when the first wave of iacxsis appeared on the southern horizon, he mistook them for the shadow of a passing cloud. Instead, he heard the buzz first, a scratching at his eardrums that caused him to shake his head as if to dislodge a gnat that had been caught inside.

By the time he looked up again into the southern sky, it was darkening as if with black rain clouds racing by on a screaming wind.

A wind moving out to sea.

It took Jacinth more than a moment to force his voice from his throat. His brain berated him to speak, but he could not comply. Rather he stood frozen, his hand on the yardarm, as the northernmost edge of the winged serpentine force flew past within a few hundred feet. When he finally found his voice, it emerged hoarse and dry, hollow, as if from the depths of his belly.

"Cap'n?"

Captain Syrus Turley looked up impatiently from his log. The sight caused his hand to tremble, sending his quill over the side and into the green water of the harbor below.

Soaring above his head was the stuff of nightmares, an immense shadow of a creature that seemed to be riding the screaming wind, high enough to have missed noticing the *Flying Sails*, only because its sights were set farther out in the harbor.

A moment later the sky darkened with similar shadows.

From all sides of the city many more great beasts appeared in the air above the houses and shops, sailing on wide, batlike wings. They were serpentine in their movements, with long barbed tails that thrashed as they flew; their legs and jaws, however, were insectoid, sharply jointed, like the plague locusts that had been one of their progenitors.

Atop each of them was a rider with a burning bundle of whey-grass stalks soaked in pitch or oil.

Turley's body was frozen in place, as if rooted to the ship's deck, but he was able to turn his head ever-so-slightly to the west, out to the harbor of

Avonderre, the terminus of one of the biggest seafaring shipping lanes in the Known World. The harbor was coming to light with the rising sun, alive with the motion and muted noise of hundreds of ships already being offloaded by hundreds more longshoremen, sweating and swearing into the early-morning wind as they reached into the cargo holds of those ships like machines, dragging forth the goods that had been transported from across the world to the shores of the Middle Continent and loading them into wagons standing on the piers, ready to continue their journeys to their eventual owners. Even more longshoremen were engaged in the loading of such goods into empty vessels, standing ready to sail forth on the outgoing tide.

At the harbor's western side, nearest the inlet, the warships of the Alliance's naval fleet were moored, guarding the harbor against incoming hostile vessels and giving them proximity to the sea.

And beyond the harbor's horseshoe-shaped inlet, flanked on either side by massive twin light towers at the edges of the seawall, the wind off the sea was bringing in a thousand ships, more, perhaps, of all types, unaware of what lay beyond the inlet's gateway.

As Time seemed to slow around him, Turley struggled to move; his legs and arms felt wooden as the horror that had washed over him settled into numbing shock. He shook it off, and turned back to Jacinth Specter.

"Ring the bell!" he shouted. "Specter—wake the sleeping shift! *Ring the bell!*"

The sailor's brain of the boatswain, long trained to respond without thought to such orders, engaged like lightning, and he jumped to obey. Specter ran aft to the enormous bell of the *Flying Sails*, seized the striker, and began pounding furiously. The ship's fortuitous placement at the high north end of the harbor gave it a surprising acoustical advantage; the resounding tone caught the morning wind that was heading out to sea and carried the alarm with it across most of Avonderre Harbor.

The great sonorous ringing of the ship's bell cut through the heavy buzzing noise for just a moment and echoed across the waterfront. It caught the attention of the longshoremen as well as the ships' crews, just in time to alert them to the waves of death that were about to rain down on them from the air.

With brutal efficiency, the squadron of winged beasts and their riders peeled off from the flying formation, the front wave heading west while the rear systematically divided and attacked, strafing the individual ships in dock or plying the harbor.

First, almost indistinguishable casks of clear liquid were fired or heaved into the mainsails of the ships, followed immediately by the whey-grass torches dropped by the riders. The sails and even some of the decks ignited where the liquid trailed, ripping into flame that crackled menacingly, burning with an unnatural insistence as the startled crews tried unsuccessfully to beat it out with their jackets and wet cloths.

As the town's bells and the voices of those in the city's streets picked up the alarm, the flying squadron divided again. The larger part of the forward wave sailed over the military fleet, heaving the same combustible liquid and torches into their sails; the warships fired their ballistae in return as the remainder of the aerial squadron flew onward past the guardian light towers and out over the sea, heading for the approaching ships that had no real view of the inner harbor.

Specter and Turley stood amidships on the *Flying Sails*, watching in horror as Avonderre Harbor caught fire. The sailors of the sleeping shift were coming topside now, and the first among them clogged the hatch as they came to the top of the ladder, then stopped, slack-kneed in terror.

The back end of the wave of iacxsis, which had set to destroying the merchant fleet moored within the harbor, turned in the air and dove, each creature at a different vessel. What missiles the merchant ships were able to fire bounced harmlessly off the stonelike bodies of the flying beasts, though here and there riders could be seen falling into the harbor or onto the decks of the ships when the heavy crossbows or ballistae found their marks. The beasts struck with insectlike efficiency, snatching sailors from the decks in their mandibles and dragging them back into the air, amid the sound of screaming and horrific crunching audible over the maddening buzzing.

"Abandon ship!" Captain Turley shouted. "Get off 'er while you can! Make for the harbormaster's office or take cover wherever you can find it." He looked around desperately for Simmons, the first mate, then realized he had been with the shift on shore leave; he summoned the boatswain again.

"Specter, take Faulring and Mitchell and get to the garrison commander. Report what you've seen, and have them send word to Highmeadow."

"Aye, sir." Specter and the other two hands took off in a dead run.

Captain Turley, alone now on the *Flying Sails*, turned his gaze back to the harbor, where surely what he was beholding could only foretell the ending of the world.

Beyond the light towers, and the view of anyone on the shore or in the harbor, the ships approaching the inlet from the open sea were greeted by the sight of the forewave of iacxsis advancing on them, riders waving the burning stalks of whey grass.

At least some of them were.

As the iacxsis crested the harbor walls, fully three-quarters of the ships beyond them spilled the wind from their sails, slowing their approach, and, one by one, raised the same billowing flag up their mainmasts.

The flag of the Empire of the Sun.

The captains of the remaining ships, caught between the oncoming waves of screaming beasts in the air, and the armada behind them flying Talquist's colors, made valiant stands against the incoming ballistae fire or sought to flee in vain. It would have been hard for the doomed crews of those trapped ships to say which sight was more perplexing—the horrifying sky force of unnatural beasts, topped by Sorbolds with fire, or the odd collection of merchant vessels, warships, and privateers, the last of which were also flying the skull and crossbones beneath the flag of Sorbold, that outnumbered them three to one.

Within the hour, the ships not flying under Sorbold's flag had been reduced to floating driftwood, flotsam and jetsam littering the sea beyond the harbor. The occasional body could be seen drifting among the charnel, though most had been snatched up by the iacxsis in the final sweep of the area before the winged squadron turned south. The next morning would find carcasses and pieces of monstrous carapace floating in much the same way as the detritus of ships had; the winged beasts had inherited the brief longevity and rapid reproductive cycles of their plague locust ancestors, along with their voracious appetites, a weakness Talquist was still working to correct.

Their riders remained unaccounted for.

The smoke from the burning ships beyond the seawall blended into the thickening clouds of debris rising from Avonderre Harbor, twisting gray and orange in the sea wind. It blackened the sky for miles up and down the western coast of the continent and out to sea, like a storm that had settled over the unfortunate harbor and had remained until it had spent its fury, leaving the nautical jewel of the Cymrian era in ashes.

Farther beyond the seawall, the combined armada of naval, merchant, and pirate ships slowly lowered their flags. The warships, braving the dissipating smoke and ash, raised their sails and moved into what remained of Avonderre Harbor, occupying it with the aid of additional armed vessels bringing reinforcements to the new Sorbold outpost. Once ensconced, the flag of the Empire of the Sun was flown at the land's edge of the port, but not from the twin guardian light towers. After the clouds of smoke had dissipated, it was as if, from the western sea, nothing had changed in the harbor at all.

The pirate vessels moved farther out to sea, forming a floating barrier, a moving blockade that monitored the sea-lanes, keeping any vessel from other parts of the Known World from advancing to Avonderre Harbor, rerouting them north to the port of Verne Hys at the western coast of the Hintervold, or south to the ports of Minsyth or Evermere in the region known as the Nonaligned States.

Or to the gleaming, massive harbor of Ghant in Sorbold.

The merchant vessels that had been Talquist's all along went quietly about their business, plying the trade routes as if nothing had happened at all.

THE CROSSROADS BETWEEN WINDSWERE AND JIERNA'SID

At the crossroads of the thoroughfare between Windswere to the south and Jierna'sid to the west, Talquist waited impatiently in the royal carriage as the regimental commander, Titactyk, rode forward on his mount and dismounted. The commander strode to the carriage and stopped before the emperor's window, waiting respectfully.

The Merchant Emperor pulled the velvet curtain briskly out of the way.

"Are we ready to proceed, Titactyk?"

"Yes, Majesty."

"You are clear in your orders?"

"Yes, m'lord."

Talquist's dark eyes gleamed intently.

"Good. We part company here. I will return forthwith to Jierna'sid. When you have finished your mission, your regiment is to report directly to Jierna Tal. Send Kymel in to see me personally. When the abbey is secured, your troops are to withdraw, leaving him alone to search and reconnoiter the grounds. He knows what to look for. Are we clear?"

"Yes, m'lord."

"Excellent. I will expect his report in no more than ten days. Travel well."

Titactyk bowed and mounted, then set off to Windswere with half of the regiment that had originally been assigned to protect the emperor.

Following the chariot of the stone titan.

36

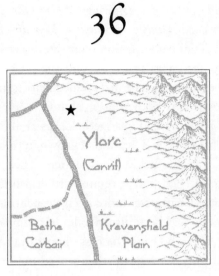

IN THE LIGHTCATCHER, GURGUS PEAK.

ℑt's cloudy today," Omet commented as he waited for Rhapsody to finish buttoning the tiny garment in which she was dressing Meridion. "I'm not sure how strong a connection you might have with just the natural light."

"That's something we always have to contend with," Rhapsody said, smoothing out the folds of the tiny shirt she had made, then nuzzling the baby's belly beneath it. Meridion cackled with delight. "If I need to, I can use the diamond. Are we ready?"

Omet glanced above him. The sun had moved into position just beyond the green slice of the spectrum of glass; the cover had been removed from the dome, and now the emerald light flooding the circle through the wheel was fading to a bluer hue.

"Any moment now," he said.

Rhapsody inhaled deeply, then let her breath out fully, willing her pounding heart to slow down. She watched above her until the slice of blue glass began to glow, shining a moment later on the floor of the instrumentality. She kissed the baby, then stepped into the light, and spoke the note of the blue spectrum and its ancient name. Then she sang the name of the room, *Eastern study off of main library, White Oak Lodge, second floor, Highmeadow, Navarne, Middle Continent, Wyrmlands, Known World.* Her specificity and detail paid off; a moment later a familiar image formed.

In the sparsely decorated office beyond the pool of blue light, Ashe was pacing. However disheveled he had seemed before, his state of dress and grooming now caused Rhapsody to gasp aloud.

She could not tell if he had changed clothes at all in the many weeks since she had seen him last. His beard had grown in fully, unkempt, as had his hair, which now reached below his shoulders. There was a sharpness to his features that frightened her; it reminded her a little of the aspect of Michael, the Wind of Death, but more alien, serpentine, less skeletal. His eyes were wild, and he was berating an aide-de-camp who stood at attention near the door, and who took the first opportunity to flee the room as soon as he was dismissed by a growl that caused the walls of the room to vibrate a little. The sound of the closing door half a continent away made her jump. Nevertheless, she stepped farther into the light and addressed her pacing husband.

"Having a bad afternoon, my love?"

Ashe looked around in surprise, then exhaled.

Go away, Aria. Please. The dragon's voice was evident, but not in control as yet.

Rhapsody blinked. "You want us to go away?"

Want? Of course not. Ashe stopped pacing and dropped into his desk chair, running his hands through his hair. *But you and Meridion should not visit me anymore. Not even when, and if, the war comes to an end.*

"Ashe—"

For the love of the One-God, Rhapsody, stop torturing me! Take him out of there—now!

The words stung like a slap across her face. Rhapsody went back to the far end of the light pool, shaking, and handed the baby back to Omet.

"Please withdraw to the far end of the room for a moment, Omet," she said, her voice shaking similarly. "We need privacy, as much as possible."

The glass artisan nodded quickly and disappeared into the shadows of the enormous cylindrical tower.

Rhapsody smoothed her hair, ran her sweating palms across her trouser legs to dry them, then returned to the edge of the light pool nearest to Ashe once again.

"All right, the baby is gone," she said. "Tell me what is going on."

Ashe shook his head, as if trying to clear it from cobwebs. *The forces of dark intent are gathering, growing every day,* he said dully. *I am keeping abreast of it as much as I can, but I fear we are outflanked, surrounded on every side, or will soon be. The warships I ordered from Manosse have not arrived—it now appears that Talquist holds the entirety of the western coast, from Traeg in the northlands almost to the shores of the Nonaligned States, and of course Sorbold, all the way to Golgarn. Any attempt to contact our allies in Gaematria or Manosse has been rebuffed, undoubtedly intercepted by the military forces that have taken the harbors, or the armed merchant fleet that patrols the seas beyond, or the pirates that run interference should anything make it past the first two ranks. We are cut off, Aria, separated from some of the most powerful parts of the Alliance, surrounded by enemies and defending a vast, open plain with no possible means to do so successfully. And while at this point I am still functioning, more and more the petulant dragon that has taken over my conscious thought is distracted, obsessing over the loss of you and Meridion as the world crumbles.*

"I'm sorry," she said softly. "We knew this was possible, but it had been my hope that our visits would serve as incentive, rather than as a distraction. I wish I had been able to be with you in the light more often."

That's just it, Ashe said sadly. *If anything, you should cease thinking about me and stay as far away as you can—even should there be a peaceful resolution, which is not looking likely at this point.*

All of her awareness of his nature deserted her, leaving her speechless. She fought back the hurt that she knew he might hear in her voice and willed her response to be calm, measured.

"Even should there be a peaceful resolution? What are you talking about?"

I—cannot risk being alone with you, or our son, ever again.

"Why?"

Ashe turned away from the light. It was not clear to Rhapsody, who was fighting to remain calm, if he was stung by the thunderstruck tone of her voice, or suffering an even deeper sorrow. A moment later it was obvious that it was the latter.

I—I am barely man anymore, Rhapsody; the dragon is rampant now. It is nearly—impossible for me to control that part of—my nature. Even my dreams of you have changed. In them I am—almost violent toward you, hungering for you. What used to be—reminiscent of our passion, our— His voice faltered.

Rhapsody exhaled quietly. "I know what you mean—go on."

Ashe's voice was barely above a whisper. *I fear—I would—ravage—you if—you were here in the flesh. I dream of—almost—consuming you—please stay away. Gods, as much as I want—to be with you—need to be—with you, if I—were to hurt you—*

"Stop. That won't happen."

You are not listening to me. His voice had changed, the draconic tones returning. *Do you think I want—to tell you this?* He held up his hands; they were trembling violently. *This is not draconic peevishness or—rage that vents itself and is gone, as it has been in the past. My dragon nature has changed. I—I fear for you, Rhapsody. The thought that anyone might harm you or Meridion is sickening enough to me. The possibility that I could do so myself is preventing me from sleep, from focus—from sanity. It rends my heart to think that you would fear me—but you should, Rhapsody. You must; believe me when I tell you that you are no longer safe around me as I now am.*

Her voice choked slightly. "I do not fear the dragon, beloved—it is part of you, and a bit of a pain on occasion but—"

You are not hearing me! The roar shook the walls of the study, causing paintings to fall to the floor, their frames shattering, and the curtains of the window to flap like flags in a high wind.

Rhapsody watched her husband in silence for a moment. He was right in that he was almost unrecognizable, his body thickening with the rise of the dragon, the angles of his face sharpening, looking almost serpentine in his aspect.

She closed her eyes and pictured the boy she had fallen in love with on a windy night in the old world, the man who had married her, once in secret, once in glorious ceremony, trying to hold on to the memory of him as he had once been in the face of the transformation of ancient lore and blood that he was contending with now. She summoned her Naming ability and spoke Truly to him, her eyes still closed, her tone as sensible and free from emotion as she could manage.

"I *am* hearing you, Ashe. It is you that is not hearing me. You will not hurt me when we are reunited, because, if all else fails, I will not let you hurt me." She opened her eyes and looked directly at him. "I am not made of glass—and you know my resources, my weapons, my strengths. We sorted this out years ago on the banks of the Tar'afel River, if you recall. Do not fear ravaging me. One of us will die before that ever happens—but it won't. I know it won't." Her eyes lost the lock with his as he dropped his head. "Remember, I have a better right cross than you do—you have said so, and tasted it, yourself. And my sword is older and more powerful than yours."

Ashe looked up again, exhausted.

Are you saying—that you will kill me if I lose control and try to ravage or harm you? Or Meridion? Even if I am only trying to express love for you both?

"In a heartbeat." The tones of True-Speaking were in her reply.

Do you promise?

"Yes." She swallowed and added a reference for emphasis. "Remember Jo."

Ashe exhaled deeply. *Thank the One-God,* he said. *And thank you, Aria—thank you for understanding. I pray that you really do comprehend the danger.*

"You're welcome. I believe I do. Will you listen to me now?"

As well as I can.

"Good enough." Her face became somber. "All right—I am advising you now; I cannot tell you what to do, but I beg you to consider my suggestions." The Lord Cymrian nodded with effort.

"You cannot successfully conduct the war from Roland anymore," she said flatly, softly. "If, as you say, the western seacoast is blockaded, in Talquist's control, to the point where you cannot reach either Gaematria or your naval resources in Manosse, you and your army—our army—are eventually going to be ringed, trapped and slaughtered as the Hintervold, Sorbold and Golgarn advance—this is not my assessment, Ashe, it is Achmed and Grunthor's as well."

The Lord Cymrian's eyes showed signs of the dragon's resurgence.

You think I don't know this, Aria?

"I am certain that you do—I am just not certain you know what I am going to suggest you do about it." She averted her gaze quickly as the dragon attempted to lock eyes with her. "Look away," she commanded, "I do not want to play games of will with your other nature. Hear me. Close your eyes and listen." She waited until he did so, after some internal struggle. "I know the primary rule is that the king must stay and hold the land—"

Yes, he interrupted bitterly. The draconic tones had fully returned to his voice. *This was why no one with any sense agreed to take the lordship.*

"Nevertheless, you must leave. You alone have the ability to pass through the blockade, to reach the Isle of the Sea Mages, and eventually Manosse, without detection—you alone can walk through the sea. Working alone, as you did for so long, shielded by the element of water, of which you are the master, you can marshal your forces of the Second Fleet and Gaematria, and bring them back to the continent, breaking the blockade."

I am well aware of this, the dragon said haughtily; Rhapsody turned even further away from her husband and closed her eyes for fear of its entrapment. *But I cannot abandon the continent. Tristan Steward would be the only possible regent at this time, but you know we cannot trust him. Anborn is likewise engaged, behind enemy lines and unreachable. You could do it, take command, but it would put Meridion in the gravest of danger. And none of you except Anborn are Wyrmril, able to maintain the Shield. What would you have me do, Rhapsody?*

She smiled. She had no idea if the dragon could sense it through the light.

"I would urge you to remember that you have a namesake. One that not only bears your name, but was named specifically for you, at a time when you were away and hidden from the sight of the world, and is your godson. He is fully vested, brave and wise—and, though young, he can hold your place until you return."

She waited for a moment, but heard only silence.

"In addition, because of everything I just said, because you and he share a name, and the fact that you are well acquainted with a Lirin Namer, even if she is limited and self-trained, you have at your disposal the ability to share your lore, your Right of Command, with him, as no other sovereign really could."

He is a child, Rhapsody.

"Nonsense," she retorted. "He is barely younger than you were when you went to the House of Remembrance on Midsummer's Night all those years ago to kill the demon in its vulnerability—"

Yes, and see how well that *turned out.*

"It only turned out badly because Oelendra abandoned you. That's not the point—he will have Gerald Owen, and Gavin, and your trusted generals, and I will send a messenger bird to Rial in Tyrian asking for aid for him as well. He can do this, Ashe—in your concern for him, you insult him and all that he has endured, learned, and already proven. If you recall, it was Gwydion who put an arrow through the head of Michael's assassin that would have killed Anborn where he sat in Haguefort's Great Hall. He has suffered even more loss than you had at his age, and yet remains considered, brave, and wise. You said so yourself at his investiture."

There was a long silence. Finally Ashe spoke quietly, his voice still draconic, but calmer.

I did.

"Trust that you, and Anborn, have taught him well. He has studied the sword with Anborn for years, he is very wise, he is an extraordinary archer, and you have included him in all the strategy sessions since the reformation of the Alliance. I wish that he might have had more time to learn the ways of Tysterisk, but if nothing else, it should give him an advantage in battle, should it come to that. Extend your protectorate to include Navarne, and have Highmeadow absorb Haguefort's inhabitants except for the garrison to protect the province against an incursion from the North. Gwydion will do better if his chamberlain is with him, as well as the other staff he trusts. If you undertake the Naming ritual I am suggesting, he will have a good measure of your knowledge and experience to aid him."

Ashe sighed. *What is this ritual?*

Rhapsody looked above her. The sun had crested the peak, and the blue section of the spectrum had passed at least three-quarters of its time.

"Listen well—our time runs short. In the old world, history purports that Vandemere, the king who reigned when I was young, was kidnapped and held hostage for a time, long after Grunthor, Achmed, and I left Serendair through the root of Sagia. Do you know of these times?"

I do.

"Good—wait, of course you do, because you are of the line of Mac-Quieth on your mother's side. One of MacQuieth's titles, appellations, was the King's Shadow, because, being related and sworn to King Vandemere, he could stand in the place of the king and hold on to his Right of Command, keeping charge of the land for him until he was returned."

I am not a king, Ashe said. *My office is elected, not inherited.*

"It doesn't matter," Rhapsody said impatiently. "You can bestow upon Gwydion any part of your lore, your office, that you so choose—and he will be the repository of it until you reclaim it, because you and he share a name. Listen carefully, and I will teach you the ritual, but only if you want to learn it."

Ashe thought for a moment. *I do,* he said finally. *I am not certain that I will ever wish to take the Right of Command back, however.*

"That's your choice, my love," Rhapsody said, smiling slightly. "If that's the case, I will expect you to begin construction of the goat hut you have long promised to build me immediately thereafter. For now, just listen."

She spoke the incantation for him, repeating the difficult parts several times, then had him echo the words. When she was finally satisfied with his rendering, she exhaled deeply.

The light is fading, Ashe said sadly. The tones of the dragon were still within his voice, but it seemed quiet, brooding. *May—may I see Meridion again?*

Without a word Rhapsody turned and signaled to Omet, then hurried to the far edge of the light. Gently she took the baby into her arms and brought him quickly across the light pool to Ashe. She turned him around and tickled him under the arm, eliciting a squeal of delight and a toothless smile, which was directed at his father.

She could almost see the dragon's hold on Ashe shatter, at least for a moment, as he stared in wonder at his son.

"Nothing you can do, at least from where you are, can harm either of us, beloved," she said. "Hold out your finger—he may try to grasp it—he's been doing that for a while."

Ashe obeyed, then looked back at her, new realization in his eyes as the baby's tiny hand caught his fingertip and passed right through it, leaving behind the thrilling buzz he had experienced before.

You bring him here to restore me to sanity, don't you, Rhapsody?

"I bring him here because he is your son, and you have a right and a need to see him, just as he has a right and a need to see you, whenever possible," she replied. "I bring him here because I love and miss you beyond description, and want you to have a chance to share in our son's upbringing, even though you have made the greatest living sacrifice I know of in sending us away for our safety. And yes, I bring him here to restore you, to remind you of what you are fighting for, what *we* are fighting for, all of us, Achmed, Anborn, Grunthor, Gwydion, all of us—a world which holds a future for him and children like him, a safe, peaceful future. Do not lose sight of this as the dragon rises, as the world grows dark. Hold on and endure, my love—we will be waiting for you."

Ashe opened his mouth to answer her, words of love that he did not get a chance to pronounce.

The image of the tiny fingers trying to coil around his disappeared as the blue light vanished.

Taking with it his sanity again.

37

Desert

Sorbold

WINDSWERE

Titactyk's regiment came to a halt behind the chariot of the stone titan, their horses dancing on the sandspit beach in the blasting sea wind. The silver light of the full moon above them danced merrily in the swirling froth of the tide, the light reflecting back at the sky.

They had ridden alongside the tower cliffwall to the east for some time, in between other spits reaching like fingers out into the cold ocean, the spring tide roaring in between the rockfaces.

Titactyk waited atop his mount until the immense stone soldier stepped forth from the chariot. It had been a terribly bruising ride, as the leader of their expedition had no physical needs to tend to, nor did he seem to give thought to those of the soldiers following him. As a result, very few breaks had been taken, and the men were suffering now, feeling the impact of the ride in their backs, bladders, and bowels. They dismounted and addressed their needs as Titactyk approached the chariot from as safe a distance as he could.

"Orders, sir?"

The monstrous statue, which had been standing with its arms at its sides and its head tilted toward the sky in the streaming light of the moon, turned slowly and regarded him thoughtfully, its milky blue eyes gleaming at Titactyk in the dark. It seemed to the commander of the regiment that the statue's lip had curled into a slight smile of amusement, which made the hair on the back of his neck stand on end. Then the stone soldier spoke, its voice harsh and shrill.

As the tide advances, the tunnel in the moraine should be shown, Faron said. *My task is but to open it for you; yours is to enter the abbey. I trust there should be no problem with a small hidden settlement of women and children, but if you are fearful, I could hold your hand, Titactyk.*

The commander swallowed the insult and rode back to the place where his men were quartering their horses. He vaulted off his mount and summoned the soldiers.

"Who has lots on him?"

"Here, sir," said Stephanus, a second lieutenant and subcommander. He ripped open the bindings on one of his saddlebags, dug around inside and pulled out a leather bag that he brought to the commander.

Titactyk took the bag and shook the gambling stones it contained into his palm.

"Determine your order of entry," he said.

One by one the soldiers cast their lots on the cold, wet sand of the beach. Kymel reached for the stones, but Titactyk shook his head.

"Refrain, Kymel; your order has already been determined."

Kymel nodded. "Last, sir?"

"Indeed." Titactyk handed the lots back to Stephanus. He turned around to see the stone titan, bathed as they all were in the light of the moon, almost as bright as day, just in time to watch the statue slam its fist into a dark depression at the base the cliff that had been revealed as the waves rolled back into the belly of the sea.

The hidden tunnel, low to the sandy ground, spat forth a small land-slide of rubble and grit that the sea swallowed a moment later.

Faron turned to the cohort of soldiers.

The pathway is long and narrow; it will take some time for me to widen it. Take this chance to organize and rest; you will not have another.

Titactyk nodded and turned to the men.

"First watch, set to," he said. "Second, third, pull out the provisions and sup quickly, then sleep."

Kymel glanced at his commander as he set to getting rations. There was a gleam in Titactyk's eye that radiated as bright as the moon, though no light touched it.

He spread his bedroll beside his mount and caught a quick round of shuteye, the roar of the sea drowning out the crash of the shattering rock and the crumbling of the stone of the moraine at the titan's hands that had been a natural barrier protecting the cliff above them provided by the All-God and nature.

He was half asleep when he thought he overheard Titactyk's command to the watch.

"Depending on what we find, there should be plenty of opportunity for recreation. The briefing said these cliffs at one time each had an ancient catapult, which should be of interest. Take your turns in order of the lots you drew. Whoever goes first cleans up."

"Yes, sir," came an assortment of voices; at least, that was Kymel's impression, though he was not certain if he was only dreaming. The light of the full moon was shining in his dreams.

Making them burn.

It only seemed a moment later when the toe of a boot roughly prodded his shoulder.

"It's done. Let's go."

Kymel rose quickly and followed his fellow soldiers into the darkness of the passageway. The stone titan stood at the entrance, watching intently. He tried not to flinch as he passed the statue, managing only to be able to keep the chill that had run down his back from being visible.

Or so he hoped.

$\mathcal{H}$e was the last one out of the new passage as the sun was showing indications of rising over the sea beyond the cliff the next morning, his face as pale as the moon that had set while they were within the abbey.

In his hand he clutched a small wooden chest, its contents wrapped in layers of cloth.

His stomach was in his mouth, threatening to spill out.

THE CAULDRON, YLORC

$\mathcal{T}$he fried potatoes are lovely this mornin'," Grunthor commented, looking down at the first seating of soldiers from the balcony of the dining hall. "Burnt to a crisp. Just the way Oi like 'em."

Rhapsody made a face. Achmed rolled his eyes.

"Oh, come now, Rhapsody, I have always assumed you enjoyed the taste of ash in your mouth."

"Are you quite through?" she snapped as the door to the balcony opened and Trug came in with the morning messages. "What in the world has gotten into you?" She shifted the baby to her lap and took the two metal tubes from the Voice Archon, breaking the seal on the first one.

It was from her husband, but the handwriting was shaky and rough, betraying the fraying of his mind she had witnessed in their last communication through the Lightcatcher. Tears came to her eyes as she read the missive, then she put it down on the table and broke the seal on the second one, sliding the scrap of parchment out of the tube.

"Oo's it from, darlin'?" Grunthor asked idly, stabbing a series of crisp black potato shreds onto his fork.

"Rial, by the look of the script," she said as she unrolled it. She read the message, then put her hand to her mouth as she read it again.

"What's it say?" Achmed asked, noting the color fleeing her face.

"Port Tallono, the Lirin harbor. It's been destroyed in a iacxsis attack, just like Avonderre."

38

HIGHMEADOW

$\mathcal{H}$alf a world away, the Lord Cymrian was slowly climbing a narrow set of curving stairs high into the tower in the center of his fortress.

In his shaking hand was a tiny metal leg container holding the message of love he sent every morning to his wife in Ylorc. The script in which it had been graphed was jagged and almost unreadable.

Which was just as well, since the words made very little sense anyway.

Ashe's head was pounding; he had just received the field report, in Anborn's curt and emotionless text, of the slaughter at the Abbey of Nikkid'sar, and had been struggling to keep the dragon in his blood from rampaging since reading it just after dawn. The darkest recesses of his mind still held the trace scars of memories from the days more than two decades before when a piece of his soul had been torn out in his battle with the host of a F'dor and used to power a humanoid construct that did the demon's bidding, including many horrific acts similar to the ones detailed in Anborn's report. He had, with Rhapsody's loving support and the use of her healing lore, managed to lock those memories away in a mental vault, to put them in perspective and only dream about them rarely.

His eyes, and his mind, had seen some very terrible things. He was almost inured to the horror of war and the evil of which man was capable.

But nothing could have prepared him for the description of what had been done to the infants of Nikkid'sar.

Especially because he could not put the image of his own son, in the care of his mother alone, inside a reputably unassailable fortress of mountainous rock, out of his mind.

When he reached the platform at the top of the stairs, he found the master of the rookery finishing up his morning tasks, the care and feeding of the birds that were so critical to maintaining communication across the continent. Ashe stood in silence as he watched the man go about his chores, cleaning out the beautiful cages, each a work of a kind of rare art that both evoked the great architecture of the continent and served to train the avian messengers in recognizing their destinations. Each building, palace, basilica, and mountain fortress, from the Judiciary of Yarim to Lianta'ar in the broken and sundered holy city of Sepulvarta, that had been considered important to maintain contact with had a birdcage, guaranteeing the Alliance's ability to keep abreast of the happenings there.

Or to warn it in times of danger.

The Abbey of Nikkid'sar had apparently not been important enough to warrant the building of such a cage.

When the master of the rookery had finished his work, he bowed to the Lord Cymrian, who looked past him as if he were not there, then made his way down the staircase, leaving Ashe alone with his leg container and his thoughts.

Almost entirely out of habit, he made his way to the cage shaped like Ylorc, the massive windows, doors, and balconies of stone that his grandfather had carved into the forbidding mountains as he shaped the world he thought of as his own possession, beautifully detailed by the artisan who had rendered them.

Ashe stared at the birds in that cage, a few pecking at the seeds left for them, or drinking from the dish of water. Finally he opened the door, almost as if in his sleep, and took out a rock pigeon he recognized as having used on many occasions before.

He held the bird up to his eyes, eyes even more noticeably scored with vertical dragonesque pupils than they usually were.

His father, Llauron, had known each of his birds' names, Ashe mused in a dark melancholy, had spoken and even sung to them as if they were his children. Ashe had not bothered to name any of his own; it had always been his plan to leave that task and honor to Rhapsody who, as a Namer, seemed the most appropriate member of the family to take over the tradition. He had looked forward to that, and Meridion's Naming ceremony, and countless other mundane and silly conventions, rites, and celebrations that they would have undertaken together as a family in the blessing of their new home at Highmeadow, a home he had spent three years building for his wife, obsessing over every detail and designing with her every comfort and amusement in mind, knowing what joy it would give her appointing and decorating it, making it their own.

The home in which she had never spent even a single night.

The home that did not carry any of her scent, or any of her music, but rather smelled of war, of horseflesh and manure, of steel and leather and smoke. The home that rang with the sound of the anvil, and the thunder of horses' hooves and wagon wheels and the ringing of swords, the twanging of bowstrings, the cursing and the shouting and the chaos of battle preparations.

The home that was not a home, but merely the largest of the military outposts of the Alliance, peopled with soldiers and servants and blacksmiths, but not his wife or his son.

I would make your happiness my life's purpose, he had said tenderly to her in the course of asking for her hand in marriage on a warm, beautiful night at the end of the most glorious summer he had ever remembered years ago.

He had not known then how capable the very world was in conspiring to keep him from even having her in his presence.

Ashe felt blood in the back of his throat.

The dragon sensed it there as well, and in his hand.

He consciously struggled to unclench his teeth; his jaw had tightened to the point where they were grinding together, rending his tongue and the sides of his mouth until they were bleeding.

Then he glanced down at his hand.

The rock dove's feathers were stained a dark red, almost black, its neck and back crushed in his grip.

The message container still attached to and dangling from its broken leg.

*L*ater that night, as Gwydion Navarne was getting ready for bed, a knock came at his door. When he opened it his godfather was standing there.

He almost didn't recognize him.

The Lord Cymrian was clean-shaven for the first time in Gwydion's memory of the time since Rhapsody had left, his hair neatly trimmed, his clothes freshly washed.

"May I come in?"

Gwydion felt himself staring, and looked away. "Yes, of course."

"I'm sorry to disturb you so late in the evening. I have something important I want to give you."

Gwydion nodded, but saw nothing in the Lord Cymrian's hand. "What is it?"

Ashe went to the window and looked out into the darkness. "My Right of Command." He tried to not see the shock on the young duke's face. "I have to go into the sea, Gwydion; there is no other option anymore. Port Tallono in Tyrian was assaulted four days ago, with very much the same outcome as the attack on Avonderre Harbor. Talquist owns the entirety of the coast; our naval vessels, those few that survived the assault, are unable to broach the blockade. We have resources and allies in Gaematria and Manosse that will come to our aid as long as we can get word to them." He looked back at Gwydion. "I mean to do that."

"But if the harbor is blockaded, surely your ship will be destroyed immediately. And even if you can run the blockade, didn't you say that Talquist has pirate—"

"I'm not going to run the blockade on a ship. I am going to walk through the sea on my own. I'm the Kirsdarkenvar, Gwydion. The element of water is my friend—my servant. The only regrets I have are that I am leaving you and the western continent alone to face forces of power that are unlike any that has been dealt with in memory. Fortunately, both your grandmother and I know you are up to the task."

"You—you do? She does?"

"Yes. It was her suggestion. And you will be able to draw on some of my lore, my experience, my wisdom, though yours is no doubt better at this point. You can do this, Gwydion. Anborn stands ready to help you, as does Rhapsody. It will take a few days to prepare for this, and I want to leave you as well prepared as I can, so I will make myself available to you as readily as I can. Now, kneel. The sooner I incant this power unto you, the sooner you can begin thinking of yourself as the Lord Cymrian—which is what you will be."

The young duke's eyes were open in stark terror, but he knelt as commanded and bowed his head as Ashe's hand came upon it, speaking words in a language he had barely begun to learn.

By the time the incantation was over, he was feeling no better.

But Ashe looked as if he did, at least.

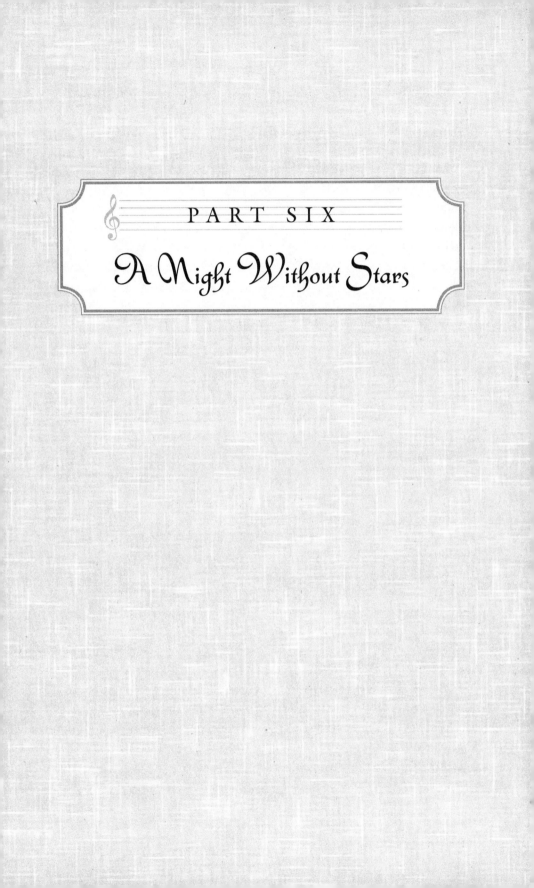

PART SIX

A Night Without Stars

39

THE MOUNTAIN PASS INTO
KRALDURGE, YLORC

*W*hether it had been half a decade or half a millennium before, the loss of Achmed's blood lore still stung in ways he could not completely give voice to, even if he had been inclined to do so.

It was an ability he had had most, if not all of his life. He could not be sure if the memory of its origin was correct, as he had been young and on the brink of death at the time, but when he sought to recall the birth of his blood-gift, the image in his mind was the face of his mentor, a quiet and unassuming monk in the old world by the name of Father Halphasion. The priest had been his rescuer, his protector, his teacher, and, in a sense, the first Namer he had ever known, despite the fact that the man was not Lirin, the race of which Namers were born, but rather Dhracian, as Achmed's own mother had been. Like Achmed, Father Halphasion was not *Zheren-ditck*, not part of a Dhracian Colony, but *Dhisrik*, one of the Uncounted, those Dhracians that were lost in the world, unconnected to their people who, more than any race ever known, were joined at the mind, like ants, able to think and act as one with their kin in vast, interwoven webs of silent vibration.

The gentle monk had come upon him, dying, in the wake of his escape from the torment of his Bolg captors who used him for slave labor and viciously cruel entertainment, in the days when his name was Ysk, the Bolgish word approximating of spittle or vomit. The word had an overtone of poison in it, likely because the only thing more grotesque in appearance than Firbolg, a bastard race of demi-humans that had been conquered by every other culture that had ever come in contact with it and had bred into it through rape and domination the ugliest of traits, was the visage of a half-breed whose other side was Dhracian.

Father Halphasion had renamed him, in the course of his reclamation and studies, calling him the Brother, a name he said described the dying boy perfectly.

Brother to all, akin to none.

Though he was uncertain when the skill of sensing and tracking the heartbeats of every person on the Island of Serendair had become his own, Achmed believed it to have been in that moment when the monk uttered those words. Not long after he was aware of a cacophony of heartbeats, vibrating on his skin and in his ears, often deafening, always maddening, but able to be singled out, isolated, and locked on to, making him an unerring tracker and unfailing assassin. But whenever the gift had actually come to him, he was certain of when it was taken from him.

It was the moment that a desperate, golden-haired half-Lirin woman had stumbled upon him and Grunthor in a back alley in the city of Easton in Serendair, asked them to adopt her for a moment, then introduced him to her pursuers as her brother.

You gentlemen are just in time to meet my brother. Brother, these are the town guard. Gentlemen, this is my brother—Achmed—the Snake.

Without even meaning to, she had snapped the chain of domination that his demonic master had around that name, and changed him forever.

He hadn't noticed the loss then; even when the power was broken, he was still tied to the sound of the heartbeats of those born on the Island. It was not until he stepped out into the crisp, bitter air of winter on this new continent, emerging from the bowels of the Earth, that he was aware, for the first time in as long as he could remember, of silence. It had been more a curse than a blessing; while he no longer was assaulted in each moment with the pounding of millions of distinct vibrations, he was now without the greatest tool he had relied on when tracking an enemy.

He was acutely aware of that loss this morning as his footsteps, normally silent, echoed up the towering walls of the mountain pass that led in to the wide circular meadow known to the Bolg as Kraldurge, meaning the Realm of Ghosts. The reverberating echoes stung his skin, making him even more irritable than he had been in recent memory.

It did not help that Grunthor's massive boots were making an even more horrific noise, a thundering clatter that bounced off both sides of the narrow pass. Even the soft treads of Rhapsody's small boots were clacking loudly; it was giving the Bolg king an excruciating headache.

"Is this really necessary?" he asked as they approached the end of the pass that opened into the meadow. "I believe Grunthor has given you several reports of the status of Elysian, Rhapsody; I don't understand your need to inspect the place yourself. Nothing survived Anwyn's attack—she set the entirety of the island ablaze, scorching the house, the boats, the gardens—everything. The smell still lingers; my nostrils are already stinging from it, all the way above the grotto. I do wish you could just take his word for it—I have an endless list of better things to do."

"Then by all means, go attend to them," Rhapsody said, stroking the head of the sleeping baby in the broadcloth sling strapped to her chest. "I wanted to see Elysian for myself—between its loss and that of the Lirin harbor of Port Tallono, I am thinking to the next steps for both of their reclamation. I am perfectly all right going down to the grotto alone—it's my duchy, I've done it a million times. It was your idea to come."

"Hardly," the Bolg king replied sourly. "It was Grunthor's idea."

"Damned right," said the Sergeant, looking around the meadow blooming to the very edges of the rockwalls in colorful heartsease. "Oi don' ever like it when you go off by yerself, Duchess; like it less when ya drag the lit'le prince with you, and especially 'ate it when you put yerself in places where dragons have been." He cast a glance around the windy veldt carpeted with bright flowers. "Don' like it at'tall."

As if in agreement, Meridion's tiny head emerged from against his mother's chest, the oil from where he had been anointed in blessing by the Patriarch still gleaming on his tiny forehead. Constantin had come to them at breakfast that morning to bless the baby before going into his last prayer vigil before departing; Rhapsody had bade him goodbye without an embrace and without speaking, knowing it would disturb his spiritual preparations. Meridion's bright blue eyes met hers.

Then he opened his mouth and screamed.

"Oh my goodness!" Rhapsody blurted, shocked. "Meridion, shhhh, now. Shhhh."

The sound rocketed off Achmed's sensitive skin, stinging it intensely. He closed his eyes, the lids of which were burning from the sound.

"Make him stop *now*," he commanded.

"Ya just fed 'im," Grunthor murmured, alone not distressed by the caterwauling. "Wonder what's botherin' 'im?"

Rhapsody bent closer to whisper soothingly to the baby.

She had just enough time to roll as she fell into the flower-filled grass, sparing Meridion from being crushed, paralyzed, an all-but-invisible dart in the back of her neck.

*W*ithin a heartbeat, the Sergeant-Major was on top of them both. Achmed made note of his movement without seeing it; he had swung the cwellan down from over his shoulder and was turning rapidly, letting loose a spray of whisper-thin disks in a spinning circle at the same height from the ground that the dart had come. In the distance he could feel the thudding of one body that fell, most likely the source of the dart, invisible to his sight.

He cursed silently and turned back to Rhapsody.

Only to find her, and her son, and Grunthor missing.

Achmed crouched low to the grass and whirled, scanning the vista of short blossoms and taller vegetation. Whatever was hiding within it in the more distant parts of the meadow was invisible to him; he tried to sense for vibrations, and found them, but they were jumbled, battered around the circular rockwalls in the wind that screamed like demons, giving the place its name. His gaze returned to the place where Grunthor and Rhapsody had fallen.

Instantly he recalled the time when Rhapsody had whispered the name of highgrass, using her powers to hide them from a troop of wandering Lirinved in the old world, and wondered if that was why he couldn't see them. But the pallor in her cheeks, the glass stare in her eyes as she fell made him certain that it had not been at her will that the two of them were hiding, if in fact they were. He looked down a short distance away to see a rich brown patch of earth that was rapidly covering itself with meadow flowers, the descendants of the heartsease the Singer had planted in this place. Within a moment, it had blending seamlessly into the carpet of blooms and taller scrub.

Good, he thought. *Grunthor has them. Good.*

Once the other two of the Three were out of sight, his ancient skill and training roared back, ascendant. Achmed sank to the ground and crawled, reptile-like, on his belly, moving without sound, causing no disturbance to the meadow grass. His instincts led him away from the center of the meadow, scanning the fields for those similarly talented at hiding, but he saw nothing. Aside from the first assassin, the one he had caught in a random sweep of cwellan disks, he could discern no one, not even a trace of scent on the wind, and grudgingly admired the skill of the assassins who had breached his unassailable fortress.

Until overwhelming fury took hold, making him shake.

Come out and play, you knobbing bastards, he thought silently.

He waited, crouched flat, but still saw no movement. The wind blew through again, howling down the rockwalls, the sound echoing until it died away.

The patterns of stalking that the assassins in his meadow were undertaking were foreign to him; Achmed cursed himself again. In the old land he made it an unconscious practice to be familiar with every trade secret employed by formal assassin's guilds and independent hunters; he had been king long enough now that those root-level survival skills were long from his mind. He turned slowly on his side again, keeping the cwellan at a wide arc of attack.

Then, as he stared into the gold-brown scrub above the colorful flowers, he thought he saw something descend, almost like the lightest of snow.

Only it was the hue of emeralds, the color of pine trees in spring, grass on Midsummer's Night. Rhapsody's eyes.

A ribbon of light was wending its way through the meadow, a wide shaft of sunlight, though unmistakably green.

What is happening? Achmed thought angrily as the radiance settled on the grass. He raised his head slightly and, in doing so, was treated to a sight that he had made possible himself, through the unrelenting and obnoxiously insistent belief in the need for the Lightcatcher's restoration.

Four shadows were highlighted, images of men crouched in a seemingly random pattern around the meadow and within the crags of the rockwalls. Each was armed with weapons of either the desert or the sea; Achmed's throat burned at the knowledge that they were assassins, no doubt, from Yarim Paar, and very likely from Golgarn or beyond. They did not seem to see him, nor did they discern the green light that was illuminating them to him, as if outlined by the light of an emerald sun.

Far away, deeper into Kraldurge, closer to the opening to the grotto of

Elysian, a dark, wraith-thin shadow was slipping away. A third curse passed silently over Achmed's lips as it rounded the bend and vanished.

One more he would have to hunt.

"Thank you, Constantin," he muttered softly. He continued the rest of his thought without speaking. *Whatever silly countersigns and oil you splashed onto the baby this morning notwithstanding, the true blessing you have given him is the use of the Lightcatcher's green spectrum, the power of grass scrying.*

He thought of Rhapsody and swallowed to ease the dryness in his throat.

Then rose slowly, almost imperceptibly, sighting his cwellan.

Within the next heartbeat, four men from the desert and the sea were bleeding their lives out into the meadow, feeding the flowers.

Achmed stood and looked around.

No other figures remained in the glowing green light, which began to disperse and disappear a moment later.

He called for Grunthor as he scanned the meadow. Closer to him than he had expected a large, blossom-covered hummock stretched and rose, shaking dirt and leaves from its greatcoat.

"Did ya get 'em all?" the Sergeant-Major inquired as he brushed away the petals and leaves.

"Lost one—he was on the way down to Elysian when I spotted him," Achmed said tersely. "There must be a breach there; it figures. Is Rhapsody breathing?"

"Yeah," said Grunthor, hauling her off the ground and into his arms, in one of which a tiny bundle was cooing. "Barely. Y'all right there, Yer 'ighness?"

A round of chirping and babbling sounds answered him.

"Must be a paralytic," Achmed said, "or she wouldn't be breathing. They must have wanted to take her alive. Here, give the two of them to me. You go down and seal the bloody entrance to that place once and for all, and meet me back in the Great Hall."

$\mathcal{R}$hapsody woke before she was able to open her eyes.

When she shuddered with panic, still unable to move, she felt the thin leather of gloves brush the hair back from her numb forehead.

"Don't try to move yet," the sandy voice said. "You will come out of this much better if you just let the poison run its course, rather than injuring body parts by making them move before they are ready to do so. Additionally, you will give me an extended respite from your prattle; the silence has been a blessing so far, please don't ruin it. I'm assuming you can hear me. Just listen.

"Your brat is fine. Grunthor has him, and he had supper before he took the baby, so Meridion is safe for the moment, I'd wager, though if I were you, I'd lie very still in the hope of dissipating the poison before Grunthor's stomach starts rumbling for his midnight snack. Yes, midnight—you've been down for a long time. I imagine your breasts will be exploding any minute now. Charming.

"You cannot stay here any longer and expect to be safe. They've broached the mountain, though they were apparently looking for you, and not the Earthchild, at least as far as we can tell. We've consulted with Gyllian, and she agrees that you and the other women, including Melisande, should travel with her under the Lightcatcher's power of grass hiding to the Nain kingdom, where you can seek refuge. It was the green spectrum that saved your arse, by the way; I never would have seen the assassins hiding in Kraldurge had it not been for Constantin's last gift to you. He was watching us through the Lightcatcher, trying to determine if Meridion was able to be seen through a scrying instrumentality; he says the cloak kept your brat from notice, though he could see each of us. He's gone now, off to rebuild his Chain of Prayer.

"Assuming you are going to agree to this, Grunthor has made preparations for you to leave day after tomorrow in the morning. You cannot risk notifying Ashe by any other means than the Lightcatcher; even the birds are of questionable security. I will expect you to return when you can, to help guard the Earthchild and lend a hand to keeping the mountain safe, but not until we find the last assassin who escaped.

"Rest now. Don't move until you are sure you can do so safely. That will most likely not happen until at least tomorrow afternoon."

Rhapsody opened her eyes, their irises the same deep green as the light from the grass-scrying spectrum had been.

"Thank you," she whispered.

40

GURGUS PEAK, YLORC

The azure hue of late evening that filled the vast room below Gurgus Peak was blotted with shadow. As the light above fled the darkening sky, pools of radiance dotted the stone floor intermittently, disappearing as the sun vanished below the horizon.

Rhapsody stood at the base of the Lightcatcher, her hand on the altar, feeling the sound of her own breath echoing in the enormous chamber. Meridion scowled, asleep in the crook of her left arm, his tiny brows drawn together, his face blue in the shadows from the sky raining down through the ceiling dome of glass.

She kissed the furrow on the baby's forehead, letting her lips linger there, breathing in the sweetness of his skin. Then she straightened her back, ran her hand over the runes in the altar, bringing her palm at last above *Brige-sol*, the symbol known as Cloud Caller, or Cloud Chaser, in the blue section of the spectrum embedded in the table board of the altar. She softly sang her Naming note.

Light appeared beneath her palm, as Constantin had promised it would.

Rhapsody exhaled. She cast a glance across the tower room to the wheel on its track, still and quiet in the darkness. Then she touched the emblem for sharp, the positive symbol from the Patriarch's ring, and sang the name of the home that had been built for her but that she had never inhabited, *Highmeadow*, followed by the specifics of the location of Ashe's office.

A cylinder of blue light appeared around her, encircling the altar. At the edge of the circle, above the silver disk in the floor, she could see the desk, the rug on the floor, the map table, but there was no sign of her husband.

Rhapsody's throat tightened. Ashe had always been in the study on the previous occasions she had contacted him through the Lightcatcher; she was uncertain how to find him now. She quickly sang his name, hoping she would not lose the opportunity before the light winked out, having misguessed where he would be.

Gwydion ap Llauron ap Gwylliam, tuatha d'Anwynan o Manosse.

The image faded, then, a moment later, a new one took its place.

In a slightly brighter evening shadow at the western end of the continent, beneath an open sky, Rhapsody caught sight of red-gold hair, gleaming in the remains of the day's light as the sun slipped below the rim of the world through the trees of the forest surrounding the palace fortress of Highmeadow.

Ashe was standing on the balcony of the central building of the complex, staring east, the fading light behind him ringing him in luminance. His beard was gone, and at first she almost didn't recognize his face; there was a sharpness to his features that she could see even in the hazy light of the instrumentality. He no longer appeared unkempt, but there was something different she could not quite place; it was as if she was staring at a stranger in the clothes of her husband.

She swallowed the knot that had tied itself in her throat.

"Good evening, my love," she said. Her voice caught in the tightness of her larynx and came out in a hoarse whisper.

Ashe started, then glanced around until his eyes found what must have been a very diffuse image of her, hovering outside the railing of the balcony. He smiled slightly.

Good evening to you, too, my love. Hello, Meridion, pippin.

"How was your day?" The words sounded inane even to her own ears.

Ashe's smile faded. *I have done as you asked, Aria. I have passed along my Right of Command to Gwydion, at least that part of it entrusted with holding the continent for the Alliance.*

Rhapsody's eyes gleamed. "Are you all right? How do you feel?"

Her husband appeared as if he were considering her question.

Lighter. And yet still worried as I prepare to leave. There have been some very awful days this week, but I will spare you the details for the sake of time. How are you both?

"We are well," Rhapsody said. Inside she flinched. *How much more well can one be, after surviving one's own assassination attempt?* she thought, then turned the still-sleeping Meridion toward Ashe and held him as close to the undulating image of her husband as she could. "Can you see him?"

The Lord Cymrian's smile returned, and for the moment Rhapsody saw her husband again.

Yes. He's beautiful, Aria. Why is he scowling?

Rhapsody sighed.

"He does that sometimes in his sleep," she said. "But he may also be sulking; we had a bit of an argument this evening."

Oh? Over what?

"I have been trying to wean him a little, to get him to take milk from a special waterskin. To say he doesn't like it much would be a tremendous understatement."

Who could blame him? Ashe said humorously. *That's my boy.* The smile left his eyes. *Why did you decide to wean him, Aria? Is his growing demand exhausting you?*

Rhapsody swallowed again.

"No," she said as directly as she could. "I am taking him to the Nain."

Ashe blinked in surprise; Rhapsody could see the dragonesque pupils, now more prominent than she remembered, reappear after his eyes opened again.

To the Nain? Why?

She steeled herself, then plunged ahead.

"To be hidden there. It's no longer safe for him here in Ylorc. Talquist is in pursuit of him through many terrible means, Sam. For all it may seem that his primary intent is to take the Middle Continent, believe me when I tell you that his real targets are in the Bolglands. I am leaving tomorrow, with Gyllian, Krinsel, Analise, and Melly. We will be traveling by night, and mostly within the mountains, so we will be as safe as it is possible for us to be. I am going to beg a boon of Faedryth: his protection of Meridion. I believe, in spite of our disagreements over the Lightcatcher, he will not deny me his fealty. Between the army of the Nain, the River of Fire and

Witheragh, the dragon who guards it, as well as the defenses of that distant kingdom, there is no place where our son will be better hidden. I am telling you because if something should happen to me, you need to know where he is, that he is safe, at least as safe as I now can make him."

The steadiness in Ashe's eyes disappeared, replaced by a similar gleam to Rhapsody's own.

The gleam of near-madness.

What terrible means? he demanded, the multitonal ring of the dragon in his voice. *What has happened, Aria?*

"Nothing that Achmed has not been able to rebuff, but I don't want to take any chances with the baby," she said quickly. "And please, be on guard against potential assassins—apparently Talquist has signed contracts with every guild imaginable, and every major Cymrian leader or figure is targeted. Gwydion is at risk, as is Tristan—please, please be careful, Sam."

Let them find me in the sea, the Lord Cymrian spat, smoke seeming to emerge from his blazing eyes. *Let them come after me, wherever I am. Have they made an attempt against you?*

"Yes," she admitted, "but as you can see, it was unsuccessful."

And is this why you are weaning our child? Because you believe the next one will be successful?

Rhapsody willed herself to be calm at the panic and ire that rose in her husband's voice.

"Of course not," she said, struggling to keep her own voice steady. "He needs to be able to take nourishment from someone other than me when I leave him."

Leave him? Ashe demanded. *What do mean, leave him? You are not planning to stay with him in the kingdom of the Nain?*

Rhapsody shook her head, trying not to meet his eyes.

Look at me, the Lord Cymrian commanded. *What are you planning, then, Aria?*

"I am the Iliachenva'ar," she said quietly, raising her eyes and meeting his glare. "I am needed in battle, especially once you have gone after reinforcements in Gaematria and Manosse, and especially in Tyrian." She saw the cords stand out in his neck, a sign of utter fury, an indication that the dragon within his blood was rising, readying a rampage.

And it angered her.

"Gwydion ap Llauron, *stop*," she commanded in return, in the ringing tones of her Namer status. "Quell your rage; there isn't time for it."

Ashe blinked again, this time in shock. The tone of her voice was as regal and excoriating as he had ever heard it. The dragon slunk away at the sound of it, cooling his wrath for the moment.

"Before you question my decision, please try to imagine what it has and will cost me," Rhapsody continued tersely. "After all the ways I have fought for this child, from convincing you of the wisdom of having him in the first place, to surviving what I have to protect him, do you think for a bloody *moment* that I would leave my baby for any reason if there was any other choice?"

I do not doubt—

"Be silent and listen. One blessing so far is that it seems Talquist does not know the baby's name; he only seeks him, as far as we know, as the Child of Time. But he *does* know who his parents are; have you had to interdict any Sorbold cohorts at Haguefort or Highmeadow?"

Even as filmy as the image of Ashe was, Rhapsody could see his face go pale in the light.

Yes. At the beginning, right after you left for Ylorc. It was the beginning of the actual war.

Rhapsody nodded slightly. "At the moment, hiding as I have been, I am more of a danger to him than a suitable protector of him. If it's not enough that Talquist apparently has scrying relics of his own, he is allied with the Diviner, and is in league with the titan, who is the host of a F'dor that is seeking to find the Sleeping Child. On top of coping with his assassins, your accursed *grandmother* is out there somewhere, injured and furious, looking to destroy me. She has already broached the mountain once, Ashe—she torched Elysian, reducing it to rubble. Can you imagine what would happen to Meridion if and when she finds me? If he is in my arms? If I am nursing him?"

Her tirade ground to a halt as Ashe began to tremble.

Pain and guilt swam through her, leaving her cold and shaking herself. Her heart stung at the horror she knew her words had caused her husband, and she took a deep breath, willing herself calm again.

"I'm sorry," she said softly. "I'm so sorry, Ashe. I did not mean to frighten you."

Too late.

In her arms, the baby began to squirm.

"Please, please don't be afraid," she said, cradling the child and trying to impart comfort to her husband through her words and her eyes. "I have pondered the situation endlessly, have in fact used the Lightcatcher to confirm my belief. Constantin has imbued it with some of the lore of the

Ring of Wisdom; I know of no better resource to consult. It was folly to believe that each of the elemental swords is not needed to be in the fray; the best way for me to protect my son—our son—is to do everything that I can to help you end this conflict. Anborn tried to keep me out of the war as long as he could, but now that he is engaged in battle, and you are leaving, I must help your namesake prosecute the war for the Alliance until you get back. But not until the baby is safely hidden away. He will have Krinsel and Analise with him, as well as Gyllian, who will support my plea to Faedryth. And Melisande will be safer as well."

Ashe nodded, subdued. *Well, that will help ease Gwydion's mind, I am certain.*

Rhapsody exhaled again. When she spoke, her voice was gentle.

"Hopefully it will ease the mind of both my Gwydions. Just as you are leaving some of your Right of Command with Gwydion Navarne, so I am planning to leave much of myself—the soul I share with you—with our son. If he is to remember me, remember us, remember the love of which he was born, I will need to give him everything, *everything*, Sam. Just as you are leaving the lordship with Gwydion, I will need to leave my true name with Meridion; I won't remember 'Emily' anymore. The only thing left of me when he is gone will be Rhapsody, the Namer, the Iliachenva'ar. And just as you said you did not know if you could take back that Right of Command, I do not know if I will be able to get back the part of me that I am leaving behind. I may be unrecognizable, just as you are when the dragon takes control of you. But it's the only thing I can do now." Against her will, tears spilled from her eyes and streaked her cheeks. "I am sorry. I'm sorry that I have failed you."

Ashe looked down and let out a long sigh.

Never, he said quietly. *Throughout two lifetimes, across two worlds, you have never failed me. Nor have you ever failed our son. I will remember Emily, even if you don't for a while, believe me. I bow to your wisdom in this matter, and I'm sorry if I seemed to doubt it. I do know what this is costing you—it is the same nightmare I took on when I realized you both were not safe here with me in Highmeadow, that I could not protect you and prosecute the war at the same time. I don't believe you understood when I sent you away what it cost me, not only to lose both of you from my life, but also to have to entrust you to Achmed for your own safety.*

"Well, I know now," Rhapsody said. "Of all the sovereigns in the Cymrian Alliance, Faedryth is the one who is most angry with me. I will have to eat the equivalent of the ground glass that he reduced his Lightforge to in order to gain his agreement, I have no doubt. At least Achmed agreed willingly to take us back to Ylorc with him."

Ashe said nothing. Rhapsody flinched at the tensing of the muscles in his cheeks as he clenched his teeth, the intensifying of the fire in his eyes, but he did not give voice to his thoughts.

"I want to tell you something," she whispered. "Something from my heart, something I barely have words for. Something I will not be able to say or feel or even understand when I—after I leave him. Something from my soul to yours, through our marital bond."

The depth of pain and love in her eyes made Ashe's gleam at the edges.

Tell me, then—I am listening, beloved.

Rhapsody noticed that the light was dimming She cleared her throat, then spoke carefully, trying not to hurry, even though she feared losing the connection.

"The night Meridion was conceived, I heard—maybe not heard, maybe *felt*, I don't know how to put words to it—a tone ring within me, a namesong different from the one I hear from you, and from my own. I believe it was the first time I was aware of Meridion in this world; he didn't begin with us, Sam. It's like we were the doorway, you and I, to allow him to come into being from where he already was. And deep within me I sense other such songs, far away; I'm not sure if it's only one, or many, because they are so distant, but it makes me believe that there are other children, other entities, meant to be born of our love, waiting somewhere in the ether."

Her words ground to a halt as she saw the change in his face. It was a softening of the sharp edges, a loosening of the hold his dragon nature clearly had on him now, leaving him human and vulnerable.

Her own eyes stung at the purity and depth of the love that she saw in his aspect.

"I've heard women of many different races say something to the effect that a woman innately knows how many children she has inside of her," she went on, feeling weak in the warmth of his gaze. "I now am beginning to understand what they mean. I asked you to consider having Meridion because I could *hear* him, as if he was calling to me, I could feel him waiting. And if there is any hope I can impart to you, my dearest love, it is this; there are others waiting, at least one other song waiting to come into this world through you and me. I can *hear* it, Sam; I can hear them." The tears spilled over again.

Ashe smiled and reached out his hand to the image of her. *I believe you.*

"And that means, I think, that we are meant to live through this, to be reunited, with each other *and* our son, to resume our lives as we have planned them, to be the doorway for whatever other souls are waiting to be born of the love between us."

I pray you are right.

Rhapsody reached out her hand in turn to him, though the images did not touch.

"The lore of the soul is as powerful a lore as there is—it transcends even Time. Hold on to that, my love."

I am doing my best, Rhapsody.

"I know. I know you are."

You cannot know how much comfort hearing this gives me, he said. *Kiss our son for me.*

The light had now left the sky, and the blue column faded to little more than an echo.

"I love you, Sam," she called as it disappeared, taking the image of her husband with it.

Along with what little peace of mind she had left.

41

When she came out of Gurgus Peak, Rhapsody took Grunthor by the sleeve and pulled him aside.

"Grunthor, will you consider doing me two important favors, please?"

The giant's amber eyes twinkled affectionately.

"O' course, Duchess—you ought to know by now Oi'd do anything for you."

Her eyes sparkled warmly in return.

"I do, but my mother always told me it was polite to ask, even if you already know the answer. Do you suppose you could make certain that the troops are not marching past my door this evening, singing grotesque cadences? Dearly as I enjoy hearing them on most occasions, tonight I need to speak with my son, and it's important that we are not interrupted."

"Good as done, Yer Ladyship."

"Thank you."

The Sergeant-Major nodded. "An' the second?"

Rhapsody's smile dimmed, and her face grew serious.

"Would you do Ashe and me the honor of being Meridion's godfather?"

Grunthor blinked.

"Godfather?"

"Yes."

A look of surpassing seriousness, and something more, crossed the Sergeant's face. "Not sure what that means, Duchess."

Rhapsody exhaled. "It's an honorary position, a sign of great love and respect," she said softly. "Offered to someone you want to be involved forever in your child's life, who will be a role model and a confidante to him, and if something happens to his parents, will make certain he is taken care of and safe. Ashe serves in that role to Gwydion Navarne, his godson." She ran her hand down the giant's arm and into his massive, pawlike palm, taking care to avoid scratching herself on his claws. "It's an honor that is not conferred lightly, because of its importance to the well-being of a child, our dearest treasure. It's one of the best ways we humans have of telling someone we love him."

The Firbolg soldier's face grew red from what looked like the warring emotions of delight and abashment.

"Ol' Waterboy is all right with this?"

Rhapsody's smile grew brighter. "It was his idea."

Grunthor grinned, but he did not look like he believed her.

"Really," Rhapsody insisted, squeezing his hand. "I knew my choice long ago, but when I asked him for his thoughts on the matter, yours was the first name out of his mouth." She looked deeply into his eyes and used her True-Speaking lore. "Our son would not be alive if it was not for you, and for what you have done, time and time again, to save and protect him, and me. His father and I are both unspeakably grateful. And Meridion loves you. Most of the time the choice of a godfather has nothing to do with the child's opinion; it's a decision made by the parents alone. But it is clear to me that if he were able to speak, my son would utter the same answer to the question 'who shall we ask to be Meridion's godfather' as his father did."

Grunthor scratched his massive head awkwardly.

"Oi don' know what to say, Yer Ladyship. O' course I will look after the lit'le prince, tend to 'is trainin' and the like, but Oi don't even want you contemplatin' 'avin' somethin' 'appen to you." He looked down into her crestfallen face. "Oi'm greatly honored, o' course."

Rhapsody squared her shoulders.

"Having a child means always contemplating what to do should something happen to his parents," she said. "You needn't worry; Meridion is the greatest insurance you will ever have that I will do everything possible to live through whatever is coming. I'm just asking you to be officially acknowledged as special to both him and to me—it's little enough to offer for how deeply I love you, and always will."

The knock on his bedchamber door roused Achmed from his reverie. He rose from his chair, went to the door and opened it.

Rhapsody was standing in the hallway, her arms empty.

Silently Achmed held the door farther open.

She crossed her arms as she came into the room, looking around at the surprising opulence. The Bolg king was a man of ascetic tastes, but the one place he had ever indulged in any form of luxury was his bedchamber. The man whose life was a constant assault of vibrations on his ultrasensitive skin had outfitted his sleeping quarters with black silk sheets and dark, thick carpets, making his time unconscious comfortable and allowing himself the respite of oblivion from the torment that was each waking moment.

"I have a request of you. Please don't grant it if you don't want to."

Achmed's brow furrowed. "You know me better than to need to say that."

"I do. I would like you to do me the honor of being Meridion's guardian."

The Bolg king stared at her.

"I do not know why you seem to hate him as much as you do," she said, looking away. "You have sacrificed much to save both him and me, twice from Anwyn, and now from Talquist. But the things you call him—"

"Stop. I don't hate him. He irritates me."

"I find that very hard to believe," Rhapsody said, meeting his gaze again. "Say I'm biased, but Meridion is the easiest, most cheerful and musical child I've ever known. Almost every time he has cried, or stunk up your sensitive sinuses, it has been a warning that we were being followed, or that the dragon was awake in the baths of Kurimah Milani, or that Kraldurge was full of *assassins*, or a dozen other things that might lead anyone who *didn't* hate him to recognize his innate magic. But you have nothing good or kind to say about him. You have never referred to him as anything but a brat, which in the language of my childhood either denoted spoiled behavior, which insults him, or illegitimacy, which insults me."

The unsettling eyes bore into her.

"Then why would you want me to be his guardian?"

Rhapsody exhaled.

"Because I love you. Because I trust you. Because there is no one on this earth he is safer with. If something should happen to me, I want to be able to die knowing that you will make sure he gets back to his father, that he will not be abused or harmed. It just makes me sad that you can't be kinder to him."

"You believe I've been unkind to him?"

She reconsidered. "No, I guess that's wrong. I think you've been unkind to me about him. And I don't know why. I don't know what I did to gain your ire, to make you angry, to make you say the things you have. But whatever regret I have about this is dwarfed utterly by how grateful I am for everything you've done to protect us, to rescue us, to keep us safe. So I ask you, please, will you do this for me? Will you protect my son if I am killed? Will you see to it that he is safe until Ashe can get to him?"

Achmed continued to stare at her for a long time. Finally he nodded silently.

"Thank you," Rhapsody said. "I'm sorry you don't know this for the honor it is meant to be, but you have my deepest gratitude. Maybe one day I will understand what I did to make you so angry and hostile about him."

She turned on her heel and left the room without a backward glance.

Achmed felt the reverberations of the door in his skin and eyelids until they died away.

"You let Ashe be his father," he said aloud to no one.

Rhapsody had taken a short walk in the evening wind to clear her head before talking to the third man she loved that night. She could hear the soft cooing noises even as she opened the door to her chamber.

Analise had already picked him up and was smiling down at him, carrying on a conversation with him in Ancient Lirin. Rhapsody chuckled; the baby responded happily to each phrase she uttered in a variety of nonsense syllables that made tears come to her eyes.

Analise, knowing what she was about to do, kissed her friend and put the baby in her arms.

Rhapsody waited until the door closed behind her, then laid Meridion down on his back on her bed and watched him for a long time, smiling down at her son. In her hand she held a tiny pearl earring.

She reached out and gently touched his ear lobe, speaking the name of mist.

For a few moments, the little boy's skin became vaporous, just long enough for Rhapsody to pin the earring through without hurting him. Then she stopped her chant, and caressed the lobe as it became solid again.

"Leaving you surely is the most difficult thing I will ever do," she said, trying to smile. "But I must be brave, as you have been so, so brave. If I falter now, how can I ever hope to be worthy of the role with which you have blessed me?"

The infant's eyes were locked on her, the look in them quizzical. Rhapsody leaned over him and kissed his forehead, then his tiny hands and belly.

"*Y pippin*," she said softly. The words came from the deepest part of her heart, in the language she had spoken almost solely with her mother, Ancient Lirin, the tongue lost to the world when the Island of Serendair sank beneath the waves of the sea. Words by which her own mother had called her. Υ *pippin.*

My baby.

She blinked, trying to keep the tears out of her eyes. With a trembling finger she caressed the tiny pearl in the baby's earlobe.

"In this pearl I am leaving you my true name and my heart, my lovely little boy, along with the memory of what I am telling you now. What better place to keep them than with the only other Liringlas Singer in our family?"

The baby gurgled and smiled toothlessly, making her eyes sparkle and fill with tears at the same time in spite of her efforts to hold them back. His clear blue eyes, almost the exact color as his father's, were still focused on her, the tiny dragonesque pupils within them twinkling as if he understood everything she was saying.

She thought back to the earliest part of her pregnancy with him, when a nightmare from her past, a demonic host, a man obsessed with her, had chased her into the sea, where she was trapped in the swirling fury of a tidal cave. The terror, the savage danger of the rising tides, the churning waves that blasted her about in the dark, scraping her against the ceiling of the cave, had been easier to bear and eventually vanquish when she had begun talking to the baby, newly conceived. She remembered the words she had spoken to him one day, floating in her watery prison, while listening to and learning the songs of the sea.

How lucky you are in a way, my child, to have this time. You are being steeped in elemental magic—the baptism of the sea, the fire that warms and dries us when the tide is low, the sheltering cave of earth that was formed in fire and cooled in water, the wind that blows through, singing its ageless song. One day you will make a fine Namer if you choose to be one.

Several times she could have sworn she heard his voice within her speaking to her, singing along with the music of the sea.

"I love you with everything that I am, Meridion," she said, the tone of her True-Speaking ringing in her words, even over the sadness with which she pronounced them. "And I swear to you, as dearly and completely as I will love any siblings you may one day have, if God the One, the All blesses us with them, you will always be uniquely special to me, because of what we have lived through and endured together."

The baby cooed as if in agreement.

She struggled to keep the tears out of her voice, but her throat was tightening to the point it was hard to swallow. "It was you that made me a mother, something I wanted to be more than anything for as long as I can remember. You, *pippin*. Thank you—I am so—honored—that you chose me. So honored to be *il mimen*, your mama."

She bowed her head, trying to keep the halting words steady, but choked with the effort of restraining her tears from the baby's sight.

Her words ground to a halt as her eyes overflowed. Rhapsody kissed him again, wiping back the tears as she did, and coughed softly, trying to keep her voice steady.

"*Il hamimen*, your grandmother, would have loved you so," she said when she could speak once more. "It was she that gave me the name I am keeping—Rhapsody—because she wanted me to have a Lirin name, a musical name—my parents gave it to me as my middle name. I need to hold on to this name, because I learned most of my lore as a Singer, as a Namer, under it. I will need that lore, those powers, in the days to come." She smiled at the baby, and received a beaming grin in response.

"But I am now going to give you the rest of my name, the name my father chose, by which I was known in the old world. It was by this name that my family knew me, both the formal and the nicknames, my human name. It was the name your father called me by when we first met. It has only been spoken one other time in this world, in the ceremony in which he and I first married in secret. It is the name I carried when I first learned how to love, Meridion—it is from that time when I was taught about family, and music, and the tending of the earth, and our tie to the stars. It was the beginning of the fulfillment of my greatest dreams which led, eventually, to your entry into this world. Keep it for me, will you?"

The baby whimpered.

Rhapsody lowered her lips to his tiny ear where the pearl earring gleamed.

"Please," she whispered. "Please, Meridion, please don't forget me. Though others will care for you, and tend to your needs, and love you, please don't forget me. Please, remember your father, too—he loves you as much as I do. Please—remember—"

Meridion whimpered again, more insistently this time.

Rhapsody kissed the tiny ear. She hummed her Naming note, *ela*, the musical tone her child shared, then whispered words, almost too soft to be heard, commanding them to leave her and be held within the pearl.

Amelia Turner, she said. *Emily. Emmy. Il mimen*—your mother.

She kissed his ear again. The pearl was warm, humming against her lips. Deep within her, she felt the fire in her soul diminish somewhat.

Leaving her internally colder.

Meridion began to cry.

The tears evaporated from Rhapsody's face. Quickly her hands went to the brads on her shirt, and she put her son to the breast, gentling him, soothing him, singing his wordless lullabye, the song they had learned in the sea together.

"Shhh," she said as she caressed his tiny cheek. "Hush now, *y pippin*. I love you."

As the baby suckled, she heard him sigh, but for the first time that she could remember, she was unable to tell what emotion he was trying to convey.

And at that moment, the realization dawned that, just as his entry into her life had changed her dramatically, the loss of him from it would do so as well.

42

The Teeth
(Manteids)

Night Mountain
Earth Basilica

Desert

THE IRON MINES, VORNESSTA, SORBOLD

The lashmen must have been tired today, Evrit mused absently as he hauled his third load of the day to the ore stockpile and dumped it onto the screen. It was almost noon, and he had only tasted the whip once; by this time on most days, his back had been striped at least four times.

He stepped out of the way of the line of his fellow slaves who were likewise waiting to offload their scuttles, and hurried back to the wall.

As he made his way to his slice of the wall of the volcanic deposit where he was assigned to scrape ore, day into night into day, with but four hours for rest, Evrit cast a subtle glance over the edge of his section. The sheer size of the area of the mine that he could see never ceased to take his breath away; the tall cave in which he spent his days beside several hundred other slaves was but one of dozens, similarly populated, on the same level of the mine. On levels above and below him, many of which he could see beyond the edge, hundreds more slaves toiled in each of dozens more caves, forming an immense, moving mass of muscle and sweat, producing a noise that had all but deafened most of them. Evrit had once tried to estimate the number just within the section he could see, but gave up quickly, because the very thought threatened to consume him with despair.

Despair was an adversary that had defeated him long ago.

Evrit returned to his labor.

In spite of the horror that was his daily existence, Evrit had managed to maintain a resolute will to survive his enslavement. Unlike his hollow-eyed companions in the mine, men who were little more than sinew and a blank expression whose very existence was nothing more than a cycle of the harvesting of iron ore interrupted by brief moments of urination, defecation, consumption of tasteless sustenance and unconsciousness, his mind was always working, always focused on one thing.

Finding his family.

Evrit was not by any means alone in this vision, he knew. All of the men who had been brought here under the lash of the emperor's guards had started out bristling with rage and murderous intent, determined to escape and find their own wives, children, siblings, parents even. The endless torture of the routine coupled with a regimen of abuse and deprivation just short of starvation had leached the anger from them, had stripped them of every bit of energy that could be put toward sustaining fury.

Evrit, however, had managed to maintain his determination.

Prior to his enslavement, trained and experienced as a tailor, Evrit had been a leader and influential member of a gentle religious sect, known as the Blessed, for most of his life. It was in that capacity that he had undertaken to hire a vessel, a ship named the *Freedom*, to transport him, his wife and two sons, along with a number of other members of their order, away from a life of religious persecution in Marincaer in search of tolerance in the land of Golgarn, a place known for its lack of a state religion and an acceptance of other points of view.

The ship had never made it there.

Evrit brought new force to bear with his diamond-edged trowel against the stone wall, remembering the *Freedom* foundering in the treacherous waters off the Skeleton Coast of southern Sorbold. As death loomed, a rescue sloop had launched from the shore and come to the aid of the sundered ship, bearing every one of her passengers to safety, only to turn out to be piloted by slavers, who had informed the pilgrims politely that their rescue would require them to serve for three years in the olive groves of Nicosi, after which time they would be released.

Evrit had thought as he sat, blindfolded and bound in the slavers' wagon, that his lot could not have been worse. It was then that a coterie of soldiers of the newly chosen emperor-to-be had come upon the slavers, had ridden them down and taken them into custody, had executed the leader, and set about unbinding the eyes of the slaves. The Emperor Presumptive had addressed them initially and apologized for their capture; Evrit had prayed in relief and thanksgiving.

Until Talquist had informed them all that rather than being indentured in the olive groves, the men would be serving in his iron mines and steel foundries, the women working in the linen factories, and the children sweeping the soot from the chimneys of the cities of Sorbold. The Emperor Presumptive had taken Evrit's own wife into his coach and ravaged her, then had returned her to his wagon, graciously allowing her to sit by her husband's side once he was done with her.

Hatred flashed and burned behind Evrit's eyes at the memory.

Then faded into the determination of survival again.

As he scratched the iron ore from the endless stone before him, he pushed away the memory of his beloved spouse's face, tear-stained but set in a rigid mien, unable to look at him as the wagon carried them away from the southern seacoast and into the mountains of the central part of the kingdom. He wondered where she was; he had been able to gain no indication from the conversations of the guards and the lashmen as to where the linen factories of Sorbold were located, except the broad implication that there were many of them across the country.

He suspected his sons were closer to him in proximity. He had been blessed to catch a glimpse of Jarzben, the elder of the two, in a line of ore-scratchers like himself, being transferred into a cave on the level below him many months before, and had been even luckier to have met his glance; his son looked thin and hollow-eyed, but in one piece, and the exchange of recognition had brought a look of shock, followed by a wan smile, to the lad's face before he was led away.

He had not seen his younger son, Selac, since he had been unloaded from the slave wagon, but suspected he was working as a chimney sweep in the capital city of Jierna'sid, if he was still alive.

That last thought shattered Evrit's brave determination.

A knot of immense size tied itself inside his throat. Dearly as he wanted to believe that each of the members of his family was still among the living, his rational mind knew that most likely he was the only one to be so.

He dug even more furiously into the stone before him, ignoring the thin tears that were streaking his cheeks, spilling what little water he had within him.

Sometimes he wondered dully if his determination to find his family alive was even crueler than what the emperor had laid out for them; at least with death would come the end of the pain and the degradation, as well as sweet rest and the chance to be reunited with one another in the Afterlife.

He was so intent in his thoughts that at first he did not notice the other slaves around him freezing in their assigned places.

When their cessation of work finally caught his eye, Evrit looked up.

Beside him, staring down at him, was an enormous soldier, a lashman of great musculature, his eyes dark and piercing, his expression forbidding. A long whip with metal falls at the tip was coiled in his hand.

Evrit's chest began to heave with fear.

The soldier looked harshly up at the other slaves, glaring them back to work, their eyes averted in terror. He seized Evrit by the leather collar around his neck and hoisted him off the ground, his black eyes boring into Evrit's wide green ones. He dragged the terrified slave up until their gazes matched. The lashman wrapped his whip around Evrit's throat, making a motion as if he were tightening it like a noose, though it did not actually cut off his air.

Then spoke to him in a soft, deadly tone.

In the language of Marincaer.

"Fear not, friend," he said, too quietly for anyone but Evrit to hear. "Your liberty is coming. Be ready when the call comes to fight. Tell no one else. For what I must do now, I apologize."

Then his expression changed to one of disdain, and he dropped Evrit harshly to the floor of the cave. He jerked the whip back, causing it to crack menacingly; Evrit could feel the other slaves, their backs to him and the soldier, wince at the sound. A red line of blood appeared, circumnavigating his neck.

But the pain from it was minimal.

"Back to work." The words were spoken in the harsh tongue of Sorbold.

Shaking, Evrit obeyed.

The lashman watched him rise unsteadily to his feet. Evrit made his way back to the wall, after picking up his trowel, and set about scratching ore again. He was fairly certain he caught a nod of the head of the lashman as the soldier met the gaze of another guard, who seemed to nod in return, but his head was spinning too fast to be certain.

After a few moments of filling his scuttle, a sense of peace descended on him that he had not felt since long before the *Freedom* had departed from Marincaer.

He had no idea why.

JIERNA TAL

Talquist watched eagerly from the parapet as Titactyk's regiment rode into the courtyard of Jierna Tal below. Delight spread quickly over his face as he saw the soldier Fhremus had brought to him in the basilica of Lianta'ar dismount, unload what looked like a small chest, and make his way toward the palace gate.

Ahead of them, Faron's chariot was coming to a halt. The stone titan stepped out of the cart and threw the reins of the team of eight horses over the bar, then looked up at the tower. It seemed to Talquist that he was smiling, but the statue was too far below to see for certain.

The emperor hurried down the tower stairs and to the second floor, where he could hear bootsteps coming echoing up the stairwell. He smiled beneficently at the young soldier, wearing the insignia of the Empire of the Sun, as he crested the top stair.

"Ah, Kymel! I have been eagerly awaiting your return. Did you locate the object from the fresco in the abbey?"

"Yes, Majesty. There were many of them."

Talquist's brow furrowed. "Many?"

"Yes, m'lord." Kymel stepped forward quickly and bowed, then handed the emperor the wooden chest.

Talquist lifted the lid and gently pulled aside the layers of cloth that had been packed around its contents, dropping them to the floor. His eyes took in the yellow shape, scored on the surface and tattered at the edges.

It did not catch and reflect the light as his scale did, however.

Talquist extended his index finger at touched the object. It felt slightly sandy and cold. He took the edge in his grip.

It snapped off in his hand, crumbling.

Irritation burned in the emperor's eyes but his voice remained calm.

"This is all? This is what you found?"

"Yes, m'lord," said Kymel quietly. "They were everywhere in the abbey. I scoured the grounds for anything else even distantly resembling the image in the fresco, but there was nothing but this."

"I see." Talquist sighed heavily. He had been accustomed to disappointment for all of his life; in the grand scheme of things, this was a small one. It was even amusing; he let out a small chuckle. "Oh, well. Thank you, Kymel. Your regiment is returning to Sepulvarta now?"

"Yes, m'lord."

"When you arrive, report immediately to Fhremus and tell him I said to deploy."

Kymel, sick at heart already, had no idea what the emperor meant, but he merely bowed.

"Yes, m'lord."

"You may go."

Kymel bowed again, turned on his heel and made his way down the stairs to the courtyard, where Titactyk's regiment awaited. He mounted up and rode off with his cohort back to Sepulvarta.

He did not look back at the magnificent palace, its towers piercing the clouds.

43

YLORC

The women set out when the first indication of the new day was apparent in the sky. The night had not yet fled, but there was the slightest hint of birdsong, and a thinning of the devouring blackness that was turning, at the very edges of the horizon, to the slightest of deep grays.

They had ridden as far north the Bakhran Pass, the last of the formal Firbolg outposts at the mountainous border of what was considered Ylorc, two nanny goats in tow, but when they came to the final outpost, guarded by Eye and Guts clan members of Grunthor's elite force, they dismounted and proceeded forth on foot, leaving the horses at the guard station but bringing along the two nanny goats Rhapsody had been using milk from for Meridion.

Analise had set the pace; being the eldest of the group, she was the slowest, though her Liringlas heritage had bequeathed her a considerable amount of stamina and the ability to walk long distances at a time. The globe of glowing blue light was in her hand from the moment that dusk came into the sky; she told Rhapsody during one of their meal breaks that she wanted to associate the outdoors with it, so that when they were inside the mountains she was able to recall the image of open sky and wind by looking at it. The Lady Cymrian had smiled broadly, understanding her need on a soul-deep level.

Once they were out of the Bolglands, or at least the part of the Bolglands with which Rhapsody was familiar, Gyllian's knowledge of the terrain became invaluable. The green spectrum of the Lightcatcher Achmed had provided to shield them with the power of Grass Hiding had given off the faintest trace of a shadow that formed a path in the air, which Rhapsody maintained by humming the note attuned with that color, but occasionally the path that the Lightcatcher projected went through areas that were impassable or too steep for them to summit, so they relied on the Nain princess and the innate lore of earth that she possessed to guide them.

It had been agreed that Krinsel would be the primary bearer of the baby so that both of them could benefit from the new cloak of mist Ashe had sent. The Bolg midwife was still a little unsteady on her feet, so Analise and Melisande took turns spotting her, watching for any sign of exhaustion, a task that was not made easy by the cloak's natural tendency to shield both the eye and the mind from its sight. The mist that rose from its folds was a natural form of obscurement, making the task of keeping an eye on Krinsel more than a little difficult.

Rhapsody and the Nain princess had taken on the responsibility of guarding the group, and shared the role of scout; both were armed with crossbows, though Rhapsody carried her white Lirin longbow across her back as well for when they were finally out of the mountains and crossing the small part of the steppes they would need to ford between the Bolglands and the northern mountains that led to the doorstep of the Nain kingdom. She and Gyllian took on the task of standing watch as well, having privately determined even before they left that none of the other women were trained or strong enough to do so.

Melisande had been very disappointed upon learning of this arrangement, so when it was Rhapsody's watch, the Lady Cymrian often invited her to join her in her task. She was given the job of maintaining the watch while Rhapsody fed the baby or did perimeter checks, a responsibility that clearly made her feel more like an adult, a need that Rhapsody remembered from her own youth and status as the youngest of six children, and the only girl in her family. Melisande frequently positioned her bedroll next to that of her adopted grandmother, too, and the Lady Cymrian would often wake to find the little girl curled up next to her, Meridion asleep in the small space between the two of them.

On the sixth day of their travel, and the second out of the mountain passes and crossing the open grasslands before the place Gyllian had indicated they would seek the entrance to the Deep Kingdom, as the sun was beginning to set, the nanny goats began bleating. They were a noisy pair, enough so that each of the women had commented on it at one time or another in amusement or annoyance, but there was a definite change in their vocalizing.

Rhapsody recognized it as terror.

She had been walking with Melisande's hand in her own; she loosed it now and looked around her.

For as far as she could see to the west there was no sign of animal or humanoid life, just a partial clay plain, and a tall sea of highgrass waving and bowing in supplication to the sun that was filling the sky with warm colors. To the north and east were endless mountain peaks, the northern peaks so far distant as to be shielded by the mist of low-hanging clouds, while the peaks to the east were proximate enough to reach with a sprinting run.

"Krinsel," she said quietly, using her Naming lore to put the sound of her voice directly into the woman's ear, "how is Meridion? Is he asleep?"

The Bolg woman pulled aside the folds of the mist cloak and peered inside, then raised her head and shook it.

From within the cloak, a whimpering sound dissimilar to any she had heard before issued forth.

"Something's wrong," she said softly to Gyllian. "Very wrong—Krinsel, step closer to the mountainside, climb up a short way. Melly, go with her, and you, too, Analise—"

Just as her friend's name came out of her mouth, the ground beneath her feet began to shake.

"Run!" she shouted to Melisande and the other women. "Get up as high as you can!"

The goats, squealing in terror, had frozen where they stood, shuddering with fear.

Rhapsody looked around her and, seeing nothing, drew Daystar Clarion from its sheath.

The elemental sword of fire came forth with a whisper and the ringing of a trumpet call.

She turned in a full circle, scanning the horizon and skies for anything other than the scrubby brush of the piedmont, the skittering, hurried flight of birds that had been sailing past on the wind a few moments before.

What am I missing? she thought, smiling at Melisande to ease the fear she saw in the little girl's eyes. *What am I—*

Her thought vanished as the ground at her feet split in twain. She jumped aside to keep from falling into the crevasse that had just opened.

Only to see an immense claw tear forth from the ground, broken talons extended, and seize the goats with a vicious, precisely aimed swipe.

Just as another ripped out of the earth beneath her, and snatched her in its grasp as well.

44

$\mathcal{A}$nwyn had been lurking beneath the loose red clay of the northern steppes for the better part of the sennight, searching in vain for fresh blood to nourish herself. She had sensed only small game, occasional rabbits and the rodents known as jurillas, small-eared, quick footed relatives of groundhogs that dug intricate and annoying tunneled nests in the ground above the ruins of Kurimah Milani. Had a large enough nest existed in the proximity, it might have been worth the risk of the jagged cwellan disk moving closer to her heart in going after them, but the ones she sensed were itinerants, crossing the clay desert in search of better resources, and would not have provided enough meat to even be noticed in her maw, or to get stuck between her teeth.

So when at dusk the sortie of women and goats came into her awareness at the edge of her waning senses, at first she thought she had been dreaming.

It had been so long since a traveler had been unfortunate enough to pass through the lands above where she had taken refuge in the broken vault that had, in ancient times, been one of the great baths of the mythical city of healing, that the dragon almost refused to believe the possibility. Hunger had clawed at her viscera for months uncounted; now, in the advent of starvation, all she felt was a dull ache around the firegems in her entrails, the source of her ability to breathe fire. Additionally, the information that her dragon sense had transmitted to her indicated that one of the traveling party was, in fact, the woman she hated more than anything her fragmented mind could remember.

So the possibility of the mirage's reality was initially dismissed in the wyrm's mind as being a fantasy, much too good to be feasible.

Until her heightened sense of smell caught wind of the goats.

*R*hapsody had just enough time to maneuver the sword out of the crush of the dragon's claw as it wrapped around her before the breath was squeezed from her lungs.

"Get back!" she shouted to the others, or tried, but the air was not there to carry her words; the command came forth as a shuddering gasp, with almost no active sound.

Out of the corner of her eye she thought she saw Krinsel, who had climbed into the rocky, elevated ground of the piedmont, duck behind a rocky outcropping; her mind made grateful note of Meridion's cover.

The ground of the steppes exploded as the dragon ripped through the clay and emerged, rampant and triumphant. Anwyn loosed a scream that echoed off the piedmont and the mountains beyond, dragging her immense body out of the ground and into the open air.

"At last!" she hissed. "At last!"

Rhapsody struggled for breath, her ribs aching as the beast squeezed tighter. She pulled herself up as high as she could among the individual talons, as the dragon lifted her into the air and dangled her body in front of the beast's tattered eyes.

"Can it be possible?" Anwyn crowed in delight. "M'lady! How kind of you to return for a visit!"

From her elevated height, Rhapsody could see Krinsel cowering behind her rocky outcropping. Analise had joined her, while Gyllian had swung her crossbow into her hands from where it had hung at her back and was sighting a bolt, but both women knew that it would not penetrate the hide of the dragon, its only possible target the beast's already injured eye.

She could not see Melisande at all.

But instinctively Rhapsody knew that all of them were well within range of the beast's breath.

Quickly she pulled the shoulder of her arm that held the sword at an unnatural angle, the tendons screaming as she did, and struck with Daystar Clarion, slashing the part of the claw that would have been a palm in a human being, dragging the sword down as far as her arm could reach, through the scarred talons that she herself had injured several years ago, severing a tendon.

The beast reacted with shock. The claw fell open and Rhapsody pitched to the ground, executing a maneuver Grunthor had taught her long ago known as a horseman's rollout. She hit the ground hard and gasped as she inhaled a storm of red clay that blasted her face, then rolled to the side, dodging the claw as it struck again.

She struggled to her feet and ran, her free arm pressed against her ribcage, due west, away from the mountains and the other women, the dragon in fast pursuit. She had made it fewer than forty paces, zigzagging, when the other claw struck again, seizing her by the back of her shirt and dragging her to a halt.

Anwyn lifted her off the ground again and dangled her in the air once more.

"Leaving so soon? Surely not."

Rhapsody flicked her wrist, bringing forward a dagger, and quickly sliced her shirt open in the front, freeing herself and falling to the ground again.

"No, surely not," she muttered as she pulled herself to her feet and took off to the west once more.

Another sweep of the claw caught her back, and Rhapsody felt the sting of her skin as it tore open. She fell to the ground, and the blow missed her, shouting to Analise in Ancient Lirin.

"Get up into the piedmont—head for the mountain!"

The dragon reared up to breathe down on her, supine on the ground. Then spun around in shock.

Melisande pulled her dragon claw dagger out of the beast's tail, where she had planted it with a two-handed overhead blow.

"Get away from my grandmother!" she screamed, burying the weapon in Anwyn's foot claw as the wyrm lashed its torn tail from side to side, splattering the ground with black blood in the darkness.

Rhapsody saw the fury in the dragon's eyes as the beast looked behind her. "Melisande, run!" she shouted, scrambling to her feet again. *"Run!"* Seeing the wyrm turning toward the little girl, she backed away to the west.

"Coward," she said, pointing her finger and using the Naming ability to place the words directly into the monster's ear. "Chasing a child with a dagger instead of a woman with a sword. You are a pathetic excuse for a dragon, Anwyn. Perhaps, rather than *wyrm*, you are actually *worm*."

The dragon's enormous head snapped back around. She crawled forward, following Rhapsody westward, where she stood alone in the open desert field.

"I will eat your eyes," the dragon whispered. "And your cursed mouth, which utters such lies."

"I suggest you eat something else," the Iliachenva'ar said.

She raised the sword above her head and spoke the name of the evening star hanging low to the horizon, a blue white one named Helaphon, named by the Lirin of this land for a warrior queen of long ago.

The open field at the edge of the steppes was suddenly blanketed with an ethereal light as bright as midday, though silver in hue. It flooded over Rhapsody, causing her hair to shine silver as well, and the beast, whose eyes glowed as they opened wide in shock.

Then, with a thunderous roar, the fire of the star blasted down on both of them, the woman and the dragon, illuminating their outlines as it flooded over them, rolling over the steppes and lighting the highgrass into a low inferno for miles around.

45

At first nothing but silence and the crackling of burning grass reigned in the desert to the west of the mountains.

Then the wind picked up, whining mournfully, whipping through the steppes in the dark. After a moment, the wind's dirge was joined by the wailing of a terrified child.

"No!" Melisande sobbed from halfway up the piedmont. "No, please, no."

"Shhh, child," Analise whispered, pulling her into her arms and letting the girl bury her face in her shoulder. "Quiet now. We are not yet out of danger."

As the words left her lips, a burning swale of grass flexed and moved.

Two enormous eyes, glowing eerily blue in the darkness amid the orange flames, opened slowly, the light from them shining like dim beacons in the fog of the sea.

Then the huge mound stretched slowly, scales falling from her hide in great chunks of black soot. She loosed a grisly sound of agony, then crawled slowly to the fissure in the earth from which she had emerged in the first place.

And slid painfully into it, disappearing into the ground.

Silence returned to the plain.

A few moments later, another, smaller ridge of grass, this one not burning, stretched as well and stood up carefully. As it did, hails of ash fell from it as well; Rhapsody was black from head to toe, her golden hair was smeared with creosote, hanging loose as the charred remnants of her hair ribbon crumbled and fell to the ground, along with her clothing.

She shook herself like a dog coming out of a lake, as even more ash fell from her now-naked body.

"*Hrekin*," the living shadow muttered angrily. "How many bloody times do I have to *kill her*?"

Melisande broke from Analise's embrace and ran, stumbling and sliding, down the grade of the piedmont and across the field, skirting the burning grass which was beginning to extinguish. She came to a halt as the Lady Cymrian held up her hand.

"Wait, Melly; could you get my pack and bring it with you?"

The little girl nodded quickly and complied as Analise, Gyllian, and Krinsel began coming forth from their cover in the rocks. Rhapsody looked around and swore again.

"Double *hrekin*," she said angrily. "I fried the goats. And I didn't even kill the dragon. *Hrekin*." She took the pack from Melisande who, in spite of the coating of soot and ash, threw her arms around her grandmother.

"It's all right, Melly," she said, kissing the girl delicately on the top of her head. "Try not to get too much of this on you—it smells terrible, and it's almost impossible to get it out of your nose once it gets in there." She looked at herself again in disgust.

"Ugh."

$\mathcal{I}$ cannot believe I killed the goats," Rhapsody muttered as she rinsed herself off in the artesian stream she found at the base of the piedmont. She had sung her Naming note into the wind, and woven the name of water into the song; the stream had answered, and Rhapsody had slipped into it gratefully.

Gyllian chuckled as the Lady Cymrian shook the water off herself.

"They were an annoyance anyway. And we have goats in Undervale. Be of good cheer, m'lady. I have seen you summon starfire once before, at the battle with the Fallen at the Moot during the Cymrian Council, but until this day I had not known that you could summon it upon *yourself* and still survive. To say that you have risen in my estimation would be an understatement."

Rhapsody was digging through her pack. She pulled forth her spare set of clothes and quickly set about rectifying her nakedness.

"Don't be impressed so easily, Gyllian," she said as she brushed away the last of the wet ashes that had once been her linen shirt, trousers, and boots, then donned their replacements. "Anwyn apparently survived it also, which makes the *second* time for her. I suppose I should have known that a dragon has all of the five elemental lores nascent in its blood, as so therefore would be difficult to destroy with a combination of ether and fire. Well, at least I now know where she is. I should have guessed she was hiding in Kurimah Milani; I hadn't realized we were near to it, coming from this direction. The last time I was here we approached from the west."

"Two little known historical points, m'lady," said Gyllian in amusement as she watched the Lady Cymrian lace up her trousers, "the legends say that Kurimah Milani was originally built, or partially built, by ancestors of the indigenous Nain that dwelt in the lands of and near the Deep Kingdom in the era before the arrival of the Cymrians, or even the humans, to the lands south of here. And one of the major resources utilized in constructing what is said to have been one of the architectural and artistic marvels of that age was the Molten River, known by a different name at the time, Fûrinazen. It is the legendary river of hot lava and liquid gold that divides the lands of the Nain of the Deep Kingdom from those of the dragon Witheragh, who guards the entrance to both. So you will be coping with not one, but two wyrms, in the space of a few hours."

"Have you ever met Witheragh?" Rhapsody asked.

"Goodness, no. But my father has had commerce with him, as well as diplomatic interaction. I can't say that he has ever enjoyed it much."

"Well, blessedly, the intelligence I have about him indicates that he is considered to be reliable in his agreements, even if he is hard to reason with and avaricious," Rhapsody said. She bound her hair back in the last of the surviving black ribbons.

Gyllian's brows drew together. "Considered so by whom? I'm not sure Faedryth would concur."

The Lady Cymrian smiled. "By those of his own kind," she said, coming over to where Krinsel was sitting and crouching down before her. "I have had a considerable amount of interaction with dragons over the last few years, including marrying and giving birth to one. I no longer am afraid to negotiate with one, even one I haven't met, as long as I have forewarning of its temperament." She waited until Krinsel gave silent permission, and then opened the outer folds of the mist cloak.

Meridion was asleep, his tiny mouth making suckling motions, a scowl on his face.

Rhapsody hid her smile and closed the folds carefully again.

"You truly are your father's son," she whispered fondly. "Only the two of you could sleep through a dragon battle and a strike of starfire."

"Another reason to be glad to be rid of the goats," said Analise.

"Unlike the battle and the starfire, they woke him up every time they started bleating."

Rhapsody turned back to the four women who were eyeing her uncertainly.

"How much farther to the Molten River?" she asked Gyllian.

"If we press on through the night, we will be there by morning."

Rhapsody smiled encouragingly.

"Then let us press on," she said.

She shouldered her much-lighter pack and took up her walking stick, putting her hand out to Melisande Navarne, who happily took it.

And followed the oldest child of the Nain king to the mountain passes that would lead them into Undervale, the hidden realm of the mysterious Deep Kingdom.

46

"The secret to talking with a dragon is to keep breathing."

The eyes of the four women across from Rhapsody in the mouth of the cave were set in four different expressions. The youngest of the group, Melisande Navarne, nodded, a steady gaze meeting that of her adopted grandmother, as if she was agreeing with her assessment of the weather. Krinsel, the Bolg midwife, was staring at her with narrowed eyes, but that was the expression that almost always would be seen on Krinsel's face. Analise's silver eyes were wide in alarm, but Gyllian's gaze was full of amusement.

"Well, I assume that's the goal *after* talking with a dragon as well," she said humorously.

Rhapsody laughed.

"All right, I put that poorly. What I meant was to keep breathing as evenly as you can. Inhale; count to ten. Exhale slowly to the same count of ten, if possible. Inhale again. And so on. Draconic conversations are almost always overwhelming, but they can be tricky and irritating beyond measure. Steady breathing helps avoid overreaction on both sides."

The light of the Molten River, the moving trail of lava mixed with liquid gold that divided the Deep Kingdom of the Nain from the realm of the wyrm Witheragh, splashed a brilliance luminescence on the earthen walls of the cavern, though the river itself was still out of sight. Even as far away as they were, the heat from the river was intense, causing all but Krinsel and Rhapsody to begin shedding their cloaks.

Analise's face had returned to its mask of stoic calm, but Rhapsody knew that being within the solid enclosure of the mountains, away from the sheltering sky, was a torment for her Liringlas soul. She handed her walking stick to Melisande, then went to her oldest friend and embraced her gently.

"I know what this is costing you," she said quietly in the language of the old world. "It is a gift beyond measure that you have given me; thank you for making the sacrifice."

"*Hrekin*," Analise murmured into her ear the word for excrement in the tongue of the Bolg. Rhapsody choked, then laughed aloud, as Analise reverted to Ancient Lirin. "It is a joy to be of service to my sovereign, a pleasure to be of help to my friend, and literally the very least I can do, given *your* sacrifice for me."

The humor left Rhapsody's eyes; she released Analise and gently patted her shoulder. Then she turned to the others.

"I suggest that once Gyllian indicates we are at the border, you all remain out of sight and out of range. Melisande, I want you to stay beside Her Highness; I am grateful for your intercession earlier with Anwyn, but this is an entirely different situation, and we need to follow Gyllian's lead in these lands." The little girl nodded. "I'll hold on to my own pack at this point; if Witheragh deprives me of my clothing as Anwyn did, I will be entering the Deep Kingdom naked anyway, as I am now out of spare outfits."

The adult women chuckled. Melisande initially appeared horrified, but once she understood the joke, she smiled as well. Rhapsody turned to Krinsel. Wordlessly she asked if the Bolg midwife was all right, and received a nod in reply. Then she came to her and opened the drape of the mist cloak.

Meridion's face lit up upon beholding her, and he let out a cackle of delight.

Rhapsody's eyes filled with tears as she returned his grin. She kissed his nose, his hands and belly, then began quietly crooning him his lullabye, the song they had learned together while trapped within the sea cave, music of the waves that carried an endless number of stories over Time.

Meridion's dragonesque eyes remained trained intently on her. Then, after a few moments, they began to droop, and his toothless grin settled into a complacent smile as his eyes closed.

"He will be ferociously hungry when he wakes," Rhapsody said softly as she closed the mist cloak around him again. "My breasts hurt just thinking about it. All right, I had best get to this. With any luck this parley will be brief." She handed Melisande her walking stick, squeezed Krinsel's upper arm, and then followed Gyllian down the brightening tunnel.

The light grew almost painful in its radiance; the sounds of the river increased until it filled the cavern with thick liquid music. Finally the Nain princess came to a halt.

"The Molten River is beyond this bend in the tunnel," she said quietly to Rhapsody. "I believe it is wise for all of us save you to remain here. We can see if we stand at the bend, but still have cover."

Rhapsody nodded. She turned and smiled encouragingly at the women who had put their lives in abeyance, and at risk, to travel to this place with her, her eyes full of gratitude. Then she rounded the bend and disappeared from their sight, though she was still within their earshot.

The sight of the Molten River caused her to take in a deep breath; it was not too much wider than a meadow stream, but flowed with a strength that belied its width. The fire lore within her sang with joy in its presence; there was a purity to it that rang in Rhapsody's soul. Its movement caused the roaring light to dance in glorious patterns around the high archways carved into the caverns on the other bank, the lands that were the beginning of the dragon's realm. Fire burned sporadically on its surface.

"Witheragh!" she called over the rushing roar of the Molten River, speaking haltingly in her best approximation of the draconic tongue. "Hail, in the name of Elynsynos."

For a long moment, all the women could hear was the echoing sound of the river and the noise of dripping high above in the cavern. Then Rhapsody was certain she heard a chuckle from the other side of the river of fire.

"Well, that's a brave greeting, in more ways than one," came a voice, sounding in the familiar tones of soprano, alto, tenor, and bass, much as every other dragon Rhapsody had heard manipulate the wind to speak sounded. "First, your draconic grammar is remarkable, but your pronunciation is appalling. I expect that's because you do not have the physiology to do it correctly; unless you have the appropriate wyrm aperture in your throat, you cannot *possibly* make the hisses and clicks that would be necessary to make your attempt anything but embarrassing."

"Sorry," Rhapsody muttered.

"Second, if you are going to pretend to know a dragon personally to impress me, it would be wise to choose one that is not of such epic status as to be impossible for you to be taken seriously. It might have been a little less amusing if you had chosen Sidus, or Mikanic, either of whom it is technically possible, though, of course, highly unlikely, that a Lirin woman might have met. You are Lirin, are you not? Though you have chosen to shield your features, I can smell you—Lirin have a sweet smell, and *taste*. But really, *Elynsynos*? One of the Five Daughters? For goodness' sake, why didn't you just come in the name of the Creator himself?"

"Because—"

The tone of the multilevel voice turned darker.

"And, finally, I'm not certain which is more foolhardy, standing at the border of my domain and *shouting* for me, as if I am a footman waiting to take your baggage, or standing, Lirin that you are, on the threshold of the Nain lands, apparently uninvited. That might actually rank up there as the stupidest thing I've heard of in several centuries."

"I apologize for my appalling pronunciation," Rhapsody said. "You are right about my physiology, but I can't help that."

"True. But the other reasons are indeed something you can 'help.' My treaty of nonaggression is with the Nain, not the Lirin. I feel pained to inform you that you are under no protection of law at the moment, and therefore in what those brighter than yourself would sense to be considerable danger."

"I understand that as well. I do beg your indulgence; if you will hear me out, I believe you might reconsider my status."

For a moment there was no sound but the hollow echo of dripping in the massive cave and the roaring of the river of fiery lava. Then, from the shadowy region beyond the painfully bright moving light, an immense form emerged, moving slowly and deliberately toward her in the darkness.

Rhapsody kept her eyes trained on the approaching dragon, but behind her she could feel the other women, who had stepped up to the bend, move farther back. She could sense their panic, especially that of Melisande, whom she had sent to a dragon's cave herself. She waved her arm encouragingly behind her.

The light splashing up from the Molten River illuminated the enormous head of the beast, a much less delicate creature than Elynsynos had been, with heavy earthen features. The dragon's hide was brown like the walls of his cave, but that hide was almost impossible to see through the carpet of thousands of sparkling jewels, carefully cut and polished, that the Nain had given him over the centuries as tribute, which the beast had set into his scales to adorn himself. The combination of the gems and the light from the river caused a visual effect much like the exploding of a dark skyful of rainbows with each movement of the giant serpentine body.

Witheragh came to a halt on the other side of the river, his red eyes twinkling menacingly.

"I'll offer you a bargain," the great beast said in a painfully polite tone, the undertone of threat unmistakable. "I will hear you out, as you have requested, and if I am not impressed enough to reconsider your status, I will give you to the Nain to flay, dress, and smoke for me, whereupon I shall enjoy the sweet taste of you for dessert tonight. I think I will have you stuffed with cheese and topped with chocolate."

Rhapsody inhaled deeply. When she spoke, her Naming lore was in her tones, along with a good deal of displeasure.

"Oh, *please*. Witheragh, from the second clutch of Mylinmacr, son of Ylsgraith, you are *wasting my time*. I have a boon to ask of you that will serve your most important purposes as well as my own, and you are playing childish games with me. Again, in the name of Elynsynos, I greet you with respect and seek your attention." She exhaled what was left of her breath. "And apologize again for my woeful pronunciation."

The vertical slits in the fiery red eyes contracted, and the enormous head stretched across the river and swung down in front of her. The giant nostrils, ringed in colorful gems and glinting brightly in the light reflecting off the Molten River, released a puff of steam that wafted over her.

"Who are you?" the wyrm demanded. "And how did a Lirin Namer come to know my lineage?"

"Well, since you have correctly guessed that I am a Namer, you know that I only speak the truth. So I will tell you again, I come in the name of Elynsynos, because she was my beloved friend and teacher—as well as being the great-great-grandmother of my child. She taught me the entirety of the lineage of the Wyrmril on one of the occasions that I went to study with her. And since I answered your second question first, I will now tell you that my name is Rhapsody." She took hold of her hood and pulled it down.

The great beast's eyes opened wide, sending a meteor shower of flashes of gem-colored light spinning around the opening of the cave. Rhapsody winced, hearing Analise and Melisande behind her cry out in pain.

"Well, well," the dragon said. "Little as I care for the affairs of man, I have actually heard your name before, in the conversations of the Nain that creep through the sounds of the river and into my lair. How unusual. Are you not some sort of queen or something?"

"That hardly matters in terms of what I have come to you for. But yes, I am."

The dragon brought its head down even lower and looked into her eyes.

"Oh, but you are mistaken, Your Majesty," the beast said, the painfully polite tone returning to the multitoned voice he was creating from manipulated air. "It matters a great deal. Because if you are a queen, you should be able to offer something of great monetary value to me in exchange for the boon you are seeking."

Rhapsody, long accustomed to dragons attempting to enchant her with their gaze, averted her eyes while remaining focused forward.

"That's a badly informed assumption. Surely you can assess the contents of our pockets and our packs, down to the last copper piece. You know that we only have traveling money and a few low-quality gems of tender."

The dragon chuckled.

"True enough, though you have quite a lovely little emerald ring on your left hand. I assume that's the symbol of a marriage vow, rather than a signet of state? At least I hope it is; otherwise, your initial description of your queendom hardly mattering was truthful after all."

The thudding silence that followed echoed in the cavern.

Rhapsody exhaled and counted to ten.

"It is, in fact, my wedding ring," she said.

The dragon tilted its head, regarding her with interest.

"Hmmm. That, and an extremely cheap locket of low quality gold around your neck, containing—" He seemed to concentrate for a moment, then shook his titanic head. "A copper piece, which at the height of its value was worth three pennies, and is not even regular in its striking; thirteen-sided, how strange." His head righted itself again. "You truly are a strange queen, Rhapsody, Friend of Elynsynos, whatever else you are. Really, Your Majesty, haven't you at least a *crown* of some sort? I like crowns."

"Not with me. It resides in my realm. And it does not belong to me, but to my people."

"What a shame. So did you plan to offer me your wedding ring in payment for this boon?"

"I did not," Rhapsody said sharply. "But if that's your price, you may have it. The vow it represents does not reside within the ring, but within my heart and that of my husband. The ring is only a symbol." She inhaled slowly.

"And, while it is of fine quality, with some very pretty sparkly diamond dust surrounding the stone, and very old, it is, as I said, very small, most likely to fit your similarly small hand," said Witheragh. "It would be insignificant among my collection. So you may keep it. What else do you have to offer in payment?"

"Do you not even wish to hear my request first?"

"No, actually," said the dragon, and the amusement in his voice dimmed somewhat. "I care nothing for the races of man, as I believe I've already stated. You are the gateway of the Unspoken into this world, an unnecessary evil and a complication in keeping the Earth safe from what lies below. That is all I care for, Your Majesty, the guardianship of what really matters. So while this negotiation has been both amusing and pathetic, you are, as you said to me, wasting *my* time."

"The boon I am requesting fits precisely into what matters to you," Rhapsody said coolly. "It may be what prevents a shattering of the Shield. And it is easy enough for you to do, if you accept my request."

"Speak it quickly then," said the beast. "And be prepared to leave quickly thereafter."

"I am asking your aid in guarding my child," Rhapsody said. "In spite of your belief that I am uninvited at the doorstep of the kingdom of the Nain, I do, in fact, have an invitation." She thought she could feel Gyllian smile behind her. "It is my intention to ask Faedryth for refuge for my child, whose lineage I have already told you of. That child is sought by one who is in league with at least one F'dor, housed in a body of Living Stone; I need not tell you what their ultimate goal is, I assume."

Again the cave was filled with devouring silence.

"All I ask is that you increase your vigilance at the doorway of the Deep Kingdom," Rhapsody continued. "If you guard this front entrance, and make it your second-highest priority to do so, I have been assured none can enter the Nain realm from any other doorway—do you agree with that assessment?"

The dragon's eyes narrowed, making the vertical pupils expand sideways. It seemed he was thinking for a moment.

"I do," he said finally.

"Let none pass that you do not know for certain belong here," Rhapsody said. "*None whatsoever.* Are you willing to do that for me?"

The draconic head raised up slightly, looking down at her at an angle.

"I suppose, as I have already said, it would depend upon the price you are willing to pay."

"I have already told you I would give you my wedding ring."

"And I have already told you that I do not want it."

"Well, what *do* you want, then?" Rhapsody demanded impatiently.

A cruel smile spread over the dragon's face.

"Nothing much," he said casually. "It's a simple request you are making, so I will be fair. All I want in payment is, hmmm, let me think, *let me think*—all right, I have it. Just to show you what a fair and reasonable beast I can be, I will ask only a lock of your hair in payment."

"Rhapsody," said Gyllian quietly from behind her, "no."

Once more the cave fell to silence.

"Why do you want such a thing?" Rhapsody asked.

The dragon rocked his head from side to side, and shrugged, a motion that she had seen Elynsynos make.

"It's pretty," he said nonchalantly. "And it's gold; I like gold."

Rhapsody exhaled evenly. She was well aware of the threat of such a seemingly mild offer. A lock of hair was the story of a person's life, and elements of that story could be retrieved and manipulated by Namers; the possibility of what other beings might be able to do with such a rich resource of personal information was staggering.

And terrifying.

Rhapsody did not care.

"When Elynsynos was teaching me the canon of the Wyrmril, she told me a little about you, as she did each of the living dragons of the world," she said quietly.

"Oh?"

"Yes. She said that you were materialistic, a hoarder of treasure, but not greedy; that you were curmudgeonly and occasionally petty, but not utterly unreasonable, as she described some others. She also said that you were a wyrm of your word and trustworthy; that the Nain had not made a foolish alliance with you, even if they pay dearly for it. So I am ready to believe, based on the word of my dear friend and a dragon of epic status, that you will not make a bargain with me that I need to fear the breaking of. Would you say that was reasonable?"

"I would," said Witheragh. "But if you doubt my word, what does any assurance from me matter?"

"I do not doubt your word. I am also not fool enough, no matter what you have come to believe, to be unaware of the risk of giving what you ask to a dragon in payment for something that should be incumbent in your stated mission anyway."

She drew Daystar Clarion.

The dragon reared up, shock on its enormous face. The billowing flames raced down the sword's blade, reflecting in the beast's wide eyes.

Rhapsody reached over her own shoulder and seized the root of the fall of shining golden tresses that she wore bound in a black ribbon. Her hair had not been cut, at Ashe's humorous insistence, for several years, and reached to just below her knees when unbound. She looked at the burning blade in her hand.

Slypka, she said. Extinguish.

The fire that licked the epic blade disappeared, snuffed for a moment.

For the first time since entering the cave, Rhapsody looked directly into the dragon's wide eyes.

With one smooth, almost vicious slice, she severed the entirety of the fall of golden hair at the base of her neck, just above the ribbon.

She struggled to ignore the gasps behind her, then held the sword at her side again until the flames returned a moment later. She sheathed the blade, then wound the long fall of gleaming hair like a rope and tossed it over the river of fire.

"Here," she said. "Take it all."

The dragon's artificial voice gagged on its words. "Wha—"

"A larger amount should serve to remind you better of your promise."

Like lightning the beast's claw shot out and seized the hair, dragging it quickly up and away from the molten river racing beneath it.

"We have a deal," Rhapsody said. It was not a question.

Witheragh stared at her. He withdrew his claw and held the hair up before his eyes on a talon as a wide smile wended its way across his face. When he looked back, his eyes were absent the condescending expression that had been there from the moment he came to the river.

"We do," he said.

"Then let us go in peace," Rhapsody said. "Remember your promise; guard this doorway, and keep my child safe."

"I will," said Witheragh. He coughed awkwardly as Rhapsody bent to retrieve her pack and turned to go. "Do you have any word of Elynsynos?"

Rhapsody stopped and looked at him again.

"I do, sadly," she said. "I sent my most trusted scout, along with the Invoker of the Filids, to her lair, bringing healers in case she was found injured. There was no sign of her at all. The lair was sealed."

Witheragh nodded. "As we all feared."

"My husband stands to hold the land as he can," Rhapsody said, shouldering her pack. "He is her direct descendant, Llauron's son. He will do the best he can, along with the Invoker, to keep that part of the Shield intact." She smiled slightly. "And he will appreciate your help in keeping his child safe, I can assure you, though he will not like the price. Farewell and thank you. Enjoy the hair."

"Wait!" the dragon called as she walked back to rejoin the other women. "Where is this child I am guarding—this great-grandchild of one of the Five Daughters? Can—can I see him?"

Rhapsody's smile was broad in return.

"Not today, I think," she said mischievously. "That is an honor that you don't deserve yet; I'm sorry. With all due respect, you've been obnoxious, and the prospect of mixing chocolate with cheese when stuffing a smoked Lirin—ugh. Revolting. And I never said the child was a boy. When I return from battle, if you have done your part and guarded my child well, perhaps then you will have merited it, and I will introduce you. Goodbye, Witheragh."

She turned and made her way back to the women, taking her walking stick from an astonished Melisande and signaling to the others to come forward and follow her.

Melisande lagged behind for a moment, rooted to the spot on which she had been standing by the look of utter shock on the face of the beast before it turned and vanished back into the shadowy darkness of the massive cave beyond the Molten River.

Then she ran to her adopted grandmother and took her hand, fairly dancing with glee as they passed by the Molten River and traveled on to the gate of the Nain kingdom.

"*Me?* I'm your most trusted scout?"

"Well, of course. Come along, now."

47

Once inside the massive tunnel that led to the gate of the Deep Kingdom, the leadership of the group changed. Rhapsody stepped back into the rear flank and took Meridion and the heavy cloak of mist from Krinsel, whose face remained stoic but whose body seemed happy to be relieved of the burden. Rhapsody took Gyllian aside before they went forward.

"How long to the gate?"

"A league and a half."

The Lady Cymrian sighed. "I'm not sure Krinsel is up to that long a trek without rest."

Gyllian nodded. "We can take refuge in one of the side-cavern barracks. If we come upon soldiers, I will address them."

"Of course; thank you." Rhapsody reached for Melisande's hand. "Come, Melly—we are going to rest for a little while, have some supper, and feed Meridion before we go on. Help me put the cloak on, will you? I need to keep him covered at all times."

The little girl nodded excitedly and helped her adopted grandmother pull her hood up. She kissed the baby's head, then stepped away, pulling up her own hood, grinning widely.

The women followed Gyllian deeper into the earth, feeling the weight of the mountains rising above them growing heavier as they traveled. The tunnels were dark, utterly lightless except for the occasional glowing spore; Analise's globe cast wide blue shadows in the dark main corridor, dimly illuminating the evidence of the rough-hewn tunnel making a slow change to smoothly engineered walls, ceilings, and floors with drainage runs and air vents.

Along each side of the main corridor smaller access tunnels yawned; before one of them to the right, Gyllian stopped, listened for a moment, then motioned her companions inside.

The four women and the little girl followed the Nain princess into what appeared to be a bunker of a sort, with a towering ceiling and side walls lined with what looked in the dark to be wide shelving.

"Close your eyes," Gyllian said. She felt around in the darkness and a moment later a series of torch sconces, much like the ones that lined the hallways of Ylorc, sparked to life, smelling slightly of rancid oil.

When Rhapsody opened her eyes again, she saw that the shelves were actually bunks, made to house fifteen score or more soldiers, stacked on top of one another and connected by a series of ladders. By her estimation of the number of access tunnels, this single main corridor housed somewhere in the vicinity of twelve thousand soldiers.

And it was but one of many such main corridors that she had seen at the opening of the Deep Kingdom.

"Sit, please," Gyllian said, indicating the lower bunks. She pulled her pack from her shoulders, laid it on the floor of the barracks tunnel, and started to pull the remains of bread and cheese stores and thin water flasks from the depths of it.

"We should eat and get back on the move as soon as we can," she said quietly, handing bread to Analise and Krinsel, cheese to Melisande, and a waterskin to Rhapsody, who had sat down on a nearby bunk and was preparing to feed Meridion. "These outer troops have the widest sweep in their patrol routes, and will be gone for longer than most of the others, but they will return eventually; it would be best if we were gone when they do."

The women nodded and set to eating, all except for Rhapsody, who took a quick drink from the waterskin, then put Meridion to the breast and wrapped him carefully in the mist cloak, humming a gentle tune of calming. Melisande came closer and sat down by her side, munching her cheese, and leaned up against her, loosing a deep sigh. The Lady Cymrian put her free arm around the little girl and smiled down at her.

"How are you holding up?"

The young Lady Navarne nodded, her mouth full, and caught a crumb of cheese as it threatened to fall from the corner of her lower lip.

"Mmmm fine."

"I had no doubt. You are so brave and strong, Melly; your brother will be so proud of you when he hears all the impressive feats you have accomplished. You will be a great woman one day, because you are an amazing young lady."

"I have an amazing example," Melisande said, brushing away the last sands of the cheese. "I cannot believe you slashed your *hair* off like that. I almost cried—but I was so proud of you. The look on that dragon's face when you threw it across the river—" The little girl stopped, at a loss for words.

Rhapsody chuckled. "It's only hair, Melly; it will grow back."

Melisande's face grew solemn.

"Ashe would have had a fatal fit if he had seen that."

"Perhaps, but I doubt it. One of the many things Ashe and I have in common is a willingness to do whatever it takes, no matter how much we dislike it, no matter how much it costs us, to take care of you and your brother and your little cousin."

The Lady Navarne's face lit up like the sunrise.

"Is Meridion my cousin?"

Rhapsody smiled.

"Well, in a way. Your father and Ashe were as close as brothers, so that pretty much makes you cousins in all ways that matter."

Melisande sighed dramatically.

"Good. The only other cousin I know that I have is Malcolm Steward, and he's a pest."

Rhapsody laughed in spite of herself. "Oh, come now, Melly, he's just a toddler. All babies are pests when they are his age."

Melisande shook her head vehemently.

"No, they're not. I am very certain that *I* was not a pest when I was his age—"

"You might ask your brother if he agrees with that assessment. I can assure you, all five of mine thought I was one."

"Well, I may have been annoying, but I didn't whine and cry for everything I wanted. Malcolm's so fat that he won't even go and get a toy if he wants it, but rather sits on the floor and bellyaches and points at it." Melisande leaned back and began a realistic rendering of the half-mewing, half-whinnying noise of her young second-cousin, to Rhapsody's barely hidden amusement. "The servants, and even his parents, grab whatever he wants and rush to get it to him just to make him stop his caterwauling. It's *awful*."

Rhapsody's face grew thoughtful.

"Perhaps he is just missing his father," she said, more to herself than to Melisande.

"Missing Tristan?" Melisande frowned. "Is he in battle?"

Rhapsody turned to her. "He's with Ashe, or at least nearby." She laced up her shirt, wrapped Meridion in the cloak again, stood carefully, and pulled Melisande to her feet. "Now, come along. We have a Nain king to meet."

The dark feeder corridor that they rejoined had gone on for almost twice as long as they had traveled already when they began to see a glow in the distance.

Rhapsody turned to Krinsel, who was following at the back of the group.

"Are you up to carrying the baby again?" she asked quietly. "Please don't fear to decline, Krinsel; I want you to feel secure." The Bolg midwife nodded, and Rhapsody transferred the mist cloak and the sleeping infant to her, then moved up to behind Gyllian.

"Is that the gate up there?" she asked the Nain princess.

Gyllian smiled slightly. "I fear not; that light is the entrance to the main thoroughfare to the capital city. But the palace is not too far past the gate." Rhapsody nodded, adjusted her pack, and took Melisande's hand.

They continued on in silence. The light from the tunnel opening ahead was brightening their way, and every now and then they could see figures passing by, their bodies of thicker mass and broader stature for the most part. As they neared the opening, Gyllian pulled her hood down.

"Follow me, if you please, m'lady."

"Without question."

The princess stepped around the corner and onto the thoroughfare, followed a moment later by the rest of the women.

Rhapsody blinked in astonishment turning to delight.

The roadway was far wider than she had imagined, and passed through what appeared to be an underground village, carved from the stone of the mountain range. Houses, shops, cathedrals, even lampposts seemed to almost grow out of the stony ground, beneath smoothly carved stone bridges that spanned the tops of buildings towering in the air above them. Gardens of shade-loving plants that Rhapsody had established in her own underground flower beds in Elysian surrounded sparkling fountains and elegant statuary, all of which had an alien style to them, like the buildings and bridges, sized to a race of people built like Gyllian.

In the center of the village stood an enormous clock, formed of multicolored stone; it was surrounded by a circle of marble benches on which mothers talking to young children and elderly men drowsing were sitting, oblivious to the ticking of the metalworks of the towering timepiece with brass hands that ended in what looked like pointing fingers.

The village apparently was outside the gate; the massive stone wall that closed off the thoroughfare in the distance ahead held an imposing set of doors, taller than four human men and bound in intricate brasswork. Many levels of scaffolding held guards on both sides of the doors, behind mounted crossbows aimed over the heads of hundreds of Nain that plied the streets, shopping, bartering, arguing, and otherwise going about the business of any upworld town.

Gyllian strode deliberately down the thoroughfare, past clusters of Nain that stopped talking and stared as she walked by, with the four women hurrying to keep up behind her. As she approached the gate the streets began to fill with the noise of murmurs and whispered excitement; by the time the group arrived at the enormous wall, the sound had swelled and risen to the upper levels of the buildings lining the streets and was bouncing off the barrier, filling the square.

The guards on the ground stepped forward to meet the arriving princess, who stopped and assumed a regal stance. She relayed a series of quiet commands in a language that Rhapsody understood a few words of, recognizing it as a modernized version of the tongue that the Nain of the old world spoke. The guards exchanged wide-eyed glances of confusion, then stared at the women behind the princess, finally assenting and opening the massive doors of the gate. Rhapsody and Melisande smiled in identical pleasantry as they passed through the doorway, causing the Nain guards to blink in astonishment and shake their heads, even after the doors were beginning to close again.

Beyond the gate the vault of the ceiling above the city was even taller, the buildings grander, and the streets wider. Gyllian commandeered a carriage pulled by a quartet of donkeys from a shocked Nain driver who, after regaining his senses, drove the coach with the princess and her odd hooded companions through the streets, beaming proudly.

Behind the heavy curtains of the carriage Rhapsody took the opportunity to feed the baby again while Krinsel leaned back against the seat and closed her eyes. Analise took Meridion and gently patted his back while Rhapsody brushed Melisande's hair and ran her fingers through her own shorn locks. She looked up and smiled at Gyllian, only to see the Nain princess looking back at her seriously.

"Don't be lulled into complacency by these sights, m'lady," she said quietly. "The Deep Kingdom has a charming exterior luster, but the vast bulk of it is martial and as cold as the stone from which it is hewn. Faedryth is as stoic and guarded a man as I've ever known, and runs this kingdom with a combination of the efficiency of the village clocks, and the grip of the forge hammers that shape the steel and brass that bind the doors of the gate. He is still angry with both you and the Bolg king, and he has an immortal man's memory. I will advocate for you as best as I can, but my father's greatest strength is not forgiveness, nor is it reasonability."

Rhapsody nodded, watching her son's head dip slowly against Analise's shoulder as he drifted off to sleep again.

Finally the coach arrived at the wide stairs of the palace. The mist cloak was wrapped back around Krinsel and the sling in which Meridion was cradled was secured on her again, then the women disembarked and followed Gyllian up the stairs and into the entryway of Undervale.

The Nain princess swept past the palace guards much in the same way she had at the gate, ignoring the protestations of both soldiers and the palace staff, herding the group of her guests into the arched corridor leading to the Great Hall.

"Announce us immediately, Faelik," she said steadily to the chamberlain, who had met them at the doors of Undervale and was struggling to keep up with her as she made her way to entrance to the Hall. She maintained an expression of serene politeness as she pushed him out of the way and pulled the tall double doors open, revealing the Great Hall.

At the end of a long aisle laid in glorious mosaic designs stood a dais atop which a heavily carved stone of black marble stood. Seated on that throne, with a look of supreme annoyance conveyed by the deepest scowl Rhapsody had ever seen, was the Nain king. He wore no crown or robes of state, but rather was attired in simple trousers tucked into sturdy boots, with a tunic belted in leather covering his upper body. He glanced at the guards standing on either side of his throne, then returned his stare to his daughter again.

"Gyllian—" The word was mostly a snarl.

The Nain princess did not blink.

"Father," she interrupted, "please be so kind as to greet our guests, the Lady Cymrian and her retinue. She has a request to make of you, and I ask that you listen without prejudice, as I support this request wholeheartedly."

Faedryth blinked in astonishment. He looked at the guards again.

Then he directed his stare at Rhapsody, looking her up and down for a long moment. Finally he gestured impatiently for her to come forward.

Rhapsody swallowed hard. She released Melisande's hand, which had grown clammy in her own, and smiled down at the little girl encouragingly. She stepped forward to the foot of the dais on which the Nain king's throne was raised from the stone floor; then, in front of his astonished eyes, she sank to one knee before him.

Faedryth blinked as undisguised displeasure crawled over his face and took up residence there. He coughed, a grumbling sound that made his guards stand up even straighter.

"Leave us," the king said to those guards in a low growl. "Now." His eyes never left Rhapsody. The soldiers complied hurriedly, closing the enormous doors of the Great Hall behind them with an echoing slam that continued to vibrate for the span of a score of heartbeats afterward.

"For the love of God, the One, the All, *get up*, m'lady," Faedryth said flatly. "Disappointed as I am in our last interaction, it is utterly inappropriate that my sovereign should kneel to me."

"I am not here as your sovereign, Your Majesty," Rhapsody said; she had not moved. "And, if need be, I am willing to add my second knee and even my forehead to my bow, to prostrate myself to you, if it will convince you to grant the boon I am asking of you."

The Nain king gripped the arms of his throne even more tightly and leaned forward. He spoke softly, an undertone of anger punctuating the single word he uttered.

"Please."

Rhapsody inhaled, then let her breath out steadily. She rose and stood in respectful silence.

"If you are not here in your capacity as Lady Cymrian, then are you here as the Lirin queen? I was under the impression that our peoples were in a fairly peaceful place as a result of your efforts at the Cymrian Council three years ago."

"No, I am not. And yes, they are."

"Then why are you bothering me?"

Rhapsody's face was solemn.

"I've come to ask you a tremendous favor, for which I will always be in your debt if you grant it. But moreover, it is of great importance to our Alliance, and, at the risk of sounding hyperbolic, the whole of the world."

Faedryth's brow darkened.

"I don't know what 'hyperbolic' means, but I find it strange that my Lady would come to me, after I made a very similar request of you not that long ago, and your *friend*, the Bolg king, only to be rudely spurned, grotesquely insulted, and outright threatened. In fact, m'lady, if you had not come to my kingdom in my daughter's company, you would have been sent away at the gate." He glared pointedly at Gyllian.

"What you just said precisely meets the definition of 'hyperbolic,' Father," Gyllian said dryly. "I would certainly hope that, given your age and the length of your reign, you would know better than to be rude to our Lady, though you are certainly treading dangerously close to it, if you haven't done so already." She bowed her head in apology to Rhapsody, then looked back at her father again. "Kindly be silent and listen to what she has to say; I would not have brought her here if I did not agree with her request. You are compromising my reputation as well as your own; mine at least still has meaning to me."

Faedryth's mouth dropped open. Gyllian was a woman of few words, even by Nain standards. Her speech was the longest he had ever heard her utter in her life. He closed his mouth, abashed, and gestured for the Lady Cymrian to speak.

"Sorbold is advancing in the south in open warfare, as I told you it would when you visited Ylorc," Rhapsody said. "The holy city of Sepulvarta fell first; the western coastline in blockaded by warships, merchant vessels and a loose fleet of pirate ships. The Icemen of the Hintervold are massing for attack on the northern borders of the Middle Continent."

"I am sure that you are very disturbed by all that. I cannot help you. I believe I made that clear when I left the Bolglands."

"She is not asking for you to commit troops, Father," Gyllian interrupted impatiently. "Be silent and listen to the Lady."

"Well, what does she want, then?" Faedryth demanded. "The Bolg king manufactures decent weapons of his own, we have no foodstuffs to supplement—"

"I am here as a mother; I am asking refuge for my son," Rhapsody said softly. "Please."

Faedryth's words ground to a choking halt.

"Son? Your child has been born?"

"You're very observant these days, Father," said Gyllian. The dryness in her voice bordered on acidic. "If you didn't take note of the Lady Cymrian's change of physical status, you might have noticed the three women behind us. One of them is Lady Melisande Navarne, the sister of the duke of Navarne, and therefore a visiting dignitary from Roland; even at ten years of age, she is no doubt accustomed to better manners in court."

"Oh, not necessarily," Melisande said. "Anborn, my godfather, is frequently at Haguefort, so I'm very used to this sort of hostile conversation."

At the mention of his old friend, Faedryth smiled slightly.

"Another guest is Analise o Serendair, a First Generation Cymrian of the Second Fleet," Gyllian continued sternly. "I am certain you do not wish her to return to Manosse with tales of the imbecilic and insolent treatment you are according our mutual sovereign.

"Our final guest is Krinsel, an Archon of Ylorc and the head of the Bolg council of midwives. In case you haven't noticed, she is holding an infant in her arms."

Faedryth rose from the great marble throne shakily.

"Why—why have you brought—a child—a royal child—to my kingdom?"

"Because I am needed in battle," Rhapsody said quietly. "I have duties as the Iliachenva'ar; Daystar Clarion's presence is critical to the survival of the Middle Continent. And though I would rather tear out my own heart and set it aflame, I must leave my child in the care of others I trust. They stand before you." She swallowed hard as the Nain king's eyes darted from woman to woman in front of him.

"I count myself among them, so you know," Gyllian added, looking sharply at Faedryth. "It would be my honor to be of service to my sovereign and her son."

"In addition to being an infant whose mother is in battle, my child is hunted, Faedryth," Rhapsody continued. "The Merchant Emperor, Talquist, seeks him so that he can consume his heart. Obviously I must do everything in my power to prevent that."

"Wait—" Faedryth stammered. "*What?*"

"My son is the Child of Time, about whom there are auguries and prophecies known to the emperor," Rhapsody said, her voice breaking intermittently. "Talquist, who seeks the longevity bordering on immortality that First Generation Cymrians enjoy, has been told that eating this child's beating heart will grant him that immortality. He has dealings with every assassin's guild of any size across the continent, and has sent them, along with his armies, in search of this child."

"Why—why did you not keep him in the Bolglands?" Faedryth demanded. "Canrif is the most unassailable fortress in the Known World—"

"It is not," Rhapsody said, her voice ringing now with a Namer's tone.

"You know that Anwyn's armies were able to assail it from without, while the Bolg were able to overrun it from within at the time of the Great War. We recently narrowly survived a breech of the Bolglands, though Achmed and Grunthor were able to repel those attacks. But Talquist will not stop there. He and his stone champion have even deeper designs on those mountains, which contain prizes that, with respect, even you do not know of, Your Majesty. One such prize, if it were to fall into his hands, would make any fear that you have of the Lightcatcher's risk pointless, if you follow my inference.

"But my son is shielded from the emperor's eyes, and from the tools he has for scrying. Talquist does not know that he has left the Bolglands, or to where he has been taken. Each of these women have gifts to care for him and to hide him from any eyes that seek him—as they have done from your own while standing in your very presence. His name, as far as I know, has not been discovered by Talquist or his forces; he is all but invisible in your lands. I have already parleyed with Witheragh on my way here. He has agreed to make the guardianship of your realm his priority second only to that of the Shield of the Earth from the Vault."

Faedryth's eyes widened. The light of the great chandelier hanging above them caught in those eyes, making them gleam ominously.

"You parleyed with Witheragh?"

"Yes."

"And he agreed to help you?"

"Again, yes."

"Why?" The king began to pace the dais, the great red gem at the base of the gold chain around his neck catching the light of the chandelier. "Witheragh has no concern for the needs of men, and never has. When the Molten River went dry, buried under a cone of ash, he could have relighted it with little more than a breath, but he refused, even though it meant the eventual death of the Deep Kingdom in winter. The steps I was forced to take were devastating." Faedryth swallowed suddenly, remembering his use of the Lightforge, and the different sort of devastation that had resulted.

"My son is the great-great-grandson of Elynsynos," Rhapsody said, her voice grave. "The Primal Lore of dragons requires them not only to not to kill each other, but to preserve their dying race, as they guard the Shield of the world from what lurks below."

The Nain king snorted. "Balderdash. What payment did he demand of you? What did you give him? I would suspect Daystar Clarion, but you have already said you are taking it into battle."

"Daystar Clarion does not belong to me; I am only its bearer. I could not have given it to him, even if I had wanted to—it isn't mine to give."

"What *did* you give, then? I want to know that you have not unbalanced the tribute that we routinely pay for the uneasy peace we have with him."

Rhapsody smiled slightly.

"I did not. The gems that adorn his hide that you have paid in tribute are astounding in their beauty and value; I had nothing like that to offer him. I gave him the only thing I had that he was willing to accept—my hair."

Faedryth's brows shot into his hairline.

"You gave your *hair* to a dragon?" he said incredulously, his eyes taking note of her missing locks. "Are you out of your mind, m'lady? Do you have any idea what sort of power he has over you now, what sort of threat he might someday be to you because of that?"

"Do *you* have any idea how little I care?" Rhapsody said, her voice straining with emotion. "It doesn't matter what he does with it; it can only harm me and no one else. You don't understand, Your Majesty; when I said that I would do *anything* to protect my son, I meant it literally, and stated it truly. Witheragh cannot, by virtue of the Primal Lore, harm my son or my husband. That is the only thing that matters to me. If he decides to make nefarious use of the power I have given him over me, I will gladly suffer those consequences if it means my child is safe." Her voice broke completely, and she bowed her head.

A devouring silence filled the Great Hall.

Finally Rhapsody looked up again, and her eyes were filled with tears.

"Please, Your Majesty, help me. It is taking every bit of strength that I have to stand before you and beg you to take my son; when I leave him I will be leaving my entire heart and a large part of my soul behind with him. I had hoped, before he was born, when I was dreaming of what the Future might hold for him, to bring him here one day, to your kingdom, to learn from you. You were at one time his great-grandfather's dear friend and collaborator in the building of the greatest nation this continent has seen in its history. Like his father, he will one day learn the deserved condemnations of Gwylliam, but it was my desire that he could learn of the good times and brave deeds of his forebear as well, from the one person who could tell him of those days with any objectivity and perspective. I don't know if he will inherit any of Gwylliam's knowledge of the forge, or architectural and engineering genius, but he has the potential one day to be a Namer of great power; he has already shown signs of it. He alone will have the chance to tell the tale of the Cymrians in a way that history can record accurately if he spends time learning the story from those who played a great part in it.

"But even if you choose to never tell or teach him anything, I beg you, *I beg you*, please, shelter him, protect him; hide him here, in your hidden kingdom. Keep him safe, please, please. I will give you anything I have, I will do anything you ask. Please."

Her spirit broke along with her voice. Rhapsody dissolved into the tears that had been welling in her eyes, and sank to the floor, her face in her hands.

Melisande, alarmed, started toward Rhapsody, but Faedryth waved her silently away. He came down from the dais and stopped in front of the sobbing queen. Gently he took Rhapsody's chin in his finely gloved hand and raised her face, looking into her eyes.

His eyes, cloudy with age and the terrible things they had seen over time, were glinting with tears of their own.

"Very well, m'lady, I will do as you ask," he said, his voice unusually gentle. "I will guard your child until you are able to come and retrieve him; my kingdom will stand to protect him with every resource it has. But do not mistake my willingness to do so with any other commitment. While we are grudging members of the Cymrian Alliance, I have said that I will not commit my forces to a war that does not threaten my lands, and I mean it still. Are we clear in that?"

Rhapsody smiled through her tears, causing the Nain king to feel pleasant warmth flooding through his body, the likes of which he could not recall feeling before.

"We are," she said. "You have my deepest gratitude, and that of his father as well."

"That's an interesting boon of its own," Faedryth said humorously. "I should assume, then, that Lord Gwydion will be more than happy to renegotiate our tariff structure once the war is over, assuming anything is left of the Middle Continent." He watched as the smile left Rhapsody's face, taking the good cheer that had come over him with it; she merely nodded in assent.

Out of the corner of his eye he caught Gyllian's glance; his daughter was watching him evenly, but there was a look of approval in her visage. Faedryth coughed, then turned to the Bolg midwife with the draping cloth emitting a fine mist that apparently held the Cymrian heir. He shuddered inwardly, then turned and offered the Lady Cymrian his hand, helping her to her feet.

"All right, let's have a look at this supposedly miraculous child," he said as pleasantly as he could. "I want to see what all the fuss is about." He gave Rhapsody his arm and walked with her to where the Bolg woman was glowering, and shuddered once again.

Rhapsody took no notice. She gently pulled the folds of the cloak of mist apart, revealing a little shining face crowned with the finest of golden curls and two tiny cerulean blue eyes, scored with vertical pupils, intently focused on the Nain king. They sparkled with interest, and his mouth widened into a grin as he loosed a musical cooing sound that filled the hollow chamber.

"Oh, my," said Faedryth distantly. A smile wide enough to crack his curmudgeonly aspect spread slowly across his face, causing his fulsome beard to twitch with delight.

"Oh, my."

48

When she finally felt almost strong enough to leave her child, Rhapsody did it quickly, knowing that if she faltered she would never be able to protect him properly.

She gave given him a warm bath, letting him splash happily as he always did, striping her laughing face with rivulets of water that served to mask her tears. She sang to him for the better part of two hours, and nursed him to sleep.

Then, after kissing him until she felt the tears return, she laid him in his cradle, rubbed his back, and left the room, not meeting Analise's sympathetic gaze.

Whereupon she snatched her pack from the hallway and broke into a dead run.

She ran through the halls of the palace, past the startled guards and servants, out into the city streets until the pain stopped.

It leaked out of her slowly, like milk from the breast; when she first had stepped away from him, she was unable to breathe for the agony of the loss.

But the farther she got away from the name she had left with him, the more she could feel that pain drain out of her, along with any feeling whatsoever.

She was almost to the mouth of the Molten River when an airy voice, sounding in the multiple tones of soprano, alto, tenor and bass, rang out in the cave.

Rhapsody, Friend of Elynsynos, tarry.

She came to a halt, her hand on the hilt of Daystar Clarion.

For a long moment, there was nothing but silence and the dripping sounds she had heard on her way to the Deep Kingdom.

"Well?" she demanded. "What do you want now, Witheragh?"

"Did Faedryth agree to give sanctuary to your child?"

"Yes."

The cave echoed hollowly. Then the voice spoke again, ringing quietly against the rockwalls high above.

"There are men, humans, four of them, on horseback, at a distance of three and a quarter leagues to the west," Witheragh said. "They appear to be searching for something, most likely the entrance to the Deep Kingdom."

Rhapsody's grip on the sword tightened.

"Thank you for the warning," she said. "Can you direct me to where I can find them—"

"That will not be necessary," the great wyrm interrupted. "I have bargained with you to protect your child, and I will take care of this. They will not enter; if they try, they will not live, and I will enjoy a supper of flame-roasted horseflesh this night. Now, I have something for you. Step away from the riverbank."

Rhapsody blinked, then obeyed.

At her feet a swirl of mist appeared, whirling vaporously, then dispersed. As the mist vanished, a solid object, long and thin like a length of rope about two-thirds Rhapsody's height with a wide, flared end, seemed to solidify in the reflected light of the fiery river. It was dark red, with a scored, mottled surface. When she looked questioningly into the darkness of the massive cavern beyond the river, the voice spoke again.

"For your use, until you come to retrieve your child."

Rhapsody bent down and tentatively touched the object. It was both warm and cold; the heat seemed to be contained deep within it, while its surface was cool and dry, almost like the skin of a snake.

"What is it?"

"It belonged to my grandmother, the matriarchal wyrm of my clutch. She was like you, in a way, a lore-tender, a keeper of draconic history. It was her greatest weapon in many ways."

Rhapsody gingerly lifted the thick ropelike object and turned it over in her hands. The wider end looked like the opening in a jousting gauntlet or the sleeve of a lance; it had a smooth, shiny interior, even darker red than the surface.

"Thank you," she said uncertainly. "I'm not sure what to do with it, how to use it. I'm not familiar with the weapons of dragons; Elynsynos did not tell me anything of them."

She could distinctly hear a chuckle in the voice.

"She probably felt no need to do so, given that you have one of your own. Yours is, of course, much smaller."

Rhapsody's brow furrowed.

"I don't own anything that looks like this."

"I didn't say it looked the same, just that you have one."

"How do I use it?"

"Put your hand inside the wide end."

Slowly Rhapsody complied.

The interior of the rope was as smooth and slippery as it had appeared, tapering into what seemed to be a hollow tube. Her fingers had just touched the inner edge when suddenly the rope collapsed with great force of suction, adhering to her arm from the elbow down.

Panic roared through her, and Rhapsody shook her arm violently, trying to dislodge the object. As she did, the rope thinned and lengthened by more than three times over, cracking and snapping in the air high above her like a whip as she slapped her arm about wildly. Where the end contacted the ground or the cave wall, sparks flew, and chips of rock broke off, tumbling to the ground amid small puffs of smoke.

"Stop!" the draconic voice commanded. "Peace—you will bring harm upon yourself if you thrash about so."

"What—what have you done? Release me!"

The commanding voice took on a distinct chuckle.

"Be still a moment," Witheragh said. Having no alternative, Rhapsody obeyed. The strange, whiplike object hung limp at her side as she stood still. She took hold of the flared end at the place where the whip grew thinner and pulled; it came off her arm easily.

"Thank you, but I believe I should leave this here with you," Rhapsody said as she bent down and started to place the weapon on the floor of the cave again.

"That would be an opportunity grievously missed." The voice of the dragon resonated through the cavern. "With a little adjustment and practice, it could be very useful to you in battle."

Rhapsody paused, then stood erect again and looked down at the weapon.

"What is this called?" she asked as she turned it over and examined it more closely.

"In your tongue, I believe it is called—a tongue."

The object dropped to the floor of the cave.

Rhapsody bent quickly and retrieved it, wincing at what she was certain was a great insult.

"I'm so sorry. Are you telling me that this is your grandmother's, er—"

"Her tongue. Yes."

"You have her tongue?"

The humor resolved quietly from the dragon's voice.

"It was the greatest thing she owned. Not only did it serve her well as a weapon, but it spoke only the truth, and was talented in the telling of the ancient lores and the history of our race. I thought it might have some meaning to you on a rather significant level. My mistake."

"No—no, I'm very sorry," Rhapsody said quickly, turning the whip-like object over in her hands. "I am immensely honored by your offer to lend it to me."

"You have just proven your understanding better than I could have hoped," said the dragon's voice. "It is but on loan, and I expect it to be returned, assuming it survives."

"Of course. Thank you. Thank you very much."

The cave echoed with silence for a moment. Then the multitoned voice spoke again.

"I also expect an introduction to your child at the same time."

Rhapsody nodded. "Of course."

"Her name was Mylinmacr, as you probably already discerned. The tongue by itself has spoken from time to time over history, but not of late. It has been silent for most of this age; I would not expect much if I were you. But you can always ask if you want to know something. Mylinmacr was said to be a great sage and gifted not only with the knowledge of our history, but with the wisdom of how to apply that knowledge. With any luck, having it in your possession may allow the same to be said of you one day—perhaps when someone is carrying your tongue about with him."

Rhapsody exhaled. "Thank you again. If it's not rude to ask, can you tell me what made you decide to loan this precious object to me?"

"You were a friend of Elynsynos," said the voice. "Perhaps carrying Mylinmacr's tongue will allow you one day to relate the tales Elynsynos told you in the way a dragon would tell them, and would be able to understand them. It may keep her lore from being lost to the Wyrmril, now that she is gone."

"Thank you," Rhapsody said again. "And thank you for what you have agreed to undertake on behalf of my child."

"Go now. I have an entrance to guard."

Rhapsody pulled forth a length of cord from her pack, coiled the tongue-whip and bound it to her sword belt.

"Goodbye, Witheragh," she said quietly. "Godspeed and may your guardianship be uneventful."

There was no reply.

She doubled her gait and hurried away from the Molten River, back to the place in the lee of the rockwall where the horses had been left.

Feeling utterly numb.

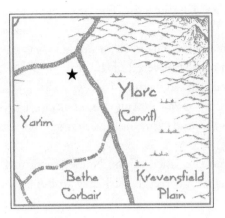

49

THE BROKEN VAULT OF KURIMAH MILANI

Deep within the sand of the northern wasteland that led to the piedmont of the Teeth, hidden in the broken wreckage that in ages past had been part of the legendary city known as Kurimah Milani, the draconic body of the being known as Anwyn ap Merithyn stirred, then opened her eyes.

She had retreated to this place to heal from the wounds of her battle, or to die, but in either case, she sought the blissful oblivion of solitude and sleep in a place that had long been forgotten by Time.

Only to be jarred from that sleep, in a way that suggested a loss of solitude as well.

For a moment, the only sound in the cavern was the distant dripping of water. The searing blue light that had gleamed madly from the dragon's eyes had ebbed to a ghostly azure shadow. An even dimmer glow shone from the wounded one, tinged rosy with blood.

The great beast lay prone, her hide still smoking, charred over the great expanse of her body. Her copper scales were tarnished by black soot and the muddy clay through which she had crawled back to the ruined cave, in ages long past a renowned place of healing, now little more than a shattered relic, a realm of broken sluiceways and smiling statuary with arms or heads missing.

The silence in what had been one of the great public baths of Kurimah Milani echoed in her stinging skin. The beast breathed raggedly, trying to control the pain.

And then, somewhere within her awareness was another vibration, an unwelcome, hated one. It hovered in the very air of the place, waiting.

The dragon recognized it immediately.

"I can—feel you—*m'lady*," Anwyn said aloud. Her scratched voice vibrated hollowly in the underground cavern, its bitterness flickering off the stone.

"Indeed," came the voice of the Namer in return. It spoke quietly, clear as the wind, slicing through the heavy air beneath the ground. "I am here."

The dragon shuddered involuntarily. She was not certain if her shivering was a result of the loss of blood or something deeper, more disturbing that she heard in Rhapsody's words.

After a momentary reflection, she realized it was the latter.

What chilled her was actually something in the reviled woman's voice that was *missing*, rather than present, a warmth that had always been nascent in the few words that the Namer had spoken directly to her, within the Great Moot of Canrif, or in the air of the fields around it, when she had the woman in her grasp, spinning in flight, raining fire down on the Cymrian people who had once revered Anwyn as their lady. Those words returned in flashes of memory now, in response to her own taunting ones.

A pretty sight, isn't it, m'lady? Look well on your people—see where you have brought them. Child of the Sky! How do you like the view from up here?

Damn your soul, Anwyn!

She grimaced as she remembered her own reply. *Too late.*

The beast closed her eyes and flexed her tattered claw, scarred from where the talon had been torn from it, recalling the delicious feel of her rival struggling, trapped within her clutches.

End it. They were your people—serve them! Save them.

"They betrayed me," the wyrm whispered, now as she had then.

The woman said nothing. Anwyn could not tell where she was within the cavern; only the slightest of vibrations even indicated she was there at all.

The dragon concentrated, trying to locate the source of that vibration.

More words echoed in her mind, spoken in the warm voice she remembered with such loathing.

I rename you the Empty Past, the Forgotten Past. I consign your memory to those who have gone before you, you wretched beast.

Anwyn had felt it then, the Namer's ancient power, older even than her own. It had reached down into her very blood and stripped every piece of her that had been able to exist within the Present, consigning her to irrelevance she could feel in her bones. Her anger at the time of being replaced as the Lady of the Cymrians by this woman had swelled to fill the holes and passageways left behind until it all but consumed her, packing her with hate.

Another fragment of memory rose up from the depths of her mind, an even more disturbing one, of the woman's voice as she banished her from the Moot after singing her a song of tribute. The kindness with which the words had been spoken left her sick with nausea.

Give Anwyn her due; she is leaving. My tribute to you is ended. Go now, m'lady of the Past. Go and sort out your memories. We will be making grand new ones for you to count soon.

By contrast, the few words that had been spoken a moment before in the resounding cavern of Kurimah Milani were cold, efficient, missing any tone of kindness, compassion, or humility.

Like Anwyn's own.

"At least you have not tried to hide, coward that you are," the dragon murmured. "How I hate you."

"You have made that abundantly clear." Within the dragon's ears, frost seemed to form on the bones. "And while you are entitled to feel however you like, your insistence on venting that hatred has threatened too many innocents. This needs to end now."

"So finally—I am—at your mercy," the dragon muttered softly. "You have—come for retribution, to—torment me—in my last moments."

"No." Wherever she was in the echoing cave, the Lady Cymrian's voice was steady. "I have come to kill you, to end your torment, not to prolong it." In her tone there was no mercy, no forgiveness, just the simple statement of fact.

"How kind of you, as always," the dragon sneered. "The beautiful Child of the Sky, the innocent heart with whom the Cymrian populace fell in love, then cast me out, replaced me. You hypocrite; you liar. They did not know of your treachery. You took over my—home in Canrif, polluted the places I once reigned undisputed. Drove—the anger out, the rage born of—righteous fury. Filled those shrines to Gwylliam's betrayal, those hallowed sepulchers of hatred, with—banal music. You planted flowers of condolence where rightfully—there should have been perennial mourning. How dare you, *usurper*."

Rhapsody said nothing.

"You sought to replace my dynastic line with your own," the dragon whispered.

"No," the Lady Cymrian's distant voice said again. "Of all the things you have said, about this you are the most wrong. I extended your dynastic line." Anwyn's gaze grew momentarily sharper and brighter. "I married your grandson. I gave birth to his child. Your line and mine are now one and the same."

"Lies," the dragon hissed.

"You know otherwise," Rhapsody said. "I do not lie; you know this."

A fluttering of tattered eyelids sent blue shadows around the darkness of the broken baths.

"I have seen no such child. If it existed, I would have been aware of it, would have seen it in the Past."

"He was born at the turn of the year, in the cave of the Lost Sea, from which your eyes have been banished. He was delivered by your own mother. You almost killed him when you attacked me in Gwynwood—and as a result, you destroyed Llauron, your own son, the member of your family whose allegiance to you was the greatest. Your son gave his life in his grandson's protection. And you would have done so again; he was with me when you attacked a fortnight ago. I have shielded my child from your eyes, for his safety. He has his own ways of doing so as well; he is not bound to your dominion of the Past. It has no power over him."

Silence echoed throughout what remained of Kurimah Milani. After a long moment, a draconic whisper echoed fragilely through the vault.

"The Child of Time."

Rhapsody remained still in the silence of the broken cave.

After a long moment, the dragon exhaled, spitting drops of black blood from the depths of her torn lungs as she did.

"Now I see," she said, more to herself than to Rhapsody. "Small wonder he is hidden from my sight; his conception, his beginning, predates my own."

"Your mind is fading," Rhapsody said. "That's certainly untrue. His conception took place but last spring. You are forgetful—it seems death approaches. You might want to prepare your last words, and whatever passes for a soul in you, if there is one."

The dragon's broken maw twisted in a hideous grin. In it was the shadow of triumph.

"Ah, *m'lady*, it is *you* that forgets," she said, her voice hoarse. "You consigned me to only the memories of what had gone before me—and yet I know of the Child of Time, and of the prophecy." Her grin became even more sinister. "How do you suppose that came to pass, if those things are not from long ago?"

"I've no idea. And I don't care."

"Oh, but you should," Anwyn murmured, an evil amusement in her voice. "I know something you will want to know. Something of the Forgotten Past, as you named me—something that, when I have gone, no other eye will see again. Something that is vastly important about the Child of Time."

The Lady Cymrian said nothing. The dragon's words reverberated in the empty cavern.

And they rang with the tone of truth.

When silence had hung heavily in the subterranean air, the dragon's parley unanswered, the beast spoke again.

"You have named me the Empty Past, the Forgotten Past. You do not even know the irony of this. Because of what you chose to call me, there is but one place in Time that I can see clearly now." The dragon's voice grew stronger, even as her scales began to pale beneath the coating of creosote. "It is an imperfection in the Weaver's Tapestry, a place where history, *Time itself*, was altered—and it changed the course of *your* life specifically. I alone know this—when I die, this lore will die with me." She smiled weakly; the dimming eyes grew brighter for a moment. "But I will tell you this lore—for a price."

There was no reply.

"Surely you, a Namer, especially the Namer for whom the world was altered, crave to know what no longer exists in Time," the dragon said. Hearing nothing, she stretched, feeling the scorched skin beneath her shattered hide of scales tear as she did, barely noticing the pain.

Knowing she had a bartering chip.

"What do you mean, 'for whom the world was altered'?"

The dragon smirked.

"Ah, that got your attention. Yes, m'lady, insignificant as you are, apparently something happened to change the course of your life, as well as the rest of the world, and not by coincidence. You should be grateful to know that lore, as the original Past, the Past that was changed, erased, held a much grimmer road for you. For your child's father as well."

For a long moment, the dripping of water was again the only sound in the ancient bath.

"I am listening."

The beast chuckled weakly.

"As I said, for a price."

"What is the price?"

Anwyn's eyes gleamed with a new light.

"Something as significant to me as this unknown lore will be to you. Something I do not wish to die without knowing."

"What is the price? I tire of this game."

"I want to know of Gwylliam's end," Anwyn whispered. "I, the victor in the Great—War, was cast out of my own domain, refused reentry to my own lands. I did not see my hated husband's corpse, did not hear his last words, do not have the story of his death behind my eyes as the life flees my body. You—the Three—took possession of—Canrif, raped the mountain where I once ruled, supplanting the remnants of the great Cymrian civilization by turning it into a midden for monsters. But I believe you know what happened to Gwylliam. Is that true?"

Silence reigned once more.

"Well?" the dragon demanded. "Do you know or do you not?"

"I do," Rhapsody said. Her words echoed in the cavern.

"Tell me, then," Anwyn whispered. "And I will tell you what only my eyes have seen."

"You first."

The beast, her mind fading until the possibility of what she wanted to know had come within her grasp, considered. Her awareness had come roaring back with the nearness of the lore she had craved for centuries, along with the knowledge that the Namer would not deny it to her if she gave her word.

"Do we have a bargain?"

"If I am satisfied with what you say," Rhapsody said. "I will not promise to tell you something as sacred as a king's last words if I determine you to be lying, or if what you tell me is insignificant."

Anwyn felt her life ebbing.

"I—can only tell you what I see," she said, her failing voice harsh. "I do not fully understand it."

"Tell me, or prepare to speak your own last words. You are wasting my time; I am needed in battle."

"Time in the Past sometimes manifests itself as a thread of a sort, the— same thread that is woven into the tapestry of history by the—Weaver," the dragon said with great effort. "For a reason I know not, there is a place in that tapestry where an imperfection, an alteration can be seen."

"I know this already. What does this have to do with me?"

The dragon struggled to speak.

"I saw that flaw when my—grandson came to me as a youth and begged me to—look into the Past to find someone. He said he had been— thrown back in Time, for less than the span of a day, to Serendair, a millennia and a half at least before his birth, and had met a girl in Merryfield—at a foreharvest dance."

She smiled triumphantly at the intake of breath she could hear, even in the heavy silence of the cavern.

"At his insistence, I looked through my—father's spyglass to the place in Time he asked about. I witnessed your meeting, your repulsive rutting in a pasture—"

"Peace," the Namer commanded. "Speak not of this; I do not wish to hear the words from your mouth—or rather, from the air you manipulate. It does not surprise me that you do not recognize the birth of love; you will never understand what you are void of."

"True," the wyrm admitted. "But I recognize the beginning of *life*— your child was conceived that night, m'lady; at least his soul was."

"Nonsense."

The dragon's maw twisted into a grim smile.

"On the night when you and my grandson met in the old world, after you let him tumble you in a field a few moments after you met, do you recall a sensation that caused you to stop walking, to need to sit for a moment— you, who could summit a hill in a dead run without breathing hard?" The beast chuckled at the silence that followed her words. "You were feeling the conception of the soul of the Child of Time. While it's true that he may not have been incorporated in flesh until recently, his soul began that night— with that meeting. You carried that soul across two worlds—why else do you think you have seen the Future, a power none but my sister Manwyn should have had?"

"I don't believe you," Rhapsody said. "You may have witnessed our meeting, but you could not have seen a soul being created. But, regardless, it matters not."

"In a way, you are right," the dragon said, grinning even as her scales began to pale again. "What matters is that it should never have been able to happen—because, on the thread of Time as it had originally occurred, you were not a child of teenaged years when you conceived him, but an aged hag, in Tyrian, not Serendair. And Gwydion was a madman, broken by life and his battle with the demon."

"What are you babbling about? What do you mean, 'as it had originally occurred'?"

The dragon grinned wider with delight. "I have told you, history was altered for you. Though I do not know by what hand it occurred, Time's threads were cut and replaced, so that your child's conception and birth was changed. In the first occurrence of Time, that conception and birth was unnatural—and led to your rather gruesome death immediately thereafter, as was prophesied. You fared much better in the second iteration of Time, sadly for me. You are, after all, still here. So, no matter what the cost was to the rest of the world, your life was saved—and improved—by the manipulation of Time. Disgusting and outrageous and reeking of hubris, but true nonetheless."

"How? And why?"

The dragon wheezed; the breath escaping her nostrils was staggered and shot with blood.

"I've already told you that I do not know this," she said weakly. "I can only tell you that the Tapestry was altered, a thread removed that affected all of the rest of history. You have seen evidence of this yourself with your own eyes, but you were not able to make sense of it. The Nain king entrusted the only record of it to you."

Utter silence took up residence again within the cave.

"I only know one last piece of lore, something heard and not seen as the time-thread of the—original Past melted into oblivion. A name that connected—you to another in your life, earlier than you came to know him or her in the second iteration of Time. The name of—someone you both cared for, and whose death brought you together. That name is *Werinatha*."

"I know no such name."

"Of course you—do not," said the dragon impatiently. "It is from the Forgotten Past, which no—eye shall ever see again. But I have been able to regale you with stories in your own memory, a Past you yourself have forgotten until this moment. Now, I have—upheld my end of our—bargain," Anwyn said with great effort. "Your turn—tell me what I—crave to know. Did you find Gwylliam's body within the mountain?"

"Yes," Rhapsody said. "Sprawled on his back on a table in the library."

"Tell me what you were able—to divine about his ending."

"I don't know how he died, though I assume it was how you arranged it with the demon. I saw a vision of his last moments, through his eyes. He called repeatedly for the horn, to Anborn and someone named Bareth. He called to you, to his 'good people,' begging to be brought the Great Seal, and water."

"And did you hear his last words?" the beast demanded.

"I did." The Lady Cymrian's voice spoke softly, respectfully in the darkness.

"Tell me," Anwyn whispered.

An exhalation of breath echoed through the cave.

"I will speak them to you, in his voice, as I heard them," the Namer said finally. "And then our bargain will be complete."

The beast listened raptly. A moment later another voice filled the air of the shattered bath, a voice with deep timbre, filled with pain and fear. A man's voice.

A voice she recognized immediately.

Ah, Anwyn, so at last you have vanquished me. What irony your sisters, the Fates, employ, that I die here, beneath the cruel visage of the great copper wyrm I had gilt in this place to honor your mother. Even in my last I am forced to see you—to leave this life with the image of you in my eyes. All for naught—all my great works, my great dreams, for naught. Hague, you were right. You were right. I stare into the Vault of the Underworld, but it is a vault of my own making. The Great Seal. Anwyn, forgive me. Forgive me, my people. The Great Seal—

The voice broke for a moment. Then, in a barely audible tone, it whispered Gwylliam's great aphorism, the words he directed Merithyn the Explorer to greet any inhabitant of the continent that he met with.

The origin of the Cymrian name.

Come—we in peace, from the grip of—death to life in this fair—land.

Silence reigned for a moment.

"Gwylliam—asked my forgiveness?" the dragon hissed. "You lie."

"You have heard his last words, in his voice," said the Namer, her voice her own again. "You will hear no more words from me to convince you of what you already know to be true."

The beast's fragmented mind was racing. "You must—heal me," she said, beginning to gasp. "There is so—much I can teach my great-grandson. And so much I can—learn from him."

Finally, the darkness shifted, and the Lady Cymrian stepped out of the shadows near the dragon's head.

"No," she said simply. "That will never happen. It is time."

"How disappointing," the dragon spat. "You are so famous for your acts of mercy, for your forgiveness; you absolved the entire Cymrian Council of its misdeeds, rinsed the blood from their hands, by telling them they needed to—forgive each other and themselves, to let the Past go. How convenient. Where is that mercy now, m'lady? Why do you—deny it to the great-grandmother of your own child?"

"It is you that has brought me to this point," Rhapsody said quietly. "There is nothing left of mercy in me; that part of me is gone. If I were to spare your life now, it would only be because it would serve my purposes to do so. That concept is not within my makeup. I don't know how to manipulate a situation to my own ends. Therefore, at least just putting an end to the threat you bring is logical and sensible. Perhaps one day I will regret it, but if it keeps my son safe, I will have to find comfort in that knowledge and live with the guilt. Right now, I feel nothing but the desire to be rid of you and your vicious, random chaos."

The wyrm sighed, hearing the truth in the Namer's words and too weak to do anything to change her mind.

"Ah, well. Your loss. I know enough—of—the Future—to know that you—will burn with your—hatred of me. That gives me comfort."

Rhapsody inhaled, then let her breath out slowly. When she spoke again, the Namer's tone of True-Speaking was in her words.

"I harbor no hatred toward you, Anwyn—but your death at my hands will bring peace to more than just my mind. In the name of my sworn knight, I end your life. I know it will bring consolation of some degree to him."

With great effort, the dragon's lip curled slightly.

"And who—is this—knight, that my death—will console him? That bastard, the Bolg king? Your slobbering friend, the—giant freak? The—mudfilth—that crawled through—the Earth with you, like the vermin you are—?"

Rhapsody's face darkened at the insults, but no wrath was evident as she drew her sword. The flames bellowed forth from her scabbard, burning with righteous anger. She stepped onto the wyrm's neck, holding the draconic skeleton steady, and sought the pulsing vein near her feet.

"Hold still, and it will be quick," she said shortly.

"Answer—my—question," the wyrm commanded in a strained whisper. "Tell—me. I deserve the knowledge as I die."

The Lady Cymrian, the Iliachenva'ar, pressed her blade to the beast's hide above the vein. She bent at the waist, so that she could speak quietly into the dragon's ear.

"You deserve nothing, but I will tell you anyway. My sworn knight, my champion—my friend—is your youngest son, Anborn ap Gwylliam," she said softly. "And, for whatever you did that turned him from a valiant young soldier to a merciless killer, for his suffering, for him, in his name, I take your life."

She heard the voice of her first sword instructor sounding clearly in her memory.

'At's right, miss. Make it a good, clean blow, now.

Then she struck. Cleanly, deeply.

At her words, just before she drove the blade of the sword into Anwyn's neck, the beast's eyes opened in shock, blazing blue fire in the darkness of the cavern. She wrenched her body to the side, slashing at Rhapsody with her undamaged claw. The Lady Cymrian stumbled off the wyrm's neck, but the blade had bit deep, and she dragged it with her as she fell back, slicing the dragon's throat open.

Anwyn's larynxless voice, a manipulation of the lore of the air around her, snarled angrily even as acidic blood spurted from her neck, showering Rhapsody in black-red gore.

"*Anborn?* That—miscreant? That *coward*, that—"

"That hero," Rhapsody interrupted, slapping the beast's cheek stingingly with the blunt of her sword, driving her onto her back. "That guardian, that protector," she continued as she drove the blade into the hollow below Anwyn's throat, eliciting a shattering roar. "That leader of men, that defender, that *Kinsman*—isn't that really what you meant to say?"

Panting with her own exertion now, she dragged the blade down toward the beast's heart, as she had once done in Anwyn's grasp in the air above the Great Moot, dodging the flailing claw and the geyser of bitter blood.

A gargling gasp was all that she heard in response.

"Your last breath is upon you," Rhapsody said as the beast's chest tore open, the flames of Daystar Clarion licking the three-chambered heart that was beating erratically below her feet. "Surely you don't want your epic last words to be a hateful lie? Even Gwylliam knew to ask forgiveness in his final moments. Remember, though I am a Namer, I owe you nothing. I will herald what you say only if I consider it to be worthy of history. Otherwise, your words will be lost to it. I know that such an ignominious end, a consignment to a truly forgotten past, would be your own eternal damnation." She let the blade of the sword of the stars and elemental fire hover in the dragon's chest, the flames licking her ribs.

"Well?" she asked politely. "Last chance."

The beast's eyelids fluttered weakly. Her claws still clutched at the air, trying to find Rhapsody, who stood now on her abdomen, bent over with exertion and in the attempt to hear what the dragon might say. The waning voice of air gurgled horribly, then spat out a curse Rhapsody recognized, having once heard it spoken by her own husband in livid anger in the language of dragons, an obscenity of mammoth proportions.

Rhapsody exhaled deeply.

"Bad answer," she said. "A waste of breath. Oh well." She leaned close one last time.

"In the name of Anborn ap Gwylliam," she said.

With a savage twist, she pierced the beast's beating heart with her sword and tore it from her sundered chest, closing her eyes against the cyclone of acidic blood that sprayed her face and upper body. With her eyes still closed, she saw that heart through her connection with the sword, no longer beating, but quivering menacingly. She set it ablaze, watching it burn to ashes, which she then tossed into the broken bed of the ancient bath where it hissed, then burned out dully.

When she opened her eyes, she beheld those of the dragon, open and staring lifelessly at the broken vault of Kurimah Milani above them.

The beast's great maw was open, her gleaming teeth spotted with drops of her own blood. Rhapsody stood silently, breathing heavily, waiting, but there was no movement, no sign of life, just the hideous sound of rancid air escaping the dragon's tattered lungs.

Rhapsody waited in the ebbing light, standing a vigil of sorts, emotionless. Finally she set about harvesting a few pieces of evidence, dipping her last clean handkerchiefs in the beast's blood, draining in a quiet river from her now-still chest cavity, removing her claws, especially the enormous thumb talon, the mate of the one Achmed had shot off with his cwellan when she was in Anwyn's grasp at the battle of the Fallen.

She wrapped the coup in burlap from her pack, then raised Daystar Clarion. The elemental blade of starlight and fire, pulsing in time with her heartbeat, filled the cavern with oscillating light.

She thought about offering a prayer of some sort, but her soul was void of any words that would be holy. So instead she spoke the word for ignition as she touched the dragon's body with the sword one final time, and then sang a word in the tongue of the ancient Lirin Namers.

Ethnegl. Consume.

As if racing, the flames leapt from the elemental blade and roared over the surface of the dragon's body. They burned intensely, filling the cavern with black smoke mingled with the occasional glimpse of copper.

As the fire consumed the beast, crackling the skin from the skeleton, Rhapsody stood, numb, pained by no regret, nor comforted with satisfaction. As the carcass's head ripped into flame, she noted that she could not even summon up the energy to make careful note for history of the death of one of the Manteids, the Seers, sometimes known as the Fates, the triplet daughters of Elynsynos, the matriarchal wyrm that had long held the continent as her own lands, and Merithyn the Explorer, her Seren lover. In the back of her mind, the significance of the moment was not lost on her.

In her heart, she could not find the strength to care.

When the fire was finally done, having burned the massive body to ash, Rhapsody sheathed her sword, gathered her pack, and left the ruins of the ancient place of healing without a backward glance.

50

YLORC

$\mathcal{A}$nborn's arrival had been reported while he was still half a league away. The lookout from the top of Grivven Peak had called down his approach to Achmed and Grunthor, who by happenchance were reviewing the breastworks on the steppes leading up to the foothills of the Teeth, and so were in place when the Lord Marshal arrived, a small retinue of armsmen behind him.

Achmed shielded his eyes from the hazy sun which had just begun to slide down the firmament of the sky to the west as the horsemen approached from that direction. He had been tracking a different arrival for the last several days, the light, steady heartbeat traveling from the north, a rhythm he had known well for more than a millennium.

While his ability to gauge Rhapsody's distance from Ylorc was minimal, he could tell that she was nearing the mountain; the song of the music within her, a pleasant vibration that soothed his angry skin and took the edge off his teeth, was beginning to quiet the veins and nerves that scored his body, however far away she was. There was something different about the song, however.

The Bolg king shook his head and refocused his attention on the Lord Marshal, who had reined his black barded warhouse to a halt at the checkpoint and was dismounting as easily as a youthful man who had never been injured.

With him Achmed recognized two of Anborn's longtime men-at-arms, Solarrs and Knapp, who remained mounted with four other unknown soldiers as Anborn approached the Bolg king and Grunthor. There was vigor in the Lord Marshal's step as he hurried toward them, the black and silver rings of his armor glinting in the afternoon sun, his flowing black cloak snapping in the wind behind him.

"Majesty, Sergeant," he greeted them, calling into the crosswind blasting the highgrass of the steppes.

"'Ow 'olds the line?" Grunthor called back. "The, er, Thres'old o' Death?"

"Strong, though dented," the Lord Marshal said, clapping the Sergeant's shoulder with his extended arm, and receiving a return salute in welcome. "Has Rhapsody returned?"

"Not yet, but she's on her way," Achmed said.

Anborn nodded, then signaled to his companions. "With your permission, my men-at-arms have a manifest for needed supplies." Achmed assented; Solarrs and Knapp dismounted and followed the Bolg soldiers to the quartermaster's tent. The Lord Marshal's gaze returned to Achmed; he looked over the king's shoulder, squinted for a moment, then broke into a wide grin.

"Well," he said, pointing north, "at least there's one woman in this world with whom I have impeccable timing."

The two Bolg turned and followed his finger.

The general's azure eyes were trained on the distant piedmont, where a moment later Achmed and Grunthor also caught sight of the silver-gray horse, atop which they could see a slight rider, still too far off to be recognizable except for a tiny shining crown of golden hair, glinting in the afternoon light.

Grunthor grinned as well.

"Well, well! This is shapin' up to be a regular party, it is. Will be good to 'ave 'er back."

"While we're awaiting her arrival, tell me of the outposts to the south," Achmed said to Anborn. "I'm worried that the redeployment of the northern regiments to them is leaving the border with the Hintervold vulnerable."

The general clicked to the barded horse and the animal came over to him, circumventing Grunthor and taking its place on the far side of Anborn, to the Sergeant's great amusement. Anborn pulled a sheaf of oilcloth maps from his saddlebags and unrolled them in front of the Bolg.

They had just finished conferring when Rhapsody finally arrived at the checkpoint down the hill from them.

As she drew her mount to a halt, Achmed noticed a severe change in her appearance, or her demeanor, or both. Her dragonscale armor, normally shining with the color of copper coins, was glazed in black blood, as was the better part of her shirt and cloak, while her trousers had been spattered with gore as well. Achmed could not tell from a distance if the blood was her own, but the diminution of the natural light that had always shone in her face and eyes, in addition to the stern look on a sallow face he barely recognized, made him fear a grievous injury. And her hair had been shorn to the base of her neck.

He swallowed heavily, trying to keep down his rising gorge.

But if she had, in fact, been badly hurt, she did not move as if she had. Her heartbeat was strong and regular, the Bolg king noted, somewhat relieved.

She dismounted quickly and smoothly, tossing the reins of her horse to the Bolg deputy quartermaster without looking back, and made her way to where the three men were standing beside Anborn's warhorse, walking with her usual ease, a large leather satchel on her shoulder.

As she came within range, she stopped.

"Well met," she said in greeting to the three men.

"Well met?" Grunthor demanded, disdain dripping from his words. "*Well met?* What the—? Get over 'ere, miss!"

Rhapsody's brows furrowed, but she obeyed, walking closer until she was within the circle, nearest to the warhorse. She came to a halt.

"Are you all right?" Achmed demanded. "What happened to you? Where's your hair?"

The Lady Cymrian's eyes met his, then followed his gaze to her chest. She looked up and exhaled. Anborn, watching the two of them intently, blinked in surprise at the utter lack of emotion in her eyes, the solemn mien on her face.

"I am not injured, at least not enough to notice if I am. My hair was the price of what I went to do in the Nain kingdom. I left the other horses at the northern outpost; they will be returned in the rotation later this month. I do, however, have something to herald, officially, Namer to king, Lord Marshal, and Sergeant-Major."

The three men exchanged a glance.

"What is it?" the Bolg king asked, his mismatched eyes watching her carefully.

Rhapsody turned to Anborn, her gaze steady.

"Your mother is dead, Lord Marshal, by my hand."

Achmed blinked. "You killed Anwyn?"

"Yes." The word was spoken without any feeling whatsoever.

"Ya sure?" Grunthor demanded. "We thought the bitch was dead three years ago."

"I'm certain of the finality of it this time. She died with your name being the last word that rang in her ears, Lord Marshal. Her last memory."

Anborn's eyes widened even more. "My name, Lady?"

The Lady Cymrian nodded.

"Forgive me—I chose to take her life in your name, for whatever atrocity, whatever it was she did to kill your valor, your idealism, your belief in the honorable tenets of selfless military service in the time of the Cymrian War. By protocol I should offer you an apology with my sympathy, but I know you wouldn't want it, nor would I mean it, so I believe my task as herald is now at its end."

The Lord Marshal stared at her for a moment longer, as did the Bolg. Then, against his will, a gurgling sound of mirth emerged from his throat. He bent his head, and as he raised it again, a chuckle of deeper origin escaped him. At last he threw back his head and roared with laughter, an almost ugly sound, full of relief. It echoed off the Teeth above them, causing small rocks to fall in a trail of dust, making the mountains ring.

The sound of victory, long denied, finally achieved.

Achmed and Grunthor looked from the laughing general to the sober face of the Lady Cymrian, then back at each other.

"Well, that's certainly good to 'ear, Duchess," Grunthor said finally. "One less random factor to 'ave to account for in all this mess."

"So that's her blood, then, not yours?" Achmed noted, pointing to her chest and cloak.

Rhapsody nodded again. She took two stiffly folded handkerchiefs from her pocket, both soaked in the same dried gore that had turned her clothing scarlet-black, and handed one each to Achmed and Anborn.

"I did not know if having this was significant to either of you, but these are the only trophies I brought back. I burned her body, all except the claws; I thought they might make good souvenirs and weapons for my Firbolg grandchildren. And, of course, her only remaining thumb-talon for you, Grunthor, for your weapons collection." She rifled quickly through her leather pack and pulled forth the enormous, gory claw wrapped in burlap, then offered it to the Sergeant, who took it doubtfully.

"Er—thanks, Yer Ladyship."

Rhapsody nodded a third time, but said nothing more.

"When you told her you were taking her life in my name, did she say anything?" Anborn asked, still chuckling, as he examined the bloodstained handkerchief.

"Not that I understood. But I was busy gouging out her heart at that point and setting it on fire, so I wasn't really listening." She looked at Achmed. "Unless you require something of me, I would like to bathe and reprovision. Assuming you haven't given away my quarters and clothes."

The Bolg king nodded slightly. "Go—but plan to join us for supper to confer and make plans, and stay this night in Ylorc."

"I had hoped to leave before nightfall. I need to meet up with Gwydion Navarne in Bethany three days hence. Ashe is leaving soon for Manosse and Gaematria, if he hasn't already."

"A few hours one way or the other won't be a significant delay." He winced at the quiet annoyance in Rhapsody's eyes on an otherwise expressionless face, so unlike anything he had ever seen there. "Humor me."

"All right." She bowed slightly to Anborn. "Deploy me as you will, where I will be of the most use, Lord Marshal. I'm ready." She turned and started toward the pathway that led up to the nearest rise in the rockface.

"Wait a bloody minute, 'ere," Grunthor said angrily as he seized her sleeve and dragged her to a stop. "What's gotten into you, miss? No 'ug, no smile? Ya kill that un'oly bitch, Anwyn, *by yerself*, it would seem, then come all this way, after all this time, and all we get is a bland report an' a bloody snot-rag? What 'appened?"

"I just told you what happened."

"Let her go," Achmed said quietly.

The giant stared at her a moment longer, then exhaled. He stepped aside, allowing her to pass. She patted his arm as she did, then made her way toward the passways into the Cauldron without a backward glance.

"Oi do believe Oi'm gonna be sick," said Grunthor after she was out of earshot, having reached the towering edifice of the ancient Cymrian stronghold. "Where's my girl, and 'oo the blazes is *that*?"

"That's Rhapsody as she is now," Anborn noted quietly. "We're going to have to get accustomed to it, I would guess."

Grunthor shook his head vigorously.

"Naw. Not acceptable. Oi don't even recognize 'er. The biggest, softest 'eart in the world, and now she's reportin' killing a dragon like she's commentin' on the weather? Tearin' off claws? Countin' coup? Since when?"

The Bolg king's eyes were following her as she disappeared from the rock ledge above into the passageways of the Cauldron.

"Since she parted with her baby."

51

Achmed's head was throbbing still at supper that night. As she silently passed him the roasted potatoes, he made note of the musical vibration that was still emanating from Rhapsody. It had changed; the soothing quality he had always appreciated was still there, but it was no longer as pleasant. She had eaten her supper more or less in silence until a word in Grunthor's report caught her ear.

It was a briefing that Ashe had sent before he left Highmeadow about the holdings that had been identified as belonging to Talquist. Grunthor was reading it aloud undisturbed until he came to the part referencing the port of Argaut, a massive shipbuilding and maritime capital on the other side of the world.

Rhapsody sat up suddenly as if she had been shot by an arrow.

"Argaut? Talquist has holdings in *Argaut?*"

Achmed shrugged as Grunthor showed her the map he had been reading from. "So says the briefing. Why, does this surprise you?"

"Surprise, no. Concern, yes. Michael, the Wind of Death, when he fled Serendair, went to Argaut as well, and established himself there for centuries. He was apparently a seneschal, some sort of judicial figure. Do you think Talquist had commerce with him?"

The Bolg king's mismatched eyes darkened.

"It's certainly possible. The implications are fairly disturbing, if it's true."

"Perhaps not," Rhapsody said, bringing the map closer. "The demon that possessed Michael died when Macquieth took him, and it, into the sea. Whatever possessions or thralls it had bound would have been released upon his death. Even if he had some sort of control of Talquist in life, it would have shattered upon his death. Not that Talquist needs any help with evil intent. But if Talquist was involved in commerce with Michael voluntarily, there may be some residual alliances, or darker plans, than we even know of or can guess at."

"So perhaps we are just going about the prosecution of this war incorrectly," Achmed said sourly. "If Talquist and the Waste of Breath had similar proclivities, maybe all we need to do is offer him a few nights with you in return for peace."

Rhapsody and Grunthor both blinked in unison.

"Excuse me?"

The headache pounding behind Achmed's eyes was making him especially surly.

"You and the memory of your—charms was Michael's sole obsession, if I remember correctly. He sailed halfway around the world for a chance to knob you again. Perhaps you can return to your old line of work long enough to satisfy Talquist—"

"That's quite enough, sir," interjected Grunthor, his eyes narrowing. His tone was deadly.

Both Rhapsody and Achmed looked at their friend, Achmed falling into immediate silence. Neither of them had ever heard Grunthor speak to the Bolg king in such a tone of voice.

"You're right," he said finally. "I stand corrected. This war will be far too much fun to waste the opportunity."

"That's more like it, sir."

Rhapsody exhaled evenly. Then she looked them both in the eyes.

"I am forever grateful to both of you for what you did to rescue me from Michael. And you both know me better, have known me longer, than almost anyone in the world. There are a few things, however, even after all these years, that you don't know about me."

"True enough—Oi don't know what ya see in Ashe," Grunthor joked. "Never made no sense to me, Oi must admit."

"That makes two of us," said Achmed.

Rhapsody's expression did not change.

"I'm guessing that neither of you knew until this moment that 'Rhapsody' is my middle name—that I had another first name, a human name, and a patronymic, a family name, as well, I believe."

"You believe?" Achmed chuckled. "You're not certain?"

"Had?" Grunthor asked.

"Had. And no, I'm not certain."

The Bolg king's brow furrowed in annoyance. "Stop talking in riddles."

"I'm not. I no longer have the rest of the name I was given at birth—just like you, Achmed. Only I wasn't renamed by someone else as you were twice. I gave my name away—to Meridion. I left it with him when I installed him in the realm of the Nain, in the care of others. So, while I believe I once had both a first and a last name, and perhaps even a nickname, I don't recall them anymore—because Meridion has them now."

"How does that affect you as a Namer?" Achmed's voice was harsh.

"It doesn't, at least as far as my abilities other than the healing of myself. I can't remember my true name, because I think I gave it to my son. But I have retained *Rhapsody,* and it was as 'Rhapsody' that I became a Namer, and the Iliachenva'ar. I kept that name because I'm fairly certain I will need those powers to deal with whatever is to come. But I was known by my first name when much of what you know about me came into being. I learned my understanding of family, to love, to forgive, to be the woman you know, for good and for ill, when I had that name. And, without it, I have forgotten those things."

"Whaddaya mean?" Grunthor demanded.

Rhapsody's eyes gleamed more intensely. At first Achmed thought it was a sign of tears welling, but within a moment had felt the cold that was behind them in his very skin. She stared at him for a long moment, then spoke slowly, each word distinct, matter-of-factly.

"The biggest mistake I ever made with you—both of you, but especially you, Achmed—was telling you on the night we met in the old world why Michael was searching for me, for being candid about my past and how I knew him. You have teased me rather mercilessly over the years about my 'old line of work,' as if it was something of my choosing, rather than something I was forced into. And because the part of me that had a sense of humor, that could love and forgive, looked past it, you always assumed it was a joke we all shared.

"Let me explain something to you that I never would have told you when my old name was my own. I did not work in the equivalent of your favorite old-world wenching spot, Madame Parri's Pleasure Palace; the brothel I was enslaved in frequently catered to a clientele of the most perverse sort. I was taken into that brothel as a means of survival; I was a slave of sorts. When I was little more than a child, about fifteen, I had a brief interaction with Michael that could only be described as torture, and I refused to see him again thereafter. So when he returned two years later from whatever maneuvers he had been on, he had a bargaining chip with him—a seven-year-old Liringlas little girl, wrapped in a bloody shawl that had probably once been her mother's. She was the only survivor of her long-house; Michael had brought her along as leverage over me, having killed every member of her family before her eyes.

"At that time Michael had two weeks of leave before he was being deployed for an extended period, most likely by Tsoltan, your hated demonic master. He had grown in power and influence in those two years; when I first met him, he was merely a thug, even if he was rising in the ranks. When he returned, he had a vast number of soldiers under him, an entire regiment, almost a hundred strong, far more than I could ever hope to escape. He wanted me to himself for that fortnight, and when I refused, he told me that the little girl would take my place. And he knew he had me then, because there was no way I could allow that to happen; it was the first sacrifice I made for someone I did not know." Her eyes dropped, and her voice darkened. "That child was Analise."

The two Bolg exchanged a glance.

"So I surrendered myself to him for those two weeks in return for the promise of her freedom. I assume you can imagine the depravity he visited upon me in that time." She paused as she saw Grunthor wince. Achmed said nothing, so she continued, her voice softer.

"But that was just when we were alone. Occasionally, when I inadvertently crossed him in a way he did not find stimulating, or when he was merely bored, his favorite pastime was to encourage—no, actually, command—his entire regiment to rape me while he watched." Her voice dropped to almost a whisper, but one without emotion. "Every one of them. Repeatedly."

She turned away for a moment; Achmed's swarthy skin had gone pale, and she could tell that Grunthor was struggling to keep from throwing back his head and roaring. She touched the giant Bolg's shoulder.

"I am not trying to torture you in the telling of this. I am only trying to help you to understand the person I am now; the part of me which allowed me endure that time, and still be able to smile, is gone. I know that you, Achmed, have survived great torment of your own, enslaved as you were to the demon. But I am also fairly certain that had you been in my position, with your Dhracian physiology, all of your sensitive nerve endings and exposed veins, that you would not have survived the abuse. I endured it, survived it, and eventually even overcame it, only because of things I had been taught in my early life with and by my family. I know that was a blessing you never had.

"But that part of me is gone now; it's protecting Meridion, keeping the memory of my love alive for him. If I don't survive this war, at least one thing that you will not have to do as his godfather, Grunthor, his guardian, Achmed, is explain to him that I loved him; he will most assuredly know, even if he won't understand for a long time. So what remains of me, the person that I am here, now, has nothing left to withstand your prodding of that awful memory. Or anything else, really.

"When we passed through the fire at the Earth's heart, I believe we were each immolated; it was our namesongs that carried us through and re-formed us on the other side, the elemental fire purging us of our scars, our wounds. The burning away of that body was a new beginning for me, your crass commentary about the restoration of my virginity notwithstanding. I tried and was mostly successful in letting all that had tormented me in the Past wither to ash with my old body, not touching my new self. Your reminders of those horrific days only drag me back in time to that torture, that depravity. And while the person who learned to love you both in spite of her kidnapping, the loss of her family and her world, forgave you that thoughtless cruelty, the Rhapsody who is with you now has none of those tools. This Rhapsody is doing all that she can to keep focused, to concentrate on the safety of her child, the memory of whom is all but gone, her own survival, and whatever she can do to ensure that of the continent."

Her voice, so steady up to that point, shook slightly as she began to run out of breath and words. "As of now, that child, my baby, is being sought by a bastard as cruel and depraved as Michael, perhaps more so—he seeks to *eat* my son's heart, alive, to grant himself immortality. And the titan who serves him desires to do something even more horrific with the Earthchild we all guard. And now I've just discovered that the beast who had visited the most torment upon me in my life, the man I thought had finally died at MacQuieth's hand, may be living on, in one way or another, through an emperor who seeks to destroy everything you and I hold dear. He is coming for each of us, for my child, and yours, Achmed—you are the closest thing to a father the Earthchild knows. I don't know how I will ever sleep again.

"I have left my own child, the center of my heart, in distant lands and the hands of others; I cannot explain what this has done to me. I am so angry I can barely breathe, and at the same time unable to feel anything good for the people I know I love. It takes everything I have to just remain numb. So, please, stop tormenting me. I have no idea what I may do if you don't."

She had to turn away again; Achmed had gone almost gray behind his mask of veils. The Sergeant's massive jaw was trembling, the tusks quivering.

"These are the last words I want to say tonight. One of the few things I still know is this: even if I can't presently feel it, I love you both, endlessly, and always will. One day, if I survive, perhaps I will feel it again. I'm going to try and reach Ashe through the Lightcatcher one last time before he goes into the sea, and then go to bed. Good night." She turned and started for the door.

"Wait," Grunthor commanded. The word came out in a voice that almost sounded as if he was strangling. "C'mere."

Rhapsody stopped in midstride, then turned back to him again.

A massive arm reached out with uncommon speed, wrapped itself around her waist, and pulled her onto his lap. Rhapsody allowed the Sergeant-Major to enfold her, disappearing from Achmed's sight into the titanic musculature of Grunthor's arms.

For a long time she remained within the dark cave of her friend's embrace, listening to the comforting beating of his heart and the occasional sniffle, quietly enduring the trickle of warm tears in her hair. Finally he released her; she stood creakily, and kissed him on the cheek.

"*Now* I'm going to contact Ashe, then go to bed," she said. "Good night, Achmed."

She blinked. The Bolg king was gone.

"Good night," she said to Grunthor again. Then she left, closing the door quietly behind her.

Grunthor waited for a moment until the sounds of her footfalls died away, then rose from the chair and made his way out of the room and down the long corridor into the Great Hall.

Achmed was there, as he had suspected, in the process of gathering supplies, laying them out on the long table. He looked up at the Sergeant-Major.

"Summon the Archons."

"Now, or in the mornin'?"

"Now. I want to be ready to leave at daybreak, right after Rhapsody departs for Bethany. I need them activated and in place before I go."

Grunthor nodded. "An' where is it you will be goin', sir?"

The frost in Achmed's voice had made Rhapsody's seem warm by comparison.

"After Talquist. As soon as she's gone."

Grunthor nodded again.

He had already known the answer.

After the Sergeant had left to activate the Archons, the Bolg king took a final inventory of his gear and began one last check of the Light-catcher. As he was adjusting the great wheel, he felt a shadow fall on him. The scent of primal wind, old and full of elemental power, prevented the need of turning around.

"Should you not be in bed, Rath?" he asked, though his tone indicated it wasn't really a question.

The sandy voice scratched against his eardrums. "Where are you going?"

"Diplomatic mission."

"Without an entourage?"

"How are the ribs?"

The Dhracian sighed silently, but Achmed could feel the exhalation of the man's breath in the sensitive web of nerves that scored the skin on the back of his neck.

"You have caught a trail? Is it Hrarfa, then?"

The Bolg king said nothing.

"I will go with you," Rath said. "I will summon the Brethren—"

"No." Achmed's voice was as icy as the wind that howled around the peak of Gurgus. "No. This time, it's your turn to stay and guard the Sleeping Child. This time, I'm hunting men, not demons."

Silence echoed through the enormous room.

"Are you certain?" Acid dripped from the words.

Achmed released his grip on the wheel of the Lightcatcher; the tension in his hands threatened damage to the instrumentality. "No one knows better than you that one can *never* be certain, Rath. But I have reason to believe that the demons are more likely to be heading here eventually than waiting in a palace, as the man I seek is most likely doing. Summon the Brethren if you like; perhaps you can lay a trap, lie in wait. I expect to be back before the titan arrives, but I can't be certain about that either."

"Your priorities are skewed," Rath said after a moment. "Can you not feel the needles in your veins, the call of the Primal Hunt? I can feel it from your words alone."

Finally Achmed turned around. He stared into the liquid black eyes of the Dhracian hunter, a man with whom he had exchanged very few words, but who shared his identity at deepest possible level.

"You may not understand this, Rath, but not every evil in this world is conceived and executed by Elder races. The F'dor may have brought the forces of destruction and chaos into this world at its beginning, but they no longer are the exclusive owners of the concept. A man wants something: a child, a woman, immortality, sadistic satisfaction—and if he has a crown, he thinks he can have whatever he wishes, and do whatever he wants with them. He doesn't have to be of an Elder race. He doesn't have to be part of a larger design, he doesn't have to desire the unraveling of the world. Your lore disregards the wretched sadist, the petty manipulator, the cruel abuser, the power-mad despot—not everyone who needs to die is a demon."

The ancient hunter's expression took on a hint of sympathy.

"No. But if the demons don't die first, everyone else will, whether they need to or not."

A slight smile crawled over the Bolg king's face, pocked with the same veins as visible on the Dhracian's skin.

"You wanted me to be more assassin than king," he said humorously. "You are getting your wish. Perhaps not in the manner you had hoped, yet, anyway. There is something unspoken in the vow of a king, an emperor, and though it's a word I scorn to use most of the time, it's a holy commitment. Those that usurp a throne, violate that vow, that stewardship, need to die in as awful a way as is possible. And if nothing else, if this man has one or more of Sharra's scales, tracking and killing him will be good training to go after the titan, assuming I survive."

"And if you don't, you will never walk the Vault—you are the only one who can."

The Bolg king merely met his gaze in silence.

Finally Dranth exhaled again. "You should perhaps let someone with more distance handle this," he said finally. "That is always the wise way in matters of revenge."

Achmed picked up his gear.

"It's not revenge, not mine at any rate," he said. "Grunthor and the Archons will see to everything in the kingdom while I am gone. Keep away from the Lightcatcher. Guard the Child."

He could feel the ancient hunter's gaze boring into him all the way out of the room.

It didn't impact him in the slightest.

52

SEPULVARTA

ſhremus was in the midst of the organized frenzy of battle preparations when word reached him in the city center of the return of Titactyk's regiment. He finished his list for the quartermaster, arranged a
delay in his fourth and fifth meeting that morning, and hurried to the
wall overlooking the barracks where the weary garrison was disembark-
ing, returning their horses to the livery and their empty packs to the
depot.

He saw Kymel almost immediately; it would have been difficult to miss
him, wandering somewhat aimlessly among his comrades who, despite the
evidence of exhaustion, were systematically breaking formation in preparation to bathe, eat, and sleep. The lack of light in his nephew's eyes disturbed him; he turned to his aide-de-camp.

"Tell Titactyk I have requested that you bring the soldier named Kymel
to my office immediately. I need to debrief him."

His aide saluted and left.

$\mathcal{W}$ithin the quarter hour his aide had returned, the young soldier in tow. Fhremus dismissed him, then walked past his nephew, closing the office door.

"Report," he said.

"The emperor was successfully escorted to the crossroads leading west to Jierna'sid and south to Windswere." Kymel stared straight ahead.

"Then what happened? What happened in Windswere?"

"Our mission was accomplished."

Fhremus slammed his hand down on his desk.

"Fine. I am done hearing your report as a soldier under my command. Tell me what happened as your uncle."

"With respect, sir, I would not do so, were I not under your command."

Fhremus's stomach was boiling at the look in Kymel's eyes. He willed his voice to be gentle but to ring with military discipline at the same time.

"Tell me," he said. "Without frosting."

Something in his last word struck home; Fhremus was not certain how he knew, but he was sure of it. The young soldier looked at him for the first time.

"We were deployed to an ancient military site that had been converted long ago into a refuge for orphans, street children and their mothers known as the Abbey of Nikkid'sar," he said softly. "A hidden place of harsh clime and gentle oversight, built atop a seacliff on a sandspit jutting out into the southern sea. I was specifically tasked with locating an object whose image the emperor showed me in a fresco on a wall in the basilica of Lianta'ar." He fell silent.

"Go on," Fhremus said after a few long moments of heavy silence in the air.

"The titan Faron was tasked with widening a small passage in a rocky moraine that had been the rampart and defense of the abbey," Kymel said. "When this was accomplished, the cohort went in. I was last; when Titactyk told me that the site had been secured, I searched and located many of the objects the emperor had shown me in the fresco. I located the one of the best integrity I could find, boxed it carefully in a wooden chest from the abbey, and transported it successfully to Jierna Tal, where I presented it to the emperor. He dismissed me, but bade me tell you to deploy. I did not know what he meant, but it was made clear that you would. This ends my report."

"Not quite, it doesn't," Fhremus said dryly. "You are showing signs of severe trauma, soldier; if I had not known you prior to your enlistment, I might not recognize those signs, but having been your uncle all your life, I do. What happened at the abbey?"

Kymel said nothing.

"Tell me," Fhremus said tersely.

Kymel inhaled deeply, then exhaled slowly.

"There was an ancient weapon, a catapult of a sort, from the days before the abbey, when the site was a defensive outpost," he said, his voice hollow. "When the cohort was finished securing the target, it was discovered that the catapult was still operational, the soldiers used it to take turns disposing of the bodies and the—"

"Halt," said Fhremus. His voice was shaking. "Bodies?"

"Yes, sir," said Kymel.

"What bodies?"

Kymel said nothing.

"*What bodies?* Tell me. That's an order, soldier."

Kymel exhaled again.

"We encountered seventeen women, one of whom was in charge of the abbey, the abbess, I believe, fifty-seven children and eleven infants. By drawing of lots, the soldiers of the cohort—"

His voice broke. Instinctively Fhremus stood in silence, waiting for Kymel to recover his calm, while he struggled to recover his own. Finally Kymel spoke again.

"In order of lot, the soldiers selected women to ravage, taking turns with some of the more attractive and younger ones. The children and infants were rounded up and used as catapult fodder; the infants were all shot from it, live, into the sea, in a game of distance and accuracy. Some of the children were used as the women had been, some just put to the sword, or shot from the catapult, live, as well. The bodies of the women were similarly committed to the sea, but not until all of their throats had been cut." He swallowed, forcing the last words to come out of his throat. "Each soldier took a turn with the abbess, sodomizing—"

"Stop." Fhremus was trembling with rage. "Did you take a turn?"

"No, sir. I was tasked with search and reconnaissance."

"For what? What was this object that the emperor was so interested in?"

Kymel looked away.

"Speak, soldier. What was so important as to send a cohort to an abbey for it?"

"It was a cookie, sir."

Fhremus's eyes opened to the size of the full moon. "A—a *cookie?*"

"Yes, sir."

"A cookie?"

"There were dozens of them, sir, on plates on the table in the main building. I heard one of the other soldiers say that the legends of this place, the Well of the Moon, had said that it was a haven for damaged or poor children where if they could find it they would also find kindness, gentle treatment, toys, cookies, and sweetmeats. I can attest to existence there of the last three; the first two seem likely from what I could reconnoiter as well. Nothing magical, epic, or significant, just—just—"

"Just what?"

Kymel swallowed again. "Just humanity, sir."

Fhremus's rage exploded. "I will have Titactyk hanged for this."

His nephew blinked. "I don't think you can, sir, at least not by the code of military justice."

"What do you mean?"

"Everything he did was fulfilling a direct command of the emperor," Kymel said without emotion. "We were told to leave no one alive."

"Did—did he know what sort of place it was, that it was an orphanage, a refuge for children?"

"Most certainly, sir. Titactyk was ordered to dispose of the bodies, but there was no place to bury them, and the wet wind prevented pyres atop the cliffs or on the beach. But even if it hadn't, the catapult was extremely popular." He looked at the floor. "I did nothing to stop it, sir. For that, I have dishonored our family and myself."

No more than I have, thought Fhremus. *Sweet All-God.*

"What will you do now, sir?"

The supreme commander looked out the window of his office, in what had once been, in the days before the invasion, a dispensary of medicine.

"Deploy," he said.

There was no emotion at all in his voice.

53

TRAEG, NORTHWESTERN SEACOAST

$\mathcal{A}$she had reached the high cliffs overlooking the crashing sea when a faint blue light appeared, hovering in the air above the beach below him.

"Rhapsody?" he called. "Is that you?"

A blurry image, filmy and almost invisible, returned his gaze.

I am here.

The voice was foreign, almost alien, bearing none of the warmth that he knew as well as he knew his own name, the beating of his own heart. *I have returned from the journey I told you about the last time we spoke. All was done in accordance to plan. In addition, Anwyn is dead; history will record me as her executioner, as her killer.*

There was no sadness in her words, just simple statement of fact blended with the whine of the sea wind. Ashe swallowed hard.

"Being victorious in battle with a wyrm, or any other opponent, does not make a killer of the winner, Rhapsody."

She did not die in battle, though one did take place between us eleven days before. I followed her into the broken ruins of Kurimah Milani, where she was hiding, injured and compromised, and put her to the sword, ig-

nored her pleas for her life. I do not regret it; I am merely telling you the truth. I took her life and burned her body; there is no possibility she will return.

Ashe's brow furrowed, but otherwise his expression did not change.

"Good," he said. "Tell me of your journey."

The look in Rhapsody's eyes grew colder. *All is in place, as I told you. If something should happen to me, you will know what to do. I do not judge it wise to say more in the open air.*

The Lord Cymrian nodded, quietly dismayed to have no specific report of Meridion, a reassurance that had sustained him ever since he had sent his wife and son away to the Bolglands with Achmed. He rubbed his hands briskly over his arms, as if to ward off the chill of the wind, or perhaps in her voice.

"Where are you going now, Rhapsody?"

The howl of the sea wind almost blotted out the sound of her answer.

Wherever the Lord Marshal deploys me. I leave on the morrow to meet up with him and your namesake.

"Please, please be careful, my love," Ashe said fervently. "I don't like the look in your eyes."

The image of Rhapsody seemed to inhale, then let her breath out steadily. She said nothing.

The gusts off the waves below picked up, whipping the Lord Cymrian's cape about him.

"Rhapsody," he said, his voice serious and grave, "listen to me. You and I have both made bitter sacrifices to fulfill our responsibilities as Lord and Lady Cymrian, but those duties are not what need to guide us now. If you and I feel the weight of every person who depends on our actions, we will surely buckle under the guardianship of an entire continent. So, having put safeguards in place, we are both wading forward, you into the fray, I into the sea—but what needs to anchor us both is our vow of love to each other. I know what you have given up to protect—"

He stopped at the furious gleam in her eyes, then dropped his gaze.

"If anything were to happen to you, it would have been better to throw myself from this cliff into the sea right now. I cannot go on until I have your assurance that you will fight with everything you have to come back to me, to us." He raised his eyes and looked at her image again.

The woman who returned his gaze was all but unrecognizable.

Within him, he felt the rise of the dragon as it began to panic.

I will do the best I can, she said. *Perhaps you can take comfort in knowing that, because I am numb, I am logical, and focused. The lack of pain should serve to keep me sensible.*

Ashe exhaled, tears filling his eyes.

"I love you," he said as the blue light faded and the image disappeared into the wind. "Gods, I love you."

There was no reply.

HIGHMEADOW

The Lord Cymrian had left without warning, telling no one but his namesake.

Not even his chamberlain.

So when Gerald Owen heard the voice in the dark of foredawn, he had no idea that its instructions would come to naught.

The voice had been nattering subsonically for some time, whispering outlandish instructions and wheedling charmingly. Owen was beginning to think he was ill from worry or succumbing to the frailty of old age, when the order that appeared in his mind sounded.

He stopped in his tracks in the buttery where he had been preparing Ashe's morning tea and the whey cereal that was one of the few things the Lord Cymrian would eat in these days of terrible news. He cocked his head to one side, hearing the directions, but for the first time since the whispering had begun some weeks ago, he did not shake it off.

And instead went back to the pantry, looking for a stronger blend of tea to hide the taste of the datura he also took from the cleaning cabinet to enhance it with.

Datura was an herbal element, deadly poisonous to the cockroaches in the nests that the Lady Cymrian had painted with it when back in the drafty keep of Haguefort.

And to anyone who might ingest it.

He had almost forgotten what he had done until the young duke of Navarne came down to breakfast.

And sat in the Lord Cymrian's place at the table.

Gerald Owen had reentered the room just in time to see Gwydion Navarne lift Ashe's teacup to his lips.

His ragged gasp caused the young man to freeze, his hand with the cup in the air in front of him.

"Er—young master Navarne," he said, trembling. "What are you do-ing?"

Gwydion summoned a halfhearted smile.

"Ashe is gone, Gerald," he said. "He has invested me with his Right of Command; I am leaving immediately to meet up with Anborn and Rhap-sody two days hence in the farming encampment south of Bethany. I thought I might keep his tea from being wasted before I left."

The elderly chamberlain's eyes welled up at the sight of the young man he had loved as a son for all Gwydion's life.

A love stronger than any demonic command could ever be.

"No, sir, I'm afraid you are mistaken. Even if you are the acting Lord Cymrian now." Gently he took the teacup from the young duke. "You see, that's *my* tea."

The tears in his eyes spilled over as he raised the cup to his lips.

And drank.

Then he bowed, excusing himself, and hurried back to his chambers behind the buttery to bed before the datura took him, so as to appear to die in his sleep.

His last act of guardianship to the family Navarne.

54

KREVENSFIELD PLAIN, SOUTH OF BETHANY,
NORTH OF SEPULVARTA

𝒜 sennight after he had numbly buried his family's beloved caretaker and left for Bethany, Gwydion Navarne stood atop the viewing tower at the highest elevation of the east-west midpoint of the Krevensfield Plain, spyglass to his eye, watching the armies of Sorbold advance. Down from the piedmont that led to the steppes to the south, long dark lines of soldiers, ten divisions mounted, another twenty on foot, and, most terrible of all, fifty or more wagons with the long boxed frames indicating the transport of iacxsis were approaching the armed farming settlement, defended only by the eight thousand or so soldiers that the Lord Marshal had deployed there.

Another forty thousand were coming, by his own command, but all intelligence predicted a three-day wait until their arrival.

By which time, the garrison was likely to be nothing but ashes.

Gwydion swallowed hard. He, like Anborn, had expected Sorbold to attack the less central, more vulnerable settlements first; their bad guess looked to be a costly one. Though Sorbold could have committed more soldiers, it was clear that the supreme commander had been confident enough to attack with the forces that had been quartered in Sepulvarta, leaving the walled city all but undefended.

In his youth, Gwydion had not enjoyed the games of three-in-hand or fiddlesticks, betting games of bluffing and intentional deception, for just this very reason. He, like his father, was by nature a straight arrow, a man with little taste for risk taking. His lack of a sense of this kind of adventure was something the Lord Marshal had bemoaned humorously when training him in field strategy, but even the great Cymrian hero had to concede that risk did not always pay off.

Anborn had taken the young duke spying in southern Sorbold and the Nonaligned States with him, and he had watched the Lord Marshal offer halfhearted crossbow support while his godfather sliced through a cohort of twenty-seven Sorbold soldiers that had made its way inside the gate of Haguefort disguised in the colors of Ashe's own regiment. Ashe and Anborn had seemed almost bored as they dispatched the intruders; it was a fascinating if unrealistic view of military maneuvers, leaving Gwydion both comforted by the level of skill of those leading the armies and navies of the Alliance, while making him worry that he would underestimate what battle really required when he himself was drawn into it.

Ashe had known of his fears, and had brought him along when repelling raids in southern Navarne, allowing him to put the skills that Anborn had been imparting to him to the test. The result was that he now had a healthy respect for his own limitations.

That real-life training was the only combat experience he had ever had, with the exception of the battle with the Fallen at the Moot during the Cymrian Council four years before, where every civilian, even the lame and children, had joined in the fray, using every possible weapon of any sort they could find, including horse whips and shovels.

The battle that had taken his father's life as he had held the gate, rescuing much of the population as it fled the Moot.

Gwydion looked down at his own hands. They were trembling.

For all that Ashe had invested his own Right of Command in his namesake, Gwydion Navarne was deeply aware that he, a human man with distant Cymrian ancestry, did not have the lineage of extreme longevity or dragon blood that both Ashe and Anborn did, nor did he have their physical training and the experience of, in Ashe's case, more than a hundred years, in Anborn's, more than a thousand, of soldiering and surviving battle.

He did not fear for his own life.

He feared that losing it easily would leave the Alliance, and therefore the Known World, in danger of destruction.

Gwydion prayed that he would be killed, rather than captured.

He looked down to his left, where Rhapsody stood, her emerald eyes gazing south as he had been.

"Do you think our ballistae will hold—I mean, will they be effective against the iacxsis?"

She did not take her eyes off the approaching army.

"I hope so," she said. "We will have a rough time of it. Don't take your eyes off the sky."

There was no confidence or reassurance in her voice, just a cold, emotionless assessment. It brought no comfort to the sick twisting in the depths of Gwydion's viscera, but he reminded himself that this was how Rhapsody was now. The warm-hearted woman who had chosen him as her first adopted grandson had been replaced by a warrior he did not recognize. But the loss of the almost parental love and reassurance she had given him over the last few years serving with Ashe as his and Melisande's guardians was well worth the cost if the steadiness was effective on the battlefield.

"How much longer do you suppose it will be?"

She did not answer immediately, her eyes fixed on the approaching army.

"It will take at least an hour before the calvary gets within missile range," she said. "No more than two, though; they didn't bring siege weapons, so they're traveling quickly. They are confident, apparently. It's time to get to down to the field."

Gwydion exhaled, looking for one last long moment at the approaching lines blackening the rolling hills of the Plain beyond the walls of the armed settlement. Then turned to embrace Rhapsody one last time before they went into battle.

She was already heading down the ladder.

The Lord Marshal was riding the line along the southern quarters of the garrison on horseback when Gwydion and Rhapsody arrived at the front.

The Lady Cymrian dismounted from her own steed and tossed the reins to a corporal from the livery as Anborn slowed his black warhorse and pulled up beside her.

"The archers are in place, the defense of the wall is forming. How many troops do you want back here in the midfort for yourself, m'lady?"

"None, thank you. For what I plan they would just be in the way. If a iacxsis is targeted at me, I don't want anyone else to suffer for it—or to prevent me from responding appropriately." She turned to Gwydion, who had dismounted as well. "The only support I will need is yours."

Gwydion nodded nervously. He had been briefed by the Lady Cymrian the night before when she arrived on her plan to work side by side with him, using their special weapons and abilities, saving any direct combat as a second line of defense. Gwydion suspected that if their swords were needed in hand-to-hand combat, the outcome would be foreordained anyway.

He was having a hard time remembering that the woman who was calmly discussing last-minute strategy with the Lord Marshal was the same woman he had known and loved for a third of his life. He barely recognized her, the golden locks she was famous for shorn to the base of her neck, her legendary beauty replaced by a sharpness that he found disturbing. He closed his eyes and willed himself to concentrate on the battle coming quickly, relentlessly toward them.

"Fair enough," said Anborn. "Good luck, both of you. We will focus on the conventional forces—the archers will hold the wall as long as they can. If we are overrun, use whatever power is at your command, m'lady. Do not spare any of your comrades—any of us. The enemy needs to die first; if you have to take some of us with them, then that is as it should be."

"Indeed," Rhapsody agreed. "Good luck to you as well."

The Lord Marshal paused for a moment, then smiled down at her. He bowed to his sovereign, then winked at Gwydion.

"Get some blood on that blade before the battle is over," he advised. "Tysterisk is an ancient weapon, and has been in many hands. It's time you started your own blood history with it."

"I will do my best," the young duke promised. "Good luck."

The Lord Marshal spurred his horse and returned to the wall.

Shremus felt the power of hearts beating behind him, those of his men, of the horses they rode. He imagined he could feel whatever passed for hearts beating in the abominations that waited in the long boxes atop the wagons.

And the beating heart of the earth itself.

He looked through his spyglass at the walls of the farming settlement.

A second barricade had been put in place, much as had been erected at every such settlement along Anborn's Threshold of Death. He suspected that, even without the iacxsis strike, the wall would have held for a very short time before the cavalry and infantry overwhelmed the settlement, sheerly due to the massive numerical advantage Sorbold enjoyed.

How sad, he thought. He had not even needed to call up troops from any of the standing mountain regiments; the occupation force of Sepulvarta outnumbered what could be seen in the Alliance settlement by more than three to one, very likely more.

And then there were the iacxsis.

It was his intention to keep the army back while the beasts decimated the wall and the interior of the garrison, sparing as many of his men as possible. By the look of things, it might not even be necessary to fire a single bolt. He sincerely hoped that the Lord Marshal was not here; even if he was Cymrian and the enemy, Fhremus carried enough respect for Anborn ap Gwylliam's soldiering career and his status as a Kinsman to deserve a better, more valorous death than the one everyone in this settlement was about to experience.

"Come to halt," he shouted to the field commanders of the mounted and infantry divisions. He turned his steed one hundred eighty degrees around and watched as the invading force slowed and stood at attention, waiting.

"Today is the first of the assaults we will launch against the enemy of Roland and the army of the Alliance," he said, his voice ringing with conviction that he did not feel. "All will remain at rest while the first wave is released; iacxsis riders, advance."

The soldiers of that elite regiment riding in the midst of the cavalry divisions dismounted and came forward to the wagons. Another group, armored heavily, came forward as well, and took up their places atop the wagons. Each team consisted of four armed soldiers whose task it was to open the boxed cage, while four more, draped and clothed with thick padding carrying heavy chains, prepared to hold the beasts steady while the riders mounted. It was a specialty unit that was becoming more popular and desirable for assignment as the aerial forces scored more widespread victories in the harbors and battlefields of the expanding Empire of the Sun.

Fhremus waited until all of the teams, as well as the riders, were in place and ready.

"Archers, draw and nock," he said. "Await my command to let fly."

The squeaking and rattling of bows being made ready almost split his eardrums.

Fhremus looked back once more over his shoulder at what a short time before had been an innocent collective of farmhouses, barns and storage silos, pastures and ponds, now surrounded by martial hardware, weapons and walls. *A shame they chose the wrong side of history to ally with,* he thought as he noted the movement on the ramparts, the sighting of crossbows and the readying of the arms of ballistae he could see through his spyglass.

He whispered his traditional prayer to the local priest of the All-God that he always undertook before leading an assault. He knew Talquist would be furious, but at least at this time the Merchant Emperor could not see into the hearts and souls of his subjects.

At least Fhremus hoped he couldn't yet. It was clearly only a matter of time.

Keep my men safe, and if I am to die, let me die bravely, he thought as he always did. *And, for any innocent that may not be spared by my hand, may the All-God be merciful to him in the Afterlife.*

"Riders, mount up."

55

"Archers, hold the wall. Ready the ballistae."

Anborn's voice, its timbre deep and thrilling, boomed out the first defensive command of the battle.

Gwydion could hear his friend and mentor from deep inside the middle of the armed settlement where he had been stationed atop the side rampart, able to see beyond the front wall and inside most of the garrison. Tears welled at the corners of his eyes; they were not from fear or sorrow, or any negative inspiration, but rather an acknowledgment that what he had trained and traded his childhood for was about to begin.

In spite of how seriously they were outnumbered, and how deadly he knew the iacxsis to be, there was an honor of a sort to be felt in being part of such a battle, where survival was as unlikely as he knew it was now. His father had told him stories at night before bed when he came into his adolescent years about doomed regiments and troops who had undertaken suicide missions in a greater cause, to spare a larger population or advance a necessary front, knowing that the cost would be their own lives. He had described it with a sense of camaraderie, of noble sacrifice.

Of immortality.

He thought back to the moment that Stephen had passed from this life, in the arms of his godfather, his grandmother singing his father a song of sustaining and passage, long enough for Melly and him to have a chance to see his spirit, whole and unbroken in the light of the rising sun, his late mother standing at his side in the doorway between life and death.

The Veil of Hoen, Ashe had called it, having been there himself.

A sense of peace came upon him now, thinking about the joy of the reunion that might be awaiting him before the end of the day.

He looked down to the ground at the Lady Cymrian, who was drawing the tongue-whip out of her pack and unrolling it carefully. She looked up at him and met his gaze calmly.

"I can offer you but one piece of advice in the bearing of an ancient elemental weapon, and only if you are desirous of it," she said. Gwydion nodded. "As vain as this concept may be in words, I have found, in training and experience, that it is best to see the sword as an extension of yourself, not the other way around. Its power, its history, and all the bravery and sacrifice with which it has been wielded in the past do not matter in your wielding of it, because, until you are part of its history yourself, it is there to serve you. Tysterisk has been carried by the man I hated the most in my life, and now is being carried by one that, when my name was my own, I have loved the most. It has accomplished great feats and committed great atrocities, neither of them at your hand yet. Be the wind, Gwydion; let the element of air assist you in your fight today, and each day you wield it hence; no more, no less. May its weight in your hand be light."

"Thank you."

"At this moment, you are, in word, and deed, and action, the Lord Cymrian, the defender of the Alliance. Believe it, for it is the truth."

Gwydion nodded again. The expression in his eyes was calm.

She smiled slightly at him. It was an expression he had not seen on her face since she met up with him in Bethany after returning from the Nain.

"Are you ready?"

"Yes."

She leaned up against the side wall. "Then let them come."

$\mathcal{L}$oose the iacxsis."

The sides of the collapsible boxes atop the heavy wagons crashed to the floor or the ground to the sides of the wagons.

A horrific sound rent the air, the screams of a hundred of the mutant beasts, their giant mandibles snapping, their batlike wings flapping wildly, a buzzing tearing at the ears of their riders and handlers.

And the rest of the army as well as that inside the armed settlement.

From the wagon beds, a great commotion of movement issued forth, rocking the vehicles violently from side to side.

Great clouds of sand rose up into the air as the monsters' wings began to beat in seriousness now.

And then, one by one, riders and mounts began to take to the air, hovering for a moment above the highgrass of the southern Krevensfield Plain before beginning to ascend, confidently now, into the sky.

A great roar of affirmation rose from the army behind them. As if buoyed on the voices of the men below them, the iacxsis gained altitude, stretched their wings, and banked off to the north in the direction of the farming settlement.

*H*old your fire," Anborn commanded as the sound of four hundred crossbows being set rattled the wood of the wall around the settlement. "Peace; await my order."

He was still atop his beautiful black warhorse, riding smoothly the east-western line in the foreguard just inside the gate. The sight of the creatures ascending into the air in the distance was a disturbing one, he knew; it was critical not to let that frightening sight generate fear that would be a weapon of its own.

He looked at the soldiers standing in wait, and a fondness beyond reason came over him. They were not the elite soldiers of the united army Ashe had recruited and trained, but rather the reserves and volunteers, the men who had not made a life of soldiering but rather had answered the call when their land was in need of them. Uniforms badly buttoned, hair not within regulation length, intense worry almost successfully hidden by miens of grim determination, they were warriors nonetheless, ready to pay the price at a greater cost than their more professional counterparts.

He felt akin to them.

"Hold," he said again. "We will get our chance. For now, let them sign their own death warrants."

He slung his own crossbow up from the horse's side, and walked the horse back to the front wall.

Waiting.

56

"They're coming," Gwydion Navarne called down to the soldiers stationed within the walls of the settlement. It was not necessary to tell the archers; they could undoubtedly see the wave of beasts gaining momentum. "Be ready."

"Stay down," Anborn called to the archers atop the front rampart. "Keep out of sight as much as you can; we want them to come in and make themselves at home."

"Ballistae set," Gwydion said as quietly as he could without his command being missed. The soldiers manning the large-armed weapons checked the torsion springs and the coils of rope attached to the heavy barbed missiles in those arms, then silently signaled their assent.

He glanced down at Rhapsody, who had unrolled the whip in her left hand, and had quietly loosed the bindings of the scabbard with Daystar Clarion with her right. She was scanning the skies above her, waiting, her face blank.

When they got within half a league of the farming settlement, the iacxsis squadron split into quarters and separated into the cardinal directions, approaching the camp from all four sides. The squadron commander signaled the successful alignment.

Then the riders pressed their knees into the hearing organs on the beasts' abdomens; the iacxsis, feeling the change in pressure, beat their wings more savagely until they were just above the encampment walls.

Then they dove.

---

*F*ire!" Anborn screamed to the soldiers manning the ballistae.

Which were, against the traditional trajectory of the weaponry, pointed almost directly up.

The heavy barbs shot forth like immense arrowheads with solid coils of rope attached. Some of the barbs sliced into the underwings, piercing the leathery hide from the bottom. Others pierced the riders, sending some of them sliding, with their specially adapted saddles to which they had been lashed, over the sides of the beasts, hanging helpless in the air. Their steeds, now out of control, deviated happily from their directions until the ropes that were attached to the barbs tangled in their wings, sending them and the men more or less atop them spinning suddenly into the ground.

Rhapsody stepped out from the safety of the wall and signaled to Gwydion Navarne, readying her whip. She inserted her arm into the flared opening, concentrating as the tongue constricted on her arm.

In the name of Mylinmacr, she thought silently, *aid our efforts.*

Another rank of iacxsis struck from the air. Three of them strafed the front rampart, seizing hapless archers in their mandibles. Rhapsody aimed at the closest one, swinging the whip over her head, then pulled back and struck.

The dragon tongue thinned, then cracked with a loud *boom*. It encircled the neck of the iacxsis as Rhapsody dragged it back and, with all her strength, pulled the winged beast and its rider from the wall along with the archer in its maw. A tangle of bodies, human and insectoid, spun and fell to the ground inside the camp.

Gwydion drew Tysterisk as the ballistae in the depths of the encampment fired again. He held the sword hilt up before his eyes, its blade all but invisible, the only evidence of its existence the tiny swirling patterns that spun in spirals where the blade would have been, closed his eyes, and concentrated.

Cease, he said to the wind beneath the wings of the iacxsis squadron that was now flying overhead.

Nine of the beasts, gliding a moment before on a warm updraft, dropped like stones out of the air.

A roar of excitement rose from the ranks of soldiers inside the walled encampment.

*F*hremus could not believe his eyes.

The last time the iacxsis had been deployed, the rout of the citizenry of Sepulvarta had been a nauseating, fascinating thing to watch from outside the gates of the walled City of Reason. The beasts had almost hopped more than flown, much in the manner their insect progenitors preferred, snatching unfortunate townspeople, civilian and soldier alike, in their great hinged jaws and had crushed them while still in flight. The riders maintained order the best they could, but iacxsis were not horses, and had primitive but stubborn minds of their own, as well as their own priorities. When the soldiers guarding Sepulvarta had come to realize that the hides of the iacxsis were impervious to their arrows, they had turned their weapons on the riders, shooting them off the beasts' backs and out of the sky. This outcome was even worse than the initial attack; the iacxsis, now freed from any sort of human direction, reverted to primitive mandates and began snatching humans, crushing their spinal columns and devouring them in the streets or the air. Recent training improvements had seen a far better result in the attack on the harbors of Avonderre and Tallono, with the riders maintaining a better record of control.

But now, as he watched through his spyglass, the assault on this insignificant farming settlement seemed to be going terribly wrong.

He could not see anything but the top of the wall, which was manned with somewhere between three and four hundred crossbowmen and archers; the rampart obscured any sight into the encampment itself. The squadron of iacxsis had achieved the directional split successfully; the diving, the first stage of aerial-to-ground attack, bordered on artistry, in his opinion. He waited for the second state, the reascent, and was surprised to see that, to a one, none occurred.

In the second wave, he saw three Alliance bowmen on the wall targeted, two of which made successful strikes, but the easternmost iacxsis had not so much as gotten its prey into its mandibles when it seemed to have been dragged off the wall and into the depths of the fortress.

What in the name of the All-God is going on in there? he wondered as nine more iacxsis dropped out of the air, as if pulled to the earth beyond the wall by a giant magnet. Another four dropped on the eastern side of the wall, one of which fell outside the rampart, its rider hitting the ground headfirst. He saw the body of the iacxsis shatter on impact, the fragile skeleton beneath its impenetrable hide breaking into a dozen or more pieces.

In vain he sat up straighter on his mount, trying to get a better view into the fortress, but all he could see was the repeated iacxsis attacks seemingly broken by an unforgiving wind, as the creatures seemed alternately to be dragged from the sky over the middle of the encampment or to fall from it from nowhere.

In the distance he could hear the muffled cheering from behind the walls, could see the archers dancing with glee on the battlements, as the squadron of unassailable winged beasts disappeared before his eyes into the bowels of the pathetic farming village.

He waited for a quarter hour longer, hoping to see the elite squadron of riders and flying mounts rise from the interior floor into the air and return, but not a single one did. The cheering on the ramparts grew louder; it was a sound that enflamed his blood and made his head pound with anger.

"All right," he said to his stunned field commanders, who were staring at the armed farming village in shock. "Let us find out what's going on inside this pathetic excuse for a fortress. Archers, provide cover—cavalry, prepare to charge. Leave one alive to render an explanation. But only one."

The stunned auxiliary soldiers of the Alliance were ruthless in dispatching both the beasts and the riders that had been dragged from the sky by the whip in the hand of the Lady Cymrian, or the wind manipulated by the sword of the duke of Navarne.

As she got a little better accustomed to the whip, Rhapsody had stepped more to the center of the encampment, seeking to make use of the ground and the wall encircling what had at one time been a small village and a handful of family farms. She saw that impact was more destructive to the iacxsis than weaponsfire, so she tried to use the whip's flexibility to not only wrap around a limb or neck, but to yank each beast from the very air itself and smash it, using its own momentum, into something hard.

Gwydion Navarne had been invaluable in the rout as well, manipulating the currents of air skillfully with Tysterisk to send the flying beasts into the ground.

When finally the last iacxsis was destroyed, the last rider killed or captured, the soldiers let up a whoop of victory. Anborn had laughed aloud, then joined them in a war cry, but called them to attention a moment later.

"This was only the first step," he warned. "There are still four times as many of them as there are of us, many on barded horseback, highly armed and trained. They will be on our doorstep momentarily, so do not celebrate too soon. But remember that these are the forces that raped the holy city, that drove the Patriarch out and defiled the basilica. You have struck a blow in the name of your land, and your God! If we do not survive what is to come, at least you will enter the Afterlife as heroes."

The ramshackle soldiers sent up another cry of victory.

$\int$hremus surveyed the horsemen who had been lined up by the field commanders across the threshold of the Krevensfield Plain. He regretted not bringing the catapults and heavy ballistae, the weapons of siege, but the thought that a tiny farming village with a hastily constructed wall would need such weapons to be vanquished was ludicrous yesterday.

Today, he had just lost a squadron of unassailable flying machines of destruction to such a tiny farming village.

He rode past the regiment, waving the banner of the Empire of the Sun.

"For the emperor!" he cried. "Charge!"

$\mathcal{T}$he cavalry charge of the Sorbolds was like the rumble of a fast-approaching thunderstorm, causing the ground within the farming settlement to shake violently.

"Archers, return to your posts and make ready!" Anborn shouted as the men on the wall sighted their crossbows again. He dismounted in a smooth leap from the warhorse and ran to the ladder, climbing the wall with the speed and skill of a man of twenty summers.

As the troops on the ground within the encampment made ready in the ranks the Lord Marshal had devised, Gwydion Navarne turned to Rhapsody.

"What now?" he asked, a mixture of exhilaration and terror on his face.

"Do you feel comfortable enough manipulating the wind that you can cause the currents to blow aimlessly, to interfere with arrow flight?"

"I think so."

"That's good enough. Come."

Gwydion followed her to the front wall, dodging soldiers and horsemen as the defenders scrambled to set up ranks. They made for the ladder and ascended the wall, Gwydion taking the time to sheath Tysterisk before starting to climb.

Anborn reached down as Rhapsody summited the ladder and offered her his hand. He pulled her onto the rampart, then did the same with Gwydion Navarne, taking a moment to clap him on the shoulder once he was off the ladder.

"Well done, young Navarne," he said. "Your father, and your godfather, would be proud." He turned back to see the Sorbold assault force barreling down across the Krevensfield Plain, almost within crossbow range; the riders were leveling their weapons as they thundered nearer.

Rhapsody was scanning the sky calmly.

"Gwydion, are you ready?"

The duke of Navarne nodded and drew his sword again.

The Lady Cymrian looked at the Lord Marshal; their eyes met, and a smile passed between them. Anborn turned and descended the ladder.

Rhapsody waited until she saw him on the ground again. Then she climbed out on top of a crossbow stand, crouched down and raised just the top of her head above the rampart.

Even amid the drumbeat of the approaching horses' hooves, she could hear the release of thousands of crossbow bolts.

Rhapsody drew Daystar Clarion and held it to her side. The flames rippled up the blade, orange and gold, blue and purple, smoldering quietly, as if it was waiting.

She surveyed the approaching charge, crouching low to avoid the crossbow bolts that were now beginning to thud in small numbers into the rampart. Then she signaled to Gwydion Navarne.

The duke of Navarne drew Tysterisk again; he rested the pommel of the sword in his palm, clutching the hilt in his grasp, and concentrated.

The sword had been Gwydion's for only a short time, and it had a harshness to its spirit that bruised and occasionally scraped against his soul. He had found it to be reliable in times of need, but occasionally petulant in its response to or tolerance of his requests. The blade sometimes appeared, a black outline defining it, sometimes remained unseen. He hoped the gravity of what they were facing would ensure the sword's easy cooperation, but he had no real faith that it would.

He closed his eyes and reached down inside himself to the newly formed elemental bond to the sword, a place of elemental lore of air that had given him a greater capacity of breath and an innate understanding he had never known of thermals and updrafts, clouds and prediction of weather. He pictured the gusts outside the wall going random, and strengthening, channeling his thoughts through the sword of elemental air.

A discordant shriek and a blasting howl blew his hair around roughly, indicating the wind had answered him.

"Ready, Rhapsody," he said.

———

Rhapsody centered her footing on the empty crossbow stand of the archer that the iacxsis had taken. "Stay down," she said to the other archers near her on the wall; the word was passed up and down the line.

Then she stood up, a solitary target, her hair and clothing flapping and rustling in the now-inconstant wind.

A sword of elemental fire burning like a brand in her hand.

A hailstorm of arrow shots sailed past, above and around her, directed by the random breezes that were spinning like a small, disorganized cyclone between the settlement and the oncoming charge.

The faces of the men atop the horses of the cavalry were in sight now. Even at the distance they still had to cross, the livid anger was apparent; she could see their teeth set in rage, their muscles corded with fury.

Another volley of arrows whizzed by her, spinning uselessly in the cycloning wind.

She searched the skies. The sun was still high.

How can I find the stars in daylight? she had asked her mentor, the Lirin Champion Oelendra, who had trained her in the use of Daystar Clarion, which she herself had carried long before Rhapsody found it. Oelendra had explained all of the sword's powers, including the ability to call fire from the stars by calling their true names.

Just because you can't see the stars, Rhapsody, doesn't mean they cease to be there, Oelendra had said. *The knowledge of their placement in the heavens, and their names, transcend the need for darkness. But you have to be able to find them, and know where they are. Even without seeing them.*

She thought she knew the location of Prylla, a star she had used to summon starfire in the Past. She raised the ancient weapon over her head, leaving her chest even more vulnerable to arrow strike, and spoke the name of the star.

Nothing happened.

A third flight of arrows were shot into the wind, vastly larger now that the charging cavalry and infantry were much closer. An arrow, misshot, grazed her shoulder, causing her to gasp in pain as blood spattered the wall. Rhapsody switched sword hands and clapped her free hand over her bleeding upper arm, then turned slightly, trying to remember where the stars appeared in the course of the day, when the world was blind to them.

The attacking force was within a league, three miles or less from the settlement. The walls were trembling now, almost as much as the soldiers on those walls were.

As Rhapsody gazed at the oncoming soldiers through the twisting winds that Gwydion, the Tysterisk'ar, was manipulating, her eyes lighted on the broken city of Sepulvarta in the distance. The city, which had once held some of the most beautiful architecture and forethoughtful governance that the nations now in the Alliance had ever seen, was no longer gleaming, but standing, stolid and stained with the soot of assault and conquest. Behind it, the Spire still towered, the tiny piece of the star Seren still gleamed bravely.

Almost as if it were offering its services.

Rhapsody blinked as she considered. She smiled slightly at the irony of the piece of elemental ether being used to exact vengeance on the army that had sacked and occupied it.

Then she raised the sword over her head again, two-handed.

And this time sang the name of the star that had once shone over her homeland on the other side of the world, as well as in the tiny piece atop the Spire.

The light of which would have shone within her own eyes had she ever been baptized in its light, something that she had been denied by the loss of her mentor and her need to have finished her Naming studies on her own.

The star that still shone down on what had been the holy city.

The city that the man this army served had despoiled and ruined.

And the star that happened to be the one she called *aria*, her own guiding star, the star she was born beneath.

The star from which she drew her power as a Namer.

The flames of the elemental fire in her weapon, and within her being, roared to life as her thoughts channeled through the sword. A clarion call began to hum, rising quickly to a loud, ringing shout.

Seren, she sang.

The winds screamed.

The clouds above rolled across the sky, breaking and frothing like the dark gray waves of the sea.

And, from the very pinnacle atop the great basilica of Lianta'ar, which meant *Bearer of Light* in the old tongue of the Cymrians, a flash of ethereal light followed by a roar of starfire shot forth from the tiny piece of the star that was embedded in the tip of the pinnacle.

It struck the advancing army of Sorbold with a bolt of elemental fire, not of the same scope that she could have called down from a living star, but a smaller, targeted blast that smashed into the very center of the cavalry troop, throwing men and horses into the air as they turned to ashes.

The battle line broke as the horses closest to the blast reared up or sheared off, tossing their riders or dragging them away from the flames.

The Lady Cymrian raised the sword again, this time pointing it over the infantry that was advancing farther back.

Seren, she sang again.

She could feel the power of its name rush up the blade in her hands as the light atop the Spire rained down again, followed by the strike of ethereal fire.

Another black pit of ash appeared where a line of soldiers had been marching on the farming settlement. At the outskirts, soldiers on each of the sides of the blast caught fire and fell to the ground, screaming.

She turned a third time, to what was now the front line of the cavalry charge, and sang the star's name one more time, delivering another targeted blast of starfire, taking out more horses, more soldiers. The light atop the Spire seemed to dim, she thought, or perhaps it was just harder to see from atop the wall of the farming settlement through the black smoke that was now filling the clear air of the Krevensfield Plain with the horrific stench of burning flesh and grass.

Grimly she watched the ripping apart of the charge.

Until a stray arrow caught her in the chest at the joint of her shoulder, piercing her dragonscale armor.

And turning the rest of the world black.

She was not aware of her body falling off the crossbow stand to the wooden floor of the rampart.

Shremus watched in horror as fire tore from the sky above him and engulfed the front three lines of his cavalry charge in an inferno.

He was even more horrified when it happened again a moment later, deep within the infantry.

And amid the cavalry again.

The fire was coming from the Spire of the city of Sepulvarta, a city his army now occupied.

Directed from within a ramshackle farming settlement that had first taken down an attack of fifty iacxsis and their riders.

"Sound retreat!" he shouted to the trumpeter, but where he looked for the soldier was a large roaring patch of highgrass engulfing the burning bodies of horses and men.

The man's trumpet lay twisted and melting in the grass, gleaming helplessly.

Fhremus was not a man easily given to retreat, but as the large gates in the settlement's wall began to open, he had seen through the billowing smoke and crackling flames of burning grass the huge black warhorse at the head of a column of soldiers preparing to charge.

Standing beside it was a man in black ringed armor, the glint of silver interlacing rings shining like tiny pinpricks illuminated by the fire's light. The man's hair was like his armor, flowing black with streaks of silver in it above a famous brow, below which azure eyes, so unlike those of the men of Sorbold, gleamed ferociously. It was a man of ancient history, a leader undisputed that had held almost godlike status in every military academy or training ground, every saga ever told of war, every historical volume, a man whose very name caused army commanders to shudder.

A man who shouldn't be able to stand, let alone walk.

And yet, before his very eyes, Fhremus saw him cross to the horse and hoist himself up onto it as if he had never been lamed, had never aged past the day he had led his own retreat from Canrif four hundred years before. The living history of the Cymrian age, and the continent.

Anborn ap Gwylliam.

He could swear the Lord Marshal was staring at him, meeting his eyes half a league away.

There was murder in those eyes.

"Fall back! Retreat!" he screamed again. "Back to the city!"

He did not have to repeat the order. The occupation force from the garrison stationed inside the walled city of Sorbold turned and fled back across the Krevensfield Plain as the Lord Marshal signaled to what seemed to be an enormous regiment of highly trained cavalry from the farming settlement, preparing to chase them back to Sepulvarta.

Fhremus didn't give him the chance.

𝒜nborn watched the remains of the attacking force of Sorbold soldiers turn tail and retreat hastily back to Sepulvarta, first in amazement, then amusement, from atop his beautiful black warhorse.

As he beheld the retreat of Fhremus's regiment, he couldn't stop the delight from welling up in him. Anborn threw back his head and laughed uproariously, to be joined a moment later by a mere eight thousand voices. He gave the sign to stand down, then rode forward to the gate and turned, surveying fondly the ragtag regiment that the Sorbolds had not laid actual eyes on. He was a shrewd strategist and a fine master of the bluff, but in a thousand years of soldiering he had never seen a hidden force of skeletal proportions so overwhelmingly convince an army that had outnumbered them four times over, with the additional advantage of a weapon of war like the iacxsis, that they were outmatched to the point of choosing retreat.

He knew it would not happen again.

Something's wrong, he thought. *That was far too easy, should never have happened. Something's wrong.*

He shook his head to clear it of the thought.

"All right," he said gruffly to the soldiers still in the throes of merriment. "Enjoy the sight of their arses flapping as they run like frightened children. Don't get used to it, however. They will be back, stronger next time. Fortunately, our reinforcements are on the way as well. But look well on this day—you were privileged to witness a *city* kicking the hindquarters of the army that ravaged it, like a woman killing her rapist. In all my days I have never witnessed such a thing." He laughed aloud again, feeling the camaraderie of the oldest of days in his memory once more.

From atop the wall, Gwydion Navarne leaned over the rampart above him, his face white as death.

"Lord Marshal," the young duke said. "Come, please, sir."

57

$\mathcal{B}$y the time Anborn had hastily climbed the ladder and reached the rampart atop the wall, Rhapsody had already regained consciousness and was slapping away the ministrations of the young duke of Navarne and a variety of soldiers who had been with her on the rampart when she fell.

They were merely trying to help her, given that she had an arrow jutting from her chest, and was bleeding copiously on the floor of the rampart.

"Leave me alone," Anborn heard her insist as he came to her side. "I'm all right."

"You have an interesting definition of 'all right,' as you do of most things, m'lady," said the Lord Marshal, signaling dismissal to the other soldiers. "Get me clean rags and calendula, if there is any to be had." He watched the men descend the ladder.

"Witch hazel and thyme would be better," Rhapsody called weakly to the descending soldiers.

Anborn laughed, though his face betrayed his worry.

"Even an arrow wound can't overcome your extraordinary bossiness," he said fondly, taking off his cloak and balling it up into a pillow to brace behind her back. "May I borrow your sword?"

"Certainly. Did you lose your own?"

The Lord Marshal drew a dagger. "Hardly. I want to sterilize my knife."

"She refused to let any of the archers remove the arrow," Gwydion Navarne said. He had regained a little of his color from when he had summoned Anborn, but was still trembling nervously.

"Of course she did; she's not a fool. Look at your hand. It's shaking like a dog coming out of a pond. Theirs would have been worse." Anborn took hold of the hilt of Daystar Clarion and pulled it, as respectfully as he could, a small ways out of the scabbard until the licking flames could be seen. He held the blade of the dagger in the elemental fire. "She's also fairly particular about who gets to see her naked." He chuckled as Gwydion blanched, but Rhapsody merely winced in pain, ignoring the comment he had expected would bring at least a blush to her face, if not ugly words to her lips. He got neither.

"Why don't you go see about that calendula—and the witch hazel," he said, giving the young duke a chance to vacate the uncomfortable scene.

"He should stay," Rhapsody said flatly. "He needs to know how to remove an arrow."

"Yes, but he probably doesn't need to see it being done to his *grand-mother*," the Lord Marshal retorted. "Go," he said gruffly to Gwydion.

The young duke bowed and hurried down the ladder.

Anborn handed Rhapsody his handkerchief. "Put this between your back teeth."

She shook her head.

"Are you under my command?" demanded the Lord Marshal.

"I believe so."

"Then you are dangerously close to disobeying orders. Put the damned thing in your mouth."

She glared at him but said nothing as she complied.

"I am not trying to abate your pain or save your tongue from being bitten off; the handkerchief is just an excuse to get you to stop talking," Anborn said as he gently removed her armor and tore her shirt open with his dagger; he winced at the sight of the wound, knowing it was painful. "On second thought, perhaps I would have achieved my objective better if I had let you bite your tongue off after all." He waited for the retort he knew was coming.

Rhapsody said nothing.

The Lord Marshal continued to wait, applying pressure to the wound, until one of the archers returned with bandages, clean rags, and calendula, a flower-based tincture used to prevent infection and inflammation. The man departed hastily, and Anborn set to removing the arrow, wishing he had taken it himself.

He cleaned and dressed the wound, then bandaged her.

"Start singing your song of healing," Anborn said, holding her shoulder to stanch the blood. "I need you back in fighting form immediately."

"I can't," Rhapsody said, her face pale but set grimly. "Thank—you for taking the arrow out."

"What do you mean, you *can't?*" the Lord Marshal demanded harshly.

She was struggling to breathe in a regular pattern.

"I can't remember my true name," she said between measured breaths. "You of all people should understand why I can't heal myself. I will just have to endure like anyone else would. Stop babying me."

Anborn fell silent. After a moment he returned to addressing her wound.

"Beloved niece-in-law," he said quietly as he tied off the bandage, "I know the loss of your son has cut out your heart. But you do know it's temporary, and that he is safe, do you not?"

"Yes." Rhapsody struggled to sit up.

Anborn's hand came to rest on her face. He turned it to allow him to look into her eyes.

"M'lady," he said softly, "you are cold—not as a result of the arrow, but of a completely different wound. I beg you—don't let that coldness ruin you. The loss to the world would be heinous, but it would be the end of me, truly it would."

Rhapsody stared at him. After a moment, she lowered her gaze.

"I will try," she said finally. "I just don't know how. I feel nothing, Anborn. Nothing." She winced in pain. "Well, nothing emotional. My chest hurts like *hrekin*."

The Lord Marshal sighed, then nodded. He had spent a thousand years in just such a state.

"I understand better than you know," he said. "How's the shoulder?"

"Serviceable. Thank you."

Anborn nodded again. "Good. Now we'll get you to a hospice in Bethany; I will arrange an armored carriage and my elite regiment—"

"No, I'm sorry. I have to get to Tyrian." Rhapsody attempted to tie her shirt up without success. "The same devastation through iacxsis attack that destroyed Avonderre Harbor has been visited upon Port Tallono as well. Rial needs me, and I need to be with my people. Unless you have specific requirements for me in the next few weeks, I want to go to Tyrian."

Anborn waited until her gaze returned to him, and met it.

"My only requirement of you at the moment is that you stay safe," he said seriously as he tied her shirt up for her. "There will come a time when, I suspect, I will specifically have need of your skills in battle." His voice dropped in volume to just above a whisper. "When your husband returns, when the ports are liberated and the blockade lifted, I want to hold a war council to assess the continent's status. I've done some calculations, and it is growing apparent to me that in order to survive we will need to harness resources other than what we have."

Rhapsody listened intently.

Anborn's eyes took on a gleam, though what it represented, Rhapsody could not tell. Excitement, perhaps. Or perhaps something more, something deeper. Realization.

Or maybe fear.

"Constantin and I had the opportunity to share and analyze the intelligence we collected or knew regarding Sorbold in the time we traveled together, before we arrived in Ylorc," he said quietly. "From without, it is essentially unassailable."

"That's what we thought about the Bolglands."

"True. But Talquist has been planning his ascension and conquest for a long time. I suspect he may have killed both the empress and the Crown Prince himself. He has resources, both here on the continent, and around the Known World, especially maritime resources, that dwarf any army we can field. At least from without."

"You have said that twice now, *from without*," Rhapsody said. "What is your plan from within?"

"I'm not certain yet. But I will say this. Talquist may have found allies and servants who share his plans—or he may have deceived some of them into believing that they do. It is very clear that he is a consummate liar. The trick will be to determine who shares his vision out of a similar self-interest—and who has been misled into believing that they are doing the right thing by throwing in their lots with him. That will be true both outside Sorbold, and inside it.

"A large and growing part of the population of Sorbold is not there by choice," he continued as Rhapsody's eyes took on a similar gleam. "Now, if the slaves who toil in his fields and factories, who sweat to death in his forges, could be convinced to join us, to throw off their shackles and rise up against Talquist, *that* would be something that might balance the scales. I have already begun to set it in motion."

"But how would you do that?

Anborn's smile brightened, along with his eyes.

"From within. But only once either you or Gwydion can hold the reins on this side of continent. Until that time, I will be your loyal coachman."

A small smile came over Rhapsody's face.

"Excellent. Now, can we see about getting me that armored carriage and regiment you mentioned—only point it southwest in the direction of Tyrian?"

Anborn laughed and kissed her hand.

"As my lady commands. Now, would you care to explain to me how you got so proficient in the use of a whip made of a dragon's tongue? I don't suspect that's training they provide in Namer school."

"No, they don't," Rhapsody admitted. "I have been practicing on crows. All the way home from the Deep Kingdom, in fact. I have great incentive—they make such a satisfying sound when they explode. I was a farm child; I hate crows. In fact, I don't recall much about those days, having given that name away, but one thing I do remember is how much I hate crows. Snapping them from the skies was the most fun I remember having in a long while."

Anborn laughed. "Well, imagine that Talquist has a caw to him, and think about what fun it will be to snap him from his tower in Jierna Tal and hurl him a thousand feet into the chasm below. Witnessing that might be the most fun *I* would have had in a long while."

$\mathcal{I}$nside the walls of the broken city of Sepulvarta, Fhremus had mustered his field commanders who had survived the rout.

"I will leave within the hour," he said to the line of men staring stonily back at him. "I must go to Jierna'sid personally to explain the loss—this is not news that the emperor should receive by messenger or bird." He scanned the line, his brain making note once again of the missing leaders in the rank beneath his, soldiers of superior skill and battlefield tactics, men he had never expected to lose in a raid on a farming village. Then his eye went to the most senior of the remaining commanders, and he tried not to let his hatred show in his voice.

"Titactyk, you are tasked with holding the city. Do not engage in maneuvers outside Sepulvarta's walls until I return, or until you receive word of my death and replacement from the capitol."

"Yes, m'lord."

"Gentlemen, you are dismissed. Return to your units and tend to the injured."

58

TRAEG, NORTHWESTERN SEACOAST

Ashe had timed his arrival at the seacoast to coincide with the darkest part of the night, when the moon was hovering at the horizon, preparing to set into the arms of the sea.

He had left his cloak, well-made but plain and without ornamentation or insignia, wrapped around one of the thin men of the northern docks, homeless and hollow-eyed, most often old sailors who had lost their souls and more to the sea. It had served its purpose in shielding his vibrational signature during his travels from Highmeadow. He had no need of it now; perhaps it would bring some warmth to old bones that rattled each night in the harsh north wind.

The clothing he wore had been specially designed, tight-fitting to the heavy muscles of his chest and legs to allow for ease of movement in the water. He knew it mattered little; when Kirsdarke was in his hand beneath the waves, his body took on a vaporous state, becoming one with the element, allowing for easy movement with the tides.

As he stared over the sea at the falling moon, he heard a sweet voice in his memory, as clearly as he had heard it on the other side of Time, so long ago, and his own in reply, so young then, so full of belief in the Future.

Sam?

Yes?

Do you think we might see the ocean? Someday, I mean.

Of course. We can even live there if you want. Haven't you ever seen it?

I've never left the farmlands, Sam, never in my whole life. I've always longed to see the ocean, though. My grandfather is a sailor, and all my life he has promised me that he would take me to sea one day. Until recently I believed it. But I've seen his ship.

How can that be, if you've never seen the sea?

Well, when he's in port, it's actually very tiny—about as big as my hand. And he keeps it on his mantel, in a bottle.

"I will remember Emily for you," he whispered into the sea wind.

Then he drew his sword and walked over the sand, down to the smooth, wet threshold of lapping froth, into the rolling waves.

He did not look back.

59

The Teeth
(Manteids)

★

● Night Mountain
Earth Basilica

Desert

PALACE OF JIERNA TAL, JIERNA'SID, SORBOLD

*L*ong before Fhremus had even reached the tower staircase, Talquist knew he was coming.

The Merchant Emperor was standing in the early-morning light, a glass of sweet milky tea in his hand, looking east, watching a profusion of twisting smoke trails, tiny in the distance, curling toward the brightening sky. The corpulent clouds hanging high in the air above the destruction were bathed in the rosy colors of sunrise, in contrast with the gray-black haze that rose from the ground, almost like foggy remnants of insistent night refusing to be banished by daybreak.

Faron had consulted the scales, and had warned him of when the change in the battle outcome would occur, before the titan had left for Sepulvarta, so he had been expecting the news, though the sight was still disturbing.

He could be forgiven for the emotional reaction, the stomach clenching, the sweat prickling on the back of his neck.

Even if his rational mind knew better.

Fhremus's footsteps were sounding now on the marble steps of the tower stairway.

Talquist took a sip of tea.

"Majesty?" Fhremus's voice held a dread that made the emperor smile.
"Yes?"

"I regret to inform you that the forward line at Sepulvarta has been routed, m'lord, driven back to within the city walls, caught in a blockade by the forces of the Alliance."

"Yes, I am aware."

The supreme commander's mouth snapped shut. For the span of fifty heartbeats he was silent. Then he summoned his voice.

"You had already heard, m'lord? How?"

Talquist's smile grew broader as he took another draught of tea.

"I knew the date and the hour of the retreat a fortnight ago, before you deployed from Sepulvarta."

"You—you did?" Fhremus was speaking slowly, because between his ears the world was turning at an odd angle.

"Of course," Talquist said smugly. "Of course I knew, because it was the plan all along."

"Our defeat was *planned*?"

"Yes. Would you like some tea, Fhremus? It's really quite a lovely blend, from Marincaer. Has a touch of pepper in it, I think."

The supreme commander put his hand for the first time on the railing of the stairway to steady himself as the emperor drained the rest of his beverage.

"Please—please explain, m'lord," he stammered as the world continued to spin around him.

Finally the emperor turned away from the window and looked thoughtfully down the stairs at Fhremus.

"Taking Sepulvarta was, in addition to the opportunity to unseat the Patriarch, the establishment of bait," he said gently, both amused and concerned at the look of shock on the supreme commander's face. "I thought you knew that, Fhremus. I needed a reason for Anborn to withdraw the army of the Alliance from the northern citadels—Bethany, Bethe Corbair, Canderre, Yarim—leaving them vulnerable. He may have managed to protect the handful of farmers who live across the Krevensfield Plain, but he's done it at the cost of his northern *cities*. As the moon disappears this night, the Icemen of the Hintervold, who have quietly been massing on the northern border of Roland, will advance while the Alliance lays siege to Sepulvarta, which is essentially an empty city to their south." His words ground to a halt as laughter spilled out of his mouth at the evolving expression on Fhremus's face.

"But m'lord—"

"The former Alliance garrisons in their northern provinces along the border have been emptied to support the cross-continental line of southern outposts, Anborn's great Threshold of Death. Senile Cymrian fool! We have continued to prod those pathetic armed farming settlements with small iacxsis attacks to maintain his belief that the south was our target all along."

Fhremus stared at him in silence.

"I'm sorry if I haven't been clear in the planning stages," Talquist said, turning back to the window. "The Diviner's army will have little difficulty taking all of those former Alliance garrisons in the north while the Lord Cymrian's forces are busy waiting for the all-but-empty holy city to surrender in the south. By the time they discover they are awaiting nothing, they will be trapped between the Icemen and the rest of your army, north and south, while the naval forces begin raining fire to cover the western advance from the sea."

"Speaking of raining fire, m'lord, you do also know that Daystar Clarion has apparently entered the fray? That the iacxsis were blasted from the skies—"

"Of course. They were deployed specifically in Sepulvarta to bring the Lady Cymrian into battle."

"Wh—if I might ask, m'lord, *why?*"

Talquist smiled broadly.

"Where do you suppose her child is now, Fhremus? Did she leave it in the care of the Bolg, or bring it with her? Either way, it will be in my hands soon. There will be an extremely fine bottle of twenty-year rum as a prize for whoever brings it to me first, you or Beliac. I told you that was my first priority, did I not?"

Fhremus said nothing, but his face went even paler than it had been when he had entered the stairwell. Finally he shook his head, as if shaking off a nightmare after waking from deep, disturbing sleep.

"Yes, m'lord. Orders?"

Talquist turned back to him slowly and smiled.

"Here are your orders, Fhremus, at least for today: take a few days' leave. Go to the gypsy district or the flesh market and get yourself a nice bedwench or two, and then to the charcuteries or the smoke grills and have a fine supper. Sleep in tomorrow. Then come see me here at the beginning of the week, and we will set to planning the slaughter that is taking root nicely as we speak."

"Yes, m'lord; thank you." Fhremus bowed over a roiling stomach and waited until the Merchant Emperor had turned back once more to the window, then turned around himself and hurried down the staircase all the way to the first-floor entryway, where he ran to the front door of the palace and out into the clear air again.

Breathing painfully.

60

HIGHMEADOW, NAVARNE

Sir?"

Gwydion Navarne looked up from the pile of battlefield communiqués littering Ashe's desk. Manus Kral, the late Gerald Owen's replacement stood at the study door, his shadow from the light sconces stretching behind him into the darkness of the hallway.

"Yes, Manus?" He tried to keep his voice steady, but only managed to sound far younger even than his years.

"King Achmed of Ylorc, sir." Manus stepped aside, allowing Achmed entrance to the room, then bowed politely and closed the door behind him.

Despite the late hour, Gwydion's young face broke into a grin of immense relief.

"Your Majesty! How good to see you. I'd no idea you had left Ylorc. To what do I owe the honor of your presence?"

Achmed smiled slightly. The young duke of Navarne had aged a good deal since he had last seen him at his investiture, and though his dark hair looked nothing like his father's, the expression in his eyes was a twin to what his father's would have held. It gave the Bolg king the rare, pleasant sensation of being in Stephen Navarne's presence again, if only for a moment.

"I need whatever intelligence you can provide about the Merchant Emperor," he said bluntly. "Did Ashe leave behind any reports specifically about Talquist?"

Gwydion nodded as he rose from the desk.

"Indeed; he has quite a sheaf of documents, meticulously sorted by category. Wyrmkin apparently have an innate attention to detail that borders on obsessive." He went to an armoire across the room and opened the doors, then pulled open a hanging file. He rifled through it, producing a fat leather portfolio a moment later, then crossed the room and offered it to the Bolg king.

Achmed accepted the file with a curt nod. He opened it and flipped through a number of the pages, then nodded again.

"If you would be good enough to wait a moment, I will summon Manus and set him to preparing a guest room and some supper for you," Gwydion Navarne said. He started for the study's door. "I don't know if you heard; we lost our old chamberlain recently—he passed away a fortnight ago."

"I'm sorry to hear that. I am just passing through; I didn't mean to disturb your review of maneuvers," Achmed said uneasily.

The young duke's smile faded. "It's a pleasant diversion; the news seems to get worse each day. Much as battle is a terrifying experience, I think I am beginning to prefer it to the direction and coordination responsibilities that I have inherited from Ashe. It's a mammoth undertaking; I don't know how he kept all these details, all these fronts straight."

Achmed's dark face took on a small smile again.

"*Dragon*," he said. "A word which in the Bolgish tongue translates directly as 'pain in the arse.' A synonym for 'Cymrian.'"

"Ah, I see. So, can you stay the night at least?"

The Bolg king considered, then assented.

"Wonderful!" Gwydion said, his enthusiasm of a moment ago restored. Then a thought occurred to him. "Actually, I have a favor to request of you."

Achmed dropped unceremoniously into a leather chair with the file. "Oh?"

"Yes, Ashe told me before he left that if you or any Dhracian were to pass through, to request that you look in on a prisoner who is incarcerated under heavy guard in the internal stockade. He said that person is suspected of being a demonic thrall, and hoped that you would be willing to make an assessment of whether that is true or not. My understanding, though it may be incorrect, is that through some sort of unscrupulous behavior, the prisoner was exposed to a F'dor's host, but no one is certain if actual possession took place, and thus all efforts are being made to restrict movement and exposure until a reliable assessment can be made. If you can clear the prisoner of suspicion, we can relocate him to a lesser security setting until Ashe returns, or, if he doesn't—" Gwydion's throat went suddenly dry.

Achmed's mismatched gaze settled on him; there was no real sympathy in it, but the look felt easy on the young duke nonetheless.

"At any rate, I don't know who it is, I'm not even certain if it's a man or woman," Gwydion continued. "I think Gerald knew, but he didn't say."

"Rhapsody made the same request of me after she spoke to Ashe a while back," Achmed said. "I don't know what makes her think I have that ability; I don't remember ever telling her that I did."

"I think she trusts you as the ultimate authority on all things demonic, given your race. I know I certainly agree with her." He smiled wryly. "But if you try and you are not certain, we can always wait until another Dhracian comes along. Or at least leave it for Ashe to deal with when he comes back."

The Bolg king sighed and rose to a stand. "All right, let's take care of it now. I need to be able to concentrate, undisturbed, once I begin reading the documents."

"Very good. I'll get the keys to the stockade cell, and on the way there I will get Manus started on your accommodations and your supper."

The lights in the stockade stairway and under the cell door were still burning dimly as Achmed and Gwydion Navarne made their way down the stairs. The full contingent of guards had been moved to other posts within the stockade, leaving only the two heavy crossbowmen at either side of the cell door.

Gwydion slid the first complex key into the smallest of the seven keyholes, springing each mechanism until he finally inserted the largest of the blades into the massive lock at the bottom. The bolt snapped back, and the door opened slightly. He stepped hurriedly back and out of the way, leaving the Bolg king clear in the middle of the doorway.

Achmed swung the door open.

Within the cell, the lanternlight fell on the auburn hair of the prisoner, making it gleam red-brown for a moment. Then the man, who was sitting in a chair facing the wall at the back of the cell, stood and turned around.

It was Tristan Steward.

The Lord Roland's mouth dropped open, then relief flooded his face.

"Achmed," he said weakly. "Thank the All-God. You've come for me!"

The Bolg king stared at him for a moment.

He exhaled and rolled his eyes.

Then he turned like lightning to the guard standing to the right of the door. He seized the man's crossbow, swung it around until it pointed toward the back of the cell.

And fired a bolt into the prince's forehead.

Tristan Steward's eyes sprang open wide just as the missile bisected his brow.

Without another sound he fell back against the wall with a sickening *crack*, then forward onto his face, the impact of the fall driving the bolt further into his brain.

A ragged gasp tore forth from the throats of all three of the other men in the hallway.

"I guess I have at that," Achmed said. "Convenient timing."

It took the span of seventy heartbeats for Gwydion Navarne to recover his voice as the Lord Roland and prince of Bethany quietly bled his life out onto the floor of the stockade cell. The young duke's face was pale as moonlight, and he struggled to keep his hands steady.

"He—*Tristan* was a thrall? You're certain? Sweet All-God."

Achmed handed the crossbow back to the shaking guard.

"I'm certain," he said. *Certain that it was well past time, whether or not he was a thrall,* he thought in disgust. *Cymrian.* "Lock the door and leave the body there for a few days, just to be sure there is no lingering demonic spirit that might be a problem for anyone else."

The guards and the young duke exchanged a wide-eyed glance.

"Let's get back to the main building," the Bolg king said, turning and walking up the stairs. "Perhaps we can bring the file to the dining table so that I can begin reading while I'm eating; I've wasted enough time as it is."

Gwydion Navarne quickly closed and locked the door, then followed him up the stairs, wishing even harder than he usually did for his godfather's speedy return.

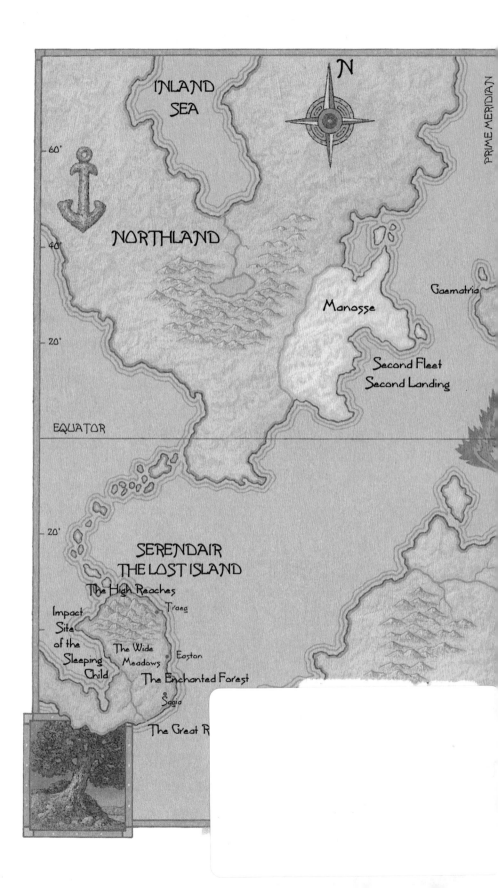